The Crimson Ribbon

Katherine Clements

headline
review

First published in 2014 by
HEADLINE REVIEW
An imprint of HEADLINE PUBLISHING GROUP

First published in paperback in 2014 by
HEADLINE REVIEW
An imprint of HEADLINE PUBLISHING GROUP

1

Cataloguing in Publication Data is available from the British Library

ISBN 978 1 4722 0422 6

Typeset in Aldine 401 BT by Avon DataSet Ltd,
Bidford-on-Avon, Warwickshire

Printed and bound in Great Britain by Clays Ltd, St Ives plc

Headline's policy is to use papers that are natural, renewable and recyclable products and made from wood grown in sustainable forests. The logging and manufacturing processes are expected to conform to the environmental regulations of the country of origin.

HEADLINE PUBLISHING GROUP
An Hachette UK Company
338 Euston Road
London NW1 3BH

www.headline.co.uk
www.hachette.co.uk

For my mother

Part One

Ely
May Day 1646

Chapter 1

Sometimes death comes like an arrow, sudden and swift, an unforeseen shot from an unheeded bow. Sometimes death comes slowly, like the first small sparks of a green-wood fire, smoking and smouldering for the longest time before the kindling flares and the heart of the blaze glows with fierce, consuming heat.

Sometimes God chooses to end a life before it is even begun.

Born on May Day, Esther Tuttle's baby should be a blessing, a symbol of fertility and hope bestowed upon the harvest to come. In these hard years of famine and war, God knows how much we need it. Instead, Annie Flowers, my mother, attending at the confinement, pulls from Esther's body a misshapen thing, slick with blood, bruised blue and purple.

The child's head is swollen, one eye unformed, leaving a gaping black hole, showing skull. Its tiny legs flop this way and that, as though the bones are gone. Its face reminds me of the graven gargoyles that watch over us from Ely's great cathedral. It does not cry. It does not breathe. A tiny coiled sprig nestling between its legs shows that it would have been a son, had it lived.

A dead baby is a bad omen, for the family, for the town, for my mother and me. The birth of a monster is even worse.

In these bleak, blighted days, when the crops fail, new lambs die of the rot and travellers report malevolent spectres wandering the Fens, we are used to bad news. But this child is unlike any other my mother has brought into the world. This creature in her arms is more than just another bad birth. I know it straight away, just as she knows it.

I clap both hands to my mouth, stopping a cry.

My mother stares at the body in her arms.

'Where is my child?' Esther, sweating and split from the birthing, struggles to sit.

My mother takes the thing and covers it with a cloth so that Esther cannot see what she has borne.

'Bring him to me.'

I go to Esther and try to soothe her. She must be calm if we are to stop her bleeding.

'Why does he not cry?'

Her eyes question, then cloud with blackness, like ink spilled across a page. She clutches at my hands. 'Ruth, where is my child?'

My mother moves to her side, bringing a dose of valerian root. I recognise its sweet, earthy scent above the meaty stench of women's blood.

'Bring him to me,' Esther demands. 'I must see him. It's a son, is it not? A boy?'

'Esther, my dear, you must rest now,' my mother says. 'Your work is done.'

Esther's face turns white beneath the blooming veins in her cheek. She huddles against the wall.

'No . . .' she whispers, kicking away the stained coverlet and drawing her knees up to her chest. 'No . . . No . . .'

My mother uses the purring tone she saves for those in her care. 'I'm so sorry, my love, but you must rest. You are very weak. This will calm you and take away a little of the pain. Come, drink.'

Esther cowers on the bed, hunched in a ball, rocking back

and forth, eyes wide and wild. As my mother leans towards her she hisses, like a cornered cat. 'Keep away from me!' Spittle, touched with flecks of crimson, flies from her lips. 'Bring me my baby!'

'My dear Esther, your child is with God now.'

Before either of us can comfort her, Esther is on her feet and across the room, dragging the filthy linen behind her. She stumbles as her wet shift clings to her legs. She goes to the trestle, where my mother has laid the child, and pulls back the cloth to see the thing lying there.

My mother moves quickly, reaching for Esther's waist to stop her fainting. But Esther is mad with grief. She picks up the child and cradles it, making an unearthly moaning in her throat. Then she spins around to face us. 'Do not touch me, witch! I see what you have done!'

'Esther . . .' I say, but she backs towards the door, snarling, showing teeth. She staggers out of the cottage and into the street, taking her baby with her.

We follow, pleading with her to return to the house, to give the baby up, but it is as if she cannot hear us, or does not care to. She lurches, barefoot and bleeding, down High Row towards the cathedral, a wild woman, leaving a trail of scarlet. Those few about the streets as dusk comes down stop and stare.

She heads for the marketplace and the Dolphin, where I know Isaac Tuttle waits for news of his first-born. There is shouting and commotion as the men outside the tavern see us coming.

I catch at Esther's arm. 'Please, Esther, come home with us. You are sick.'

'Let me go, Ruth!' Her eyes are fierce, her mouth twists. She bears no resemblance to the mousy, mild-mannered girl we attended at daybreak.

People spill from the alehouse, Isaac Tuttle at the fore. He is drunk, swaying, eyes unfocused. He is a big man, hardy from labouring in the Fens. It takes a lot of ale to make him that way. But it is May Day and, though we have not had maypoles and dancing for all the long years of war, old habits die hard in these parts. The men have been sinking their drink since noon.

Isaac's cronies gather, bringing their tankards, eager for some new distraction.

'Wife?' Isaac gawps at the bloodied woman before him.

Esther trembles. Her gaze darts madly; her hair is loose and tangled. She holds out the baby in her arms. 'Here is your son!' she cries. 'Here is the evil thing that *she* brought forth from me.' As she flings out an arm to point at my mother, she loses her grasp on the child. Slippery as it is with gore, it slides across the ground like an eel and lands in the dust at Isaac's feet.

There is a pause, an intake of breath, a moment of dawning understanding. Then, horror, catching hold like flames in a haystack. I watch a puddle of crimson bloom on the ground between Esther's feet.

'She did this!' Esther says. 'Just as she killed Goody Woodrun and her boys, just as she cursed the Taylors.'

'The Woodruns died of a fever,' I say, but no one is listening.

'Help me, Isaac . . . I swear she lies with the Devil. She uses me as his vessel. She brings forth his foul offspring from me – and now she means to kill me with her potions and her spells . . .' Esther sinks to her knees.

My mother goes to her and tries to put her arm around Esther's shoulders but Isaac will not have it. Dim-witted and lumbering with the drink, he bats my mother away with one swing of his arm, thundering, 'Do not touch my wife, whore!'

I hear a crack like splintered wood as my mother falls. She clutches at her ankle, the colour draining from her face.

I run to her side, feeling the crowd bristle. Her ankle is broken. I need no potion or charm to know that. Already it is swelling and turning blue, just like the bloated body of the poor child that lies discarded like a scrap of offal.

Esther is babbling to Isaac: 'I didn't want her with me, but you asked her to come and now see what she has done. I told you she was bad. I didn't want her in my house and yet you left me there alone . . .'

I can see she is fading, the strength going from her fast. Someone picks up the dead child and brings it to her. She whimpers and hides her face against Isaac's chest. He waves the tiny body away, holds his wife and pulls down her shift to keep her decent as blood pools around them.

There is muttering from the crowd. More have gathered now, onlookers and tipplers from the inn, throwing poisonous looks our way, among them our neighbour Samuel Ward, a mean, brutal man who has never been a friend of ours.

I know that this is dangerous. I know that we cannot ignore them and walk away, as I have been taught.

'Ruth . . .' my mother whispers, clasping my hand. I see fear in her eyes and it pierces my heart, making it thump, making my skin prickle and my ears ring. Suddenly my body is not my own. I cannot control my breathing, which comes shallow and fast, just as Esther's own breath gives out.

Esther dies, there in the street, in Isaac's arms, her ungodly offspring in the dirt at her feet, all the time spitting hatred and lies at the one woman who might have saved her life.

Cradling my mother, I search about me for help. Among the gathering are many who come to us for cures and remedies when their families are sick. There are faces I know from the market square, fellow servants, quick to gossip but even quicker to ask for my mother when their children are ailing or their wives struggle in a difficult confinement. They all know her skill with the old wisdom. More than one may owe his life to her.

But they all turn from me now. None will meet my gaze.

Martha Featherstone, a thin, watery-eyed girl I know from my time at the free school, begins a high keening.

'Will someone help me?' I beg.

Isaac looks at me. His skin is red-raw and his eyes are glazed with something more than drink. 'Help?' he says. 'You have cursed my child and put my wife in the earth, and now you ask for help?'

He stands, leaving Esther's limp body on the ground. He steps over her, making a trail of red footprints as he comes towards us. The other men push and jostle behind him, leaving the women to deal with Esther and the child.

'She has broken a bone,' I say, stroking my mother's head. 'She cannot walk.'

My mother is faint but somehow gathers strength enough to wave Isaac away. 'Let us be,' she says.

The men surround us.

'You must answer for your sins,' Isaac says. 'I will have justice for this.'

'And justice for the Woodruns,' Samuel Ward says.

'And the Taylors.'

'And my husband,' Edith Cobbett adds. It is no secret that she blames her widowhood on my mother.

'Dead, one and all,' Isaac says, 'all tended by you, Annie Flowers. Esther was right. You are a curse upon this town.'

His eyes speak of the turmoil of grief. The veins in his forearms bulge like ropes as he swings his fist and knocks me aside with a single blow.

I sprawl in the dirt, spitting out dust, my jaw a lightning bolt of pain. He has hold of my mother's hair, fingers tangling with the red ribbons bound into her dark curls. He yanks her head back hard.

'What have you to say, witch?' he snarls into her face. I can smell the drink on him even from a distance. My mother's eyes show white, like a frightened animal's, her words caught in her throat.

'This town is plagued by evil and unnatural things!' Samuel cries. 'Sickness and death rain down upon us, ever since the Cromwell household came here.'

There are murmurs of agreement.

'Our crops fail, year after year.'

'She consorts with the Devil.'

And then I hear Edith Cobbett's voice raised up: 'She lay with my husband and cursed him when he would not pay her for it. She is the reason he is dead!'

'She's a whore,' Edith's son, Will, says. 'Cromwell knows it better than any!'

'She brings the Devil's work to Ely!'

'We must cast her out!'

Isaac drags my mother to her feet. She cries out and crumples as she puts her weight on her broken ankle. 'We will settle this!' he roars. 'You will swim, witch!'

Will Cobbett pulls me up and pins my wrists behind my back. He is not much older than I, barely a man, but I cannot escape the strong grip of his farm-boy hands. My head throbs and my vision blurs. I am pushed forwards, following the hulk of Isaac Tuttle, who takes my mother towards the river. Will kicks at my legs, making me fall, then beats me until I walk again.

My mother claws and scrabbles, her hair coming out in clumps as Isaac tears at it. He punches her jaw and I see her swoon with the shock, as I had done. All the time he yells at her, 'Whore! Witch! Devil!'

We reach the Ouse and Isaac wastes no time. He drags my mother away from the quay to where the muddy bank slopes into the water and heaves her into the deepest part of the flow.

I battle against Will, but he holds me fast.

'Stop! Please stop!' I beg, only to be silenced by a thump in the stomach that winds me and makes the world turn blinding white.

She splashes and struggles, pale limbs flailing, caught up in strands of riverweed.

'She floats!' someone cries. 'See how she floats!'

Isaac watches and waits as my mother's head remains above the water.

It is all done in seconds. The mob, mad with the horror in their midst, cannot be stopped. I scream. I yell. Will knocks me to the ground and pins me down until Samuel grinds my face into the dirt with his boot.

'She is a witch!' comes the cry.

A rope is brought and Isaac wades into the river until it is up to his waist. He flings the rope to my mother, who grabs hold of it, clutching at it as if it is her last chance of life. It would be better if she did not. As soon as Isaac has hold of her, I know what he means to do.

Samuel pulls me up to my knees and breathes liquor fumes into my face, making me retch. 'Now you'll see what happens to witches.'

Isaac has my mother by the hair and wrenches her arm behind her back, forcing her up the path. He tears at her sodden clothes, slashing at her stays and exposing her breasts for all to see. I think for one moment that he means to defile her. But instead he shouts, 'Here is Satan's whore! Who here would see an end to her evil? Who here will see justice done?'

The crowd bays its consent. A lone voice calls, speaking for all, 'Aye! Let it be done!'

A couple of the men loop the rope over the low branch of a willow that stands at the water's edge.

I begin to wail. I can barely hear the poisonous things whispered in my ear.

'Have mercy,' I plead. 'She is all I have! She is all I have ever had!' But they have no pity.

As they drag her to the tree and tie the noose around her neck they call her witch, harlot, devil-wife. They spit upon her with their stinking alehouse breath and one man opens his breeches and pisses upon her naked skin. She fights for her life but Isaac and his men are too strong, lost in drunken rage, eager for retribution – this is God's work after all. Martha Featherstone comes forward from the crowd and drops to her knees, calling upon the angels to take the witch back to Hell where she belongs.

And there in the shadow of the great cathedral, with their God watching, they hang my mother by the neck.

Chapter 2

Have you ever seen a person hang? There are few, I think, who have not been witness to a painful death in these last years of strife. Who has not been to an execution in the market square on hanging day? Who has not cheered and clapped at the violent end of some common thief or some bandy-legged slattern?

It is different when it is someone you love. The person at the end of the rope is no longer an object, to be mocked and despised. They are not the enemy. They are a part of you. They are a part of your wholeness, and when the breath is choked from them, so a part of life is choked from you.

Will Cobbett holds me back as I watch my mother's perfect face bulge and swell. Her eyes run with red tears. Her legs twitch like those of a freshly slaughtered fowl. I watch as she stops fighting it, as her arms fall limp by her sides and her tongue lolls. I stand by, powerless, and watch my mother die.

As her spirit leaves her battered, broken body, so the fire seems to go out of Isaac Tuttle. His shoulders sag and his snarling lips slacken. He watches his victim swing, as if surprised at what he has done. Then he turns and slumps down the riverbank until he reaches the water's edge, where he kneels and begins washing the blood from his hands.

Martha Featherstone continues her vigil, her voice a thread, wavering above the hum of the crowd. Samuel orders the rope cut down and my mother's body falls into the mud like a jumble of discarded rags.

'What about the girl?' Will says. He pushes me forwards, and I feel eyes slice me, like knives.

Isaac doesn't answer but carries on wiping the stains from his skin.

'Send her to Hell, like the witch,' Samuel says, to a buzz of agreement. 'She is a cursed bastard, a witch's child. She will go the same way as the mother.'

'Swim her!' comes the cry, as I knew it would.

I am pushed towards the river, the mob gathering, not yet sated.

Isaac stands in their way. He comes close to me and eyes the welt that spreads across my jaw. He leans in, puts his cold fingers up to my cheek and turns my face away from his. Then he runs his hand down my neck and over my bodice, squeezing my breast beneath my stays.

'A little whore . . . just like your mother,' he says.

Will's grip slackens a little. No doubt he wants nothing to do with Isaac's perverse lusts. I see my chance and stamp my foot down hard on Will's boot. He yelps and I pull my hands free and claw at Isaac's face, feeling the soft, wet give of his eyeball beneath my fingertips. He bellows and swipes at me but I twist and tear away from them both.

I run, almost blind, stumbling but escaping the hands that reach for me.

'Let her go!' I hear Isaac shout behind me. 'She will not get far.'

He is right. I run to the only place I know, the only place where I might be safe. I run home, to the big house on the green – the Cromwell house.

★ ★ ★

News travels fast in Ely. Servants will always make it their business to know the latest, especially when it concerns one of their own.

It is Old Bess who finds me, as night falls, shivering on the mattress in the servants' quarters that I have shared with my mother all the years I can remember. It smells of last summer's straw and the rosemary she wore in her hair.

Although I know what I have seen, I swear it cannot be true. Without my mother I am alone in this world. She was all to me – my protector, my comfort, my closest friend. I cannot fathom what life may be without her. I want to dream, and wake to find her next to me, sleep-warm smiles banishing my nightmares, telling me that all is well, that today is the same as every day before. Any other truth is too terrible to bear.

But there is a pain, beginning at my heart, seeping through my limbs, thrumming in my head like poison. When I close my eyes, all I see is my mother's face, bloody and lifeless. My body tells the truth, even if my mind cannot.

Old Bess is the master's mother. She is ancient, with white hair, parchment skin and the deep brown eyes of a much younger woman. It is she who rules the house in the master's absence, not the simple dough-faced wife. Old Bess is the anchor that keeps the household docked in this world of stormy seas.

She swoops in, like a great bat, rustling in black damask. 'Is it true, child?' she asks gently. She enfolds me in her arms.

My body trembles as though I am taken with a fit. I spew up a strange, strangled whimpering. My eyes are dry; though I long for tears, they do not come. Instead I feel turned inside out. My innards seethe so much I begin to think I will die of it.

'My poor girl.' Old Bess rocks me, like a babe. 'You are safe now.'

But I am not safe, and she knows it as well as I.

* * *

They come with weapons and torches. They take up their place on the green before the house. They call out to God and to his angels. They call out to the master. They want me surrendered that they may mete out justice as they see fit. They want me dead.

'Stay here,' Old Bess whispers. 'And be silent.'

She leaves me cowering on the mattress and goes into the main part of the house, where the mistress and her two youngest girls huddle before the fire. I want to obey her but I am too afraid to be left alone. There is only one door to the servants' quarters and it has no lock. Fear sharpens my wits. I gather myself and tiptoe after her, sliding silently up the front staircase, choosing the boards that do not creak. I find myself a shadowy spot by the window that overlooks the green. From here, I see the men gathered below.

Their number has dwindled to a dozen or so, but now they carry weapons – poor men's arms – axes, clubs and long hunting knives. Isaac Tuttle stands at the fore, alongside Samuel and Will. They look savage, swaying from drink, braying like a pack of dogs. Martha Featherstone and Edith Cobbett are with them still. Martha weeps and holds up her arms to the heavens as if beseeching God. I cannot tell if it is my death or my deliverance that she prays for.

There is a banging on the street door. It is Isaac, fists curled and ready. 'Give me the witch! She is rightfully mine!'

I imagine the Cromwell family gathered downstairs, Mary and Frances clinging to their mother's skirts. With the master and his sons away, we have only one man in the household. The stableman, Christopher, is a quiet, gentle sort and no match if it comes to a brawl.

Isaac pounds on the door again and my heart thumps in time with it.

'Bring her out, or we will burn her out!'

Samuel whoops a battle-cry, brandishing the flaming torch he holds. Others join him. Some are army men and no strangers to slaughter.

I hear the front door open and Old Bess steps out onto the green. The men howl and laugh, pleased at such easy prey.

'You will leave this house and go home to your wives,' she says.

'We will have justice,' Isaac slurs. 'Bring the witch to me and we'll leave you in peace.'

'There is no witch in my household, Isaac Tuttle, and there never was.'

Isaac sways closer. He grins and a string of tobacco-stained slaver drools from the corner of his mouth. 'We have proof.'

Will Cobbett steps forward. He carries a sawn-off pike. At the pointed end of it I see what looks like a slab of meat, wet and glistening in the torchlight. Then I realise: it is Esther's child. They have skewered the tiny body like an animal on a spit. I gag, covering my mouth with my hands.

'See the demon that the witch brought forth from my wife! What more proof is there? We have dealt with the mother and now we will finish this. We will deal with her bastard!'

Old Bess raises her voice: 'There is no sin on the girl's part, or on the part of Annie Flowers. It is you who have sinned greatly this night and you who will pay for it.'

She jabs him in the chest with a bony finger. 'It is God who has given you this unfortunate child, Isaac Tuttle, as punishment for your own lusts. You are known for your drunkenness, your fornication and your violence. Annie Flowers is not the first to suffer at your hands. If your wife lived, she could vouch for that. Now God has punished you. Think on it.'

Torches flicker and crackle as the Fenland wind gets up.

'And as for the rest of you,' Old Bess says, 'you can be sure I know you all by name. When my son hears of this there will be retribution indeed. Lawful and just retribution. Do not doubt it.'

At this mention of the master and his powerful influence, a few of the men lower their weapons and look to one another.

But Isaac is undeterred. 'You do not scare us, old woman.'

As he speaks, Christopher steps up behind Old Bess, holding the axe he uses for chopping firewood. He blocks the doorway.

'Leave this house,' Old Bess says, 'or you will be the ones who hang. You know I have the power to do it. God knows it would be right to do it.'

Already some of the men are backing away, the fight clearly gone out of them, preferring the thought of their tankards, or their beds, to the future that Old Bess predicts.

But Isaac roars and pushes up his sleeves as if preparing for a fistfight. Samuel takes hold of his arm and says something I cannot hear. Isaac shrugs him off. Even in the shifting torchlight I can see his face, flushed with fury. He draws out a short blade and swipes wildly at the air, missing Old Bess by inches.

A cry goes up from the men as she staggers backwards. Before he can strike out again, they are on him, pinning his arms, holding him back. Even drunkards are wiser than to attack their betters.

Christopher bundles Old Bess into the house.

The men have hold of Isaac. He fights against them but they are too many. They force him to the ground and Samuel holds a knife to his neck until he is forced to submit.

'Not this time, then!' Isaac shouts, and I know he is talking to me. 'But I can wait! I will not rest until I have justice! I will see you dead!'

I watch, letting go of a breath I do not even know I'm holding, as they drag him off into the night.

The floor beneath my feet shudders as the door slams and the bolts slide across. Then comes a child's cry I recognise as that of

Frances. She is the littlest, only seven years old, and my favourite. Her tears usually make my heart falter, but fear has purged all other feelings.

Isaac's threats echo. He meant what he said. He means to see me hang.

The mistress sends both girls upstairs and Christopher tries to soothe them as he leads the way. I crouch in my hiding place beneath the lintel. I do not want them to see me like this, wretched and desperate, for they will read the story in my eyes.

How I wish the master were at home, for none of these Ely men would dare go against him. He has the power of Parliament's army and the righteousness of God on his side. It is his good name, and his good heart, that has kept us safe until now. But instead I must beg the protection of my mistress. The Cromwell house has been my cradle all these years; now it must be my sanctuary.

I need the kindness of Old Bess too. She will understand. She will hold me close and tell me I am not alone. She is the only one I can trust in the master's absence.

My legs shake as I stand and try to still my breath. I creep down the stairs and pad to the door of the parlour. What I hear makes me freeze.

'She must go tonight.'

'Calm yourself, my dear. You are upset,' Old Bess says.

'I always knew Annie Flowers would bring shame upon this house and I was right.'

'We cannot turn Ruth out into the street. She would not last the night. Do you want her to meet the same fate as Annie?'

'It is not my concern.' I hear the scrape of a chair as the mistress sits.

'It is very much your concern when you've already lost one servant. Would you lose another?'

'I would have my children safe in their beds.'

I hear footsteps pacing and the swish of Old Bess's skirts. 'I will send word to Oliver by first light. He will know what to do.'

'No!' The mistress is adamant. 'I have charge of this household and I say that she must go. I will not have her here for one more day. You saw those men. You heard what they said. If they dare to trespass so far, nothing will stop them. Men like that think nothing of the law, nothing of sin. They will attack us as we sleep. They will burn the place down!'

'I cannot send her away. Oliver will want to take this to the law . . .'

'Oh – Oliver! I have never understood why he insists upon housing and feeding the pair of them. He knows my thoughts and disregards them. Well, now I shall have my way.'

'You are mistress of this house, my dear, but are you sure this is the Christian thing to do? Do you feel no responsibility for the girl?'

'You heard those men. They will come back. And what then? Are we to live in fear, night after night? Are we to be hounded and mocked in the streets? We are a respected family and I will not have the taint of witchcraft upon us. I will not have the Cromwell name dragged through the dirt along with that of Annie Flowers or her bastard.'

Old Bess hushes her. 'Have compassion. Annie served us well these fifteen years. Ruth has lived with us all her life. She is a friend and companion to your little ones. We cannot abandon her when she needs us most.'

'She is a servant, nothing more. Oliver would agree. His position is precarious and any hint of scandal would damage us. There is too much at stake. And you, Mother, are forgetting your place, as well as hers.'

Old Bess sighs. 'I suppose, for Oliver's sake . . .'

'And the family. Think of them. Would you put a servant's needs above those of your own grandchildren?'

'Very well, for the sake of the family, then, for Oliver's sake, she must go.'

Chapter 3

Christopher knows the safe roads through the Fens and rides hard, stopping only once to water the horse. We reach Cambridge by nightfall the next day. He takes me to a hostelry called the Devil Inn. The sign, swinging above the door, shows a red impish creature with horns and a barbed tail. I wonder at his choice, but am too weary to care.

He leaves the horse with the ostler and secures a room for the night, but when we are safely seated in the taproom, supplied with trenchers of yesterday's bread and maggoty cheese, he tells me that he will not pass the night.

'The mistress was clear. I'm to go straight back, no waiting.'

'But you can't travel in darkness,' I say. 'Besides, the horse is tired. It needs rest, as do you.'

I look around the room, thinking that I cannot bear to be left alone in such company. Groups of young men carouse at tables laden with tankards. The women among them are gaudily dressed and painted with white lead and rouge. A couple sit before the fire, kissing openly. This place is aptly named.

'That's true, but I dare not anger her further. I have to take my chances.'

'Then you will leave me here, alone?'

'I'm sorry, Ruth. Those are my orders. I must obey them.' He picks at his food and will not meet my eye.

I never did like goodbyes. Even as a small child I would run and hide rather than bid farewell to my mother whenever she went out to market or to tend one of the townsfolk. It became a game to me. In the end, she gave up trying to leave me behind and I trailed everywhere with her, learning her skills by mimicry.

Now I cannot stomach another parting and fall to dumb sulking as Christopher finishes his meal. As he stands to leave, dusting crumbs from his lap, I feel the last shred of hope that he will change his mind and take me home snap like a twig underfoot. I stare at my plate.

'Farewell, then, Ruth,' he says, holding out his arms to embrace me. He waits a while before letting them drop to his sides and picking up his hat. 'May God go with you, child.' Grim-faced, he dons his cloak and leaves.

I watch a maggot crawl from the hunk of cheese and worm its way across my plate.

Sitting alone in this stinking place, I realise that the people I have grown up with, and shared my life with, are no substitute for true family. The ties of blood are absent. To them I am just a servant, and that is not the same thing at all. I have deceived myself into believing that they care about me. I have collected every kind word from Old Bess, every smile from Master Oliver, all the hours spent playing happily with Mary and Frances, and thought that these things meant as much to them as they did to me. It all means nothing. The only person who really loved me is dead.

I began to understand this as, just hours before, I pressed up against the panelling in the passageway outside the parlour and listened to the mistress dismiss me, as if I have less value than a squealing new piglet, born in the slop of the sty.

'She must go tonight,' she said. 'And Oliver must know nothing of it.'

'You cannot mean to keep this from him?' Old Bess said.

'His regard for our servants is unseemly. Ruth is a grown girl now, a young woman. People will talk, just as they always have about her mother. It did not matter when we had nothing, when we were nothing. But now Oliver has risen so high. He has such power. He is a gentleman. He must behave like one.'

'You would have him act the Cavalier, wanting everyone to bow and scrape, just because he has a general's position and a few coins in his pocket?'

'Of course not. But he has more pressing matters to deal with. He has the future of the country in his hands. We should not trouble him with domestic concerns.'

'Perhaps you are right. I know my son and I know he will be compelled to act. He cannot afford distraction at such a time. Better to tell him Ruth left by choice. We will keep her whereabouts between us, for now at least. London is best, I think. I have an acquaintance there who will help.'

'There must be no connection. Nothing to tie her to us.'

Then the scratch of a quill, the sizzle of sealing wax.

'She will need money,' Old Bess said.

'Give her only what she needs. And make sure she knows she is not welcome here. I do not want to see her again.'

The food on my plate sickens me but I reach out for the ale and drain the pot, swallow the lump in my throat and wipe away the tears that swell.

I put my hand on my satchel to feel the hard, square shape inside and draw some comfort from it. This is all I have left of my mother: a book, bound in tattered brown leather and tied with a cord. On the curled yellow pages, in a spidery hand, she noted a lifetime of knowledge – the spells and charms and herb-lore that condemned her. It is my only record of her and her only gift to me. I have no belongings to speak of, no chests full of clothing, no keepsakes or vanities, so it is this book that I clung to as I set off through the cold damp dawn to try my luck with the Fen spirits. But it is of little use to me now. Even with all the charms in the world, I cannot bring her back.

I watch the couple before the fire. I watch how the man's hands move over the woman's bodice. I see how she breathes, head tilted back and eyelids quivering. She wears a length of crimson ribbon in her hair, a sliver of blood-red opulence, just like the ones my mother favoured. A leery-eyed old man watches the couple too. He catches my gaze and nods knowingly. I look away, shamed.

Just then, a man comes swaying towards my table and leans heavily against it. He is young and handsome, with the confidence of one who knows it. His smart clothes are dishevelled, his undershirt open to the waist, displaying a slice of pale, smooth skin.

'What have we here?' he drawls. 'A pretty lady, all alone?'

His two companions follow. Like him they are richly dressed and reeking of liquor.

'Mistress, it pains me to see such a face without a smile,' the man says. 'Pray don't cry, for we have the means to cheer you.'

His friends snigger.

'I wish to be alone,' I say.

'Lord Jeremiah Lytham never leaves a damsel in distress.' He makes a low, mocking bow and slides onto the bench next to me. 'How can I be of service?' His eyes are bright and blurred with drink.

'Thank you, but I'm not distressed.'

'On the contrary, pretty one, it's quite plain that you're in need of good humour.' Lytham claps his hands for the serving girl, who comes running. His friends pull up stools and ogle her as they order wine. She leans forward across the table, simpering, her lacings half undone, flesh spilling. One of the men slides a finger between her breasts, draws it out again, puts it into his mouth and sucks. The girl chitters and pretends to be shocked, but her eyes are lusty, hungry.

I back away, clutching my satchel to me. 'Please, sir, I had rather be left alone.'

Lytham scoffs. 'Any girl who comes into a place like this is surely looking for some fun.' He walks his fingers up the sleeve of my dress. 'Don't be shy. You're in good company – the best in the place.'

I shake his hand from me. 'I'm not a whore.'

'Of course not. None of these estimable ladies is a whore.' He sweeps his arm wide, indicating the drabs about the place. 'We're in search of a little companionship. And when I see a comely young thing like yourself – a country girl I'll wager, like a breath of fresh country air – well, I delight in such a companion.' He strokes my neck and leans in close. 'What do you say?'

His breath stinks of stale beer and onions. I push him away and try to stand. 'You are mistaken.'

'Sit down, bitch,' he hisses, pulling me back to the bench. 'Do not raise your voice to me. Do you know who I am?'

'I don't care.'

'Oh, but you shall. No common slut refuses me . . . and I am losing patience.'

'Sir, I tell you, I am not a whore!'

He pulls me towards him and grips his arm about my shoulders. 'Not a whore? A virgin, then. I'm in luck, boys!'

His friends laugh and leer as I tussle with him.

'You'll sell me your wares this night,' he whispers into my ear, 'or I shall have you anyway, without recompense. You will remember my name and you will remember this night.'

He wrenches the satchel from my grasp and throws it to the floor. He pins me to the bench and tugs at the lacings of my dress, his fingers fumbling with the strings.

I could struggle, I could call out for help, but I do not. I give in, close my eyes and pray for oblivion. I have no fight left in me. What does it matter anyway, if he takes me right here on the trestle? I have no life, no friends and nothing I recognise as my own. I am as good as dead.

I am no stranger to the ways of men.

He was a farmer's son: at sixteen, only two years my elder, but the very picture of a man to my unripe eye.

For one long, hot summer my days were sweetened by dreams of him. He had the looks of a prince, with shifting eyes, one moment blue as a robin's egg, the next grey as floodwater at leaf fall.

The first time I curled my hair and went to market without a cap, I did it so he would notice me. When I strayed from the causeway into the plush drained fields tenanted by his father, I did so hoping to cross his path. When he smiled at me, I smiled back.

He came to me one day at the end of that summer and told me he was destined for Parliament's fight. He laid me down and whispered words of love in my ear. He told me I would make him the happiest of men.

But when he was done with me, he was done with his pretty words.

'So it's true what they say. Like mother, like daughter.' He shook himself clean, spotting my skirts. 'Little whore . . .'

That day, I swore no man would have the heart of me again. But what do I care now, if a man takes my body?

There is a great thwack of metal upon wood and I feel Lytham's prying fingers jump with shock.

A male voice says, 'Leave the girl alone.'

I open my eyes to see a tall man dressed in a sackcloth cloak.

With his hood drawn up, I cannot see his face, just dark, straggling stubble and a stern mouth. He towers over us, a rusting sword held out across the table, pointing at Lytham's groin.

Lytham takes his hands from me and leans back in his seat. 'And what business is it of yours?'

'I said, leave the girl alone.'

Lytham's companions, shock-eyed, flounder for their weapons. One pulls out a short dagger but drops it, clattering onto the flagstones. He goes down on his knees to retrieve it.

The hooded man raises his blade and holds the tip of it to Lytham's throat.

Lytham falters. 'Touch me and you'll hang for it,' he says.

The hooded man shrugs and indicates the door with his blade. 'Be gone.'

Lytham slides from the bench and stands, swaying on his heels. 'Come,' he slurs to his friends. 'I tire of this game. There's better sport to be had elsewhere.' Then, turning to the man, 'You, sir, had better watch your back. I won't forget such a slight.'

The hooded man watches them leave. Then he sits down opposite me and slips the cloak from his face.

He is younger than I'd supposed, no more than twenty years. He has swarthy looks, dark eyes and dark hair shorn in the fashion of the New Model Army. A broken nose gives him the look of a brawler.

'Are you all right?' he says, as I rearrange my dress, fingers trembling.

Before I can answer the landlord addresses him: 'I'll thank you not to be scaring off my best paying customers, sir.'

'Why are you serving that Royalist scum anyway?' the man says.

'A paying customer is a paying customer. My establishment is a place for relaxation and refreshment, not politics.'

'Nothing political about those braggarts.'

The landlord accedes. 'You'd have done better not to make an enemy of Lord Lytham. I've seen him draw swords for less. If I were you, I'd keep my head down for a few days.' He nods to the flagon of wine that the group have left on the table. 'That's already paid for. I reckon the young lady has had a shock. It's yours if you want it.'

The man pours two cups of the deep red liquid and passes one to me. 'It'll help,' he says. He slugs his serving and pours another.

I drink and feel the bittersweet heat of it run through me.

He sits, eyes fixed on me, until I feel as uncomfortable as I had under Lytham's gaze. 'I thank you, sir,' I say.

He shrugs. 'Men like that still think they have rights over the rest of us.'

'I can look after myself now.'

'You're shaking like a leaf in autumn. Drink.'

I do as I'm told, glad of the warming and softening of my body. 'You've done me a service,' I say, 'but I've no means to pay you for it. You have my gratitude, but that is all. I'd rather be left alone.'

'What – so some other drunken fool can try his luck?' He leans across the table and lowers his voice. 'Or am I mistaken? Are you hoping for a finer catch than Lord Lytham and his merry men?'

I pull my shawl around my shoulders. 'Of course not.'

'Well, then, what's your business here?'

'I . . . I'm on my way to London.'

He raises an eyebrow. 'London. Why?'

'To stay with friends,' I lie.

'At such a time as this, the roads swarming with thieves and beggars? Some friends, to let you travel alone. Have you a horse in the stables?'

'No,' I admit, thinking of Christopher, already on his way back to Ely.

'Then how do you travel?'

'I have a pass.'

'I see.' He pauses and looks me over. 'Who grants you permission?'

'My mistress arranged it.'

'A pass is all well and good, but it'll not buy you a horse.'

I have no answer to that. I drain my cup and refill it from the flagon.

He strokes the dark hair on his chin and when he speaks again, he seems to be talking to himself. 'Full of secrets and determined not to share them. We've much in common. That will make us good companions, I think.'

'But I told you—'

'You admitted yourself, just now, that you're indebted to me. Is that not so? And you cannot pay me. So, I would strike a bargain with you.'

'Sir, I never asked for your help. It's unfair that you make demands of me.'

He laughs. 'And you were coping with those louts so well on your own.'

'I'm grateful to you, but that is all.'

He holds up his hands in supplication.

I drain my second cup of wine. On an empty stomach it makes my head swim but I draw courage from it.

'I travel to London too,' he says. 'I've a place on a carter's wagon, leaving at dawn tomorrow. It has taken three days to find someone willing to take passengers. And thank God I did – if I'm to have Lytham breathing down my neck, I think I'd best be on my way. You'll travel with me.'

'I cannot.'

'Why?'

'I do not know you.'

'That's easily remedied. I'm Joseph. Joseph Oakes.' He holds out his hand for me to shake it, as if I am a man and his equal. I ignore it.

'I can find my own way to London,' I say.

'Forgive me, but even before those scoundrels approached, I noticed you cowering in the corner, like a frightened lamb. You're easy prey. You'll not last a day on the London road.'

'And you would be my protector, I suppose?'

He shrugs. 'I can help you.'

'So that I may become further indebted to you?'

'I have need of a travelling companion and you're as good as any. We can travel as brother and sister. I won't lay a finger on you. Think on it. You're unlikely to find a better offer.'

'Brother and sister?'

'Why not? Yours is a Fenland accent like my own. No one will suspect us.'

Until then I had not noticed the familiar round tones in his voice.

'Where are you from?'

'Hilgay. A small village, not four miles from Downham Market. And you?'

'Ely.'

He smiles to himself. 'I knew it. You have the look of a Fenlander.' He pours the last of the wine into his cup, without offering it to me. 'Ely is a fine town. I know a little of it. I've friends from there. Why leave?'

I am silent.

'Ah, more secrets,' he says, holding up his cup as if to make a toast. 'Well, it has been interesting, but I have business to attend to and if you're determined to reject my offer . . .' He stands to leave and turns away from me.

'Wait,' I say, thinking of brigands and bandits on the journey ahead, or worse yet, a second night at the Devil Inn. 'Will you promise that no harm will come to me? That we will travel as brother and sister? That you will make no claim on me once we reach London?'

He pulls up the hood of his cloak and leans close. 'I can promise you only this. No harm will come to you by my hand.'

'Then . . . I will come with you.'

He smiles. 'Good. The cart leaves at dawn. I'll call here for you at first light. Be ready to leave.'

Again he holds out his hand and this time I take it.

'And what is my new sister's name?' he asks.

'Ruth. Ruth Flowers.'

'Ruth.' He lingers over my name, as though savouring it on his tongue. 'Have you a bed here tonight?'

'Yes.'

'Then I suggest you retire to it. And bolt your door.'

I nod.

'Until morning, then.'

Before I can reply, he turns and sweeps out of the inn, leaving me staring at the empty flagon and wondering what I have done.

Chapter 4

Joseph Oakes keeps his word and comes for me a quarter-hour after the first crow of the cockerel. I am awake and dressed. I have snatched only moments of sleep, plagued by hot, fervid dreams and the topers in the taproom until the early hours.

Joseph takes me away from the Devil Inn and leads me through a maze of alleyways with high red-brick walls, speckled with leaded casements, until I have quite lost my way.

'Where are you taking me?' I ask, but get no reply.

I make a silent prayer for mercy. If I am walking to my death, then at least make it a swift one. I notice that Joseph carries a sword, the one he used to threaten Lytham, strapped to his pack. The slash of a blade across the throat is preferable to the end that haunts me. I have no desire to jerk and jump at the end of a hangman's rope. Whether that rope belongs to Isaac Tuttle or some deceitful stranger makes no real difference.

But then we come to an open tract of land that adjoins one of the colleges and beyond it a road, stretching south. Sure enough, a cart waits there: an open wagon, loaded with barrels and pelts, all tied over with canvas. A sore-looking nag stamps and snorts snatches of breath that float up and away to meet the dawning clouds.

Joseph greets the carter with a handshake – a welcome more civil than any I have received. 'Siddal, this is my sister, Ruth,' he says, rough-handling me forwards. 'She will come with us.'

Siddal is the sort of man who stays ruddy and rotund against the odds. I wonder how much of his cargo he siphons to keep his belly so plump.

He takes off his hat, displaying a round bald spot on his crown. The skin there is as red as fresh beef. 'Well, now, Mister Oakes, this is not part of our bargain.'

'We will make it worth your while.'

'A man who can handle a weapon is a useful thing, but a woman?'

'She's small, as you can see, so she won't add much to the load. And, besides, she has a pass, issued by her mistress.'

Siddal raises an eyebrow and holds out his hand expectantly. I push Old Bess's note, my one safeguard, into his rough fingers and he looks it over, his eyes flickering to my face. I doubt that he can read it. 'I'll need extra, for the trouble,' he says, passing the document back to me.

'Two shillings more a day,' Joseph offers.

'I'll have you understand that I can't answer for her safety. It's work enough travelling with a load, these days, with all the trouble on the roads. She's your sister. You look after her.'

'Understood.'

'Make it two crown all in and I'll take her.'

'Do you have it?' Joseph whispers to me. I nod, even though it will leave me with very little. I will be a beggar by the time I reach London.

'You are a kind and generous man, Master Siddal,' Joseph says, clapping the carter on the back.

The London road passes through lush, rolling country. Not half a day out of Cambridge and we meet with views very different from any I have seen before. The carter hauls us up hills and plunges down slopes, making me queasy. The day has turned hot for May and I swelter in my winter layers, imagining myself seasick. I am glad when we stop at an inn and I can buy bread to still my stomach. It is the first I've eaten in two days yet I am not hungry and have to force it down.

It is well into the afternoon, once Siddal has handed the reins to Joseph and snores among the skins in the back of the cart, that I dare to make comment on our progress.

'I don't see any bandits, Mister Oakes.'

'Pray God we don't. What Siddal said is true. The roads are crawling with troublemakers. Beggars, gypsies, soldiers.'

'Soldiers?'

'Aye, the worst of the lot. Runaways mostly. Parliament men, disaffected and run wild. The King's men tend to drunkenness and whoring, as they've always done, but the rebels? They've had no pay, no thanks and little satisfaction. Desperate times make desperate men.'

'How do you know?'

He looks off into the distance. 'I was one of them.'

'You're a soldier?'

He turns to check that Siddal is still sleeping, and lowers his voice. 'I was.'

'For Parliament?'

'Yes. Eastern Association. Under Cromwell and Rainsborough.'

At the mention of Master Oliver I feel a thin vine of fear twist up my spine. I remember him discussing discipline among the troops with his guests at table. 'Once a soldier, always a soldier,' he had said, talking of duty and honour. He thought deserters were godless men and should be punished, even given a traitor's death.

'Are you a runaway?'

'Injured at Naseby Fight.' He pats his chest, just below his ribs, to illustrate. 'Never went back.'

'So that's why you need me,' I say. 'You have no pass to travel so you need mine, and my purse too, no doubt.'

'Something like that. Naseby was my first battle. God willing, it was my last.'

I've heard tales of Naseby Fight. Accounts swept through the Fens in the wake of the battle. Parliament men rejoiced at stories of such conquest. Master Oliver had returned home not long after and had been grave and silent on the matter of the multitudes of dead. But those who visited him, Eastern Association men in leather coats with booming voices, slapped him on the back and drank to bravery and daring. They had all thanked Providence for the result.

'But it was a great victory, was it not?' I say.

Joseph shrugs. 'Victory comes at a cost.'

'But to fight for God's cause, to die by God's will, surely—'

The fire in his eyes cuts me short.

'What do you know about it?' he snaps. 'You know nothing.'

'I know what will happen if you are caught.'

'London is a big place, or so I'm told. Big enough to hide me. Besides, I might be done with army life, but I'm not giving up the fight.'

With one hand holding the reins, he reaches into his pack and pulls out a sheaf of papers. They are dirty and ragged, looped with string. He unties the bundle and passes the first few pages to me. Printed in black ink, the front page is torn almost in two; he must have been carrying them for some time. They remind me of the pamphlets strewn about Master Oliver's desk. Across the frontispiece, dark, lopsided letters spell out 'England's Birth Right Justified'. I turn the first page and read, 'To all the Freeborn people of England . . .'

I am no stranger to pamphlets such as this. Many of the apprentices and labourers about Ely trade in them on market days. Sometimes a man would read aloud from such a piece in the market square or outside one of the taverns. In the first days of war, Parliament recruiters seduced our local boys with such talk.

'Can you read?' he asks me.

'Yes.'

'So, you understand?'

At my blank expression he reaches across and points to the smallest words at the very bottom of the page. They are smudged and difficult to make out but I read aloud: 'Printed in London, 1645.'

'I aim to be a printer's apprentice,' he says. 'London is where the presses are. I'll carry on the fight in a different way.'

'So, you believe that words will win the war?'

'The war is almost won. They say that Oxford will surrender any day now. And once the King's strongest centre is taken, there is nowhere for him to go. What comes next is the fight for people's sympathies.'

I brandish the pamphlet. 'And you think people want this Levelling talk?'

'Aye. Don't you?'

'I think people want food on their tables and their men at home.'

He snorts and gives me a mocking smile. 'Tell me, what do you do in Ely? How did you earn those pennies in your purse?'

'I'm a servant. You know that.'

'And do you like it?'

I shrug. 'It is my lot.'

'Would you change it if you could?'

'I . . . I don't know.'

'Would you like your own home, your own piece of land to work? No mistress with a hold over you, telling you what you can and can't do? How would you like that?'

'That's impossible. Things have always been this way.'

'It *was* impossible. But this is what we're fighting for. The world is turning and now is our chance.' He turns to me, animated. 'There are men in the army, good, honest men, who would secure such things for the people. A voice for the common man in Parliament, rights for the common man and everything in its natural place. No longer will Englishmen be held down by kings and lords and squires.'

He sounds just like the guests at Master Oliver's table, sloshing their wine and rattling the pewter in heated debate. I hush him as Siddal stirs. 'I do not know politics,' I say.

'But you are alive. To be alive in this time is to witness the changing of the world. You cannot help but be caught up in it. The army has such power now and the people are ripe for change. The King will have to compromise. You'll see. Soon things will be better and we will all be glad of this war.'

How blind he is.

'I will never be glad of this war,' I say.

He snatches the paper from my lap. 'Those who fight must have something to believe in. Would you take that away from them?'

'It has already taken too much from me.' It was the war that took Master Oliver away and, with him, the protection that might have saved my mother.

Joseph's eyes are scornful. 'And what of those who have lost everything – even their lives? Would you have all this blood spilled for nothing?'

'I just wish . . . I wish it had never begun. I wish things were as before.'

'Then you prefer the old order? You prefer to stay a slave? Pray God, tell me my new sister is not a Royalist.'

I do not have the courage to tell him the truth. I know little of politics, understand few of the arguments that led Charles Stuart to wage war on his own people, but even so, I belong at the very centre of it all.

I have tended the man who led those poor soldiers to die in the fields for God and for Parliament. I have laundered his war-soiled clothes, scrubbed the blood from his breeches and scoured the battlefield mud from his boots. I have endured the lecherous stares of his army friends. I have played sister to his children and tended his wife when she was sick. I have been privy to his private rages and his tormented prayers. I know better than most what it means to be loyal to Oliver Cromwell.

But what does it matter? That part of my life is over and I cannot trust this deserter with the truth of it. I am not ready to answer the questions that will follow. I understand that much at least.

Despite my companion's stories, we make good time that day, free from the threat of vagabonds and highway robbers. I wonder if Joseph has been telling tales to frighten me, to bind me to him. The contents of my purse have already proved valuable. Only God knows what other uses he might have in mind for me. It seems that every man I meet wants to take something from me. Still, there is something in Joseph Oakes, something in his manner, that seems more like truth than deceit.

By nightfall we reach Puckeridge and stop at an inn there to rest the horse and find a bed for the night. The Old Bell is a place made for travellers, worn out and filthy, populated by transients. The innkeeper saves his best rooms for those with the coin to pay and the rest are forced to make do with a draughty chamber, tightly packed with pallets and barely warmed by a sputtering central hearth.

I claim my place, between Joseph and Siddal, and pull my skirts and shawl tight around me. I lie still for some time and listen as it begins to rain. Thunder rumbles in the distance. Filled with the human stench of unwashed bodies, the snores and grunts of the sleeping, the room makes me uneasy. But despite my wakefulness, Nature gets the better of me and, before long, I sleep.

★ ★ ★

It is still dark when I wake. The fire in the room has faded to embers and the air is chill and damp. The rain is still pouring, in that way saved for summer storms. Water drips from the eaves and pools under the window where the paper covering has come loose. At that moment a great crack of lightning brightens the room, a roll of thunder answering it. The storm is close.

The others stir and shift in their beds, burrowing under blankets and huddling together where they can. And then I notice – the pallet next to me is empty: Joseph is gone.

Chapter 5

Downstairs the fire still blazes in the hearth and a couple of men doze, stagnant tankards of ale and the remains of a meal on a table next to them. I find and light a lantern and duck into the yard, hiding in doorways and under eaves until I reach the stable block where I can see the glow of a brazier.

Someone has made a fire and a few lads rest nearby on bales of straw, but Joseph is nowhere to be seen. Staying under cover, I skirt the boxes, some of them housing stamping, steaming horses, disturbed by the storm. I curse the mud that seeps into my shoes, knowing the roads will be bad tomorrow.

I reach the far-most point of the inn, just where the open road begins and the blacksmith plies his trade to passers-by. After that, there seems to be nothing but a few shacks and open fields, dark and blurred through the rain.

I do not know why I feel compelled to search Joseph out. My satchel is still stowed safely under my bed and my purse is still hidden in the folds of my petticoat. Siddal still snores on his pallet. Free from the binds of our arrangement, I should be glad, but thinking he may be gone, I feel more alone than ever.

With my courage faltering, I turn back, and then I see him, perched on an upturned trough, just inside the open door of the forge. He is staring out across the fields, shoulders hunched, one hand cupping his injured side. Despite the light I carry, he does not seem to notice me: he is lost in his own world.

Suddenly I feel as though I should not be there. I'm guilty, like an eavesdropper caught bending to a keyhole.

I turn to go but the sound startles him and he looks up, his expression blank, as though he does not recognise me. Then he shakes himself from his trance. 'Ruth?'

I come forward and nod towards the hand that clutches his ribs. 'Does it hurt?'

'Aye, at times. It has not healed well.' His voice catches in his throat.

In the cast of the lantern I notice the hollows under his eyes. 'What are you doing out here?' I ask.

'Cannot sleep with the storm.'

As if in answer, the sky is rent with a crack of white fire and the yard reverberates with thunder. Joseph winces. I duck under the shelter and sit next to him. We watch the rain come down, listening to the slurp and suck of the gutters.

'I can help.' The words escape me before I think better of them. Easing the suffering of others was my mother's way of serving God; it comes to me as naturally as prayer.

He raises a brow, eyes questioning.

'I have a little of the healer's knowledge,' I say. 'I have tended wounds before . . . If you show me . . .'

He hesitates for a moment, then shrugs off his jacket. He stands, flinching as he straightens, and turns to face me so that we are both held in the circle of lamplight. He tugs his shirt free and lifts it high, looking steadily ahead into the darkness.

The scar is jagged, the colour of a ripened plum. It begins at his chest and runs down his left-hand side, over the flesh of his belly, ending somewhere beneath the ties of his breeches. Even by candle flame I can see where the skin has puckered and knitted together unevenly, and the angry raw welts where it has still not calmed. The cut was not a clean one, and it was deep. I have never seen worse on anyone still living. By rights, he should be dead.

I stay seated, my face level with his hip, and reach my hands up to his chest. Sometimes I can tell more by touch than by sight. As my fingers meet his skin he glances down, surprised. I feel his heart jumping.

I work my fingertips slowly down the length of the scar, feeling the hardened ridge where the wound has come together. I pause where the flesh is soft and the scarring is worse. I can feel a knotted thickening there, as though pebbles are sewn beneath. I press my flattened palm gently and feel his muscles tense. I know this must pain him, though he refuses to show it. Lower down, the scar is smoother and has healed better, its edges seamless and fading to silver, a dusting of dark hair beginning to conceal it. I run my fingers down as far as I can, meeting with the line of his breeches. The skin here is hot to touch. I catch the scent of him, the scent of the road, but sweet and musky.

I look up and find that he is watching me intently, watching my fingers on his skin. For a moment I am snared by his stare. I cannot lift my hands. My mouth is dry; words will not come.

When at last he breaks the silence, his voice is strangled. 'Have you ever seen a man die?'

I shut my eyes as memories cascade: the faces of Ely towns-folk, marked with the purple bruises of plague, fevered with the pox; infants cramped with colic, wheezing their last feeble breath; Esther Tuttle's stillborn child; the kicking of muddy ankles and the baying of a bloodthirsty crowd. My stomach turns.

'Yes,' I say.

'Was it a bad death?'

'Yes.'

'Then you know how it is. I've seen many men die, most of them in blood and pain. Most did not deserve such an end. Many's the time I've asked why I was spared. Better men than I were not.'

I drop my hands to my lap and sit in silence.

He lets his shirt fall and sits back down. 'Have you family?' he asks.

I falter before I shake my head. It is the first time I have admitted it.

'I had a brother. His name was Jude. I lost him at Naseby, the day I got this. Every day since, I've had this pain upon me. The wound will not heal until I've put his soul to rest.'

'There is much that may be done,' I say. 'A poultice will help the healing and a dose of comfrey—'

'There is nothing to be done, nothing that you can help with. The wound is deeper than you can ever know.'

My own heart aches as though it is cut. I want to tell him that I do know, that I understand what it is to have a loved one taken so suddenly, so violently. I want him to know the real reason I am here. I want him to understand that I, too, am fleeing for my life, with wounds just as deep, and fresher than his. Most of all, I want to have him reach his arms around me, and tell me that I am not alone in this.

But I do none of these things. The truth chokes me as I say, 'They took my mother . . .'

For a moment he does nothing. The muscles in his jaw twitch. Slowly, he reaches out and takes my hand from where it rests in my lap. He enfolds my fingers in his palm. I cannot speak, or meet his gaze, for fear that the sorrow will come spilling out of me, and never stop.

We sit in silence. The rain is easing, leaving behind the biting chill of a fresh spring morning. In the distance, the sky is turning from black to grey. The clouds flash every now and then to the south, towards London and our journey's end. And over that great city, the sky trembles with thunder, like the sound of distant guns.

Chapter 6

By morning the storm-soaked roads are muddy and spoiled by puddles. But the rain brings one blessing: the heat of the day before is gone and the sky is hazy and pale blue, the sun tempered by a fresh breeze. My clothes, still damp and itchy from the night-time rain, begin to dry, and I tie my shawl to the side of the cart and let it hang loose, fluttering and catching the wind, like a flag.

Every now and then the mud holds us back, our wheels caught axle deep. I spend the better part of the morning climbing down from my perch among the pelts to tug at the reins of the horse while Siddal and Joseph clear the spokes.

Joseph is gruff and churlish. By sunrise any trace of the sad, unguarded man I came to know in the night has vanished. He grunts in answer to Siddal's orders and refuses to meet my eye. I suppose he is ashamed. After all, I am a stranger to him, pretending siblings or not. I imagine a fighting man like him will suffer to be seen so weak and troubled. Still, the change in his manner is so marked that I cannot help but be hurt by it. I did not choose his company, or ask for the burden of his secrets. The burning of my own grief leaves little room for sympathy, but I am puzzled that whatever affinity moved me by darkness seems such a dreamlike thing in the light of day.

* * *

During the afternoon, as we pass through Waltham Woods, Joseph is dozing in the back of the cart. I loll next to him, marvelling at the tall trees that stretch their boughs towards the sky, making a green and gold canopy overhead, like the hangings on the master's old four-poster. Joseph lies with his hat pulled low over his brow. The light trickles from above, making the leaves glow so many hues. I watch shadow patterns dance on Joseph's clothes and skin. I notice the hairs on his chin spark deep red as the sun hits them.

After a while his jaw grows slack and his lips part. They are full lips, well shaped. His looks are softer with the innocence of sleep. I long to lean across and raise his hat from his face, to see him vulnerable again. I want to feel the comfort of my hand in his. Instead I touch his sleeve lightly with my fingers.

'I'm sorry for your brother,' I say quietly.

He stirs and lifts his hat. 'What?'

'Naseby, your brother, your poor wounded belly . . . I'm sorry for it all.'

He scowls. 'I have no brother,' he says. 'And I never was at Naseby Fight.' He pushes himself up, twisting away from me to check whether Siddal is listening. Satisfied we are not overheard, he leans in so close that as he whispers I feel spittle land upon my cheek.

'I should never have told you aught of Naseby. Promise me you'll not speak of it.' He grabs my arm insistently, fingers digging into soft flesh. 'They'll shoot me for deserting . . . I should never have told you. Do you understand? Promise me . . .'

Siddal turns in his seat, disturbed by the movement, and Joseph releases his grip. I nod, rubbing my arm where the bruise will colour. Siddal smirks.

I understand better than Joseph knows. The name 'Witch' will follow me to London if I do not hold my tongue. My own life depends upon my secrecy. I'm suddenly glad that I did not share the truth with him. I see it clear now: I must tell no one, trust no one. I must lock my secrets inside so they cannot be used to hurt me. I turn away from him and do not speak another word until we near London.

My first glimpse of the great city comes just as the sun begins to wane. I'm starting to wonder if we will arrive in darkness when, cresting a hill, Siddal calls out, 'London ahead!'

Before us, the land flattens, low hills rolling away into a valley. And there in the distance is a grey smudge of buildings, haloed by a puddle of smoke.

'An hour or two more,' Siddal says, giving the horse's rump a rap with his switch.

Soon there are houses alongside the road. These are different from the Fenland homes I am used to, where hamlets are grouped around a well, or common land, and huddle together, centred on themselves, villagers protected by a circle of timber and stone. Here the buildings skirt the track, as if the road is the lifeblood of their world. Kitchen gardens and small farmsteads fill the country; pigs and goats live in roadside pens.

Inns and alehouses pepper the route. We stop at one to water the horse and are instantly surrounded by pedlars selling beer, maslin bread and pottage. They seem to come from nowhere, like rats to scraps, ragged, with haunted eyes and shabby clothes. They press around the cart until Siddal, fearing for his goods, swipes them away with his whip.

Twilight is falling and the road is become a steady stream of carriages and carts and men on horseback. We can see the city proper now, glimpses of great buildings and spires each time we reach higher ground. And so many chimneys, spewing dark smoke skywards.

At last we reach the city gatehouse. Stretching away on either side is a great ditch, some yards across. It puts me in mind of the earthworks that criss-cross the Fens, built by the adventurers who came to drain the land. I wonder what city men want with such excavations. Beyond the ditch the city defences rise bleak and grey, pointed with iron spikes, like rotten teeth. Siddal, all puffed up with his knowledge, tells me that the works are only a few years old, put up by the people in the early days of war to protect themselves from the King's army, after Parliament had routed him at Turnham Green. Already they look as though they have stood for decades, crumbled in places and shored up with wattle and timbers. I gape at his stories of the city's women and children clawing the mud with bare hands, shouldering great stones, making their homes safe from their king. Joseph sits, grim and unspeaking, as Siddal weaves his tales.

The road is barred here with a chain. I hold my breath while a soldier peers at Siddal's papers, and at my pass, before nodding us on. Siddal is to take his cart to a merchant who lives near the Royal Exchange. From there, he tells me, it will be easy to find St Paul's.

When at last we reach Cornhill, Siddal, pretending a gentleman at the end, helps me climb down from the cart.

'Well, now,' he puffs, eyes glittering, 'I have made my end of the bargain. You are arrived.' He nods and glances about, as if expecting thieves and pickpockets to appear like wraiths and spirit away his fee.

Joseph is by my side, nudging me. 'Two crown for Master Siddal, Ruth.' I count the coin from my purse into Siddal's damp palm. Siddal nods at Joseph in thanks.

'There is Cheapside,' he says, pointing to a broad street that leads away to the west. 'And yonder is St Paul's. Now, if you'd lend a hand in the unloading of my goods. Such is the extra danger I have put myself under to bring you here, I expect you can spare a minute or two . . .' This last he addresses to Joseph, who begins unlacing the ropes that fasten the barrels.

For a short while I work at the knots and watch as they fling back the canvas and begin to sort the bundles. As they turn their attention to the work, I take my chance. Grabbing my satchel, I dart across the street and into the dark stretch before the shop fronts. I pick my way quickly through the gloom, keeping to the shadows, towards Cheapside. As I reach the turning I glance back and see that Joseph is looking about him. I press myself into a doorway, hidden by the heavy wooden frame. From there I watch as he circles the cart, then ducks to peer beneath. He calls out, 'Ruth . . . Ruth!'

Siddal comes out of the shop and laughs. He slaps Joseph on the back, saying something I cannot hear. Again Joseph calls my name, louder this time, and people in the street turn and stare. In the neighbouring house an upstairs casement is flung open and a pale female face peers from within.

Siddal leads Joseph back to the cart to begin the unloading. Joseph doffs his hat to another man, who must be the merchant. He takes up a bundle of skins to carry inside. All the time he looks about for me, cursing under his breath. Siddal and the other man go inside, and Joseph follows. As he passes the threshold, he turns back to search for me one last time. Instead of the frown he has worn all day, the furrows in his brow speak of disappointment, as though, believing himself unobserved, his true feelings are written there.

For the briefest moment, doubt flickers, and I think perhaps I should go to him, but he does not linger: he disappears into the darkness of the house.

I slip from my hiding place and hurry into Cheapside. This is the last I shall see of Joseph Oakes. I feel none of the relief I had expected, but oddly desolate and alone. I pay the feeling no heed – I am becoming used to it.

★ ★ ★

Cheapside is the broadest street I have ever seen, wide enough for carriages to pass each other twice over, wide enough for shopkeepers to set up trestles before their doors and sell their wares on the street.

Although night is falling, there are still people abroad and I'm thankful for the gentle mill of bodies outside the taverns as I move away from the Exchange and set off to find St Paul's Cathedral. According to the instructions that Old Bess gave me, it is from here that I will find my way.

On Cheapside the houses are built up three or more floors, each level leaning further out over the street than the last. I keep to the side beneath the overhang. Looking up makes me feel giddy. There are fine, large buildings in Ely, but not so many and not so large as these.

The ground is soft beneath my feet. My nose tells me it is covered with muck. Timbers have been laid out in places to make byways over the stinking drains that run from side-streets into the main thoroughfare. Glimpses of those side-streets show them to be dank, unwholesome places, almost closed overhead by the tunnel of houses. I have the feeling that I might fall into one, as if into a badger set, burrowed into the roots of a tree.

There seems to be no sky here, only a low grey blanket draped over the houses, firewood and hot coals smoked up through the chimneys – and there are so many chimneys – choking the moon and the stars.

Further along, a gang of lads laze on the steps of a stone monument. They are drinking and singing in slurred cacophony. One clambers to his feet and dances an unsteady jig across my path, making his friends cheer and hoot, but I pass them by.

Soon the road opens into a wide courtyard. St Paul's Cathedral sits in the centre, a huge hulking building of soot-stained stone. Here there are no tall houses but instead row upon row of timbered shacks, all built up against the walls of the place, tacked on as an afterthought. Some are barely more than tents, made from canvas and wooden stilts, pegged down with large grey boulders. More lumps of stone lie here and there, waiting in the mud to trip me. Dogs scavenge, growling at each other in the bid for scraps, yelping as they are kicked away.

The cathedral glowers in the darkness, its outline smudged against the billowing sky. It is big, like Ely, but somehow it seems penned in. Where Ely Cathedral seems to soar heavenwards like a great pale bird, this place is captured and tied down, feathers plucked, waiting for the pot. I can just glimpse the tower, crooked and broken, the spire either missing or lost in cloud.

I feel a weight in my chest as I think of Ely and the palace of grey stone that sits above the wet green flats of the Fens. I remember the sun peeking from behind towers, sparkling from the eyes of gargoyles, sliding across the faces of carved saints and swirling flowers until the building seems to breathe and swell. It is beautiful. It is terrible. Towering over the little church of St Mary's, where we worshipped every Sunday, like a judgemental grandparent, its presence ever reminds us to beware the Catholic threat in our midst.

But there is one thing I love about the place.

Sometimes, when I was old enough to know better, I would slip from my classes at the free school and run there. I would tiptoe silently among the marble pillars, gazing up at the arches and curves of the ceiling, before finding my way to the winding staircase that leads to the top of the tallest tower. Almost touching the clouds, I would watch people, like beetles, in the market square. Sometimes I saw my mother, pinning laundry in the yard or feeding scraps to the pigs. I could see the gypsy boatmen on the Ouse and travellers on horseback as they crossed the safe passages through the floods. I saw swallows catching insects, free in the great open sky that goes on for ever. It made me feel lightheaded, powerful, knowing that I saw all of this and yet no one saw me. This must be how God feels, I thought, understanding why those ancient churchmen had built such a place. They, too, had wanted to reach the clouds and play at being God.

But there is no such wonder here, just a broken-down building and a press of people. I can see where the rocks on the ground have come from. Statues and stonework are missing from the walls and lie ruined underfoot, as though the Almighty himself has taken a cleaver to the stone.

Groups of men gather around one or other of the stalls, drinking and talking. As I pass a doorway into the nave I see the flicker of candles and the movement of bodies inside but I shy away, too afraid to explore.

I see people preparing for a night outside, hunkering down among the shacks. Hollow-eyed children stare at me as I pass. Afraid of thieves, I press on, clinging to my satchel with both hands.

Soon, at the western end of the church, I ask a lone ragged woman for directions to the Poole household. She does not speak but flaps her arm in the direction of a narrow alley that leads off the churchyard.

The street is in darkness and I'm blind as I step into it, hearing the squeal of rats alongside. I wait a moment for my sight to return, then begin to make my way from door to door. Here and there a nightlight burns in an upstairs window but most houses are shuttered against the chill. Behind bolted doors I hear voices raised in argument, someone playing a fiddle, a baby crying. Outside, there is the stench of rotting vegetables, and the rhythm of my own heartbeat, rushing in my ears.

I find a door with a plaque affixed to it. With my nose almost touching, feeling the shape of the letters with my fingers I read

'Robert Poole Esq., Tailor and Haberdasher'. This is the house I'm looking for. I draw myself upright and do what I can to tidy my skirts and fasten my hair beneath my cap. I take Old Bess's letter from my satchel and, clutching it before me like a talisman, I knock upon the door and wait.

Part Two

London
May 1646

Chapter 7

I wait a long time for an answer.

'He is a tailor, a Guild man,' Old Bess had told me, as I mounted the horse behind Christopher. 'I knew him once, long ago. He is a good man and respectable. He will keep you safe, if you give this to him.' She pressed the letter into my hand. 'But remember, no one must know of this. Your safety depends upon your silence.'

I knock again and begin to think I will spend a night under the smoke-clouded sky when, from behind the door, I hear a coarse female voice.

'Who's there?'

'Please, is the master of the house at home?'

'Who wants to know?'

'I've come very far to see him. Please, I have a letter . . .'

Iron scrapes against iron as the bolts are drawn back. Then I hear the turn of a key in the lock and the creak of ungreased hinges. A sliver of candlelight casts shadows.

'And what time is this to be calling? It's past ten and the master is abed.'

'I'm sorry, but I must see him. I have nowhere else to go . . .' Suddenly I am overwhelmed with tiredness, and at the thought of a bed among the beggar children of St Paul's tears well.

'What's your name?'

'Ruth Flowers. I have a letter from Bess Cromwell.'

I don't know if it is the quaver in my voice or the mention of Old Bess that does the trick, but the door opens and I am facing a woman dressed in nightclothes, with arms as thick as hams. Her hair falls in dusty brown tendrils from under her cap, as though she has thrown the thing on in an attempt to be decent. She has a round, ruddy face and squinting sow-like eyes.

'You'd better come in. The mistress is still up.' She ushers me inside. 'Give me this letter.'

I hand it to her.

'Wait here. And do not touch a thing.' She waddles into the darkness, taking the candle with her.

Now I'm inside I will do anything to stay. I will sleep on the flagstones beneath my feet, I will curl up before the hearth like a kitchen-boy, I will eat nothing but scraps meant for the slops. I will beg if I must.

The woman soon returns, muttering to herself. She comes towards me and lifts the candle to my face. 'Let me look at you. Hold out your hands.'

I do as I'm told and she inspects them, nails, knuckles and wrists.

'Well, you look healthy enough. This way . . .'

I follow her down a narrow passageway that leads to the back of the house. We pass more chambers to each side and a staircase that marks the way to upper storeys. The house is bigger than I had first thought. It smells of mouldering laundry and vegetable broth. At the end of the passageway, we come to a large room, lit by a good fire and candles on the mantel. I recognise the glint of copper skillets and the sheen of well-fired pottery: familiar signs of a well-appointed kitchen.

But all this is nothing compared to the woman who sits by the fire. She has the loveliest face I have ever seen. She has wide, clear eyes, a high forehead and pale skin, sprinkled with freckles across the nose. She has a small pink mouth. Her hair, red as the blush of an autumn russet, is shot through with gold. The light of the fire seems to glow around her. I'm instantly reminded of the statues in the cathedral at Ely: false gods with shining ivory faces, ageless in their perfection.

I know right away that she is a precious thing. I know she is different from other women, and I have never met anyone like her before.

When she speaks, her voice is soft and prettily clear. 'Margaret tells me you are come here with this letter for my father.'

'Yes, madam.' I curtsy to her, and she beckons me forward with a small amused upturn of her lips.

She breaks the seal and tilts the page towards the flames to read. In the light I can see that she is some years my senior, but her brow is unlined, either by age or by worry. Her figure is slender. She wears a dress of deep red serge, darned carefully in patches with a paler yarn. She has fine thin hands with long fingers and clean nails. I feel small and dirty beside her. I hide my own calloused palms behind my back.

As she reads, she bites her lower lip and a tiny crease appears at her brow. When she has finished, she holds the letter in her lap. 'Well, Ruth, it seems you need a place to stay,' she says.

'Yes, madam.'

'This lady, Mistress Cromwell, claims you are an orphan.'

'Yes, madam.'

'I do not know this lady myself.'

'The letter is for Master Robert Poole. This is his house, is it not?'

'Yes. He is my father.'

'Please, madam, if I could speak with him . . .'

'You are quite alone in London?'

'Yes.'

She refers to the letter. 'And you are come from . . . Ely?'

I nod.

'Come closer. Let me see you.'

I step into the light of the flames and stare at the floor.

'Let me look at your face.'

I tilt my chin, burning with shame at my unwashed clothes and filthy skin. I cannot bring my eyes to meet hers, but I can feel her gaze on me. It makes such fierce fire in me that I can hardly breathe.

'Well, Margaret, it seems we have a visitor.'

The red-faced woman named Margaret snorts. 'Are you sure? We know nothing about her. Should we not wake the master?'

'The Good Lord has sent us a soul in need and we cannot fail him. Set a bed in one of the upper rooms, the one next to Charlotte's. And see to it that there is water to wash. I shall speak to my father in the morning. There is no sense in disturbing him now.'

Margaret shuffles from the room, tutting under her breath.

The woman stands, comes to me and takes my hands in hers. 'You will stay here tonight. I shall speak to my father tomorrow and we will see what can be done. Oh, you are trembling. Please, sit . . .'

'Thank you . . . thank you.' I take a seat on the bench and feel the welcome heat of the hearth.

'My name is Elizabeth. Those who know me call me Lizzie.'

I look up and meet her eyes. They are full of life, the kind of eyes that can see deep inside a person. They shine a pale, gold-flecked green, like Fen water sparkling in the sunshine. My heart quickens. Elizabeth. Lizzie. My saving grace.

It is gone midnight by the time I'm left alone. Margaret shows me to a tiny room under the eaves where there is no window and no fire. There is barely room for the truckle bed and the small cabinet where a basin sits, filled with cold water. But I do not care. I lie on the bed fully dressed, listening to the rustles and creaks of a strange household settling for the night, glad for every moment I am safe. Eventually, when all is silent, I rummage in my satchel and bring out my mother's book. I hold it to my chest as though it is my own babe in my arms, and I sob myself to sleep.

Chapter 8

I wake to find Margaret, basin of water in hand, grunting at me, as though she knew she would find me still fully clothed in the grime of the road.

'Mistress says you're to come down to the parlour. I've brought you some clean things.'

She puts down the steaming basin and picks up the cold one from the night before, her meaty body consuming what is left of the space in the room. Then she produces clean clothes. I stand to let her lay them on the bed.

'Bring your old 'uns down and Charlotte will see to 'em.'

She is gone before I have the wit to thank her.

I strip and wash as best I can. The hot water feels like a blessing. I dress quickly: a loose white shift, a brown dress of thick worsted and old worn stays, threadbare in places, darned and mended, but clean and smelling sweetly of lavender soap. I wonder if they belong to Lizzie.

Margaret has brought a cap and boots too, and I do my best to untangle my hair, plait it and tuck it under the cap. The boots are ill-fitting, but they are clean and dry.

I say a prayer and let my fingers wander over the mottled leather of my mother's book before stowing it safe beneath the bed, out of sight. Its gifts must be used sparingly and I must wait for the right time.

* * *

I find Lizzie in a room at the front of the house that looks onto the street. She is sitting by the fire, deep in conversation with a man I take to be her father, although you would not know it by the look of him. He is frail and grey for a man in his middle years, with none of the presence or beauty of his child. That must come from her mother, I think, as I hover by the door, afraid to disturb them.

'It is not only the money we must think of,' Master Poole is saying. 'We do not want the old rumours to surface again. We must be wary. We cannot trust outsiders . . .'

'Oh, Father . . .' Lizzie talks to him as if he is the child and she the parent. 'Must we always return to that? She is gone, long gone, and forgotten by all but those who loved her. We must think of the future. Think what a connection to the Cromwells might do for business.'

'Mistress Bess is clear. She asks particularly that no one else in the household must know the girl's origins. If you had not opened this private letter, Lizzie, you would not know either.'

Lizzie rolls her eyes.

'I suppose, out of respect for past ties, I must do it,' he goes on, 'but she will stay in the kitchens. And you will tell her nothing of what has gone before.'

The remains of a good breakfast sit on a table next to him and he reaches for his mug.

Fearing that they will notice me standing mute on the threshold and think me a sneak, I reach out and rap upon the door.

'Oh, Ruth! There you are.' Lizzie smiles. 'Come in, come in.'

I go into the room, keeping my eyes to the flagstones.

'Ruth, this is my father.'

Master Poole nods at me and wipes his whiskers with a linen kerchief.

'Did you sleep?' Lizzie is up and at my side, guiding me to her chair by the fire.

'Yes. Thank you.'

'And will you eat? I had Margaret prepare plenty. There is bread and meat and cheese.' She goes to the table and carves a great hunk of crust before I can answer. I watch her pale hands wielding the knife. She is soberly dressed this morning in dark skirts, her lovely hair tucked away beneath her cap like my own, tiny copper strands escaping at the nape of her neck. Next to her, the table is strewn with swatches of fabric, so many hues of wool, silk and velvet, as if a rainbow has fallen from the skies and landed there.

'Well, child,' Master Poole says gravely. 'I have read the letter you brought with you and I believe it to be genuine.' He pauses and looks me over. 'Bess Cromwell was a friend to me once, many years ago, when I found myself in need. She tells me you are orphaned and need a home. Well, I find myself able to return her favour. We are not a wealthy household, but if you are willing to earn your keep, we can manage one more. What kind of girl are you?'

'A good girl, sir,' I say.

He suppresses a smile. 'Kitchen? Laundry? Can you sew?'

'A little. I was kitchen maid for Mistress Cromwell.'

'Then you will help Margaret.'

'Yes, sir.'

'And, Ruth, there must be no mention of Mistress Cromwell, or your previous place, to anyone. No mention at all. Her letter is quite clear on that. It must be a secret between the three of us.' He tucks his napkin into his jacket pocket. 'Are you a gossip?'

'No, sir.'

'I cannot abide a gossip. If I hear of any idle talk, you will be out on the street. Do you understand?'

'Father!' Lizzie exclaims, bringing me a plate of food. 'Do not be so harsh. Ruth deserves our pity.' She flutters around me like a butterfly, setting down a mug of small beer and fetching a stool for herself. I am hungry, I realise, and unable to stop myself falling on the meal as if I am starved. Between mouthfuls I thank them both.

'There is no need for that.' Master Poole flaps his hands at me and stands, dusting crumbs from his coat. 'I understand you have nothing of your own. Clothes and the like.'

'Very little, sir.'

'Lizzie will give you what you need. We keep an orderly house, which is good for business. Mind you keep out of the customers' way.'

'Yes, sir.'

He nods at me and leaves us, crossing into a room beyond the passageway and closing the door behind him.

As soon as he is gone, Lizzie jumps up from her stool. She comes to me and places her hand on my head for a moment, as though giving benediction. 'Do not worry about my father,' she says. 'All will be well. You'll see.'

I am placed in Margaret's care and spend the rest of that day in the kitchen, learning the tasks and rhythms of the house. At first she is churlish with me, but when she sees that I'm good for the work, she softens. Her distrust gives way to grudging acceptance as I prove to be useful and free from plague, against which, she says, we must be on constant guard.

I have taken Master Poole's warning to heart and when Charlotte, the maidservant, asks me questions, I fumble my way through an invented history while she and Margaret exchange doubting looks.

Margaret is easy to make out. I know that if I work hard and keep my own counsel, I will win her over in the end. She is mistress of the kitchen, and set in her ways, but sentimental loyalty spills from her eyes whenever she speaks of our mistress.

Charlotte must be only a few years my elder and I hope at first that she might be an ally, but she treats me with suspicion. She is stout and rounded, with fair natural curls, and must have been pretty once, before the pox scarred her.

The three of us servants are in the kitchen, Charlotte and I taking the first rest of the day, while Margaret kneads the dough for tomorrow's bread.

'Will we see the mistress tonight?' I ask, thinking of Lizzie settled before the hearth, as I had first seen her.

'I don't know,' Margaret says. 'Oftentimes she spends her evenings here, but sometimes her father wants her with him.'

'Have you known her long?' I ask.

'Her whole life, since she was a babe.'

'You like it here?'

'Aye, 'tis a good enough place. The master don't interfere and Mistress Lizzie, well, I could not leave her now even if I had some other place to go.' She wipes the back of her hand across her forehead, leaving a dusting of flour.

'She seems kind,' I say.

'Oh, yes, she was the kindest, sweetest child, and she has grown into a fair mistress.'

Charlotte snorts.

'There'll be no cheek from you,' Margaret says.

There is one question that I must ask, for I have been wondering about it all day.

'Where is her mother? Where is Mistress Poole?'

Margaret does not answer but pummels the dough. I look to Charlotte, who chews her lip. 'Shall I tell her?' she says.

Margaret sighs. 'I don't doubt she'll hear the story soon enough. It may as well be from you.'

'Your answer is, nobody knows,' Charlotte says, eyes glittering. 'It is a famous mystery hereabouts. Mistress Poole was a great beauty and came from a rich family, so they say, but she ran away to marry the master and was cast off without a penny. They say she could only manage the one child – Mistress Lizzie ruined her for good – and after that she became sickly and unstable in her mind.' Charlotte taps a finger to her skull. 'Then, one night, she disappeared. She was ill and took to her bed, and the next morning she was nowhere to be found. No one knows what happened. No one heard a sound, all her things were here, just as she left them, and all the doors were bolted on the inside. It was like she was spirited clean away. Some people blamed Mistress Lizzie, said she was peculiar, that she had strange powers. There was talk of witchcraft—'

'That's enough,' Margaret snaps. 'You can gossip all you like outside this house, but I'll not have you speak ill of the mistress in my kitchen.' She has coloured, a ruddy flush mottling her throat.

'When did it happen?' I ask.

'A long time ago, when the mistress was young,' Margaret says. 'We do not speak of it before her, do you hear?'

'Of course,' I say. This must be the secret that Master Poole was so keen to hide from me, the old rumour he is so determined to quash.

Margaret shakes her head. 'A thing like that is hard to forget. It has left my girl delicate, poor child. She is not always . . . clear-headed.'

'Is that why she has never married?' I ask.

'Oh, there have been suitors . . . but none could tempt her away from us.'

Charlotte is looking at me sideways, with a smirk.

Before I go to bed that night, I step outside into the yard. There are no stars and no moon by which I can right myself, but I scratch a circle in the dirt with my foot and step inside it. I whisper a prayer to the Fen spirits, and to the four corners of the wind, hoping that my words will be carried to waiting ears.

Now I know that Lizzie has felt the same pain that gnaws inside me. Her loss mirrors my own. My mother can never be replaced, but I long so much for a kind word, a gentle touch, the sort of comfort that only another person can give. The fading memory of Joseph's hand in mine feels a poor substitute for what I need now. I whisper my wish that Lizzie will be the one to comfort me.

But I do not know if the Fen spirits will hear me, muffled by coal smoke, so far from home.

Chapter 9

The Lord's Day is a day of rest, but there is no such thing for a woman, especially one employed in a kitchen.

My first Sabbath at the Poole household, and I'm dressed and sweeping the front parlour before dawn. It is the first time since the night of my arrival that I have been left alone in this room. It is usually out of bounds to all but Lizzie and her father, and Charlotte, who answers the street door and keeps the place neat through the week. This is where Master Poole receives his customers, where he and Lizzie work during daylight hours and where he displays his finest wares.

As the sun comes up and pale dawn light filters through the casement, I marvel at the samples of fine cloth, the rolls of coloured ribbon and intricate bobbin lace, laid out on the table, like offerings upon a harvest altar. Dishes of buttons lie on the sideboard – perfect discs of pale wood and bone, like tiny moons, and shining silver and brass too, for the wealthier clients. There are little cushions pricked all over with silver needles, like a family of hedgehogs, and all manner of fine yarns, measuring sticks and thimbles. In one corner of the room an upright chair wears a dress of the palest blue satin.

I have glimpsed Lizzie at work upon this dress when passing the door, her fingers glittering with needle and thread as she applies fine lacework to the collar. It is a commission from a local merchant's wife, a Mistress Cutler, who is a good customer. I know this from hearing father and daughter in discussion over breakfast. The workings must be perfect, the best quality, for the fee alone will keep us in eggs and butter all summer long.

Alone with the dress, I caress the fabric, my fingertips tracing the stitching that betrays the path of Lizzie's hands before my own. I stroke the lace, so delicate, like dew-soaked spiders' webs draped from a branch.

I kneel and lay my cheek upon the folds of cool satin. It is like gazing into a morning Fenland sky – the palest of blue, sheened with wisps of cloud. I think of Lizzie's hands moving over the cloth, folding it, stitching it, and making it into something beautiful.

'What are you doing?'

Charlotte stands at the door, hands on hips.

'Oh . . . I – I'm sweeping.' I struggle to my feet and brandish the broom.

'Don't much look like it to me.' Her mouth twists into a sour half-smile. She nods at the dress. 'Touch that again and there'll be trouble.' Her cap, always askew, tips down over her right eye.

I make as if to sweep the flags around the skirt.

'A word of advice,' Charlotte says. 'Never let the master catch you in here, not with your hands all over the goods. Anyway, let it alone now. You're to come to chapel.'

I expect a visit to one of the local churches but instead Lizzie leads Margaret, Charlotte and me to a house in Devonshire Square, near Bishopsgate. Master Poole stays at home. Lizzie explains, as we pick our way through the quiet early-morning streets, that the distance is too great for him. She chooses to travel for she has found a special place among God's chosen people. Her eyes shine as she speaks and her hands hover in the air like turtledoves.

Our place of worship is a simple room. The parlour of a London leather merchant, fashioned as a chapel, it is large enough to hold two score bodies. Wooden benches are lined up like pews and a table at one end of the room serves as a makeshift lectern. There is no altar, no candle, no cross. The walls are whitewashed and unadorned. Two small windows let in a shifting, gloomy light. There is no fire in the grate and the room smells damp. For people who choose not to worship in church, they have created a fine impression of one.

Twenty or so souls are already gathered and each one seems to take note of our entrance. Men doff their hats. Women fall silent and stare. Lizzie glides through them all as though she is a duchess, and we her ladies-in-waiting.

Until now I thought that only I recognised Lizzie's special goodness. But I see I am not alone. The men look upon her with admiration. In the eyes of the women, I see something deeper and more complicated. They are reverent but uneasy. I wonder how many of them feel as I do and am surprised by a stab of jealousy at the thought.

There are eyes on me too. Eyes full of questions. A small boy tugs at his mother's skirts, pointing and asking, 'Who is she?'

Reaching the front of the room, Lizzie greets a tall man with soulful brown eyes and soft chestnut curls falling to his collar. He enfolds her hands in his own and inclines his head.

'Mistress Poole. We are glad to have you with us, as always.' His voice is deep and full-toned. He pronounces each word with precision, as though he is an actor upon the stage, and wants all his audience to hear.

'Pastor Kiffin.' Lizzie glows in his presence. 'You are well, I hope?'

'Well enough.'

'And Hanna? Is she not with us this morning?'

'Unfortunately my wife has taken to her bed.'

'Oh. I hope it is nothing serious.'

'Serious enough to keep her from worship.'

'Is anything to be done?'

'The physician says she must rest. That is all. She will be well again soon.'

'And the child?'

Kiffin cast his eyes down. 'Gone.'

'I am sorry to hear it.'

They stand, wordless, for a few moments, hands clasped together, heads bowed, as if in silent, private prayer.

'But here is some good news to cheer you,' Lizzie says, breaking the spell. 'We have an addition to our group this morning. Ruth, come forward.' She slips her hands away from his and unfurls a palm towards me. 'This is Ruth Flowers, my new maid. Ruth, Master Kiffin is our pastor here. You will not find a finer preacher in all of London.'

Kiffin waves away her praise as though he is batting at a fly. He moves a few steps towards me and takes my hands in his, just as he had Lizzie's moments earlier. 'Welcome, Ruth.' His eyes search mine until I have to look away for fear of what he might find.

'Mistress Poole has a habit of bringing lost souls to me. I think perhaps you are another.'

I long to pull my hands away but his grasp is insistent. His palms are warm and slightly sticky, despite the chill of the place.

'Where did you worship before?' he asks. 'Which church?'

'I'm not from London,' I say.

'Ah! A stranger. I thought so. You have done well to find a place with Mistress Poole.'

'Yes, sir. I am blessed.'

'And now you would take up a place within this congregation.'

I dart a look at Lizzie and she gives me an encouraging nod. 'I think so, sir.'

'Then you will need instruction. Do you know your scriptures? You would do well to learn from your mistress. You could not have a finer example . . .'

'Be gentle, William,' Lizzie whispers, lightly touching his sleeve. 'Remember, it is only her first time with us.'

'Do not fear,' Kiffin says. 'If you seek God and your heart is true, we will never turn you away. I welcome you wholeheartedly to our gathering. May you find spiritual sustenance here.'

Then he smiles at me. He is blessed with good teeth, like a row of tiny pearls. He is handsome when he smiles. I find myself inexplicably comforted.

At last he lets my hands drop and turns back to Lizzie. 'And Charlotte is with you still.' He nods to the girl, who curtsies and simpers. 'Forgive me, but is not one maid enough for a woman of your standing? I fear for the well-being of any woman who needs two. We must protect ourselves against vanity and the trappings of indulgence.'

Lizzie laughs. 'Do not fear for me, Pastor Kiffin. My taste for finery and fripperies has not run wild. Charlotte is my maid still and keeps a close watch on such things. Ruth is helping Margaret in the kitchen. And a fine cook she is. If you would care to visit my father this week, perhaps Ruth will prepare her oatcakes for you – they are particularly good.'

'I would be honoured, if your father will receive me.'

'He will.' Lizzie's lips part and she raises an eyebrow almost imperceptibly.

As we make our way back to West St Paul's, thoughts of the beer and bread that await us running through my mind, Lizzie asks me to walk alongside her. 'Tell me,' she says, 'what did you think of our little congregation?'

'Wonderful,' I say, sensing the answer she wants.

'How does it compare to your worship in Ely?'

'It was much longer.'

She laughs. 'You will get used to that. Pastor Kiffin is a fine speaker, is he not?'

'Very fine.'

'And a good man.'

'He seems so.'

She looks pleased. 'What else did you like?'

I am aware of Charlotte, trailing just behind us, collecting every word, like dropped pennies.

'I liked how the people were towards you.'

'They are good people. God's most devout.'

'I mean, how they respect you. They see you for how you are.'

'And how is that?'

I cannot put my thoughts into words. Then, 'Good. You are a good person too.'

She laughs again, like a trill on a pipe.

We walk on and I notice how she holds herself, ready to meet the gaze of those in our path, proud, almost defiant.

'You made a good impression, Ruth,' she says. 'New faces are rare and always remarked upon. You did well today.'

She reaches out her hand and touches my sleeve. 'I'm weary. May I take your arm?'

Charlotte hurries to her side. 'I'm here. Let me.' She offers hers, but although it is perhaps sturdier than my own, Lizzie does not choose it.

'I will do well enough with Ruth,' she says, drawing me closer.

Glancing back at Charlotte, I see her give a sullen look in my direction. But I do not care. I feel my chest swell a little and flush with gladness, even though I know Lizzie's actions have brewed trouble to come.

Chapter 10

Summer stays with us longer than usual. At home, I loved this time of year. The last dry days before the floods bring a flurry of activity – the sedge harvest, the salting of meat, early apples coming in from the orchards. Labourers round off their days singing the old songs outside the taverns. Servant girls laze on the green before the Cromwell house, taking off their slippers and wriggling their toes in the grass, snatching the last of the sun's heat on their way home from market. Ely smells of baked earth. We wait for the scent of salt in the air and the cry of gulls.

London is different. There is no space. No air.

In September, Lizzie fades like a rose without rain. She takes to her bed on the first of the month, claiming a weakness in her limbs and an agitation in her heart. There is plague in the city and Margaret will not allow visitors, apart from Pastor Kiffin, who spends hours ministering to Lizzie at her bedside, but she entrusts Lizzie's errands to me.

Negotiating the city's warren of side-streets, and bartering with the cloth merchants may have frightened me at first, but as days turn into weeks, and it becomes clear that Lizzie will not soon leave her bed, I start to enjoy my new duties. It is the first taste of freedom I have had for months.

As I grow bolder, looking forward to my outings, my grief seems to lessen. The bad dreams that plagued me nightly during the summer fade to memory, memory that I quash with new dreams of Lizzie.

Cheapside is sticky in September swelter. Hawkers, dulled by the heat, wear kerchiefs around their faces, like bandits, protection against the pestilence. Fruit-sellers flick away flies with horsehair switches. I ignore the familiar flutter of fear as I do the ragged children clamouring for pennies.

I find my way to Cornhill and the Pope's Head and pause there, pulled up short by a gathering of men in the street outside the tavern. They lounge, mugs in hand, pipes puffing lazy smoke into the thick air. A few look me over. I press on, head down, feeling their eyes follow me into Pope's Head Alley.

The narrow passageway bustles with activity. People jostle for space outside the shops. Building work is going on overhead, houses stretching their eaves towards the thin streak of light, as if gasping for air. Moon-eyed children sit in a huddle on planking that has been laid down before a toymaker's shop, waiting for the day's puppet show. A rainbow of bottles, ointments and balms sparkle in an apothecary's window.

The high walls of the tavern thwart the worst of the midday heat but the air is still stifling and smells of rot. I have heard from Charlotte that fear of plague causes the night-soil men to abandon their rounds and the evidence is here: a thick mulch of dirt festers in the drain along the centre of the alley. I balance on the planks that give safe passage and make my way to the print shop.

Master Stukeley, licensed printer and bookseller, sits at his desk, quill in hand, scratching away at his ledgers. As I enter he sizes me up, completes the line he is working on, places his quill in the pot on the table and blows on the paper to dry the ink. He smoothes back his hair with both hands and clears his throat, in no hurry to attend to me.

The place is sultry and full of dust, with the pungent stench of hot leather and the privy. One wall is covered with shelves of books, some with fine bindings. Beneath them are stacked wooden crates, a chaotic assortment of pamphlets, newsbooks and tracts. This is a man's world of politics, sealing wax and strong, sweet sack.

Through a doorway towards the back of the room, I can see another man, dressed in a leather apron. I watch the back of his head as he moves in and out of sight, working at the printing press.

Stukeley stands up. 'Good day to you,' he says. His coat is patched and his stockings mismatched; his hair flies wild about his head.

I bob a curtsy. 'Good day, sir. I am to fetch a packet for Mistress Poole, of West St Paul's. She sent me in her stead.'

Lizzie's message delivered, I find myself breathless.

Stukeley wrings his hands. 'Ah, yes, Mistress Poole. She is well, I hope?'

'She is not, sir, but it is not the plague.'

'You look a little flushed,' he says.

'It's hot.' I fan my cheek to prove my point.

He indicates a chair opposite his worktable. 'If you would . . .'

I sit down.

'Boy!'

There is a clatter from the back room and the man comes to the doorway, wiping his hands on a dirty rag. He has taken off the apron and his shirt hangs loose from his breeches. His dark hair has grown since the spring and stands out around his head like a dandelion clock, but I know him at once.

'Ruth?' He drops the rag he is holding and stands there slack-jawed, open-palmed. 'By God, I thought I had seen the last of you . . .'

'Attend yourself!' Stukeley's hands flap, as though he is trying to scare a goose. 'Is this how you greet my customers?'

Joseph spits on his hands and dries them on his breeches. He holds out an ink-stained palm. I do not take it. 'I searched for you,' he says.

I cannot hold his gaze. The air is close and so full of motes I can hardly breathe.

'Well, thank God you are safe,' he adds.

'The girl is here on business, not pleasure,' Stukeley says. 'The parcel for Mistress Poole. Is it prepared?'

'Yes, sir.'

'Then fetch it.' He shoos Joseph into the back room.

I gather myself, stand and pace, my skirts making a tiny dust storm on the floor, while Stukeley offers platitudes I cannot hear because my mind is whirling.

When Joseph reappears he carries a small, square bundle, wrapped and tied with thick string. He moves to the shop door and opens it.

I thank Stukeley and turn to leave. As I reach the threshold Joseph whispers, 'I must speak with you.' His eyes search mine earnestly. He hands me the package and taps his finger deliberately on the top before he lets go. He has tucked a note beneath the string.

With Lizzie's parcel under my arm I make my way back towards the Pope's Head, my breath catching in my throat. My heart is thumping. As soon as I reach Cheapside, where the wider street and the shadows cast by the sun afford me a little privacy, I slip into a doorway and take out the piece of paper. I unfold it and read the scribbled words:

Tomorrow after dark. St Paul's.

I tear it into tiny shreds and leave it on the doorstep in the dust.

Chapter 11

I have not thought of Joseph often since we parted ways at Cornhill, the first night I came to London. Not even half a year has passed but already that journey seems like another lifetime, one in which I was altogether different, and upon which I prefer not to dwell. I had sometimes wondered, seeing the printers and booksellers in St Paul's Churchyard, whether he had found the apprenticeship he hoped for. Now I have my answer, but I find I am not satisfied. I saw such urgency flash behind his eyes in the half-light of Pope's Head Alley that all the next day my insides churn with curiosity. It is past eight o'clock when I have done with my chores and, despite my better instinct, decide to hear what he has to say.

The cold stone of the cathedral gives welcome relief from the heat of the day. Charlotte has told me rumours about the great church and Margaret refuses to enter, claiming it is a hotbed of plague and pestilence, a holy place turned unholy by popery and fashion. Now I am here, it seems little more than a meeting place, its once sacred spaces long spoiled and forgotten. During these late-summer evenings, when soot settles on cloaks and caps, no breeze to blow it away, people gather in the cool shadows of the interior to gossip and hear the latest news of the King. Street traders jangle their bells in a mockery of the silent chimes in the tower. Criers bellow a roll call of that day's plague dead, for anyone with nerves strong enough to listen.

He appears, shabbily dressed, sweat-stained, dark smudges of ink across his cheek.

'I wasn't sure you'd come,' he says, with a smile. 'Are you well?'

'Well enough.'

'The Poole household is a respectable one, I understand. The master is a Haberdashers' Guild man, is he not?'

'Yes.'

'A good trade, if you can attract the business. Not much call for finery, I dare say, with the Court scattered about the country.'

'The shop does well enough.'

'So I see.'

I scuff my toe in the dirt between the paving slabs and watch as a crow-headed clergyman in a leather plague mask passes by, swinging a smoking ball of sage.

'But the daughter is making a name for herself.'

'What do you mean?'

He takes in my frown. 'I've heard her name on people's tongues. Probably nothing. Just gossip.'

'Mistress Elizabeth has been good to me.'

He nods. 'I'm glad to hear it. Stukeley is not a wealthy man, but it's good work and he lets me sleep in the back room. I'm learning the trade. I'm lucky. There's a thousand more like me in London and not all can find work. There's not enough to go around.'

I did not come here to exchange pleasantries. 'What did you want with me?'

He glances about. 'Not here.' He takes my hand and leads me down one side of the nave, past faceless saints and the tombs of long-dead bishops. A group of men watch us go by, some of them gaudily dressed in lace cuffs and feathered hats, seldom seen on the streets these days. They nudge and snigger, sucking at pipes in a cloud of cloying smoke.

'Pay them no heed,' says Joseph, as I flinch.

He leads me into a small chapel, away from the main chancel and mercifully empty. It has been stripped of all decoration, the altarpiece smashed, the odd fragment of stained glass still glimmering in a corner. It stinks of mould and decay. But at least it is private. We sit, side by side, on a low bench.

'I looked for you,' he says. 'I know why you ran off the way you did, and God knows I'm sorry for it. It was my own fault.' He shakes his head. 'I've cursed myself for my selfishness. I should've been kinder.'

'No matter now,' I say. 'You had what you needed from me. I paid my way. That's the end of it.'

'You think that? It was not only the money.'

His eyes search mine, and for a moment I am drawn in. Despite his passion for all things modern, there is something of the old days about him. In the Fenland lilt of his voice, in the solidity of his presence, he is like an anchor, weighed deep in the silt of the marshes. He feels comfortingly familiar.

I manage a smile. 'I have forgotten what you said then,' I lie, 'so you may forget it too.'

He nods slowly. 'That's good to hear . . . because I must ask you again if I can count on your silence. There are things I told you that must remain between us.'

I think back to that dark wet night in Puckeridge and the livid scar upon his body.

'Since the King's men surrendered Oxford, the army looks for trouble within their own ranks. There are rumours that those who were not loyal will be brought to justice. The grandees are afraid of spies, I think, and turncoats. I must be wary. I must know if you've told anyone else about me.'

'I've told no one.'

Relief passes across his face. 'I should've known you wouldn't tell. You, so good at keeping secrets.'

'What do you mean?'

'You keep yourself so closed. If you are ever in need of money, you should try your hand as a card sharp.' He smiles. 'With those mysterious eyes, you'd put even the most hardened gambler off his game.'

I pull away from him and stand up. 'Have you said all you wanted?'

'Oh, come now, Ruth, I was making a joke, that's all.'

'I must go.'

'Have you heard the news from home? I hanker for it, picking up titbits anywhere I can, like a street-corner gossip.'

'My mistress will be waiting—'

'Have you heard about the witch killings?'

My breath catches as though I am plunged into icy water.

He reads my shock. 'Aye, one hundred witches were hanged at Bury St Edmunds this year and now there are cases come up at Cambridge and into Huntingdonshire too, towards Ely.'

'Witches?'

'At least a hundred, maybe more, at Bury Assizes. And now there's a plague of it, infecting the eastern counties. Sad to think of it, so close to home.'

I sit back down, my heart hammering. 'Is it true?'

'There are pamphlets about it. I printed one myself. I've seen some fine pieces of work, with wood-block pictures and all. We could walk out right now in the street and buy at least a dozen. They sell well, you see. The public has an appetite for such things. Some say it's a sign of the times, that the Devil is at work among the most godly, rooting out the weak and the sinful.'

'And what do you say?'

He shrugs. 'With the Court all but destroyed and our precious Pope-loving queen fled to France, perhaps it's time to find out where else the threat lies. I'm all for purging the country of ill-doers. I just wish the witch-finders would peddle their trade somewhere other than the Fens. God knows there are more than enough tales about the water folk without scaremongering.'

'How do they find them out, these witches?' I ask.

'There are plenty of people willing to point a finger. Enough to fill the gaol at Colchester ten times over.'

'And what happens to those accused?' I ask, trying hard to keep my voice level.

'They're watched, day and night, until the Devil comes to them. Or they're examined. If the marks of the Devil are found upon them, they're tried at the assizes. They're the lucky ones, though. They've a chance at life. I've heard stories of lynchings would turn your blood.'

I let out a small cry and he frowns. 'Are you unwell?' he asks.

As I turn away from him to hide my distress, two men stumble down the steps of the chapel. They giggle and clutch at one another, clumsy with drink. They don't see us, crouched in the shadows, and before we can move, one pushes the other up against the wall and kisses him full on the mouth. The other moans and drops the bottle he is holding, ignoring the splinters of glass that explode across the floor, his hands going straight between his lover's legs.

I choke back my tears and Joseph stands, holding out his hand for mine. The men notice us then and break away from each other. 'Looks like we're not alone,' says one, coming towards us.

Joseph drags me to my feet and pulls me to the steps.

'You've caught yourself a big fish there, lucky girl,' the man says. 'Don't you want to join us?'

I stumble up the steps, their hoots ringing in my ears.

Joseph's cheeks are aflame. 'I should never have brought you here.'

I set off for one of the side doors that lead out to the churchyard, Joseph trailing after me. 'Let me take you home,' he says.

I round on him. 'You ask me to come here, thinking only of yourself and your dirty secrets. You tell me you fear for your life when all you really want to do is spread evil gossip—'

'I'm worried, Ruth. What would you have me do?' he hisses.

'Leave me alone.'

I push through the jumble of debris and discarded newsbooks and reach the door.

'Wait! I just thought . . .' He pauses, gulping a breath and clutching his side as though it pains him. 'Let me see you safe home.'

'No. I go alone.'

'It would be safer . . .'

But already I am running, fighting tears. I don't turn back or stop until I am locked behind the Pooles' kitchen door.

Chapter 12

I have many secrets. They can be a heavy load to carry alone. I
long for a confidante. My mother knew everything about me.
She knew my whole story, from first breath to the day her own
ended. She knew all, except one thing.

There is a certain charm that can be woven only on the darkest
nights when the moon hides her face from the sea. My mother
forbade it and would not teach me how best to cast it. She said
that the old wisdom should be used only for healing, for saving
lives, not for meddling with them.

Some would call it a love charm, a binding charm, designed to
catch a human heart and tie it to another for ever. What my
mother did not know was that I had learned that charm by rote,
and I have been waiting for the right moment to use it. I always
thought that one day I would find a man strong enough to make
me forget the hurts and doubts of the past. Then I would use
what I had learned to make him mine.

Now, in the blackest hour of the blackest night in the month,
I lie awake while the household is sleeping. When I hear the
church bells strike midnight, I rise from my bed, wrap myself in
a hooded cloak and pad softly down the stairs. Outside, I have to
creep in the shadows, avoiding the Watch, who keep the curfew,
but it does not take long to reach the river. The charm needs
water. It needs the tide.

On the banks of the Thames, I whisper my wishes to the

waves. I go down on bended knee and release a talisman – a tiny pouch, made up from linen scraps, sewn and bound with silver thread. Inside I place a silver penny, the remains of the coin that Old Bess gave me, and a single strand of Lizzie's hair, collected from her bolster when no one was looking. It will go with the tide and meet the Fen spirits, who will take their payment and send their magic back to me by the time the moon is full. With every turning of the moon, the thread is wound that little bit tighter, drawing her closer to me.

I never dreamed I would cast this spell for a girl, but I find it does not seem to matter. All the fantasies I shared with my girlhood friends, of husbands, the hearth and the marriage bed, seem nonsense to me now. All the things I have been waiting to feel, I feel for Lizzie.

This charm needs patience and the belief that it will work. I send my love out with the tide and trust that it will come back to me twofold.

In the autumn rain, St Paul's Churchyard turns to mire beneath the endless parade of pamphleteers and gossips. Londoners flock there by day and night, ever hungry for news of the King and the fate of the country. With Parliament in disarray, there are no censors or justices to stop the cascade of newsbooks, pamphlets and tracts that flies from the presses springing up in damp alleyways and hidden cellars around the cathedral.

Lizzie revels in the new freedom, eager for knowledge. She is one of the news-sellers' most regular customers. As soon as she recovers from her illness, in early October, she spends hours flitting from stall to stall, picking out the latest papers from the great thinkers of the day. Nothing is too extraordinary for her: preachers, politicians, army men. All have their right to a voice now and Lizzie wants to listen.

Her favourites are the many tales of supernatural happenings.

Here a devil-child born with two heads, there a spectral army sighted in the sky, elsewhere a plague of flies destroying the apple harvest. It seems there is no end to the signs of God's displeasure at this country at war with itself.

Lizzie devours the stories, sitting before the kitchen hearth in the evenings. She draws me in and makes me a part of it, reading aloud as I go about my business, scrubbing pots or working the flour for the morning's baking. This is how I come to learn that Joseph told me the truth that night in the cathedral. A hundred or more witches have been hanged this year in the eastern counties, and more await trial at the assizes. Such a plague of sorcery has never been seen before. The sign of the witch is truly a sign of the times.

I listen carefully, waiting for the day when I will hear a name I know. I keep my secrets close and my fears to myself.

But whatever bad news I hear, I treasure these moments with Lizzie. While Charlotte gossips in the street with the neighbours' servants and Margaret takes to her bed with her caudle, these times alone with her are precious. I am filled with such feelings. The tiny hairs on my skin crackle and stand on end. My breath comes shallow and fast. My senses are heightened, attuned to every shift of her body, every nuance of tone. I am so aware of her, and it thrills me to the core.

Better still are the days when Charlotte is busy with the laundry and Lizzie asks me to go with her as she browses the wares in the churchyard. Sometimes she takes my arm and walks from the house, chattering as if I were her sister. At these times the distance between us, as servant and mistress, shrinks and I can forget my place. I can pretend that we are equals. I feel her drawing near.

It is on one such day, some time in December, that Lizzie and I spend an hour in the churchyard, exchanging gossip and picking from the best new pamphlets on offer. There is a chill in the air and Lizzie walks arm in arm with me, keeping me close. I can feel the heat of her body, even through her cloak. Our breath steams and mingles. Although the churchyard is busy, it is for me as though no one else exists. I am wrapped up in her; all others seem pale shadows by comparison. At moments like this it seems that the world is made anew, just for us. The world is ours alone. I am lost in this dream when I hear a high, girlish voice calling my name.

Then, as if spirited from the heavens, hands clutch at my skirts and two little bodies twirl about me calling, 'Ruth! Ruth!'

For a moment I do not recognise them. They are dressed in fine frocks and matching dark capes, their hair ringleted; they are like miniature ladies. But their faces, bubbling with childish joy, are so dear to me I cannot mistake them. It is Mary and Frances, Master Oliver's youngest girls, my own sweet charges.

'Ruth, is it really you?'

I fall to my knees, not caring about the muck. 'Oh, my girls! My girls!' I wrap my arms around them both.

They giggle and chatter. 'Is it really you? We thought you were dead!'

'What are you doing here?' I ask.

'We live here now,' says Mary, the eldest and always the most confident.

'Here, in London?'

'Yes. We came to be with Father.'

'You've left Ely?'

'Yes, the house is all shut up.'

'Oh . . .'

'We packed our trunks ourselves,' Frances butts in, pulling at the strings on my cap.

I hug them both close.

'And now we have found you, and we can bring you home,' Mary says, burying her face in my neck. 'Father said I would be happy here, and now I am.'

I glance about for Lizzie, longing to introduce her, but instead my eyes fall upon another familiar figure, pushing her way through the crowds towards us.

'Girls! What are you doing?' It is Mistress Cromwell, their mother, thunder in her eyes.

Mary pulls away from me and hops up and down. 'Mama, Mama, look! See who we have found! She is not dead after all.'

Mistress Cromwell stops short. Her eyes meet mine for the briefest moment, long enough for me to see her shock turn to malice. 'Girls, stop pestering that poor woman and come back to my side at once.'

'But, Mama, it's Ruth. We've found her.' Mary dances a hopping step towards her mother.

'The woman is a stranger. Leave her be at once.'

Frances looks up at me, confused. I tighten my grip on her.

'But, Mama—'

'Come away at once!' She grabs Mary's arm and the girl winces, bottom lip quivering.

'Frances!'

I struggle to my feet, with Frances's arms still wrapped tightly around me. 'Mistress Cromwell, please . . .' I start to speak but find no words. I have only one thought – my love for these girls, like a string, winding me back to Ely and a life that no longer exists.

People are staring.

'I do not know you,' she says. 'My children are mistaken. Frances, come to me at once.' Then she speaks to a bulky older woman who stands at her side. 'Sarah, help me.'

The woman takes hold of Frances.

'It is Ruth! It is!' Frances bawls, clinging to me. A crowd begins to gather.

I put my hand upon her head, feeling the warm softness of her hair. 'Do as your mother says.' The maid pulls Frances away and the child sets up a long wailing cry. Mary joins in.

Mistress Cromwell comes close to me then. I look down at Mary and see the red welt around her wrist, where she twists against her mother's grip. 'I do not know you,' Mistress Cromwell says, loud enough for others to hear. 'You will leave my children alone or you will see the inside of Newgate. Think on that before you make untruthful claims.'

Then she turns on her heel. I watch as the girls are led away, blotched faces twisting back to see me sink to my knees in the dirt.

I cry myself dry that day. I cry for Mary and Frances and their screwed-up faces, spilling tears like gargoyles after rainfall. I cry for myself, for my losses and loneliness. My heart is breaking all over again. The frayed thread that keeps me tied to my old life is finally snapped. I see there is no going back. Now it is only Lizzie who keeps me from despair. Curled up in a ball on my truckle bed in the windowless attic, with Lizzie's fingers stroking my hair, the world does not seem quite so cold.

She is gentle with me, cooing and holding me as I sob out my grief, almost as if I am a child myself. And then, when the tears have stopped and the tearing pain dulls to the ache that I am used to, she stays with me still, like a guardian angel.

'You must think me very foolish,' I say, when eventually I am calm.

'Not at all.'

'Those girls, they are . . .'

'I know who they are. There is no need to explain. I saw their love for you in their eyes.'

'Then you believe me?'

'Of course.' She smiles.

'I'm sorry I caused such a scene.'

She shakes her head. 'With such stories and scandals every day, you'll not be news for long. It will be forgotten tomorrow.'

'Then you are not cross with me?'

'Of course not.' She pauses for a moment and holds my gaze. 'Sit up, Ruth. I have something to ask you.'

I pull myself up to sitting, my legs curled beneath me.

Lizzie takes both of my hands. 'I have watched you closely these last months. I have seen how hard you have tried to fit in here. You have lost so much and yet you hide your pain. You are so strong.'

My heart warms a little.

'I would like to keep you closer to me,' she says. 'I want you with me at all times. I've decided that you will become my personal maid. Would you like that?'

'Oh, yes . . . yes, very much.'

'Good.' She squeezes my hands before letting them drop.

'But what about Charlotte? If there is to be a place at your side then she has the prior claim. She will expect it.'

'I'm sure Margaret can find some use for her in the kitchen.'

'She will be upset.'

'I have decided.' Her voice is smooth and calm. 'The household is my concern. You need not worry.'

'I don't know what to say. Thank you . . .'

She waves away my gratitude. 'Rest a little. I need you strong for tomorrow. We will start your instruction in the morning.'

She leans forward and cups my face in her hands. Her fingers are cool on my cheeks. 'Do not worry about a thing. All will be well, you'll see.' She stands then, but before she leaves me, she brushes her lips against my forehead in a tiny kiss, as gentle as fairies' wings.

Through my pain I love her then. She is the one kind soul in my sadness – the one who will cradle me, who can make me whole again, the one who can save me, if only I can make her love me back.

Chapter 13

It is three nights before Christmas and I am alone in the kitchen, using the light from the fire to hem lengths of fabric, when Charlotte bursts in through the back door, wrapped up and red-nosed from the cold.

'I've bad news,' she says, unravelling her shawl. 'Mistress Cutler is fallen ill. I found out from their kitchen lad. He says she's abed.'

Just a few days before, I had taken a package to the Cutler house. Mistress Cutler, one of Master Poole's regular and most affable customers, had ordered a bolt of cloth for new servants' clothes and she'd slipped me an extra penny, winking and wishing me 'the spirit of the season'. Her husband is one of the few men doing well for themselves out of the war, a gunpowder merchant with orders from the army.

'What's wrong with her?' I ask.

Charlotte pants, getting her breath back. 'Fever, I think. The quack has been there all afternoon, bleeding her.'

'It's not the plague?'

'I don't know. Maybe. Has she been here lately?'

I nod, and Charlotte claps her hand to her mouth. 'Lord, don't tell Margaret or she'll have us stinking the house out with sage again.'

I sit awhile listening to Charlotte prattle, but I cannot focus on the simple stitching before me. I keep thinking of the sick woman, of the three little girls who cling to her skirts and gaze at the rainbow of ribbons in Master Poole's front parlour with eyes like jewelled buttons. I run a list of ailments in my head, coupled with a corresponding list of remedies. I mentally measure the herbal stocks in the Poole kitchen, hellebore, hyssop and pennyroyal, and conjure up dosages in my head until I can no more concentrate on the work before me than on Charlotte's gossiping.

Eventually I rise, wrap my shawl around me and slip out into the street, with Charlotte in tow.

I find Mistress Cutler in bed. Just a few days before, she had colour in her cheeks and fat, laughing lips. Now she looks like one of the wooden mannequins that her daughters drag about, shrunken and desiccated. Her skin is grey and sheened with sweat. Her lips are pale, beginning to crack and seem to shrink back against her teeth. She lies without a cap, her hair matted and spilling across the bolster in tangled ropes. Her nightdress is stained with her own blood where the doctor has been at his work, and the air is acrid. I recognise the sickroom stench of decay.

Her husband stands at the door to the room, a cloth pressed over his nose and mouth. 'The physician said that the best thing is to stay away, in case it develops.' He speaks as if his wife can't see or hear. 'And pray. He said we must pray.'

I go to her. 'Mistress Cutler?' I reach out and touch her forehead. It is flame hot. 'Mistress Cutler, can you hear me?'

She stirs, her eyes unfocused. 'Who's there?'

'It's Ruth, from Master Poole's house.'

She groans. 'Stay away . . . Keep them away . . .'

'She means the children,' her husband says.

I fold the coverlet back and check her skin for marks. There are none. This is not the plague. 'Master Cutler.' I turn to him. 'Is there hot water in the house? And wine?'

'I'm not sure. I'll call the maid.' He leaves, shouting for assistance.

Charlotte peers around the doorframe, her face twisted in disgust. 'Ruth . . . what are you doing?' she hisses.

'Will you do something for me?' I ask. 'Go home and fetch pennyroyal and nightshade. Margaret will help you. And tell the maid to bring clean linen.'

'It's not your place to be here.'

'Please, Charlotte. Do as I say.'

Soon after, Mistress Cutler's maid comes in, carrying a jug of hot water and clean strips of linen. I send her to empty the stinking chamber pot, then set about bathing the sweat from Mistress Cutler's face and arms. The rest of her will have to wait until after the purgative.

It does not take long for the foulness to come out of her and I'm ready with bowls and pots when it does. I banish the pacing husband, and Charlotte, with her incessant questions.

The poor woman bucks and kicks as the herbs do their work. She vomits and writhes in the brown stickiness of her own mess. Master Cutler is beside himself, hearing the wails of his wife behind the closed door. He strides up and down outside the room, cursing me and ordering me out, threatening to call the Watch, but I will not go until my work is done. I have seen this before. I am good at it. I was birthed to it.

In the throes of her agony the poor woman is crazed. She clutches at my arms and digs in her fingernails, her eyes rolling back in her head. She pulls me close and whispers, 'I know who you are. I know why you have come . . .'

I try to soothe her by cooling her forehead with strips of soaked linen but she looks at me with eyes half full of wonder and half full of fear. I have seen cases of delirium before and have often been mistaken for another while attending a sick bed – an ancient crone's long-dead daughter, perhaps, or a farmhand's first sweet-heart. Even, once, a visiting angel. So I think nothing of her ranting. But she is persistent, and surprisingly strong, wrapping her fingers around my wrist with an iron grip and pulling herself up until her face is level with mine.

'I know you are hiding,' she hisses, her voice parched. 'I see it in you. But he will find you. You belong to him.' She fixes me with a stare as deep and powerful as a preacher's. 'You belong to him and you don't even know it. But I know it. Oh, yes . . . I know it . . .'

She must be talking about Our Lord.

'We all belong to Him, Mistress Cutler,' I say. 'And He is with you now.'

'He is with us now?' Suddenly she seems confused, as innocent as a child.

'Of course. He is always with us.'

For the briefest moment, a look of horror passes across her face and then she shudders and relaxes. She sinks back to the bolster, her grip sliding away from my arm, closing her eyes.

It takes all the darkest hours of the night, but at last it is over and her body stilled, the cramps lessened. Slowly, I wipe away the mess from my arms and face. With the help of her maid, I change Mistress Cutler's nightdress and we clean her up as best we can. The poor woman is exhausted, moaning and looking at me with hollow, desperate eyes. She lies back and I stroke her head and make soothing noises until she sleeps. Her breathing is shallow and stilted but it is not the rattle of those near their time. I call for her husband.

'She must sleep now,' I tell him. 'When she wakes, give her hot water and a little warmed wine. Then, if she is stronger after a day, broth or caudle. And, please, no more bleeding.'

Master Cutler looks at the grey-faced woman in the bed and at my dress, spattered and crusted. 'Will she live?'

'I don't know, but I think she is past the crisis. I have seen worse cases than this come through.'

He is puzzled. 'Where? How?'

I look down at the floor. 'My mother was a healer.'

'It is not the plague?'

'No. You can go to her without fear.'

He slips past me and falls to his knees by her bedside. I leave him there and walk home in silence. Charlotte is quiet, a small crease between her brows as if she is trying to make sense of what she has seen. As we turn in to snatch a few hours of sleep before dawn, she stands at the door to my room, watching me peel the soiled clothing from my body.

'I'll see to those in the morning,' she says.

'Thank you.'

'Ruth, how did you know what to do?'

'It was something I've seen done before.'

'By your mother?'

'Yes.'

Charlotte bites her lip. 'Where is your mother now? Why are you not with her?'

'She is dead.' I feel the usual cold blade slide into my chest.

'Oh. How did she die?'

I move to the door. 'Now is not the time. Good night.'

I close the door and climb into my bed, the stench of the sick room still filling my nostrils.

The next afternoon, Mistress Cutler sits up in bed and demands small beer. Her husband praises God for her swift recovery and the servants gossip about how I have saved her from a certain death.

It is both the end and the beginning of something for me. It is the end of my anonymity. People in the marketplace begin to address me by name and point me out to their friends. The Cutler girls peep at me from behind their mother's skirts, more fascinated by me than by the ribbons. When Lizzie hears of it, she hugs me and praises me to her father, saying that I am the saviour of the business and that she cannot do without me.

I am finally finding my place in the vast city. It is next to Lizzie. I think she knows it too.

Chapter 14

Pastor Kiffin makes it clear that those in his congregation do not celebrate Christmas. During our Sunday sermons we learn that the old festivities are but leftovers of superstition and idolatry. Christmas does not fall on the Lord's Day so it holds no sway with us, God's chosen ones.

Master Poole does not have the stomach to argue with Kiffin, no matter how much he misses his plum pottage and honey cakes. It is Lizzie who rules the house now and we are all subject to her whims. But I don't mind. This year, the first without my mother, I would rather forget.

When Twelfth Night comes, it is just another day in the Poole household. We sup with no ceremony and the family retire early as usual. I am finishing in the kitchen, elbow deep in oily water, when there is a tentative tapping at the back door. Margaret and I frown at one another. It is too late for visitors and the household is not expecting company, especially the kind to arrive after dark.

Margaret makes her voice gruff. 'Who's there?'

A male voice returns, muffled through the wood. 'I'm here to see Ruth Flowers.'

Margaret darts a glance at me. I shrug.

'Who calls at this time of night?'

'My name is Joseph Oakes. Please, madam, is Ruth there?'

I have seen Joseph only once since our argument in St Paul's and I made sure that he did not see me. When I had spied his dark head bent over a bookseller's stall in the churchyard, my heart had pounded and tightness had crawled up my spine to squeeze the breath out of my lungs. I had turned away and put the encounter out of my mind as quickly as I could.

'Shall I let him in?' Margaret asks.

'Ask him what he wants.'

She unbolts the door and opens it a crack. 'What do you want with Ruth?'

'Forgive the late hour, but I wish to speak with her. There is a gathering, held in honour of the season. I would like her to join me.'

'We don't observe the festivities in this house,' Margaret says, but she looks over her shoulder at me. I shake my head.

Joseph notes the exchange. 'If I could just speak with Ruth, it would save us both time, madam.'

Ever one to be charmed by young men, Margaret gives in. 'You may as well come in,' she says. 'There's caudle in the pot that'll spoil if I don't attend to it.'

She opens the door and arches an eyebrow at me.

Not long after, I am strolling through St Paul's Churchyard, Joseph at my side. Before I could argue, Margaret had bundled me into her warmest cloak and pushed me out of the door with a knowing glint in her eye. Still, it's good to be outside and although it's cold, the sky is, for once, clear enough to see stars blinking in the blackness.

Joseph takes me east along Cheapside before plunging into the warren of alleyways that lead towards the river. The city teems with people, all ignoring the curfew and celebrating the last night of the season. Along the way Joseph tells me rumours that Parliament are planning a Bill that will make Christmas unlawful, but you would never imagine it by the gangs of revellers in the streets around Cornhill. Part of me thrills to see people out on the streets. To be part of it, on this night of all nights, when the veil between the worlds is thin, makes me feel something between regret and excitement. It is a part of me that I thought long dead. I miss the celebrations of my youth.

When I was very young, Master Oliver would bring all the servants and farmhands inside the house on Twelfth Night for a good meal and merriment. The parlour would glow with the fire stoked high. The smell of sweet pastries mingled with rosemary, bay and the meat roasting on the spit. My mother would work at preparing the feast for a week, then dust off the flour and dress her hair ready for the dancing.

I remember one year most of all. I have a clear memory of my mother, radiant, hair tied with her favoured red ribbons. She danced all night long and even stood up with the master himself. He danced rarely and it was quite a thing to see them both, he, red-cheeked and roaring with laughter, and she, dark hair streaming as she spun. That was the first time I noticed the special power my mother had to catch a man's eye and to hold it. They were all pleased with her – except the mistress, who stalked from the room with a sour look upon her face.

But that was a long time ago and over the years, as the master was away more often, and he grew older and more serious, Christmas faded from the house. The farmhands still found time to get drunk and rowdy, but that year was the last that we were invited into the parlour to sup with the family, and the last that I saw Master Oliver so carefree.

Before long we reach a tavern, lit up like a lantern, smoke and soot billowing from the door. I hear pipes, a fiddle and voices raised in song.

'This is what I wanted to show you,' Joseph says, taking my hand and leading me inside.

The taproom throbs with people. Wealthy merchants from Cheapside sit side by side with market boys from Smithfield.

Children weave between legs. Milkmaids and servant girls giggle and preen, darting evil looks at the painted bawds working the room. I recognise several faces from the bookstalls at St Paul's. Pipe smoke catches in my throat and makes my eyes smart.

Joseph pushes through the crowd towards the sound of the music. In the back room we find dancing – couples squashed up against each other in the throng. A gang of apprentices link arms and spin each other about, trying not to spill the contents of their mugs.

A couple of men call to Joseph and we make our way towards them.

'These are the twins, Benjamin and Charlie,' Joseph shouts. 'No one knows which is which.'

I take in their matching friendly faces as one jabs Joseph in the ribs and laughs. It's true that they are the mirror of one another, with mouse-brown hair, snub noses and mischievous smiles. I notice how Joseph's hand leaves mine to rub at his side, though his face betrays nothing. Is it habit, or is his old battle wound still unhealed?

He cups his hand to my ear. 'They have a new press, just off Lombard Street. Good men – more worldly than they look.'

I nod to them and they take turns to shake my hand. It is some time since I have found strangers so unguarded.

A girl moves through the crowd, carrying a jug of ale. 'Lord, what a rabble!' She nods towards the apprentices. Two have climbed onto a table and are encouraging the crowd to join them in song. 'Here we are, gentlemen.' She has the clipped accent of a local woman, smiling eyes and a gap-toothed grin. I like her immediately. 'I'm Sal.' She pumps my hand up and down, as if she is drawing water from the conduit.

'I'm Ruth.'

'Oh, I know who you are. We've heard all about you.' She winks and nudges me with her elbow, making me blush.

We drink the ale and watch the dancers. Joseph and the twins are soon deep in discussion about a new pamphlet, something to do with wealth and property, and I am happy when Sal rolls her eyes and turns to me. 'They might as well be talking in Latin,' she says. 'Joseph tells me you're a maid in a house near St Paul's.'

'Yes.'

'Is it a good place?'

'Oh, yes. The mistress is very kind.'

'Good. Take care to keep it, then. Don't go making mistakes.' She flicks her eyes towards the three men, now in earnest debate. I'm puzzled and Sal sees it. 'Joseph is a good lad, but once they've got a few drinks inside them, they're all the same.' She pauses and swigs her beer. 'We both know that girls like us can't afford mishaps.'

I colour deeply. 'Joseph and I are not . . . I mean, we're not . . .'

'Of course, my lovely, of course. I'm sure you can look after yourself.' She grins at me, then tugs at Charlie's sleeve. 'Enough of that. This is supposed to be a holiday.' She drags him into the centre of the room and they join the dancing.

The ale is stronger than I'm used to; it makes me a little lightheaded. The music is fast and loud. I feel the rhythms inside my chest, making my feet move in time.

'I see you've made friends with Sal,' Joseph says, in my ear.

'She is . . . very lively.'

He laughs. 'Aye, she has a good heart. She's Charlie's girl. They're hoping to marry if he and Benjamin can make a go of the press. She likes you, I can tell.'

Some of the apprentices have joined their fellows in song and voices pick up around the room.

'Dance?' Joseph sweeps a low bow in front of me and I cannot help but smile. It is such a long time since I have felt myself moved by music, and after the drink I am bold.

He takes my hand and we leave Benjamin with his pot and step into the crush.

I don't know if it is the press of people, or the ale, or the dizzying flash of candlelight but I feel a kind of release. With Joseph's hand in mine, and his arm circling my waist, I feel both safe and free, free from the demons that have followed me these last months, free from duty and obligation, and free from fear. Perhaps it is the easy anonymity among strangers or just the infectious joy of so many, but as I dance, I feel a little of what they feel, swept up in the moment. Even if it is only brief, I think I understand why we are all here, and why Joseph brought me.

Later, after we have said our goodbyes, Joseph walks me back to West St Paul's. It is past midnight and the streets are quieter now. The frosted ground glitters as if sprinkled with gems.

'Do you forgive me?' he asks.

'For what?'

'The last time we met, in St Paul's, you were upset.'

The argument seems a long time ago. 'Oh . . . yes. You are forgiven.'

We walk on in silence, my mind running ahead, thoughts tumbling over one another so that I can barely hold on to them. Fixing on a question that has plagued me all evening, I ask, 'Why did you come for me tonight?'

His eyes search mine. 'I thought . . . I should make amends. You have not come to the shop since we quarrelled, so . . .'

'My mistress likes me close at hand.'

'I'm sure she does,' he says, a note of sarcasm in his voice. 'But there is more to life than duty and work. I hope tonight showed you that at least.'

I smile. 'It did.'

'How did you like Sal, and the twins?' he says.

'Very much.'

'They have such grand plans. And they would like me to join them, when I can, with the new press. They have so many new ideas.'

'What kind of ideas?'

'Well . . . they believe, as do I, in the power of words. The time for the battlefield is over. People are weary of bloodshed, so they turn to the newsbooks for their politics. There is such influence to be had. People's minds to be won.'

'But who would you win them for? Yourself?'

He laughs. 'You think me as unworthy as that? My God, do I have any hope of winning you over?'

I say nothing.

'We would fight the cause of the Army Agitators,' he says. 'Those good, true men who want nothing more than we were all promised. Pay, voting rights, equality. They are the true crusaders in this fight now.'

The passion in his voice spills into his eyes and makes them shine. Despite my own good fortune, I feel the cold slide of envy. He has kindled a new life for himself here. He has a future that burns bright with the promise of better things. 'And do you think you can win this war of words?' I ask.

'It's worth fighting for. There is always something worth fighting for. There is always something that can be changed for the better.'

'Perhaps that is the difference between a man and a woman,' I say. 'You have more freedom than I. You are free to achieve such things.'

'You think you are not?'

'I know I am not.'

'You have more freedom than you imagine, Ruth Flowers. Look at Sal. Do you think she is powerless?'

I remember Sal's clever eyes and wicked grin. 'No. But she is . . . she is different.'

'Why?'

'She does not have my past . . .'

Joseph stops suddenly and pulls me around to face him. His fingers dig into my flesh. 'Will you tell me what you are running from? Whatever it is, I don't care.'

Damn the drink. My mouth is running away with me. I tug away from him and start to walk. The magic of the evening is broken now. He keeps pace by my side.

'You can trust me,' he says. 'I've trusted you. Can you not do the same for me?'

'Please, let's talk of something else.'

'It may help you to unburden yourself of your troubles.'

'Please . . .' I beg. 'I was glad to be with you this evening. Please don't spoil it.'

He sighs and shakes his head. 'I'm sorry. I always push too hard. It is a fault in me, I know. Sal is always telling me so. She says I'm like a dog with a bone.'

That makes me smile, despite myself, and I soften. As we reach the churchyard he takes my arm and tucks it into the crook of his elbow. After the dancing it feels natural to be close to him and we walk the rest of the way in companionable silence.

There is something different in the souls of these people, something pure and honest. The twins have it, Sal has it, and now Joseph is transformed with it. It does not matter that they dance and drink and blaspheme. Underneath their ragged clothes and coarse manners, they have something precious. I recognise it, and covet it, even though I cannot put a name to it.

I remember what Joseph told me that night of the storm in Puckeridge, of the things he had seen and suffered. I marvel that a man can recover so swiftly and find a new reason to live. I would do well to learn from him, I think.

When we reach West St Paul's, we stand wordless for a few moments, cloaked by the night. Then he takes up my hand and brings it to his lips. Such a gesture should be awkward on him, but it suits well, in place of the goodbye I find I don't want to hear. He turns and walks away. I watch him go, the darkness taking him like winter fog. It may just be the effects of the ale, but I swear I feel my heart pull towards his, just a little.

Chapter 15

As I lock and bolt the kitchen door, my head spins with the drink and the cold night air. I rest my forehead against the wood for a moment.

'Where have you been?'

Lizzie sits by the hearth, swaddled in a thick shawl. The fire is fading and the red glow from the embers lights her features, casting dark shadows beneath her eyes. She stares at me, unblinking, like a falcon.

'Oh! You startled me,' I say, moving towards her. 'May I fetch you something?'

I realise that her eyes are swollen. She has been crying.

'Where have you been?' she repeats, her voice hard.

'I've been with a friend.'

'Margaret told me you went out with a man.'

'Yes . . . a friend called. You were abed, so . . .'

'You told me you had no acquaintance in London.'

'He is someone I know from . . . before.' I crouch down and reach out a hand to touch her arm. 'You don't look well. Let me help you upstairs.'

She shrugs me off. 'You stink of the alehouse.'

Then she stands suddenly, knocking me backwards onto the floor. 'You seem to have forgotten your place, Ruth. You are a servant in this house. You are *my* servant. I will not have any servant of mine going about with strange men of whom I know nothing. I will not have you drinking like a common slattern and I will not have you celebrating papist festivals.'

She is so cold, so angry. I have never heard her voice knife-edged like this before. She towers over me like a gorgon, her hair streaming over her shoulders.

'I have given you a home here, Ruth. I have treated you with charity and generosity, and this is how you choose to repay me – by disappearing without a word and gadding about with a man. We are a respectable household and I will not have my servants bringing disrepute. These are dangerous times – gossip and scandal have ruined better households than this. Is that what you want? To bring the fires of Gomorrah to our very door?'

Her anger shatters me. I have been stupid. I should have known that Lizzie would not approve. I have risked my place by her side on a whim.

'Well?' Lizzie says. 'Have you anything to say, or shall I leave you to gather your things?'

'I'm sorry . . .' My voice quavers, brimful of tears. 'Please, don't make me leave. I couldn't bear it . . .'

She stands over me unmoved, taut as a bowstring. Shame bears down on me like a weight. Any joy I have felt in the evening is crushed to dust.

'Please . . . I know it was wrong . . . I do so want to be good. Teach me how to be good.' I reach out and touch the hem of her skirt, like a penitent.

'Do you see that you have sinned against me? That you have betrayed my trust?'

'Yes . . . yes. I will do anything to make it right. Please show me how . . . Please let me stay.' Sobs rock me, doubling me over on the floor by her feet.

She leaves me there, giving me time to languish, and paces the kitchen. I think of all the kindness she has shown me. She has taken me in and given me a home. She saved me when I was desperate. She cared for me when I had no friend left in the world. She has made me her maidservant, when she could have treated me as a kitchen drudge. She has trusted me. Without her, I have nowhere to go, no money, no family to save me from the streets. And, far beyond all of that, I cannot bear to be away from her. I feel a deep, yawning void open in my chest, filled with nothing but bitter blackness. I tremble with the horror of it. I had thought I was in control of this – the casting of the binding charm slowly stitching her heart to mine – but I am not in control of my own heart. Of everything I stand to lose in that moment, it is her company that matters most. I will do anything to keep it.

Eventually she comes to me, kneels down and puts her hand on my shoulder. 'Sit up, Ruth.' Her voice is measured.

I try to dry my eyes.

'If you are truly sorry, I suppose I can forgive you. Come now, it gives me no pleasure to see you so. Let us begin again. We will not speak of this to my father, or to anyone. But I will be watching, Ruth, and I will be speaking with Pastor Kiffin, to recommend that he give you special attention and instruction. If you are willing to learn from this, then that will be an end of it.'

'I will do anything you ask.'

'I want you to do this for yourself, Ruth. I need to know that you are committed to the true faith and are willing to work hard to banish your sinful thoughts and actions.' She takes my hand and helps me up.

I meet her eyes. 'I would do anything to stay with you.'

Her features soften as she looks at me and she cups my hand in hers. 'And do you promise not to see that man again? Or any man, without my presence or my permission?'

'I promise.'

'Then, we have an agreement.' She turns to leave the room. I stand, shivering, alone. But then she throws a glance back at me and says, 'There is one more thing, before we retire. I have something for you.'

She beckons. I follow her up the stairs and into her bedchamber, meek as a lamb, grateful for any scrap of goodwill that she is willing to throw me. She crosses the room to the chest where she keeps her private things, opens it and draws out a small package. Then she closes the door to the room, indicating that I should sit down upon the bed.

'I planned to give this to you tonight. That's why I came to the kitchen looking for you. Part of me thinks that you do not deserve it. Perhaps I am being too lenient. But I believe you are sorry, and I do not want to spoil our friendship. For we do have a friendship, do we not?'

My heart picks itself up from the pit of my stomach and grows wings. It flutters against the cage of my chest. 'Oh, yes!'

'Then this is for you. We do not celebrate the season here, but I like to give a token to those I care about.'

She hands the package to me and I unpick the strings and unfold the linen. A pair of crimson satin ribbons gleams like rubies in the candlelight.

'I thought they would look pretty in your hair. It is our duty to appreciate God's natural beauty and a little adornment will do no harm, if we are ever wary of vanity,' Lizzie says, and I hear Kiffin's voice in hers.

The ribbons nestle in my palm, coiled like shining snakes. They speak to me of my mother, twirling with red ribbons in her hair. Red – the colour of passion, the colour of the army, the colour of blood. I finger them. They are slippery, silky, the best quality that Master Poole sells. I have often coveted them as I cut a length for some lady in the shop.

'They are beautiful. Thank you.'

Then the idea takes me. 'I have something for you too.' Before she can speak, I race upstairs to my room and pull my mother's book from its hiding place beneath the pallet. I hold it to my chest and breathe in the familiar scent of the binding. My mother is on every page of this book, her life woven through the paper, steeped in the ink. I falter. Must I part with all I have left of her?

I sit down on the pallet, rocked yet again by the strength of my memories. I can almost see her before me, brow furrowed as she bends over the bed of a fever patient; smiling and slapping out the first cry of a newborn; reaching for a sprig of herbs over a steaming cauldron, face hot and shining; salting the meat for the barrels, arms red and itching. In every task, her book was always somewhere within reach.

I have my memories and that will have to be enough. All those things are in my past. Lizzie is my future, I'm sure of that now. I owe her my life. I so desperately want to repay her and this book is the only thing of value I own. To me it is beyond value. If I give the book to Lizzie, then I give her everything. Then, suddenly, I am resolved – I know this is what I must do. It is the best way of proving my word.

Back in her bedchamber, I place the precious thing in her hands as though it is a piece of the most delicate lace. 'This belonged to my mother.'

She looks astonished and then her eyes blur with tears. 'Oh, Ruth, I cannot take this from you.' She opens the cover and scans the first few pages. I see her face alter, a shadow passing behind her eyes. Her hands close around it, as though she possesses it already.

'I want you to have it, if you will promise to keep it safe,' I say.

'Indeed . . .' She is thumbing through the pages now, intent on the contents. 'What a fine gift.'

'Please, take it.'

She looks up at me. I see that she understands. 'Then let us agree that our exchange of gifts seals our pact. Our agreement stands. No more lies and no more harsh words. We will be the very best of friends.'

'Yes.' I take up Lizzie's gift to me and run the ribbons between my fingertips. The satin is smooth and gossamer soft, like her skin.

She reaches over and clasps my hand. 'You are special to me, Ruth.' The ribbons lace our fingers, crimson lengths falling, coupling our wrists. For the briefest moment she squeezes my hand tightly, then lets it drop.

I go to my bed lightheaded and exhausted. As I reach my door Charlotte is waiting on the threshold of her room, candle in hand. My weeping must have woken her. Perhaps she has heard it all. She does not say a word but closes her door with a scowl.

Chapter 16

The ice that binds us over Christmas remains well into February and people stay indoors, hiding from the cold. The streets are quiet and the fallen snow dulls the clamour of the hawkers. The war continues outside the walls, now a game of hide-and-seek for the King, who has escaped the Parliament men and is sought by the army. There can be no fighting in this season when men must stay at their fireside to survive. The brutalities of the battles at Marston Moor and Naseby begin to fade in people's minds. The newsbooks still feed the fire of the New Model Army, and people still talk of a better future, but somehow, inside the city walls, it seems a long way off. Westminster could be a hundred miles away for all I care about it. My concern is with my life at West St Paul's, and I feel no threat from any army, Parliament's or the King's.

I love winter-stilled London. I love to walk the streets, all swathed in white, icicles dripping from eaves, windowpanes frosted. The sky is clear, chimney smoke dispelled by biting winds. The vile filth beneath my feet is frozen, the stinking drains encased in ice. Like this, the city has a melancholy beauty that suits my mood. My grief lingers but the pain is dull now, as though the cold has numbed the cracks in my heart.

These quiet months are a blessed time. Lizzie keeps her word and makes me her constant companion, banishing Charlotte to the kitchen. She teaches me how to help her dress in the morning and how she likes her things put away when she is abed. Each day I brush her hair until it shines, then plait it and pin it up under her cap. I lay out her clothes and lace her into her stays. I am close to her for most of the day. Master Poole allows me to sit in the front parlour. Now that I have one or two of Lizzie's old gowns to wear, I look almost like a lady myself and I'm learning the trade. My needlework will never be as perfect as Lizzie's but it is good enough for the rougher jobs, so I sit alongside her, tacking and hemming as if I were born to it.

Young men come calling, dropping into the shop to make enquiries of Master Poole or to buy buttons and trimmings for their wives. But for the most part they come to see Lizzie. I watch them, their eyes sidling over her as she measures out some length of ribbon, their lips wet and cheeks flushed. I see their hungry gaze linger on the graceful turn of her neck, the trimness of her waist and the swell under her stays. In watching them I learn what a precious thing I have, and secretly triumph over them, for I alone can touch her. I feel no threat from these dribbling oafs, for they will never have what I have. They will never catch the scent of her hair as she pulls a shift over her head, or feel the brush of her clean skin, fresh from her bath, or the morning heat of her body. These things are mine alone now.

And, more than that, she is become softer and more open with me. She honours her promise – there are no more arguments and no harsh words. We are the best of friends. I have bound her to me. I thank the Fen spirits for heeding my prayers, whispered to the waters, and I promise I will not let her go. No one will ever replace my mother, but at least I am no longer alone.

I am almost sorry as the season turns, spring arrives and I can no longer take refuge beside the kitchen hearth at West St Paul's. The days are longer, the air turns milder and, with it, Lizzie's energy is renewed. We spend our days at work in the parlour, making trips to the churchyard or the market, or visiting Stukeley at Pope's Head Alley. Encouraged by Kiffin, Lizzie is writing a treatise and loves to discuss the printing of it with Stukeley. She spends her evenings at the kitchen table with paper and ink, but I never see a page completed, though many find their way into the fire.

One day, Lizzie is busy working on a new dress for Mistress Cutler, the second of two commissions granted in thanks for my ministrations at Christmas. She sends me out on an errand to Stukeley's, claiming she does not have time to go. She finally has some pages that are ready for the press. Stukeley is expecting them.

'Surely you would prefer to see it done yourself,' I say.

'He knows what I want,' she says, 'and I trust you to do as I ask.' She smiles at me and I think how beautiful she is today, in her red serge with unruly copper curls escaping her cap. 'Besides,' she says, 'I prefer to be alone for this work. I must concentrate. I do not want to be disturbed before supper. Please tell the others – I am only at home for important callers.'

Lizzie does not know that a visit to Stukeley's means I will see Joseph. She does not know that Joseph is the man I have sworn not to see. God forgive me for the deception, but I have chosen not to tell her the whole truth. I reason that sometimes silence is kinder, and safer all round.

Since our quarrel on Twelfth Night I have visited Stukeley's shop several times, always as Lizzie's chaperone. I sit in the corner, near the window, while Lizzie and Stukeley mutter in low voices over some new setting or woodcut. Although Joseph has made sure to catch my eye, we have not been free to talk, and I am glad of it. I burn with guilt when I think of this secret, but I burn with fear even more, when I think of Lizzie's wrath. It is better that she does not know.

Today when I arrive at the shop, I find Joseph alone. He listens

patiently as I detail Lizzie's request and takes the papers she
has given me for printing. Then he leads me to the back room.
He pours a cup of small beer from a bottle that stands open
on the mantel and hands it to me, indicating that I should sit
upon a stool next to his workbench. I watch him for a while as he
sets letters into a tray. I study the press, running my eyes over its
oily black hulk. To me, it is nothing but a jumble of levers and
pulleys and wooden panels, stained with smudges of grease
and black ink. I cannot make sense of it, of how this new-
fangled machine can make the crisp white pamphlets that Lizzie
loves so much. It broods in the centre of the room, keeping its
secrets from me.

Joseph breaks the silence. 'Why do you not speak to me, when
you come here with her?'

'She forbids it.'

He frowns.

'My mistress forbids me to speak to men she does not know,'
I explain.

'She has no such rights over you.'

'She is my mistress.'

Joseph snorts.

'She is good to me. I will not disobey her.'

'Then why do you linger here?' He smirks, knowing he has
caught me out. He looks me over, taking in the good dress I am
wearing, the new leather boots on my feet. 'You think you are too
good for the likes of me, now you've moved up in the world. Is
that it?'

I shake my head. 'It's not that. It's only . . .' I look at his big
labourer's hands, stained black with ink, and his patched and
darned clothes. 'Lizzie would not understand.'

'She's not so fine herself.'

'What do you mean? She is as fine as any lady.'

'I measure a person's worth by their deeds, not their bearing.'

He stops his work and looks me full in the face, as if searching for something. Then he shakes his head. 'I don't want to argue. Let's talk of something else,' he says.

I drain my cup and eye the contraption in the centre of the room. 'How does it work?' I ask.

His eyes brighten. He sets aside the tray before him and fetches an empty one. 'See these letters?' He picks up a tiny metal block and holds it up to the light so that I can see a delicate letter M cast upon it. 'I make up the words with these. Often I work from a handwritten text, like those your mistress sends, or I'll be copying something else that has been printed before.' He points to a document on the table covered with ink. 'I read each word in turn and select the letters from over here.' He strides to a large wooden cabinet, which has drawers from top to bottom. He pulls one out and I see row upon row of tiny squares. He takes his time, choosing four of the larger ones and carrying them back to the bench. 'I line the letters up in the frame to make the words. But, and here's where the skill lies, the letters are formed backwards, like looking in a glass, so you have to set the type in reverse. When the words are printed, they come out the right way around.' He slots the four letters into the tray.

'And we use blanks to fill the spaces.' There is a jar filled with unmarked blocks on the bench top. He picks up a handful and places them in the tray, arranging them around the word he has spelled. Then he carries the tray to the bed of the machine. 'Each frame corresponds to the size of paper you are using and each set of letters to the size of the type, you see? It's delicate work. Took me three weeks to print a page with no mistakes.' He smiles, with something like pride. 'Do you want to work the press?' he says.

'Really?'

'Yes. But not a word of it to anyone.'

He slots the tray into place and fastens it down with a little wooden frame. 'We coat the blocks with ink. See?'

I watch as he uses a leather pad to blacken the metal letters, surprised by his dexterity. He wipes his hands on a rag, then fetches a fresh sheet of paper. He slides it onto a flat plate above the bed, nudging it gently to straighten and flatten it, tightening screws to secure it.

'Now, come here.'

I stand and go to his side. To my right there is a long iron lever. Joseph puts his hand on my waist and guides me until I am alongside it. 'Take hold.'

I put both hands on the cold metal. He stands close behind me, so that his arms circle me and he can reach the lever too. I am enfolded. I sense the warmth of his body and smell the leather of his apron with the distinct spiciness of male sweat. His face is at my shoulder. If I turn my head now my lips would brush his cheek, I would feel the scratch of his stubble on my skin.

'Now, we push the handle down. Not too fast or too slow.'

He places his hands gently over mine and guides me as I apply pressure to the lever. It is heavy and as I grapple with it, the weight of his grasp increases. I feel the flex of his forearms. His palms are hot and damp.

Together, we haul the lever down. The press makes a creaking, clunking sound, and the paper is pressed down upon the waiting ink.

'And now slowly back up . . .' Joseph says, gradually lessening the pressure until the lever finds its resting place.

For a few seconds I am breathless, my hands glued into place beneath his. And then he is away from me, attending to the press.

He peels the paper from its holding and reveals a sheet of creamy whiteness, stamped with four letters in perfect glistening print:

RUTH

I have never seen my name in print before. The letters are stark and lonely on the page. But he has used a curling script the like of which I have not seen on the newsbooks. It is strangely beautiful. I reach out to take it from him.

'Careful,' he says. 'We must let it dry.'

'It's wonderful,' I say, and he grins.

'The skill is all in the setting and knowing how to handle the press. And patience. You must be careful and patient. There are some men so skilled they can make masterpieces. Beautiful pieces from Germany and Holland sometimes pass through this shop. They say it takes years to learn the real art of it.'

'But you will do it, I'm sure,' I say.

He puts the paper down on the workbench and his eyes rest on my name. 'Ruth . . .' he says, under his breath, and then he raises his gaze to meet mine. The air between us is alive. 'If things were different . . . if I were a richer man . . .'

Just then the shop door clatters open and there is stamping and blowing as Stukeley warms himself. Joseph pushes the printed paper towards me. 'Take it,' he says.

I pick it up and hold it behind my back. Joseph is suddenly panic-eyed. If we have done something wrong, I do not know what it is.

When Stukeley sees me, his face turns sour. 'What is happening here?'

'Mistress Flowers has come on business, sir.'

'We have talked about this, Joseph.'

'Master Stukeley, I'm sorry . . . Mistress Poole sends—'

'It is not for discussion. See her on her way.' He does not acknowledge me. He stalks across the room and thumps up the stairs.

Joseph cannot meet my eye. He takes up the papers I have brought from Lizzie and holds them out to me. 'Please tell Mistress Poole that we cannot take her work.'

'What? Why?'

'We're too busy.'

'Nonsense. What do you mean by this, Joseph?'

'Stukeley will not print Mistress Poole's work. He must decline.'

'But it has been arranged. They have spent hours discussing this. How can he withdraw now?'

He sighs and beckons me closer so that he can whisper. 'There has been gossip . . . about your mistress.'

'About Lizzie?'

'Aye.'

'What kind of gossip?'

The sound of Stukeley moving overhead chases us into the shop and Joseph opens the street door. 'You must go.'

'What gossip, Joseph? Tell me.'

'God knows I'm not one to believe in rumours, but I've heard things. People say she's not to be trusted.'

'What do you mean?'

'Some are saying she does bad things. That she is sinful.'

'What?' Anger bubbles in my chest.

'I know how much you like her, and that she has been good to you, but I think perhaps—'

'Stukeley believes it?'

'He says we need to be careful who we associate with. It could damage the business if we're seen to deal freely with someone who is . . . a known sinner. If we print her words we could be implicated.'

I bristle with indignation. 'But she has done nothing wrong. How can you say these things?'

'I'm just telling you what I've heard.'

'But Stukeley knows her well. How can he believe it?'

'He is being careful.'

'I thought he was a friend.'

'He has his reputation and his business to think of.'

'And you? Do you believe it?'

'All I see is that she has you beguiled.'

I am furious now, the anger giving me strength. 'How dare you talk to me of sinning? You of all people, with your secrets.'

'Please, Ruth, don't—'

'I'm such a fool that I had begun to think better of you, but now I see I was right about you from the start. You are the one who cannot be trusted. Elizabeth Poole is the best person I know. I will not stay here to listen to this from you, when you don't even know her.'

'How can I know her, when you keep her so much to yourself?'

I pull my shawl tight around me and am out of the door before I can hear another word. I still clutch the paper with my name printed upon it. I have smudged the letters in my haste, where the ink is not yet dry. The beautiful thing is ruined. When I reach Cheapside, I scrunch it up into a tight little ball and toss it into the street drain. I push away tears with the back of my hand as I walk, keeping my head down so no one will see my face. I feel the old conviction that I am watched. There are eyes everywhere in this city.

I walk a long tangled route back to St Paul's, and by the time I reach home, I am calmer. I am resolved. I will not mention what I have heard to Lizzie, or to anyone. I'm angry with Joseph for believing gossip, but I see no reason to cause Lizzie any worry – at least, not yet. Perhaps he is mistaken, or perhaps Stukeley is deceived. Perhaps it is a different Mistress Poole whose name has been blackened. Whatever the case, I'm determined to protect Lizzie as she has protected me. I will do nothing to disrupt the haven I have built for myself.

When I get back to the house, Lizzie is with William Kiffin in the parlour. There, I think. What more proof does the world need? A godly woman, deep in debate with her pastor. How can anyone doubt her?

It is only later that evening, when Margaret remarks on my dirty face, that I remember Lizzie's papers. I left them with Joseph. I cannot go back for them now. I will have to tell her they are lost. But not yet, not tonight. Tonight I cannot bear the disappointed look she will give me. Looking at my image in the bottom of a shining copper pot, I see two dark smudges under my eyes, where ink has come away from my hands as I dried my tears. 'Soot,' I tell Margaret, but I know she doesn't believe me.

Chapter 17

I spend the next few days worrying about the missing papers, but I dare not admit the truth to Lizzie. I know this dallying will only make my fate worse, when it comes, but I am scared that the careless loss of Lizzie's precious words will be one folly too many. I am scared that she will send me away. What will I do if I am cast out? I have no money, save the few pennies left in my purse, and nowhere to go. I have no acquaintance in London, except the Cromwells, and nothing could induce me to try their charity now. So I stay silent and pray for a miracle. And a few days later it comes, with banging on the kitchen door after dark, unshaven, ink-stained and reeking of the alehouse.

Master Poole is at his account books in the parlour, and we women are gathered before the kitchen hearth. When Margaret answers the door to Joseph, with a smile of recognition, I glare a warning at her. She has been at the ale herself today, but she is not too far gone to read my meaning and says nothing.

'I'm come from Master Stukeley's, with a delivery for Mistress Poole,' Joseph says.

Lizzie looks up from her sewing. 'Let him inside, Margaret.'

Joseph crosses to the hearth and hands a bundle of papers to Lizzie. He does not look at me. It is odd to see him here. He looks different somehow, out of place. My heart is suddenly leaping in my chest.

He gives her a polite little bow. 'Your pamphlets, madam.'

Lizzie unties the package and flicks through the pages. 'You are Stukeley's man, are you not?'

'Yes, madam.'

'And did you print these?'

'Yes, madam.'

She peels a pamphlet from the pile and holds it up to the firelight. 'They are well done,' she says.

'Thank you.'

I risk a glance at Joseph and find that his eyes are already on mine. He understands what is at stake. He has done this to save me.

'Margaret, fetch him a drink,' Lizzie says. 'Will you sit awhile, Mister . . .'

'Oakes. Joseph Oakes.'

'Please sit, Mister Oakes. I have some questions for you.'

Margaret does as she is told and scoops a good measure of the hot caudle she brews nightly in the pot on the fire. Joseph seats himself on a low stool, his long legs spider-like. He cradles the cup.

Lizzie introduces Charlotte, who simpers and bats her eyelids, and Margaret. 'And Ruth, of course, you know,' she says.

I do not trust myself to greet Joseph. I'm grateful to him, of course, but fearful that one ill-chosen word might give away the betrayal of my promise to Lizzie. Seeing him here is part comfort, part torture. I am like a child who has stolen delicious fancies from the master's table, but knows a price must be paid when her thievery is found out.

Lizzie and Joseph discuss the pamphlet. They talk about the settings and the bleed of the paper he has chosen; they talk of where she will distribute it; they talk of its subject. I have not read it – Lizzie has not yet chosen to share her words with me – but I gather it is a religious work, similar to those produced by Kiffin. Lizzie means it to reach the poor of the parish.

I listen to her talking with great passion of her thoughts and wishes. How close she came to losing it, I think, and now she will never know. Joseph is easily her match in conversation and, as I watch them, I am jealous. I understand little of these things. I am not a dolt, but sometimes it's hard to find the right words when I need them most. Besides, this world of politics and the press is a mystery to me. It does not take long for the talk to turn to the war, as it seems it always does.

'You know they are saying that he should be captured, held prisoner and forced into agreement. There is no other way,' Joseph says.

'The King? To be held like a commoner?' Lizzie is shocked.

'The army believes there's little option, for his word cannot be trusted.'

'Will they put him in the Tower with the thieves and the traitors?'

'I don't know.'

'Of course the King must be tamed, and the threat of popery must be stamped from the Court – I believe that with all my heart – but surely there is still hope that he is a reasonable man. He may be brought to govern *with* Parliament.'

'Many say the time for that is long past. He has proved himself unreliable. But there are some in the army who still want to try – Cromwell for one, and Fairfax. But he must be captured first, to force him to an agreement, and who has the guts to try that?'

That is so like my old master, I think. Always looking for the good in a person, even a wayward king.

Lizzie shakes her head. 'And what do *you* think, Mister Oakes? You come armed with the opinions of a hundred newsbooks, but which are your own?'

'I believe that the bloodshed we have endured these last few years is not truly God's way. The horrors of the battlefield do not lead to salvation. The King is a traitor, madam, who has turned against his own people. He must be made to account for that, but the deaths of honest men and women are not the means.'

'Amen to that. But what then? What would you have the army do?'

'Debate is the way forward now, and agreement within the army, without more war.'

'You are a passionate man, I can see. I understand your reluctance to draw innocent blood, but tell me, why is it that you are not moved to fight? You are of age. You are fit and well. Why not the army?'

Joseph pauses and drains his cup. 'I prefer to work for freedom in other ways.'

'With comedic pamphlets and superstitious stories?'

'With respect, madam, the press can work just as hard as a sword. I know you believe that too. The paper you hold in your hand makes that clear as day. And why should a man be expected to go to battle just because he is a man? There is no such expectation of women.'

'Mister Lilburne fights in the New Model Army and writes his Levelling pamphlets too. Or are you saying that women should fight? I do not see Mistress Lilburne drawing a sword and rushing to the fray. No, she stays at home to keep her house and children, because that is what is expected of her. Just as it is expected of a man to fight for a cause, if they believe in it strongly enough.'

Lilburne. I know the name: he is an army radical, the author of the pamphlet that Joseph carried with him from Cambridge to London. A name I've heard on the tongues of the news-sellers in the churchyard.

'There are other things a woman might do,' Joseph continues. 'Such as?'

'She has a voice. She may not be able to preach from the pulpit or stand up in the Commons and debate with the Members. She may not be asked to pick up a sword and drive it through the heart of her enemy, although God knows many enough have been forced to do so, but she may still have a voice.'

'How so?'

'With these.' Joseph takes up a pamphlet and brandishes it. 'And this.' He points a grubby finger at his own lips. 'Mistress Lilburne has a hand in her husband's words. I see a woman's sensibility in his arguments. And you, Mistress Poole, why spend your time and your pennies on such things if you don't believe you can make a difference?'

Lizzie feeds him a slow smile. 'You like your women strong, I think.'

'I like a woman who knows her own mind and has strength, even if she does not always show it.' He shoots a glance at me and I feel a blush rise as I look away.

'Well, we can all agree with you there at least.'

Charlotte, who has been listening avidly, nods. She is red-cheeked, captivated by the exchange. She cannot take her eyes off Joseph.

'A woman must be good too, don't you think?' Lizzie goes on.

'Of course. But that's no different for a man. There is little difference in the qualities that make up a good person, regardless of their sex, or their status in life.'

Lizzie muses for a second. Her eyes glitter. She is at her most beautiful when she is fired up. 'You are a good Protestant, are you not, Mister Oakes?' she says.

'That I am, by God's grace.'

'Then you believe in God's chosen people, in those who are elect?'

'I do.'

'And does it not follow that there are others who are damned? Those who will never truly know God's grace, no matter how godly they may appear.'

'So we are told.'

'And should we not all work to find His grace within us, before judging others?'

'Yes.'

'And, having found it, should we then declare ourselves, man or woman, in this battle against the Antichrist?'

'Of course.'

'Do you believe this is a duty, to speak one's mind, to tell the world of what you know?'

'I believe that it's a man's duty to follow his conscience. To seek out good from evil and to help others see truth where they find it.'

'What about man's baser instincts? What about greed and envy? What about lust?'

'These things are sent to test us, I suppose.'

Lizzie leans forward, her eyes flashing in the firelight. 'And do you find yourself tested, Mister Oakes?'

Joseph shifts in his seat, leaning back and away from her. 'That is a matter for me and my conscience alone.'

She has pushed him too far, I think. They are at a stalemate. But then his lips twitch in amusement and he holds her gaze for just a second too long. I see it. I see something pass between them. It is beyond my understanding. All I know is that a cold, sliding feeling has entered my heart.

But then Joseph stands. 'I must thank you for your hospitality, madam.'

Lizzie bows her head.

'And I have a favour to ask. I would like your permission to call upon Ruth two days hence, on May Day, providing that your household will observe the holiday.'

No one is expecting this, least of all me. Lizzie frowns, just for a second, before she gathers herself.

'I'd like to walk out with her,' Joseph goes on. 'A picnic, perhaps, as is tradition.'

I feel my face flush and I stare at the sewing in my lap. Beside me, Charlotte is making little puffs of indignation.

'I know little of you, Mister Oakes,' Lizzie says.

Joseph places his hand over his heart. 'You know I am Stukeley's man. You know where I live and work. You can trust me to look after Ruth.'

Lizzie does not even glance at me. I am not consulted.

'Well, it's true that I do not need Ruth on May Day. We do not observe the old holidays here and I will spend the day in devotion at Devonshire Square with Pastor Kiffin. You may take her when she has performed her morning duties.'

'Thank you, madam. You are generous.'

She offers her hand to him as if expecting him to press his lips to it. Instead he takes it in a handshake and this seems to please her. Their eyes lock and they exchange a nod, as if they have just bartered at one of the bookstalls in the churchyard.

Chapter 18

May Day dawns bright and mild. As I dress Lizzie's hair, ready for her appointment at Devonshire Square, she snaps at me and snatches the comb, claiming that I am hurting her.

'You are thinking of your outing, I suppose,' she says, bottom lip pouting. 'Thinking of your young man.'

'He is not my young man.'

She hands back the comb to me. 'Be more careful.'

I brush her hair, then begin to plait it and pin it up, ready for her cap.

'Pagan nonsense. No doubt you will wear your best dress, and tie ribbons in your hair, and go along with all the other simple country maids, hoping to come home with a husband.'

Her words wound. If she is so piqued, why has she bade me go?

Joseph is waiting for me in the kitchen. Margaret clucks around him while she carves great hunks of cheese and bread to make a picnic. She has plied him with her best beer and he compliments the brew. She is pink-cheeked with pride. I notice her trying to hide her gnarled naked feet beneath her skirts.

My body prickles with queasy anticipation. I am plagued by sickliness these last two days and cannot make sense of it. It seems this is what Joseph makes me feel. I am not afraid of him, as I was when we first met at the Devil Inn. I'm sure now that he means me no harm. But I am afraid of what this day may bring.

Last night I visited the river to cast my wish that nothing would change. I want my life to stay as it is. It is not so much that I am happy. God knows I have not felt joy this long year past, but here, at West St Paul's, at least I am safe. And with Lizzie I have the chance of joy, even in the smallest snatches. It is better than nothing. I do not want anything to change this. I do not want anything to take me away from her. I do not trust Joseph to leave me be. And I find that the more I see of him, the less I am able to trust myself.

Joseph and I walk northwards, towards Bishopsgate. Today there is a mood abroad that alters the busy London streets. According to Parliament and the Church, it is just another day, the May Day holiday having been cancelled a few years before, but here, as in the countryside, people seem determined still to mark it. It is as if something of the holiday mood is buried so deep that, despite the lack of maypoles and dancing, people will not, cannot, give it up.

Already there is a gathering of apprentices on Cheapside, at the spot where the great maypole once stood. They hand out pamphlets calling for their rightful holidays and rest days. Joseph takes one in return for a penny. There is laughter and back-slapping, and pewter tankards flash in the sunlight. There is a guilty delight about them, drinking so much, so early in the day, like schoolboys playing truant. As we pass Smithfield, the fish-wives call out their wares to the accompaniment of a fiddle playing an old maying tune that echoes in my memory and stirs my heart. Hawkers smile and doff their hats to each other in a display of neighbourliness that is usually absent. Joseph and I are not the only couple to be out for the day: a great number of people are dressed in their good clothes and making for the gateposts. Parliament might pass laws and edicts but it cannot erase the past. It cannot change what has gone before, for generation after generation, with its pieces of paper. Even in this most modern of cities, some of the old ways still hold sway.

We reach the gate and take the north road to Ware. Suddenly it strikes me that I have not been outside the city for a full year, and I feel superstitious about going beyond the walls and into the countryside. I am surprised at myself. Just a year ago, I was terrified by the great city and its people. For months I have gazed up to the smoke-hazed sky and longed for the deep blue of the Fens, and clouds like the exhalations of angels. I have pined for the smell of green things growing, craved to slip my bare feet into dew-glistened grass at dawn and catch the scent of salt on the wind. But here I am, squirming as we broach the gates and follow the broad, dusty road that brought us here. Joseph falls silent as we do this and I know he is thinking the same thing.

Before long, we turn off the main road and take a track that leads to higher ground. Joseph points out landmarks and turns back to view the city as we rise above it. The May sun cannot burn off the haze that hangs over London, like a sea mist, but I can still see the great broken tower of St Paul's, standing like a beacon at the city's heart. It comforts me to see it and know that I can never be lost while I have it in my sights. To the west, along the river, I glimpse a glitter of gold, as sunlight catches the windows and flagpoles of Westminster Palace and the Abbey. To the east are the plague pits of Spittle Fields, diggers at work again after the lull of the fierce winter. The summer months will always bring plague but I pray that this year will not be as bad as the last.

We walk for most of the morning, turning northwards along a narrow track that crosses fields and skirts a wild, dense wood. Here and there we pass farm labourers, hoeing the fields for sowing. They straighten up to watch us pass, glad no doubt of the excuse for a rest. It is good to smell the earth again, to feel the cushion of moss beneath my feet, to hear birdsong instead of raised voices. I want to keep walking all day, but I begin to ache with hunger and exertion so we find a place to sit, where we can lean against the trunk of a tree and look back towards the grey smoke of London. In the meadow before us, the grass is grown long, strewn with buttercups and cowslips. I stretch my legs and spread my skirts to hide my ankles. I lean back on my hands and tilt my face towards the sun. The warmth feels so good on my skin. How I long to tear off my cap and let my hair spill down my back like a girl. How I long to take off my boots and race barefoot across the grass.

So I do. It feels dry and warm on my feet and the sun beats down on my bare head. I run and I am laughing. Joseph calls after me but I ignore him. He strips off his own boots and chases after me, making great whoops.

I sprint all the way across the meadow until I have to stop for breath, and then I stand and turn my face up to the sun, spellbound by the light dancing on my closed eyelids.

As Joseph reaches me, I turn from him. We run, laughing like children, and he tries to catch hold of me, but I will not let him.

Margaret has done herself proud. The bread is fresh and the cheese is the good sort, flavoured with cloves, that she usually saves for Master Poole. There are two fat slices of honey cake, sweet, tasting of summer, and a flask of ale.

We are quiet as we eat. I think of the last time we were alone, of our quarrel in Stukeley's shop and the gossip that caused the fight. I will not be the one to smooth over that hurt. Despite Joseph's kindness over Lizzie's papers, despite his lightness today, I am still a little angry with him for the things he said then.

'Was Mistress Poole pleased with the pamphlet?' he asks.

Sometimes, I think, it is as if he reads my mind. 'Yes,' I say.

'She has some fine ideas. A little muddled, perhaps, but there is good intent.'

'Do you believe me now? You see that she is genuine?'

'It's not for me to judge. She's difficult to read.'

'There is nothing untruthful about her, if that's what you mean.'

'All I see is how she presents herself, what she puts down on the page. I don't know about anything else.'

'But she is so devout.'

Joseph laughs then. 'Oh, I don't doubt that. She is the most devoted of Kiffin's circle, I'm sure.' He takes off his jerkin and folds it into a pillow, then lies back with his head upon it. I notice that the sun has already coloured his skin.

'Her ideas have some worth, I'll admit that,' he goes on. 'Peel away the godliness and there is a political mind at work. A keen mind at that. Whether she knows it or not, I can't say, but I've a feeling she probably knows exactly what she's doing. She is . . . interesting.'

'She is good. I know it. Goodness shines from her.'

I check myself. I recall the flicker of understanding I saw pass between the two of them, and Lizzie's contrary mood this morning. Suddenly my heart constricts. Perhaps it is better if he does not think so well of her. I think of her pure white skin, the burnish of her hair, and the plumpness of her breasts. I cannot compete with her. Until now, I did not know that I wanted to compete.

'I know you're loyal to her,' Joseph says, 'and that's to be admired. But I've seen God's goodness, how it can work through a person, and I don't see it in your mistress.'

He closes his eyes and is silent for a few moments. He has washed the ink stains from his hands and face as best he can, but they are so deeply ingrained now that they cannot be scrubbed away. He has the shadow of them streaked across his cheek. It makes me smile.

'Sometimes I wonder how life might be if all this was over,' he says. 'If there was no war, no fight.'

'What would you do?' I ask.

'Go back to the land. My own land. That is what we're fighting for, after all.'

'Do you think you will get it?'

He sighs. 'One day. Not here, somewhere else. I'm still a farmer at heart and a man must follow his destiny.'

'Will you go home?'

'Back to the Fens?'

'Yes.'

He shakes his head. 'I cannot go back. I must go forward. Besides, there is better land elsewhere.'

'Where, then?'

'Some little corner, tucked away from the rest of the world. Somewhere a man might be free. Perhaps America.'

He breathes the word as though he is embarrassed to say it, as though even the thought of abandoning England is sacrilegious. It is as though the New World holds some kind of secret power over men. I have heard others use the same tone of awe and hope, tinged with guilt, when talking of it. A place where there is land for the taking, where a man may begin again, may live as he pleases. It sounds a dreamlike thing, a place that captures many an imagination. My own Master Oliver would speak of it at times with a self-conscious wistfulness that was unusual in him. I see that wistfulness now in Joseph.

He turns onto his side and props himself on his elbow to look at me. 'A small farm, a couple of fields, just enough to keep a family. Maybe some livestock in time. Pigs, or a cow. What do you think?'

'If that is what you want,' I say.

He plucks a clover leaf and twirls it between his fingers, staring at it as he says, 'And you? Do you think of the future?'

I have. I do. And it does not include America. I think of endless days at West St Paul's. I think of Lizzie's hair splayed across her pillow when I wake her in the morning. I think of her hand squeezing mine as she pulls me through the throng in the churchyard, and I think of her lips, soft on my forehead as she bids me goodnight. 'No,' I lie.

'Everyone has dreams,' Joseph says. 'I've told you mine. Won't you repay me in kind?'

I shrug.

'Sal tells me that every girl dreams of a husband, a house of her own, a brood of children about her feet.'

'I am not every girl,' I say resolutely.

'No, you're not.' Joseph pulls himself up and comes to kneel beside me. He reaches out and softly touches my hand.

My heart quickens. This time I do not snatch my hand away. I realise that this is what I have been hoping for, and dreading. How can a person feel two such opposite things at the same time? I cannot think. I do not know what I want.

Gradually he intertwines his fingers with mine. 'You are no fool.' His voice is thick. 'You must know how I . . .'

My mouth is dry and I cannot speak. My body leans towards his. It is as though I am not in control of it, this leaning in, this draw of my body towards his. His face is so close to mine I feel his breath on my cheek as he whispers, 'Ruth, you and me—' but his words are cut short as his lips meet mine.

His mouth is hot. He tastes of cloves. I put my hand up to his neck and feel the pulse there, swift, like my own. His rough stubble grazes my chin. But he is gentle, tentative, his mouth exploring mine a little at a time.

I close my eyes and try to give myself up to it, but all the time my mind is racing ahead, thinking of what a life with Joseph might mean, thinking of Lizzie, thinking that I cannot give her up.

I barely notice the walk back to London. Joseph holds my hand and talks about the great plans he has for the future. He tells me about the press that the twins, Benjamin and Charlie, are running in some dank, candlelit basement and how he works alongside them through the night, printing the works of London's radical thinkers that no licensed press will print. This is how Lizzie's pamphlet was done. He talks of the good men in the army, who fight for voting rights for all men, land for all men, and how, if the army grandees will listen, there is a chance of such things. And he talks again of life after the war, of settling, of a simpler way. He tells me stories of America, of bad men come good and fortunes made by a fresh start in that unspoiled land. His face has a new light to it. The darkness in him is gone, washed away by the sunshine. Washed away by a kiss.

When he turns his gaze upon me, I see myself reflected there. He looks at me with wonder, as if I am some extraordinary thing. There is tenderness of the sort I have not seen since my mother held me close and told me how much she cared for me. I am seduced by it. I want it, this love – if that is what it is. I yearn for it. I see it in Joseph's eyes, there for the taking.

But if I take it, what will I lose? Lizzie is foremost in my mind. She will not permit this, and I cannot bear to leave her. I will not leave her. She is there like a shadow, a question to be answered, but I push the thought away and let myself enjoy the moment. I let myself be carried away by Joseph's dreams. All those things I thought I would never have are made possible by his words: a home, freedom, a sanctuary from my memories. I deserve these things, I think. And I deserve to be desired, just for today. Just for now.

* * *

The sun is setting when we reach Bishopsgate. The road is busy with people returning before curfew. But London looks different. I do not see the muck and poverty of the streets. I see only the smiling faces, and the pretty children playing, and the sun's last rays bouncing a honeyed light from windowpanes.

Joseph holds my hand, and as we make our way towards St Paul's he stops and puts his arms around me, squeezing me and laughing, almost lifting me off my feet. There are sideways looks from passers-by, but I care nothing for their judgement. I am enfolded, protected, by a secret, golden glow. For the first time in a long time, I feel truly wanted, truly safe.

Joseph insists he will walk me back to West St Paul's but we stop by Pope's Head Alley along the way. He has a new pamphlet to show me, one that he is proud of. I see he wants to share it with me, like a child flaunting a treasured new toy. I can indulge him this once. After all, this is what it means to care for someone.

Stukeley is seated at his desk in the shop, poring over papers by candlelight. He glances up as we enter through the street door. He sees me and frowns. I see his mouth open to protest, but then his eyes slide down to our linked hands and he falters. He does not greet us but bows his head over his papers, and says, 'You have a visitor. Back door.' He flaps his hand towards the room that houses the press.

'Thank you, sir,' Joseph says, and pulls me along behind him.

There is a door beneath the turn of the stairs that I have not noticed before. It is propped open and a lantern glows on the step. Joseph gives my hand a quick squeeze, then steps outside.

'By God!' I hear him cry. 'I did not expect you till next week!'

There comes the sound of a good-natured welcome, of back-slapping and hand-shaking. I peep through the door and, in the gloom, I see a big man, his hand on Joseph's shoulder. He wears a hat, pulled down low, and smokes a pipe. His coat is shabby and patched, and covered with the mud of the road.

'Come inside,' Joseph says, and I slip away from the door, resisting the urge to straighten my cap and pinch my cheeks to give them colour before I greet this stranger. I wonder how Joseph means to introduce me – as his acquaintance, his friend, his sweetheart? I flatter myself it will be the latter.

As they enter, I keep my eyes to the floor. I catch the scent of male sweat, stale liquor and tobacco.

'Ruth,' Joseph says. 'Meet an old friend.'

I look up and find I am standing face to face with Isaac Tuttle.

Chapter 19

The last of the daylight fades and a low mist creeps over the water. The river is busy. It is always busy, even at this late hour. The tides are not controlled by the curfew and the tradesmen are at their whim. The tide is low and cargo-laden barges make their way slowly downstream, lantern-hung wherries darting between them like fireflies. The lighted windows of Southwark glimmer on the south bank. Shouts and cheers echo across the water from the bear pits. Lights, too, in the houses on the bridge. The smells of cooking drift from open windows, mingling with the fishy, unclean scent of the Thames.

My chest burns from running, so I climb down the river steps and slump to the ground by the water's edge, amid the slimy silt. A few feet away, rats tear at the carcass of a dead dog. It is bloated and fleshy and stinks of decay.

I am as dead as that dog. Isaac Tuttle will do his worst. I saw the hatred in his eyes. He will not stop until he has seen me hang.

At first, he is as shocked as I. He reels with disbelief. The two of us are mute, while time stands still. My mind whirls away from that room, from Joseph and the gladness of the day, and I am back there again, on the banks of the Ouse, watching the last laboured breaths of my mother's broken body.

Joseph's voice pulls me back. 'Ruth?'

Isaac smiles, a terrible, triumphant smile. And then I run.

★ ★ ★

I sit here in the mud and the grime. Joseph has not come after me and I'm certain that I will not see him again. Once Isaac has told his tales, once he has spread his lies, the love I saw in Joseph will die. He will not want me so tainted. He will not think me so perfect then.

It is the injustice that hurts most. My mother was innocent. I am innocent. But the world will not believe it. I know that much. The world will believe Isaac Tuttle. The world is ready to credit a man like him. He puts the fear of the Devil into people and they believe him, as he believes his own lies. In this world a man's word holds more weight than a woman's. Joseph will trust his friend, just as the townsfolk of Ely were ready to trust.

It is borne of fear – fear that has been bred by the long years of hardship and hunger, by living daily with the threat of war, of never knowing when the fight might reach your own door. Fear makes folk so keen to believe in the evils of this world. How can they not, when they see evil at work all around them? They are looking for someone to blame for the things they suffer. It is the same fear that hangs witches by the dozen in the eastern counties. The same fear that tore my life apart, and will do so again.

I lose track of time. I sit and watch the rats fighting over the flesh of the poor drowned dog. I could do Isaac's job for him. I could sit here and wait for the turning of the tide, wait for the icy grey waters to carry me off to the sea, back to where I belong, in the marshes with the Fen spirits. Or I could climb up onto the bridge and jump. Plunge myself into the city's lifeblood and let it take my own. I am alone. There is no one to watch my end. It would be easier, quicker.

A ferryman passes by, close to the bank. His boat is empty and he whistles a bawdy tune to himself. A wind gathers and I shiver as the dampness seeps in. I listen to the lapping water, the sound of revellers at some nearby tavern, the scratch and scurry of river rats. Nothing is constant in this world. Nothing except the beating of my heart. And one day even that will end. I decide today is not that day. As the water washes the shore, it speaks to me. There is life even here, and I hear it echoing within me, and I know I am not yet beaten.

But I must vanish. I will leave tonight. It is my fate to be alone. Although the thought of leaving cuts like a dagger, I know it must be done. I will creep back to West St Paul's one last time, collect the few coins that are stowed under my mattress and then I will be gone. I will go to where the sky is not always covered with smoke and fog. Somewhere I can see the moon and the stars. Somewhere Isaac Tuttle cannot find me.

Candles are still burning at the windows when I get back to West St Paul's.

Charlotte is in the kitchen, ladling strong-scented caudle into cups. Her face is pinched and her hair sticks out from under her cap like straw.

'Where've you been? Mistress is asking for you.' She pushes a cup into my hand. 'Take this up to her now.' Her eyes widen as she notices my skirts, blackened with river slime. 'Lord! You're filthy!'

I find Lizzie pacing her room in her nightgown, holding a sheaf of papers, a wild look about her. She sees me and wrinkles her nose.

'What on God's earth – Where have you been? I did not give you leave to abandon me the whole night long.'

I offer her the cup, but she waves it away. 'How dare you go about the place all dirty and stinking? What will people think? I told you to be back here before dark. Charlotte had to help me undress and you know how she fumbles and pulls at my hair. You know how I hate it!'

She slams the papers down on the bed; they waterfall to the floor.

'Why were you not here when I needed you?' She slumps onto the bed, covers her face with her hands and starts to cry. Despite her years, she looks like a child.

The ties that bind my heart to hers begin to tug. I sit down next to her.

'Oh, Ruth, what am I to do?'

'What's the matter?'

'Pastor Kiffin and I have quarrelled,' she whispers, as though she is afraid the others will hear. 'Such bitter words, Ruth, such hurt.'

'What about?'

'This!' She kicks at the papers scattered on the boards. I see they are copies of her pamphlet. 'This stupid thing.'

I pick one up. 'But this is your work. Your own words.'

'Stupid!' she cries. 'Unthinking, he said. Blasphemous. Oh, Ruth, I have displeased him so.'

'But you're proud of it, are you not? There is worth in it, so I hear.'

'What do you know? William says it is full of pride and conceit and not God's word at all. He said it demeans a woman of such high standing within his congregation. He said only a woman of low morals would proclaim themselves in such a way. He says I bring shame upon his church. The Devil's work, he called it. The Devil's work!'

She begins to sob again. 'How can he think such things of me, when I believed in him?'

I put my arms around her and she leans against me, her head on my breast. She does not seem to care now about the riverbank stench coming off me. The cloud of her hair tickles my face. I hold her and feel the shudder of her body.

What would my mother say?

'You meant only to do good,' I offer. 'Pastor Kiffin will surely see that in time.'

'He spoke such poison. He was so fierce. He is so angry with me.'

'His anger will fade, as anger must.'

'I meant only to spread God's word, His love.'

'Then your intention is good. If your intention is good, then surely good will come of it, in the end.'

She sniffs and looks up at me. 'Do you think so?'

'I know so,' I say, even though I do not believe it.

'Then what am I to do? How will I mend it?'

'You must go on as before. You must hold fast.'

'How so?'

'Show Pastor Kiffin that you feel no guilt, no remorse, because you have done no wrong. You must go back and face him, with your own conscience clear. God will see into your heart and do the rest.'

She takes hold of my hand and looks into my eyes. 'You are right. I have done nothing wrong. My heart tells me so. Yes, I shall go to worship tomorrow, just as I always do, and I shall show him that my heart is pure before the Lord. Then he will see. And you will come with me, Ruth. I will have courage, with you by my side. You see how it is? I cannot do without you . . .'

Later I lie in my bed and stare at the cracks in the ceiling until dawn breaks. I know I should run. I should bundle up what remains of my possessions, creep down the stairs and vanish into the night, like Lizzie's mother before me. It is the only chance I have of life. But I think of Lizzie, calm now and asleep in her bed below. I think of how the touch of her head upon my chest filled me with such tenderness, such sweet sympathy, her tears drawing out my own. And I think of the look in her eyes when she spoke of her need for me, her belief in me. How it swells my heart and fills me with such glorious feelings. I always thought it was my love for her that kept me here, but I find instead it is her need for me that has that power. To be needed is sweet indeed.

My body will not move. My limbs will not do as I bid them. The coverlet binds me like a winding sheet. I stay because she needs me. I stay because I cannot go.

Chapter 20

As we make our way to Devonshire Square, the city seems made of a thousand eyes. In traders and churchgoers alike, I see suspicion and disgust, the falsehoods of Isaac Tuttle. He is there in the turn of a head, the tip of a hat, the yell of a hawker. The church bells call out my name, sounding his lies. He is there, even as we reach the chapel, and the faces of our people are stone, turned to gargoyles by what they may know.

About thirty men and women are gathered inside, and as we enter, they fall silent. Can Isaac's word have spread so fast? My breath is tight, my body prickling with fear. Every moment I expect the call of my name, a rough hand upon my arm.

William Kiffin stands at the far end of the room, in earnest discussion with two men. He looks up and sees Lizzie. His mouth is a grim line, his eyes impenetrable.

Lizzie holds her head high and walks between the benches towards him. I realise I have done a wrong thing. I have let her come here unawares. I thought I was protecting her, protecting myself, but now she will hear lies from Kiffin, not the truth from me. She will think I have deceived her. By hiding the truth, I have condemned myself.

'Good day to you, sirs,' she says, and holds out her hand, expecting Kiffin to take it. He does not. There is no warm smile today, no kindness in his gaze.

'Mistress Poole,' he says. His eyes slide to the floor. 'I must speak with you, if you please.' He indicates a low doorway to the side of the room.

Lizzie's hand hangs there and, as she realises he will not take it, she falters. It is fleeting, but I see it. I have an unpleasant taste in my mouth, bitter and caustic, like poison.

'Of course,' she says.

I follow her into the room.

It is a small antechamber, lit by a casement high in the wall. Through it I can see only soot-stained brick – no air, no sky. There is a battered old desk and a chair but no fireplace. The desk is covered with books and papers, all neatly ordered. There is ink and a quill, and sealing wax, lined up ready for use.

Kiffin closes the door. When he speaks, his voice is brittle. 'Mistress Poole, I must tell you that you, and members of your household, are no longer welcome here.'

'What?'

'There have been allegations of a most serious nature. I'm sure you understand that, as pastor of this congregation, I cannot allow—'

'I know you are angry with me, but I can explain.'

'I am not angry.'

She steps towards him and puts her hand on his arm. 'You will forgive our little quarrel when you understand.'

He pulls away from her and turns his back. 'Elizabeth, this has nothing to do with that.'

She frowns. 'What, then?'

'There are those among the congregation who have made claims against you.'

I think of the men, red-faced and angry, and the disapproving stares of the womenfolk.

'What claims?'

'Just know that you are no longer welcome here.'

'What claims?' Lizzie demands.

Kiffin turns to face her and his eyes are thunderous. He uses his pulpit voice. 'You are accused of committing grievous sins, both spiritually and bodily. You have let the Devil into your house and your heart. In short, madam, there are those who would have you tried for a whore and a witch.'

Witch. My breath catches at the word. Not her. He cannot mean her. Surely he means me.

'I don't understand,' she says.

'Elizabeth, you are found out.'

She laughs at the idiocy of it. 'And you believe this?'

'They have evidence.'

'What evidence?'

'You have been seen with men. Many men, so I am told.'

'You know that is not true.'

'They say that you conjure spells and put the Devil into men. Drive them mad. Make them do things . . . sinful things . . .'

'How can you speak such nonsense?'

Kiffin pauses. 'I have seen what you are capable of,' he says bitterly.

I should speak out. I should try to right this wrong. But fear binds my tongue.

Again Lizzie tries to go to him, tries to touch him. 'William, surely you cannot believe this.'

'What am I to think?' he says. 'When you have proved yourself so wanton.'

He goes to the desk and picks up a paper. It is a copy of Lizzie's pamphlet. 'You say you know God. You say He speaks to you.' He unfolds the pamphlet and jabs his finger at the page. 'Here, you say God has shown you how the world should be, and here . . .' again he points '. . . you speak of love. You speak of the love between a man and a woman as if it were some base thing. You say women should be free as the angels in Heaven and not be tied down by a marriage contract. You say they are equal to men, and should give their love, and their bodies to whom they choose. These are not God's words, Elizabeth, they are your own, and they come from a darkness in you.'

He is angry now, the glorious passion I've seen in him when he preaches replaced by fury.

'I meant only to spread God's love,' Lizzie says.

'This is not God's love. This is carnal love you speak of. You are an unmarried woman. To write of such things . . .'

Still Lizzie does not quake. 'Will you not stand by me in this? Have I not been the most devoted of your followers?'

'I thought so, but now I see I have been deceived. I must act in accordance with the wishes of Our Lord and my church.'

'Will you not refute these claims?'

'Madam, it is my true duty to protect my flock from any kind of scandal or devilishness. For a man in my position . . .'

'You can stop this, William. One word from you would silence them, such is your power over these people. Will you not refute?'

'No, madam, I will not.'

She stands tall and proud but I see the flush in her cheeks, hear the tremor in her voice. 'Why have you turned against me?'

'They are angry. They talk of bringing in the magistrate. They demand that I send you away. It is my duty. If I do not, I will have a mutiny on my hands.'

'You know there is no truth in this, but you will choose them over me. To keep the peace, to keep your power, you will condemn me.' Lizzie's lip quivers as she speaks.

'You doubt me,' Kiffin says, 'but my people do not. It is you they doubt.'

For a moment they stand face to face, both unbending.

'I see you are set,' Lizzie says, 'and I will not beg forgiveness for something I have not done. But Our Lord knows the truth of it. You know the truth of it, though you will not admit it. You will answer for the wrong you have done me.'

She moves towards the door. I think she has forgotten me, so I step after her. As I pass Kiffin, he catches my arm. 'If you stay with her you will be tainted,' he says. 'It is not too late for you.'

Oh, how mistaken he is.

Chapter 21

Later that day a letter arrives. Although there is no seal, I know that it is from Kiffin. Lizzie takes it and asks for privacy. I expect indignation, fury, but no sound comes from her room and she does not call for me. For hours there is nothing but silence and the quickening in my chest. When I can bear it no longer I go to her with an offering of small beer and oatcakes as my excuse.

She sits on her bed, staring at nothing. The letter is nowhere to be seen. Her eyes are red-rimmed and I know she has been crying, the quiet crying that happens when a heart is broken and there is nothing to be done. I do not need to ask the questions that have burned inside me all afternoon. I can see that nothing has changed. Kiffin will not save her. She is named a whore and a witch. She is outcast. She is like me.

It is not until dusk, when I am tossing the dishwater out into the street drain, that I notice the woman. She is hovering in the shadows by the kitchen door like a cutpurse, wearing a dark cloak, the hood covering her face. It is only by the primrose yellow curls, escaping at her collar, and the flash of green and red skirts, that I recognise Sal.

She and the twins, Benjamin and Charlie, have often been in my thoughts since we met on Twelfth Night. Joseph speaks of all three with affection, as though they were siblings, but it is not he who keeps them alive in my mind – it is the memory of how I felt that night. Sal had seemed so brave, and so carefree. For a moment I had felt those things too. It seems a fleeting, unreal thing now, but I have sometimes wished to see them again, and to know Sal better.

I hiss her name, startling her.

'Ruth – thank the Lord it's you at last,' she whispers. 'I've been waiting here an hour or more.'

'Why did you not come to the door? Come inside.'

'No. I mustn't see anyone else. Just you.'

I glance behind me. Margaret is tending the hearth and I've left the door open. 'What is it?'

She tugs at my sleeve and we move away from the house until we are hidden from view.

'The Watch will have me for the King's spy, skulking about like this,' she says, smiling. In the fading light, her eyes sparkle momentarily before she is serious again.

'I'm come with a message from Joseph.'

'Oh . . .'

'That fool of a boy has got into trouble with Stukeley. He would have come himself but he can't get away.'

'What kind of trouble?'

'Stukeley's in a rage because Joseph was off with you all day yesterday. He has him working round the clock, fearing for his place. If you ask me, it's just an excuse. Stukeley suspects he's up to something.'

'And is he?'

'My boys are always up to something.' She smirks. 'If I wanted a quiet life, I wouldn't have set my cap at Charlie.'

'What does he want?'

'You're to meet him tonight. He can't get away until Stukeley is abed. Ten should be safe enough. Meet him at Broken Wharf, outside the tavern, by the river steps. And come alone. He says it's important.'

She reads my silence and is suddenly straight-faced. 'Ruth, what's happened?'

'Nothing. Nothing for you to worry about.'

'I'm no fool. I know the signs of a lovers' tiff. Lord knows I'm on the wrong side of one often enough.'

'It's not that, Sal.'

'What, then? The whole thing is making me twitch. Joseph looked dreadful, like he hadn't slept. And he had that manner about him again – troubled, like a man with the Devil snapping at his toes. He seemed that way when I first met him, and I don't mind saying that he scared me a little back then. You don't cross a man like that. Of course, I know him better now . . .' She pauses and searches my face. I must not give myself away, but she sees my struggle anyway. 'If there's something I can do for you, Ruth, you must ask. They might be a troublesome lot, but they're good men, and Joseph is as good as any. God knows I'm a fool, but I'd risk much to help him.'

'I can't explain.'

She frowns and makes a sound of exasperation. 'Well, then, I must get back before I'm missed.' She takes my face in her hands and leans in. For a moment I think she means to kiss me, but she brushes her lips briefly against my cheek and whispers in my ear, 'You're a sweet girl, Ruth. You could make him happy, if you've the heart for it.'

I watch her go. As she turns the corner she looks back and smiles before slipping into the darkness.

I don't blame her for the part she plays in the trap, for I know it *is* a trap. What other reason can there be for a moonlit meeting by the river, for such stealth and secrecy? I am just sorry that Isaac's web has drawn her in, even if she does not know it. I envy her trusting nature. I envy her simple life. Although I do not know her well, I feel bonded with her in a way I cannot explain. I'm sorry that I will not see her again, that I will not have the chance to know her better, once they take me away.

So, Joseph has believed Isaac's lies. Even though I expected this, it hurts to think that he can be turned so swiftly, his love transformed to hate by a falsehood. If he can believe a man like Isaac, then I am much mistaken in him. I curse myself for my stupidity, for allowing myself to think of him at all. I have let my guard down. I should have known better. I should know, by now, that men like him cannot be trusted. I have been a fool, flattered by the longing in his eyes, seduced by his talk and his dreams, like a naïve girl hankering for a husband. Joseph's dreams are not my own. When he kissed me, it was Lizzie's face I saw in my mind's eye.

Of course I do not go to Broken Wharf, and it is past midnight when they come for me. Isaac Tuttle's messengers do not come with weapons and warrants, as I have imagined it. There is no bloodthirsty crowd. Instead, two men come and rap upon the street door.

I'm still up, sitting with Lizzie in her room, and I'm at the window before Margaret has answered. In the dark street below I see them waiting patiently, as though they are invited guests. They wear buff coats, swords hitched at their hips. There is no cart, no chain and no gaoler. I suppose they think that one young girl will cause them no trouble and I suppose they are right. I have nowhere to run to, nowhere to go.

'Is it the Watch?' Lizzie thinks Kiffin's cronies have turned her in. I know better. She paces the boards. 'How can you be so calm?' she says. 'Don't you care?'

I care more than she can know. I care so much that I will give myself up for her. I did not flee when I had the chance. I stayed for her. It gives me some small comfort to know that she will understand this when the truth comes out.

Downstairs, Margaret lets the men in and takes them into the front parlour. I hear the scrape and clatter of their weapons against the doorframe. Then she goes to Master Poole's room, and I hear him complaining about such late callers. As soon as the parlour door is closed, Margaret comes puffing up the stairs. She does not knock.

'Mistress, there's army men here, asking after Ruth.'

'Ruth? But surely they are come for me?'

'No, mistress. I heard it rightly. It's Ruth they want.'

They both look at me.

'Ruth?' Lizzie is confused. 'What do they want with you?'

I do not know how to reply, where to begin. But she must hear my story before she hears Isaac's lies. This might be my only chance.

'There is a man,' I say. 'A man who wishes me dead. He named my mother a witch and he killed her for it. Now he wants to kill me too.'

'What man?' Lizzie says.

'His name is Isaac Tuttle. He is here, in London.'

Lizzie starts to laugh as though it is a joke, but her laugh soon dies.

'I'm telling the truth,' I say.

They both stare at me as if it is the first time they have ever seen me, as if they do not know who I am. I hear muffled voices from below, men's voices, deciding my fate. It is too late to flee.

'You say this man killed your mother?'

'Yes.'

'Why?'

'He believes that she killed his wife.'

'And did she?'

I am hurt that Lizzie could even ask the question. I shake my head. 'We were trying to help her. She was in childbed, but her baby would not breathe. Her baby was . . . unfinished. We couldn't stop the bleeding . . .'

'So it happens every day. That does not make you a witch.'

'There were other things. My mother was unwed. She was not well liked. The townsfolk thought . . . It was an excuse.'

'What did this man do?'

I do not want to remember, but I must.

'He hanged her.'

My legs are weak as I speak. I want to sit down, right there on the boards, and go to sleep. I want to run from the memories.

'And where were you?'

'I was there. I saw it all, and then I ran.'

'Is that why you came here? To hide?'

'I suppose so.'

'And now he has found you.'

Before I have the chance to answer, there are raised voices below and Master Poole is calling for Margaret. She flings me one last astonished look, then hurries down the stairs.

Lizzie and I are alone.

'How long have you known that this day would come?' she says.

'I have feared it all this time, but I saw him only yesterday. I knew then.'

'Why did you not flee?'

I answer her with a look. There are no words.

Master Poole stands in the corner of the bedroom, wringing his hands. I notice for the first time that he stoops when he walks and, under the lower ceilings of the upstairs room, looks hunched and old.

'Really, Elizabeth, are you sure this is the best course of action?'

Lizzie is flying about the room, pulling things from chests and closets and piling them on the bed. 'Yes, Father. Please don't argue with me.'

He turns to me. 'I'm sorry, Ruth, but I could not lie to them. They say the order comes from their colonel, and I dare not disobey.'

I bow my head. 'I'm grateful for what you have done.'

'It is only one night's reprieve. They will be back to take you in the morning.'

'We will be gone by then,' Lizzie says.

'My child, whatever they want with Ruth, you have no part in it. Why must you go rushing off into the night?'

'What have I to stay for?'

He seems crushed, but she is too excited to see it. The idea has taken hold of her and nothing will change her mind.

'This is your home.'

'It is not safe. I must go somewhere new. Somewhere away from the lies and the accusations. Somewhere I can work to clear my name.'

'You are running away.'

'Can you not see that more scandal will ruin us? Will ruin you and the business. Ruth must go and I must go with her. It is to save *you* that we must go.' Lizzie comes to me and takes my hand. 'We will be safe if we go together.'

I leave Lizzie and her father to their farewells. I drag my old satchel from under the trestle, where it has lain untouched for the last year. Into it I squeeze my one good dress, the red ribbons that Lizzie gave me and the last of the pennies I have saved.

I pause for a few seconds and look around this tiny space, the four walls that have cosseted me as the year has turned. I will miss this house. I will miss the life I have had here. But a life on the road is better than no life at all. Besides, I am taking with me the one thing that matters most. It is so much more than I had hoped for.

★ ★ ★

And so we fly, like two outlaws, bound together by the crimes we did not commit. Before dawn we are at Cornhill, looking for a carter to take us west. We are to go to Abingdon, a place where Lizzie says she has connections. There are people there who may help us.

For the second time I am running for my life, but this time I am not alone.

Chapter 22

As we go west, beyond the city walls, we pass Tyburn Tree. The gallows stand stark and empty against the sky. I have heard of this place many times, muttered as an oath or spoken of in hushed tones by the goodwives in the market, but it is the first time I have seen it. I cannot help but stare at the place where so many have met their end. I hope I have escaped the same fate.

The countryside beyond is pretty, blooming with late spring, cleared to make way for the farmsteads that feed London's clamour for food. The carter is a man of few words and that suits us. We want no conversation, no enquiries. Even Lizzie is silent as we watch London shrink into the distance. I ask her if she has ever left the city before and she shakes her head. Her mouth is pinched into a tight little O. Now I'm the one with worldly experience. I reach across and squeeze her hand. We must help each other to courage. I cannot fail her but, at the same time, I cannot bear her to fail me. If she crumbles, and wants to turn back, I do not know what I will do.

We travel through the day and at nightfall snatch a brief, disturbed rest at a nameless inn on the wayside. The next morning the carter takes us as far as the great castle at Windsor. From here we must find another transport. The castle, huge and proud above the town, grey stone warmed by the sun, puts me in mind of the cathedral at Ely. It is not a match in looks. Instead of Ely's soaring beauty, the walls are thick and squat, built for siege, not prayer. But the castle has the same presence, power made in stone, watching over the town as it has done for centuries. I imagine that the people of Windsor love it and hate it in equal measure, just like those at home.

No royal flag flies above the great round tower. This is a Parliament town now, like so many others that once held to the King's cause, and it shows. Soldiers with stained coats the colour of tilled earth check the carter's pass and give us the eye.

We pay the man and look for the night's lodgings, but everywhere we go there are more soldiers. They lounge outside the inns and fill the taprooms within. People stare at us. Men stare at us. Men always stare at Lizzie, but this time they follow us like hunting dogs, sniffing out prey. It is not safe here.

It is Lizzie's idea to go on by foot. As the day wears on, we leave the town and set off on the Oxford road. I'm keen to gain more distance from London and, travelling alone, we cannot be traced by soldiers with bribe money to loosen tongues. It is warm enough to find an outdoor bed for the night.

The track takes us into the woods, and as the sun begins to set, we stop to find a place to eat and sleep. We leave the road to find a safe harbour within the trees that cannot be seen by bandits and thieves. I am afraid to stray too far, so we settle in a small clearing, near the track, hidden by a high bank of knotted brambles that make a hollow in which we can shelter from the worst of the chill. We will have to do without a fire here, but at least we will not be discovered.

We eat our supper, bought from the market in Windsor, and watch the light between the trees turn deep summer gold. Little pockets of warmth dance across my skirts as the breeze gets up and the leaves shiver, making the sound of rushing water above my head.

'I have something to show you before it gets dark,' Lizzie says. The bundle she carries is much larger than my own and from it she pulls a neatly folded set of men's clothes – a pair of grey woollen breeches, a jacket and a hat.

'I took them from Father's room. He won't mind. He has plenty.'

'But why?'

'I'm as tall as any man, and with my hair tied up inside the hat, we will be safer.'

'But you do not look like a man,' I say.

'You'll see. Help me . . .'

She tugs at the lacings of her stays. I unbutton her dress and she pulls the breeches on over her shift.

'There – see? They almost fit.'

The jacket is too big for her but she puts it on anyway and we struggle to pile her hair up inside the wide brim of the hat. When we are done she looks misshapen and mismatched, a tatterde-malion. But her face is lit up. 'You must be my looking glass.' She spins around and makes me a bow. She smiles, nose crinkling, freckles aglow in the gilded light.

'Quite the gentleman,' I say. I spread my cloak on the ground, making ready for the night. We must bed down before the sun is gone.

But she laughs and swaggers around the clearing and between the trees, kicking up pine needles. Then she starts to sing.

I have heard her sing in worship, at Devonshire Square. There, her voice was fine and high, soaring above the others in a quest to reach God. Now she chooses an old tune, one I know well, one I heard often from my mother's lips. She sounds like a bawd, sing-ing for the loss of a lover. She could be sinking ales with the 'prentices outside the Pope's Head, her tone so round and ripe. I sit, leaning back on my hands and watch. She likes having me as her audience and climbs onto a fallen tree trunk, her voice ringing out.

It can be no coincidence that she has picked a song that fills me with feeling. It reminds me of a long-ago time, when my greatest ills could be mended by a pretty lullaby and the promise of sweetmeats before bed. She cannot possibly know it, but there is magic in her choice.

As the song ends, she finishes with a flourish and a deep bow, her hat in her hand and her hair spilling down her shoulders, ablaze in the yellow light. I clap and call for more but she shakes her head. She jumps down from her perch and begins to spin round and round on the spot, her head tilted back to catch the last of the sun that trickles down through the leaves. I think of Mary, Frances and me, playing in the field behind the house in Ely, joining hands and spinning each other until we were dizzy and almost sick with it. There is a kind of freedom in such simple things. I want to get up and link hands with Lizzie, but instead I sit and watch her. The air is filled with tiny flies, their wings catching the rays and making them glow like candle flames dancing around her head. She is glorious. She is queen of the fairies.

Then she stops, sighs, and comes to sit next to me.

'I feel quite different,' she says, her eyes fixed on something in the distance. 'Like a different person.' She sits with her legs wide, unrestricted by her skirts. 'Tomorrow I shall be *Master* Poole and we shall travel together, as sweethearts.'

My heart leaps. She sits awhile, looking at me, her breath still coming fast. I cannot meet her eyes. I hope the twilight hides my burning cheeks.

'Come,' she says. 'The light is fading. We must make ourselves ready.'

I tidy the remains of our meal and store it deep inside our bags. Then we fashion a bed from our cloaks and Lizzie's discarded skirts. The hollow is mossy and smells of earth and damp. As we lie down together, my heart feels as though it strains towards hers and my skin prickles at the brush of her clothing against my own.

We lie face to face and I curl up into a ball, a little afraid of the gloom that creeps through the trees. There is still enough light for me to see her face and I study it as she tries to sleep. Although perhaps she is tall enough to be mistaken for a boy, her face will always give her away, for her features are delicate. Her jaw is too fine, her skin too smooth. I watch as she relaxes into sleep and her mouth falls open slightly. I trace the line of her lips in my mind, so that I might remember this moment. Then she opens her eyes.

I hold her gaze, emboldened by the encroaching night. I think I feel a little of whatever has been freed inside Lizzie. In this place, the same rules do not seem to apply.

She reaches out her hand and gently strokes my cheek with a finger. This time she does not move her hand away. As if she knows what I have been thinking, she draws her fingertip to my mouth and delicately traces the line of my own lips. The sensation sends a bolt of feeling straight through me, warming my insides.

She wriggles closer to me then, until our bodies lie together, tangled in layers of cloth. Her knee, unencumbered by her skirts, nudges its way between my legs. As she presses against me, my whole body turns to liquid, golden as the sunset, syrupy as honey. Her face is so close to mine that as she whispers I feel hot breath upon my skin.

'Will you do something for me?'

'Of course.'

'Call me Lizzie. No more "Mistress". I want us to be real friends now, for I fear I have few left.'

'I'm always your friend and nothing will change that.'

'I know you are, Ruth. I knew the moment you came to me. I said to myself, "God has brought someone here for me." Promise you will never leave me.'

'Never. I will never leave you. I promise.'

My heart sings, I promise, I promise. I made such a promise the day I met you and I will never break it.

'My angel,' she breathes.

And then she tilts her mouth towards mine and I feel the wet tip of her tongue on my lips.

As she kisses me it feels as though my whole body is shaken awake after a long time sleeping. I pulse with a thousand fragments of light and colour behind my eyelids. Desire heats every part of me. My chest feels too small to hold my heart.

I do not know how long we stay like that, kissing and touching each other's faces with cold fingertips, but I want it never to end. By the time she sleeps, the night is as black as Fenland peat. I cradle her in my arms and watch for snatched glimpses of the stars through the canopy. I cannot sleep. I will be tired tomorrow, but I do not care. It is more than I have dreamed of, to know that we will enter Abingdon not as lady and maidservant, not only as friends but as lovers too.

The silver thread is wound so tight. I thank the Fen spirits for binding her to me. I thank God for the part He plays in all earthly mysteries. I pray only that the thread knotting us together proves as strong as real silver. In this fragile, shifting world, we must cling to the things that are solid. I swear that I will not be the one to let it break.

Part Three

Abingdon
July 1647

Chapter 23

Abingdon is a Parliament town. Although not a day's ride from Oxford, it is a shadow of that wealthy city. There are no rich colleges here, no fine buildings filled with scholars, no gentlemen with lace cuffs and feathered caps, none of the King's favoured clergy. These days, Oxford is a Parliament town too, but by force rather than will. For the long years of fighting, it sheltered the traitorous King and his Court and drained the land all around, like a leech.

The people in Abingdon are poor, made poorer by the billeting of soldiers, by failed harvests and epidemics, by menfolk lost in the battles at Newbury and Basing House. The goodwives are careworn, the houses tumbledown and the market stalls scanty. On market days, beggar children scratch in the dirt for grain, competing with the chickens. The congregation of the church of St Helen's, where Lizzie and I go to worship, is made up of those few souls who still have hope, and the rest, who come to beg for a few crumbs of bread and a cup of broth, made of scraps from the vicar's table. I thank God I am not one of them.

I see the beggar children and the poor creatures seeking charity. I see the plague victims, the survivors with scarred faces and wasted limbs. I see them every day and I pity them. They are no worse off than the vagrants I used to see about St Paul's Churchyard. They are no different from the paupers who tugged at my skirts and asked for scraps in the alley at West St Paul's.

They are no different from any penniless servant making his way in the world on his master's whim. But here I notice them all the more. I feel the gap that widens between their fate and my own. For here, in Abingdon, I am free. I am happy at last. I am in love.

July is hot. In the little cottage that Lizzie and I have taken, I spend my days in household tasks. I clean the street dust from the casements and sweep the floor in our one good room, where Lizzie sits bathed in shafts of sunlight, her needle fast at work on whatever sewing she can take in. I fold back the coverlet on the bed that we share and shake the mattress free of moths. I strew it with rosemary and lavender, so that our dreams will be filled with the sweet scent of summer.

Along the riverbank, I search for flowers and bring home wild roses for Lizzie's hair. It is hard to believe that this same river flows all the way back to the city we have left behind. London barges drift lazily upstream, taking goods to Oxford. When they stop in Abingdon, there is sugar and spice from the New World, for those with the means to buy, and barrels of sack, destined for the Oxford colleges. The bargemen bring penny broadsheets too, and pamphlets from the churchyard, ever reminding those with the mind to care that the war is not yet won. The King no longer has the power to rule and no one will stand in his stead. The country is without a captain.

But for me the cares of Westminster seem far away. Here, I am in another world. Here, the waters of the Thames are clean and brilliant in the sunshine. The banks are laden with blooms. Among them I find real treasure – comfrey, sage and garlic, borage and agrimony. I bring home the herbs and boil them in a cauldron over the fire. I make cordials and remedies, as my mother used to do on summer days in Ely. I hang herbs to dry, bunched over the hearth, and the kitchen smells of meadowsweet and catmint – the savours of my girlhood.

On market days, I sell my wares from a basket on my arm. Trade is not brisk in this beaten-down little town, but it brings me a few pennies to add to the money that Lizzie makes by her needle, and between us, we scrape a living.

A letter comes, delivered to the Bell by the Oxford carrier, and finding its way to us, hand to hand, in the market square. In neat clipped words that reveal nothing of the emotion he must feel, Master Poole asks for news of his daughter, wishes her safe, offers her what money he can spare. Lizzie will not reply. She wants to cut herself off from the past. She says I am her family now and we must make our own way in the world. I'm glad to leave the past behind and I don't argue when she tosses the letter onto the kitchen hearth, as though it means nothing.

We live as cousins or, at least, that is what the world outside these walls believes. Within, we are much, much more. Our claim to be kin may be a lie, but we are close, as close as blood. Each night when darkness comes and we take a candle to our bed, she kisses me before we put out the flame. She strokes my hair and tells me that I am her own angel, sent down from Heaven to watch over her. Sometimes, when the evening chill creeps in, we hold each other, as we did that night in the woods. Our limbs tangle, she puts her head upon my shoulder and I fall asleep with her breath upon my neck.

Sometimes we are so close that I feel her heart beat against my chest. On nights like this, I lie awake and my body yearns. It is as though my own heart, pounding and jumping, strains to meet hers. I long to touch her, to make her heart quicken, and for my own to match its pace. Surrendered to sleep, she is all innocence, unaware of my desire. I lose myself in the scent of her and fall asleep to dream of things I would never dare to say or do. The dreams I have are full of sin and I pray that God will cast them out. When I wake, sweat-drenched and unsatisfied, I curse myself for what I cannot control, but still my body burns.

★ ★ ★

It is a fine day and I have been out wandering the riverbank since sunrise. The best time to gather herbs is at dawn, when they are crisp and fresh in the dew. I have had a good morning and my basket is full.

Back in the cottage, I lay out my finds on the kitchen table. I fetch water from the conduit in the square and put a pot on the fire to boil. I will use some of the herbs, the borage and the burdock, to make a cordial for the market next week. The hot weather brings on the ague. Those ailing will be looking for relief. It might be a profitable day.

As the pot begins to bubble, Lizzie comes home. I hear her voice before she reaches the house. She is talking to someone.

I panic. We never have visitors. Save the acquaintance we have made at church and the few customers Lizzie has found, we do not know people here. This suits me. I want no one knowing our business.

I am dusty from my morning's work, my skirts carrying burrs and dandelion seeds. My hair is loose, tumbling down my back, tangled with leaves from pushing through undergrowth in the woods. There is no time to tidy myself or fetch my cap.

Lizzie welcomes her guests and leads them into the kitchen. The first is a tall, dark woman I recognise as the vicar's wife, and the second is her maid, a small, lumpen girl with plump cheeks and darting eyes. Chattering happily, Lizzie is unaware of the tall woman's disdain as she looks about the place.

Lizzie takes in the state of my dress and smiles. 'What did I tell you?' she says, to the tall woman. 'Always tramping about the woods, quite the wild thing. Always chopping and boiling and concocting magic out of nothing. Is that not so, Ruth?'

The woman has a long, straight nose and she peers down it at me. She has large eyes that match the Puritan black of her dress. I feel their depths. She has the uncanny knack of reading thoughts that sit just below the surface, just behind a smile or a frown. I know it, just as I used to know it when Master Oliver looked at me. He has the same gift. I look away.

'Ruth, this is Mistress Pendarves,' Lizzie says.

I feel as if I am a maidservant again. I fight the urge to curtsy. Women like her are no longer my betters.

She holds out her hand to me.

'Thomasine,' she says. 'Please, call me Thomasine. We do not stand on ceremony here. This is not London.'

As I take her hand, she squeezes it, just a little, and gives me a smile. Her smile changes her face, softening the sharpness of her cheek and jaw. She must have been a great beauty at one time. Haughty, perhaps, but striking, and there is a trace of warmth in her smile.

'And this is Dot, my maid. She is mute, poor child.'

Dot shuffles her feet and stares at the floor.

Lizzie is animated. Her colour is high and her eyes are merry, as if she has been supping at the Bell Inn. 'I have wonderful news,' she says. 'Thomasine has agreed to write to Pastor Kiffin.'

'What for?'

'To answer the claims made against me, of course.'

'My husband has a long-standing acquaintance with Pastor Kiffin,' Thomasine explains, 'and I myself have had some correspondence with him, on spiritual matters. I flatter myself that I may have some influence. I can see what good work Elizabeth is doing here, how keen she is to join the work of our church, and if I can be of help . . .'

I do not see how this woman, whom we barely know, can make a difference to something that feels so far away, so unimportant to me now.

'Is that not good news?' Lizzie says.

'Of course.'

Lizzie is pleased and so, I suppose, I must be too. After all, if I truly love her, I must want what she wants.

'I have told Thomasine all about the lies that were spread. I'm sure she can help us.'

'It is my duty to help a soul in need.' Thomasine puts her hands together as if in prayer and bows her head. Behind her, Dot copies, like a shadow.

'Come, we will sit in the parlour and Ruth will bring us something to drink,' Lizzie says. 'We must discuss what is to be said. What have we for our guests? Thomasine, will you take some beer?'

She leads them into our one room, shabbily furnished with a settle and stools before the hearth, and shoots a look over her shoulder that says, 'Do as I ask.' I listen to her chatter, recognising the excitement in her voice: she sounds just as she did on my first day in London, when I was her latest cause.

I take them weak beer. It is the best we have, but Thomasine's cup sits untouched. Dot eyes her portion, as though she longs to drink, but dares not.

I sit with them and watch Lizzie devise the letter that will go to Pastor Kiffin. She has such a passion to clear her name. In London she is branded, she is outcast, and she cannot rest in that knowledge. She cannot be happy while there are people in this world who think so ill of her. I am used to this. I do not have the desire to be loved by all. As long as I have Lizzie's love, I need no other.

Chapter 24

Thomas Rainsborough is a slim man of middling height, with a presence that overshadows his stature. His brown hair sits high on his forehead, with grey at the temples – a telltale sign of the struggles he has witnessed as a colonel in the New Model Army and thorn in the Army Council's side. His eyes are large, heavy-lidded, and shine, like chestnuts in autumn; as I watch him eat at the Pendarveses' table, I can barely look away from them. Their colour seems to shift with his mood, as does his complexion. Both are quick to change. I'm struck by the easiness of his manners. But I also sense earnestness, passion perhaps, for his beliefs – beliefs I have rarely seen so stoutly defended. When angered, he is all flashing eyes and scything tongue. In this, he reminds me a little of Lizzie.

Lizzie and Thomasine have fast become friends, and Lizzie is jubilant when Thomasine suggests the meeting. The invitation to sup with their guest is the first real sign that Thomasine recognises her as an equal and a fellow soul on the path to righteousness. It is an opportunity for us to establish ourselves here, one that Lizzie is determined will not go to waste.

Returning one morning from an early errand, I find her cutting a length of fine green brocade. She stays indoors all day and all night, stitching by the light of a single candle, to make herself a new dress. I'm sure she must have spent the last of her father's money on the fabric and I worry about the expense. But she pinches my cheeks and calls me a skinflint, saying that after the dinner we will be assured of a home and hearth for years to come.

I have a horrid, hard feeling in my stomach, and when I see her in her new clothes, I fall into a black mood, for I'm sure that no man could resist her. The emerald cloth makes her eyes blaze, and her hair, curled and dressed, looks like spun copper. The neckline exposes her collarbones and the swell of her breasts – the sight makes me breathless.

Lizzie does not know that I have heard of Colonel Rainsborough before. The mention of his name brings back memories of Joseph and the stories he told of his time in the army. I do not like to dwell on my friendship with Joseph, although my thoughts turn to him more often than I would like. I know there is no point in this. He belongs in my old life. The dreams that captured me that day in the meadow are dead and gone. I have chosen a different path, and I know what this means. There will be no husband for me, no children, none of the things that I was taught to want at my mother's knee. But there is no room for regret, when I am filled by Lizzie's love. Besides, I am sure Joseph hates me now. Isaac will have made sure of that.

John Pendarves pours the wine. 'Colonel Rainsborough has recently returned from a meeting with the King, so I'm told,' he says.

Master Cheyney, Abingdon's mayor, splutters, his knife clattering to his plate. 'Really, Colonel? How so? Was it army business?'

'Indeed, sir. I attended with a delegation from the Army Council,' Rainsborough says. 'We presented the King with our grievances and our proposals.'

'And how did he take it?'

'Not well, sir. The King will not compromise. As you can see, I am still the colonel of a defending army.'

'What were the terms? They were too harsh perhaps. Cannot a compromise be met?'

'Sir, I believe that there has been too much compromise already. We ask only to consolidate the power of Parliament, and for a promise that the King will rule alongside his people's elected representatives.'

'And will he not agree?' Pendarves asks.

'I fear not. And if he will not accept this compromise, put forward by established men of power and wealth, then there will never be a chance for the rights of the people – of the common man.'

'And what rights are those, pray?' Cheyney leans back in his chair, red-cheeked.

'Of the right of each and every man in England to choose the government under which he lives. There are many men in the army who have fought for that right, have lived and died for it. I fear that those who now have the power in their hands would rather have a broken and stitched-together peace with the King than risk losing all for the rights of the people.'

'You speak like a Leveller, sir,' Cheyney says.

His wife lays a hand on his arm. 'Surely any peace is better than none.'

'Is it better, madam, that our countrymen fight and die only for Charles Stuart to take up his crown once more, and for us to return, slowly but surely, to the world whence we came?' Rainsborough's tone is gentle but his eyes spark. 'It pains me to think that all this blood has been spilled for so little. No . . . Better war and more killing than the slow and inevitable death of our dreams.'

His words stir me. I am swayed by the passion in his voice. In Rainsborough's speech, I hear echoes of Joseph. I wonder what he would make of my sitting down at table with his hero, listening first hand to the ideals that spurred him, and so many others, to the battlefield. I have a sudden longing to see him, to tell him I understand now the fire that drives him on.

'But with the power of the King reduced, surely Parliament will have a rein on him,' Lizzie says, leaning towards the colonel.

'I, too, thought it possible, until I met him. Now I see he will not compromise. There is no such middle point for him. He is not a reasonable man. He will live and be king or he will die in the trying.'

'Then is he not to be pitied?'

'Pitied? How so?'

'He is God's representative on earth, is he not?' Lizzie says. 'Surely we must pray for him. Pray that Our Lord will see fit to direct him, for he must be misguided. Perhaps he is overly influenced by his advisers. They say that the Queen—'

'He truly believes that his way is the only way. I saw it in his eyes, in his bearing. He is as unbending as . . . as castle walls.'

'And walls may be broken down, sir, with cannon fire and flames. That is your way I see.' Lizzie leans back in her chair, takes a sip of wine and holds his gaze over her cup. 'Tell me, what kind of man is he?'

Rainsborough shrugs. 'He is a king.'

'Come, sir,' Cheyney says. 'The lady wants an account of him, his dress, his person.'

But Lizzie shakes her head. 'With respect, I was wondering what Colonel Rainsborough makes of the King's religion. Is he a pious man? Is he popish, as they say?'

'That I cannot tell,' Rainsborough says. 'It is his queen who is Catholic. The King remains a Protestant, in public at least.'

'But he is not godly, I think,' Pendarves says, 'with his gaudy attire and debauched ways. We heard such stories when the Court was at Oxford, of masques and plays and festivities, as if the King had not a care in all the world. And the so-called ladies of the Court displayed themselves like common slatterns.' He sends a sly glance towards Lizzie. 'And here we are, his people, starving and suffering not ten miles hence for want of food.'

'All I know is what I believe in my heart, and I believe there will be no agreement between the King and Parliament,' Rainsborough says.

'Then what will become of the King?' Lizzie asks.

'I cannot tell. Perhaps there will be more killing before this argument is settled.'

'Do you mean to kill the King?'

'No, madam. Even the army would not go that far, I think. But exile, perhaps, or imprisonment. A trial by law would be my way.'

'You cannot try the King!' Cheyney's nose glows as red as his wine, and spittle showers the table as he speaks.

'He is a citizen of England, is he not, like any other?' Rainsborough says.

'But he is the King!'

'Come, come, let us not squabble,' Pendarves says, playing the good host. 'I'm sure that Colonel Rainsborough has enough of these arguments daily. We are here to enjoy ourselves.' He turns to Rainsborough. 'Tell me, sir, have you a family?'

'Aye, a boy and a girl.'

'And your wife?'

'She is at Worcester, awaiting my return to take her back to London. She finds travelling around the country wearisome, but we cannot be apart for long.'

Secretly, I rejoice. He is married, and happily.

'How unusual,' Thomasine says. 'Is it not the case that army wives stay mostly at home?'

'Yes, but my Meg has a strong will, and although I would prefer her away from all dangers, I cannot persuade her when she is determined. And she is determined to be at my side, when duty allows.'

Cheyney snorts. 'Perhaps you should have a firmer hand, sir, with your wife as well as your troops.'

Rainsborough smiles, as though he has faced this argument before. 'With my men, I have a position of command, but I cannot answer for their individual consciences and I cannot always control them. In the same way, I would not dictate to my wife's conscience. I could not control her if I tried, but I have no desire to do so. She is her own person.'

'You have an unconventional view of marriage, I think,' Pendarves says, a prickle in his voice. 'Do you not agree that a wife should submit to her husband, as directed in the Bible?'

'Meg is not my servant, nor mine to command, however the law of the land would have it. Our marriage makes us one and the same in the eyes of God. She is who and what she is. I am blessed indeed to have her.'

'So she is your equal?' Lizzie asks.

'Indeed. Granted, we have different roles to play, but over the last few years I have seen women just as strong and brave as any man. I have seen women fight to the death to protect their babies and their homes. Why, I have even seen women hold their own as equals on the battlefield.'

'Catholic witches and baggage whores,' Cheyney mutters.

'Far from it. I have come to believe that, despite their natural weakness, women have a strength in them that, for the most part, goes unnoticed. I have merely chosen as my wife a woman who shows that strength, rather than keeps it hidden. Some say she is a woman of spirit and that is something to be admired.'

Lizzie's eyes are fixed on the colonel as he speaks. I see she is captivated.

'Beware, sir, you are close to causing offence,' Pendarves says.

'Then I'm sorry. But let us not forget that the saints include many women of moral courage. Have we not witnessed, on these very shores, a queen of such power and holiness that she quashed the Catholics in this country? There can be godliness in a woman of strength, a woman of power.'

Lizzie's cheeks are flushed, making her even prettier, but Rainsborough is looking at me.

'This is a fascinating topic, sir,' Lizzie says, draining her cup. 'I'm glad that some men have faith in the female sex. I, too, believe that women have a part to play in these times, as much as any man.' Her eyes flick to the faces around the table. 'Our bodies may be weak, but that simply means we need God's grace all the more. I believe the strength you are referring to is God-given. Our bodily weakness makes it easier for God to find a home within us.' She puts her hand on her heart. 'I pray daily that He will find a home in mine.'

Rainsborough turns to me. 'We have not heard what you think, Mistress Ruth.'

My cheeks burn. 'Me?'

'Aye. You have been quiet as a mouse all evening.'

'I'm sure I do not know, sir.'

'Come now . . .' His eyes are kind. He smiles.

'I . . . I think that, as women, we may have many thoughts and feelings that we are not able to express. We are told they are not . . . proper. But I think that as God gives us our lives, so He must give us our thoughts and feelings. If our thoughts and feelings are God-given, how can they be wrong?'

'But what if those thoughts and feelings are the Devil's work?' Pendarves says. 'If a woman's weakness may allow her to be close to God, so she must also be more susceptible to the Devil. We need only look to the current cases of witchcraft in the east, to see those poor wretches, too weak to withstand the Devil's tempt-ations. Beware these "thoughts and feelings" of which you speak, Mistress Ruth. Trust only Our Good Lord's word, as written in the Bible and as preached from my pulpit.'

I cringe with shame. I cannot raise my head for some time, but when I do, Lizzie's eyes are the first to meet mine. She looks at me with an admiration I have not seen before. It is only a moment before she turns her attention to the mayor, who has begun a long story about a woman burned as a witch in Abingdon market when he was a boy, but I see it and I cling to it.

All this talk makes my stomach churn. I am hot and long for the safety of our cool and empty house.

Then Rainsborough leans over to me and whispers, 'Are you quite well?'

'Yes . . . yes, sir.'

He pauses for a moment. 'Pay no heed to Master Pendarves's scolding. I liked what you said.'

'Really?'

'We must all protect ourselves against the Devil's work. Man or woman, it makes no difference. But we must have the freedom to live according to our conscience.'

'Thank you.'

'Where are you from, Ruth?'

'London.'

'That is not a London accent, I think.'

'The Fens, originally.'

'Ah, good Parliament country. I do not know it myself, but General Cromwell speaks fondly of the place. Perhaps you know of his family there.'

'I . . . I do not, sir,' I say, praying that he will not notice me falter.

'And who are your people?'

'I have none.'

He nods, looking thoughtful.

I realise my mistake. 'Except for Mistress Poole, of course. We are cousins.'

'Cousins?'

'Yes . . .' Under his inscrutable gaze, I feel exposed.

Cheyney finishes his story of the witch burning and returns to the present day. 'Never since that time have I seen such strange goings-on, such proof of the Devil at work, until now,' he says. 'Hundreds tried at the Bury Assizes, and now more cases up into Norfolk, and at Downham and Ely. Why, Master Pendarves, you have your work cut out in these trying times.'

'Ely, you say?' Lizzie glances at me.

'Yes. That case is a diabolical one indeed. Some of the local farmers say they are bedevilled by the spirit of some local witch, some foul whore who was brought to justice by the townsfolk last year. Cattle are dying and their children are falling sick. There is talk of a curse upon the town.'

My heart constricts. I stare at the food before me. The meat swims in bloody juice, making my stomach turn. I can only hope that Cheyney is right. I can only hope that the Fen spirits have listened to my silent prayers and will take their revenge for Annie Flowers, who served them well for so long.

'No doubt the justice will get to the root of it,' Cheyney says. 'Such lowly people, the Fenlanders, always susceptible to superstitious nonsense.'

Rainsborough catches my eye and throws me a small smile.

'Indeed, these are wondrous times,' Pendarves says. 'I have heard reports of such strange events all around the country. Thunderstorms that sound like battlefield drums, with hailstones the size of a pigeon's egg, and a plague of flies sent down upon the sectaries in the West Country. And some speak of spectral armies, fighting in the skies above Kineton and Naseby. Let us pray that these are all signs that the Lord is preparing to walk among us once again.' He holds up his cup. 'To this, the year of miracles.'

We take up ours and echo thinly, 'The year of miracles.'

Chapter 25

It is late when we leave the Pendarveses and summer rainclouds have broken over Abingdon. I'm glad of the cool wetness soaking through my cap and turn my face up to the sky, catching raindrops on my eyelashes. My head swims a little with the good wine I have drunk.

Back in our kitchen, Lizzie unpins her hair and lets it fall over the sea-green shine of her dress. She lights a candle from the embers in the hearth and puts another log on the fire. It will burn and smoulder until morning. For a few moments we warm ourselves.

She stands there, watching the flicker and dance of the flames, deep in thought.

'You should be more careful, Lizzie,' I say. 'The things you said. You don't want to make a name for yourself as a radical. We are doing so well here.'

'Oh, I know you're right, but I cannot help it. John Pendarves is a godly man but a pompous one, with worn-out philosophies. Even Thomasine says so, behind his back. How silent she was tonight, playing the good hostess. And that mayor, with his little mouse of a wife. It will do them good to be shaken up. Colonel Rainsborough is just the man to do it.'

'Then leave it to him. He has nothing to lose here.'

She reaches out and runs her finger down my cheek. 'Oh, my angel, always so careful, so cautious. Our good colonel will be gone in a day or two, and then who will speak up?'

She is right. I have learned to be cautious. There is a fear in me that runs deep in my bones. I always thought that as I grew older I would not be so afraid of the world and the people in it. But instead it is the opposite. I wonder what happened to the wild, carefree girl I left behind in Ely and whether she is a part of me still.

Lizzie picks up the candle. 'Come, let's go to bed.'

The room is chill and dank without a fire. I feel my skin shiver into goose bumps under my wet clothes.

Lizzie begins to undress. 'So, what did you think of our colonel?' she asks.

'He is a good man. He has kind eyes.'

She laughs. 'Everyone is offended by his politics, and you notice his eyes. I might think you have a liking for him.' She is spiky in her jest.

'Well, he said too much, more than was sensible in the company.'

'So, you listened.'

'Of course I did.'

I cross the room to her and help her unbutton her dress. Lifting her hair aside, I notice the tiny curls at the nape of her neck, soft as down. I long to put my lips to them, to feel them against my cheek. She steps out of her dress and stands in her shift. Then she turns and begins to unfasten my stays. Feeling her fingers working the lacings at my chest, my breath comes fast.

'And what of his views about women and marriage?' she asks.

'Is not his talk of equality blasphemous? If God and the law tell us that a wife must submit to her husband, surely that is the right way of things.'

She helps me out of my stays, then works at the ties of my dress. 'There is something William taught me. Pastor Kiffin, I mean. "From the beginning of creation God made them male and female. And they twain shall be one flesh: so then they are no more twain, but one flesh.'" She stops and looks me in the eye. 'One flesh, Ruth . . . one and the same. Equals.'

I step out of my dress and lay it on the chair next to hers. We stand face to face, neither of us making for the warmth of the bed.

'But if Eve was made from Adam . . .' I say.

'Eve was weak and fell to temptation, but in doing so, she changed the world. She had power, you see, beyond that of Adam. We may be weak in body but there is power in women that men are afraid of. Men keep us shackled because they are afraid of that power. They call us witches and whores – they tell us we are wild in the mind when we speak out. Colonel Rainsborough is not like other men. He sees us not as weak and fragile women, to be cosseted or controlled, but as equals, with the capacity to think and to feel and to fight as boldly as any man. He is no ordinary soldier, I think. He is truly brave.'

'So . . . temptation is not always wrong?'

'I suppose it depends on the nature of our temptation.'

'Suppose it is another person. Suppose it is love. Suppose it is . . . desire.'

'There is a difference between love and lust. One is a gift, the other a sin.'

'How do you know which is which?'

She looks at me. Her voice is steady. 'I think, sometimes, they can be two parts of the same thing, so intertwined that they cannot be unravelled.'

Perhaps it is my passion, perhaps it is the wine, but I feel a rush of daring. My heart begins to pound. I slip my chemise down over my shoulders, let it puddle around my feet and stand naked before her. Love or lust – I may not know the difference, but my longing for her is my master now, and I want her to know it.

She is silenced. Her eyes slide over my body. A great wave of wanting sweeps from the very pit of my stomach. I cannot move. I am pinned by her gaze. Then she takes a step towards me. I reach out for her and press myself against the rough cotton of her shift. I put my mouth to hers and kiss her deeply. I will die if she does not kiss me back. But her arms come round me and her hands are on my back, pulling me closer. I shiver as she runs her fingers down my spine and over my hips. Then I am untying the fastening at her breast and touching her skin as her shift falls to her waist.

I pull back, clasping her hands in mine, our eyes locked. Hers are half closed, her lips parted. The candlelight catches the gleam of her pale skin. Her chest is scattered with freckles, gathered here and there in constellations, a map of the heavens written on her body.

I did not know how much it is possible to want another person, how the hunger takes over until there is nothing else. All these months I have yearned to take her into my arms and make her mine, and yet I did not know how. And now she is here, opened up to me, showing herself like one of God's angels in a painting.

It is her eyes that give me the strength to do what I do next, to take her to the bed like a wife to her husband or a whore to her john – her eyes, blazing with love, questioning me and making my body burn in reply.

Chapter 26

Trade is quiet at the Monday market. Even with a good summer behind us, grain is scarce and apples from the Abingdon orchards rot in their barrels, infected with some flying pest that the farmers cannot name.

In the market square, gossip is the favoured currency now. London newsbooks exchange hands as if they are precious stones. The King is held prisoner, captured by the army, and some say that the country cannot prosper. There can be no progress without God's elect on his throne. Others blame Charles Stuart for the years of war and call for a new government to set the country straight.

All I care about is whether there will be wheat to see us through the lean months and whether I can afford a scrap of meat to tempt Lizzie, for she eats little these days and she needs the strength.

As autumn comes in, I dig for burdock roots and nettles along the riverbank and in the woods. I boil them with vinegar and make ointments with pig's fat begged from the butcher's boy on Ock Street. I take down bunches of dried lavender that have scented my kitchen for the long hot summer, and sell them as nosegays to ladies in the square. But my stocks will not last for long.

Lizzie does not seem to worry. She is much engaged with Thomasine and spends her time preaching to the debtors and drunkards in the Gatehouse Gaol. God will sustain us, she says, if we do His will. We need nothing more.

But she changes her mind on the day that *he* comes.

I am returning from the woods, swaddled in my cloak. A grey drizzle saps the colour from the world and I do not notice the two red-coated men until I'm almost home.

They are stationed at either side of our front door, armed with pistols and swords. One is holding a large white horse by the bridle, and is petting the beast to calm it.

I put my head down, pull my cap low over my eyes and walk on towards the church. As soon as I'm out of sight, I duck between the buildings and make my way down a siding to the path that runs along the back of the house. As in London, the cottages are close together here and the alley is used for dumping waste. There is no street drain and it stinks of rot and vomit. I hesitate as I feel the squelch and suck of the filth beneath my feet, but Fate pulls me forward.

I reach the kitchen door at the back of the house. Ankle deep in mire, still clutching my basket, I press my ear to the slats. Silence. I lift the catch and slip soundlessly into the kitchen. The room is empty, the fire smoking, just as I had left it.

I put down the basket and stand in the middle of the room, straining to hear the sounds of struggle or distress. There is nothing but the whooshing of blood in my ears.

Then I hear it: high and fluttering, like birdsong, the unmistakable sound of Lizzie's laughter. And then another in answer, but deeper this time and male.

The door to the front parlour is closed and I creep up to it and listen. A man is speaking, I'm sure of it now. It comes again – her laughter, pretty and light. I open the door.

Lizzie is seated on the settle by the fireplace. The hearth is cold but she stretches out towards it as if she is warming her toes.

Her cap is missing and her hair is tied up, as though she has attempted hastily to dress it. She is smiling at a man who sits with his back to me on the stool opposite.

He has broad shoulders and straggly brown hair, curling over the collar of his buff coat. A black felt hat sits on the floor beside him, with a sword.

I know him immediately. I know the set of his shoulders, the stoop of his back, the stillness of his bearing. I know the soft Fenland burr of his voice. I have answered to it all my life.

Master Oliver turns, sees me, stands.

Lizzie beams. 'Ah, Ruth, here you are at last.'

I am struck dumb.

'We have been waiting,' Lizzie says. 'General Cromwell has come to find you.'

He has aged since I saw him last. His face is careworn, crumpled like an unlaundered shirt. His hair is thinning and losing its colour.

I do not know what to say.

'Are you well, child?' he asks. His voice is husky with the cough that always plagues him at the turning of the seasons.

'Yes . . . yes, sir.'

'I'm glad to hear it. I have been concerned for you, ever since you left us so suddenly.'

'I'm grateful that you think of me, sir.'

'It pains me to think on it, but I would honour the service done by your mother. She was a fine and faithful servant. I pray for her still.'

'I too, sir.'

'Good girl.'

'Come, sit,' Lizzie says, patting the settle beside her.

Master Oliver returns to his stool and I move a few steps closer, but I cannot sit easily in his presence.

Lizzie frowns at me. 'Have you nothing to say?'

I bow my head. I don't understand why he is here, or how he found me when I have tried so hard to be lost.

'Ruth is humbled by your attentions, sir,' Lizzie says. 'As you can see, we live a simple life here. I'm sure that she—'

He holds up a hand to silence her. 'Sit down, Ruth.'

I obey him. He studies me with grey, fathomless eyes.

'How . . . how did you find me?' I ask.

He smiles. 'Mary. She never could hold her tongue. She told me she had seen you, back from the dead, in the churchyard at St Paul's. I thought it fancy at first, but she told the tale over and over, so earnestly that I knew it to be true. By and by, my mother told me where to find you. I sent for you at West St Paul's, but by then you had moved on. After that, well, it is not so hard to find two girls like yourselves, especially when I have men in my service all about the country.'

I think of the soldiers who stare at me in the market square. I think of Colonel Rainsborough. I had thought that no one really noticed me here; I do not feel watched, as I always did in the city.

'The men who came for you that night at West St Paul's, they were General Cromwell's men,' Lizzie says.

I remember the night we fled London, the night I thought I was running from Isaac Tuttle and his lies, running for my life. Is it possible that instead I was running from it?

'Your mother was a good woman. I'm sorry for what happened, that I was not there to stop it,' Master Oliver says. 'I have done what I can, but the perpetrators have gone to ground. There is scant justice to be found in these times.'

I want to scream out loud, *I know where Isaac Tuttle is – I have seen him*. But the words will not come.

'I will do what I can for you.'

Lizzie opens her palm and shows me the shining silver shillings she holds. 'You are to have twenty pounds a year,' she says. She cannot hide her smile.

'We don't need it,' I say. 'We are managing on our own. You said—'

'I will brook no argument,' Master Oliver says. 'I have prayed on it. The Lord has guided me here. If I cannot bring justice to those who did you harm, then, by God, I will make sure no harm comes to you again. You spent your life in my service, and if the tide had not turned, you would be in my service still. It is right and proper that you are provided for. It is the will of God that guides me in this, as in everything.'

'Amen,' Lizzie says.

He smiles. 'Besides, Mary will have it no other way.'

I see he is set in this. I find I cannot argue against the man I once called master.

He retrieves his hat and sword from the floor. 'And now I must leave you. I must attend to some pressing business.'

'Of course,' Lizzie says. 'We shall be for ever grateful, sir. As simple as our household is, please consider it your own, while you are here.'

'Alas, I can stay no longer in Abingdon. There is trouble within the army ranks that must be put down. But I will try to come again, if time and duty allow.'

'I hope this trouble will not keep you away long,' Lizzie says, 'and that Our Good Lord protects you from all danger.'

'It is an unfortunate matter and we must move swiftly to quiet any discontent, but I trust that Providence will keep me safe.' He takes her hand and presses it to his lips in a gesture that makes him hunch-backed and ungainly. 'Things will be as we discussed, madam,' he says. 'You have my word.'

He comes towards me, awkward and bulky in his thick coat. He puts his hand on my shoulder and I notice dirt under his fingernails. There is something of the farmer in him still. 'I am glad to see you well, child,' he says, his voice low. 'And I promise I will not forget her. I will find him out, God willing, when the time is right, and he will pay for his sins.' He does not need to say the name of Isaac Tuttle for me to know what he means.

'Good day to you both,' he says. And then he is gone.

Lizzie runs to the window and watches him mount the white horse, then clatter off towards the square with the redcoats in tow.

She claps her hands. 'Oh, Lord, thank you for your kindness! Oh, my angel, such good luck you bring me!'

I cannot join her in her happiness. I feel strangely flat. 'I don't understand. Why would he come here?'

'Because he cares about you.'

'But I'm no one to him. A servant . . .'

She comes towards me and cups my face with her hands. 'What does it matter, the what and the why of it? Twenty pounds a year! We will have a table to match Thomasine's. You will have a new dress at last and we can hire a girl to cook and clean.'

'I need no help. You said we were better left alone . . .'

'Things are different now that we know we are safe. And we will be safe, Ruth. Just think how word of this will travel. We will be the general's girls now, and no one will dare question that.' She catches my hands and squeezes them tight. 'We will be free to speak our minds and live as we please.'

'What do you mean?'

'There is so much good work to be done here, and now I am free to do it. No more stitching by candlelight, no more fingers pricked sore with needles. Don't you see? Your Master Oliver is truly a godly man, and God has brought him to us for a reason. I will work only in God's name, and I will show Kiffin that he is wrong about me. Oh, Thomasine will be delighted! I must tell her.'

She runs to fetch her shawl, humming to herself as she covers her head and ducks out of the street door, stopping only to plant a kiss upon my cheek. It has been a long time since I have seen

Lizzie so excited and it raises a smile in me, despite my misgivings. I'm glad to be the cause of her happiness. I know only that seeing Master Oliver has stirred something I had hoped was put to rest.

Lizzie is right, of course. Master Oliver can bring me coin, and coin can bring us safety and comfort. Coin will put food on our table and buy fuel for the fire. Coin will keep Lizzie by my side. Coin can bring me everything, apart from the one thing I want most. It cannot bring my mother back.

Chapter 27

In the weeks that follow, the tumult caused by Master Oliver's visit settles, but he has wrought changes that cannot be undone.

Lizzie is good to her word. She takes in no more sewing but spends her days in preaching or prayer. I worry that she will grow tired of our small life here and want to return to West St Paul's, but we talk little of London, or the past, despite the truths that Master Oliver conveyed. I do not want to go back. Even with such an ally, there is still much to chance in a city where gossip and slander send people to the gallows. And I have too much to lose here. In Abingdon, I am mistress of my own home. There is surprising satisfaction in the knowledge that Lizzie and I live by my pocket alone. I feel a sense of freedom that is new to me, and a sense of hope too, for if Lizzie depends upon me utterly, as I depend upon her, it can only strengthen our love.

Some nights, when Lizzie has spent the day with Thomasine, she prefers prayer to pleasure. On these nights our bedtimes are chaste, and it feels as though she is far away from me, shut off in another world – a world I cannot reach. But I try to reach her with kisses and small gifts – winter violets from the riverbank, sweetmeats and cake bread, bought with Master Oliver's pennies. I try to bring her back to me, with elaborate meals and a clean-swept house, for I will not have a servant girl to do these things, but she does not seem to notice my efforts.

Other times, the heat from our bodies warms us so that we need no fire. Then she is mine and mine alone. I love these nights. I live for them.

One such night I lie on my back while Lizzie props herself up on one arm and plays with the tendrils of hair that stick to my damp skin. I love to lie like this, enjoying the rare peace of the early hours, knowing she is mine until dawn.

'How things have changed between us,' she says.

'Yes,' I reply, thinking that my feelings for her have not wavered since the first day we met, except to grow and burn with a fiercer passion.

'I'm so glad that we can be together like this,' she says. 'No pretence, no lies, no secrets. We do not have secrets, do we?'

'Of course not.'

'Good, for I would hate to think that you keep things from me.'

I turn on to my side to face her. 'Do you think I keep secrets from you?'

'No. It's only that . . . there are some things I long to ask. But you are so quiet and never speak of them.'

'What things?'

'The book you gave me, in London, your mother's book. Do you ever think of it?'

'At times.' The truth is that I think about it almost every day. Although I treasure the ribbons that Lizzie gave me in exchange, I have felt the lack of the book. I do not regret my gift to her exactly, but I have missed the surety it holds. Many a time I have guessed at an ingredient or a dosage for a cure. Not everything is embedded in memory. And more than that, I miss the possession of it, as if ownership of some physical thing had linked me to my mother in a way that memory alone cannot.

'I would like to know more about it, and the woman who

penned it,' Lizzie says. 'Will you tell me what you remember of her?'

'One day I will tell you everything, but not yet.' The past is my own and I do not want to share it, not even with her.

'Did you read the book?' Lizzie asks.

'Of course. My mother used it all my life.'

'I have been looking at it these past weeks. There are some pages that I do not understand. Will you explain them to me?'

'You have it here?'

'You did not think I would leave it behind?'

She is out of bed and across the room before I know it. She has kept it well hidden, buried deep in the chest in which she keeps her things. I feel a prickle of excitement, of joy, as she returns holding the book.

She puts it into my hands and straight away I feel the warmth and love it contains. I cradle it against me for a moment.

'It is very special to you, is it not?' Lizzie says.

'Yes, it is.'

'Then it means all the more to me. Let me show you . . .'

I give the book back to her and she turns a few pages. Over her shoulder I see the familiar handwriting, black ink fading to brown.

'Here,' Lizzie says, pointing to a page dense with scribbles. 'What does this mean?'

At the bottom of the page is a list of instructions numbered from one to ten. There is a circle opposite, drawn in an unsteady scrawl, with crosses marked around the rim. An inner circle is marked with a list of herbs. I remember this one. We used it often.

'It's a charm,' I say.

'I thought so. What can it do?'

The knowledge I have of these things, passed down from my mother and by her mother before her, I keep close. I have seen how it can be mistaken and misunderstood. I have found out only too cruelly how, in the wrong hands, it can bring devastation and grief. I have learned from my mother's mistakes. But it comes spilling out of me now, as if Lizzie herself has charmed me.

'This is a spell for protection, to be used against curses,' I say.

'And this?' Lizzie flicks forwards a few pages and finds another diagram.

'A charm to harness the power of the full moon.'

'And this?'

'This one is to ward off death. See the crossed scythes? It is good for the plague.'

'So your mother was a cunning woman,' Lizzie says.

I do not like the term. 'My mother did not call herself a cunning woman, although there were those who called her such, and much worse. She was a kind and godly woman. She made no covenant with the Devil. Of that I am sure.'

Lizzie reaches out and strokes my hair, soothing me. 'I know the memories must be hard. I'm just trying to understand.'

'My mother was a good woman, from a simpler time and with simpler ways. War and politics were not for her. This time of fear and suspicion and recrimination was not for her. It was not her way. She taught me things, simple things – ways to heal, ways to pray and ways to speak to God that no clergyman tells of in church. She believed that God is all around us, in every flower and herb, in the rivers and the clouds, and in every one of us. She used her charms and rituals as ways of speaking to Him.'

'I know she was a true believer. Scripture runs throughout. See here, this is what I wanted to show you . . .'

Near the back of the book, where the words are not so crowded, she has found a scrap of gold. Even I have never noticed these words, spelled out in a tiny delicate hand, as though a spider has scuttled across the page:

Whither thou goest, I will go; and where thou lodgest, I will lodge: thy people shall be my people, and thy God my God. Where thou diest, will I die, and there will I be buried: the Lord do so to me, and more also, if ought but death part thee and me.

Beneath, my mother has drawn a tiny scrawl of arrows and crosses. I know it is the ancient symbol of everlasting love. I am taken aback for a moment. I wonder whom she had in mind when she made such a charm. Lizzie reaches out for the newly printed Bible that Thomasine has given her. She finds a page and hands it to me, pointing to the same words, mirrored on the page.

'It is from the Book of Ruth,' she says. 'I believe you are named for her.'

She is right: the words match exactly.

'It is a pledge,' she says. 'A pledge between two friends, two women, whom God brought together. Listen . . .'

She lies back against the bolster and reads the story of Ruth, a widow and outsider who promised her loyalty to Naomi and, in her devotion, found her way to a new love and a new life. I have heard it before, of course, but never had it spoken to me as it does now.

Lizzie finishes and closes the book. 'Why do you think your mother would pick out such a passage, if not for you? These are Ruth's words. They were written for you to see, I think, when the time was right. Your mother had a special wisdom.'

I take the book in my lap and run my finger over the words. Are they really meant for me?

'It's beautiful,' Lizzie says.

'Yes.'

She comes close to me and brushes my hair away from my face. 'I would make such a pledge. Would you?'

I look into her eyes and see the love and hope that live there. I want her to look at me like that for ever. 'I will do anything you ask, you know that.'

She smiles. 'Then we will swear it . . . on the memory of your mother.' She takes my hand and places it palm down next to hers on the page. 'Together then . . . until death.'

'Until death.'

As I reach for her, my mother's book slips from my lap and falls to the floor, but I barely notice.

Chapter 28

Lizzie does not leave my side for weeks. Through December, we sleep late and spend our days about the house. She walks with me in the woods to find the last of the ripe juniper berries and we come home laughing, sucking pricked fingers, with pine needles tangled in our hair. She comes with me to the wharf and we pick out the best freshwater eels for our supper. She reads aloud to me while I stew them, the kitchen steaming with the scent of tarragon. She tells me the news from London. Since he became our benefactor, she has a keenness to follow the general's every move, and asks me question after question about the man I once called master. And I talk, more than I have for months. I tell her about my life before, about Ely and the Fens. I tell her about my mother, and her knowledge of the old ways, as she pores over passages in the book. I tell her about Mary, Frances and the others, about Old Bess and her small kindnesses to me. Before, this would have made me homesick or angry, but now there is no need. I have a home, and it is filled with joy.

It is the smallest things that bring me the most happiness – her arm through the crook of mine when we walk out, the sight of our intertwined fingers fitting together so perfectly, the laughter in her eyes at some shared secret joke. Since the day of my mother's death, there has been a chasm in my soul that no amount of prayer could sate. Now it begins to fill once more, drop by drop, with each smile, each touch, each kiss.

These weeks are blissful and I cherish each day because I know they cannot last. They will pass, as all things must.

Two days before Christmas, Thomasine comes with a letter from Kiffin. I can tell by the look in her eyes that his answer is not what Lizzie has hoped for in these long months of waiting.

Lizzie reads it, screws it up into a ball and tosses it into the corner of the kitchen. 'He will not help me,' she says, her voice tight. She sits at the table, head in hands.

Thomasine sits down next to her and puts her hand on Lizzie's shoulder. 'I could try again,' she says. 'I can tell him of the good works you are doing here. I will ask John to put his name to it.'

'It is no use,' Lizzie says, standing. 'Do what you will, but William Kiffin has made up his mind. You will not change it.' She goes upstairs, slamming the door to our bedroom.

Thomasine fetches the letter and smoothes it out on the table. She sits and stares at it, saying nothing, as if I'm not in the room.

'Thank you for coming,' I say, wanting her gone. 'I can look after Lizzie now.'

Thomasine looks up at me. 'Tell me, Ruth, how well do you know Mistress Poole?'

'We are the best of friends.'

'Does she tell you her secrets?'

'Yes.'

'Then you will know that she is right. This is a hopeless cause. Her name will never be cleared while Kiffin is against her.'

'Surely not,' I say. 'Lizzie has done nothing wrong. You must try again, for Lizzie's sake. The truth will come out in the end. It always does.'

'That is what concerns me.' Thomasine stands, wrapping her shawl around her shoulders. She folds the letter and tucks it into her pocket. 'Your faith in her is admirable, but perhaps you do not know her as well as you think.'

'I know her better than anyone.'

'There are things you do not understand. Elizabeth is much troubled. Do what you can for her. Treat her well. She is more fragile than you know.'

She leaves without saying goodbye.

Secretly, I glory over Thomasine. She thinks that she understands Lizzie's heart when, in truth, she is the one kept in the dark. She does not know where Lizzie's passion truly lies.

After Kiffin's letter, Lizzie becomes snappish and fretful. She tells me that her best chance of forgiveness is to help Thomasine in her work. She must prove her worthiness. There are people who need her more than I do. God needs her. So, of course, I must let her go.

I'm curious about the work that keeps her from me for long hours at a time so one evening I ask to go with her. She is surprised but I sense pleasure in her hesitation. She kisses me and tells me she is glad I take an interest at last.

The very next day she takes me to a prayer meeting where a preacher from Oxford, an acquaintance of Thomasine's, will speak. I am surprised when she leads me to the back room of the Bell. A tavern on the market square, it is most often filled with traders and their lackeys. It is not the place I would choose to speak to God. But Thomasine is here, deep in conversation with Crowley, a fat, red-headed fellow who looks as though he has had too much ale and not enough sleep. She looks up as we enter and, seeing Lizzie, a rare smile twitches at her lips. Dot is here too, sitting meek in a corner, hands folded in her lap, pink-rimmed eyes buried in her cheeks.

Those gathered are mostly men. A few of the more respectable townsfolk, no doubt here at Thomasine's invitation, stand together, talking in low voices. Others laze on stools and sup their beer, laughing and smoking pipes. There are only two other women, sisters I recognise from Pendarves's congregation at St Helen's. I have seen them about Abingdon. They are always together and stand out because of their sameness – the same complexion, the same clothes, the same meek manners. I can barely tell them apart. They sit quietly, waiting. Their eyes follow Lizzie and me as we find empty stools near the fireplace and warm ourselves.

After a few minutes, Crowley shakes Thomasine's hand and clears his throat, coughing up spittle and hawking it into the fire. Thomasine joins us, greeting Lizzie warmly. Crowley begins to speak.

'My brothers and sisters, let us join together in worship.'

His voice carries surprising weight. He spreads his arms as though he would embrace the whole room. Titters from the drunkards do not distract him.

'I know you are all here for good reason. You are seeking solace. You have questions in your heart. Let me speak to you, my brothers and sisters. Let my words offer you some balm. I ask not for your agreement or your argument, only that you may listen with an open mind and an open heart and ask yourself whether what you hear is the truth.'

He takes a swig of ale.

'Who has not suffered the yoke of poverty these last few years?' he asks. 'Who here has not strained against the shackles of hunger and despair? Who has not seen proof that we are living in unprecedented times? There are those of you here, I know, who once lived quiet and peaceful lives. You thought never to have a care for high politics or matters of King and State. Oh, how those times have changed! Every man and woman has been touched by this war. Every person here has seen misery and hunger and bloodshed. Am I not right?'

There are murmurs of agreement around the room. People are listening.

'Let me ask you, my friends, where is God in all of this? What for these terrible days? The two sides of this great fight both say they are led by Our Lord. Both sides claim their killings and their victories as providence. How can they both be right?

'I tell you now, God is not with those rich men, cosseted and fattened on the profits from taxes and estates, who wear velvet and feathers on the battlefield. God is not with those iron-skulled generals who slaughter innocents in the name of the people. The blood of English men has been spilled on these shores to teach us a lesson. These men, these powerful men, have risen up and made themselves into gods! They are pretenders to His throne! Is this how it should be?'

The air bristles. Beside me, Lizzie's head is bowed, her eyes closed. She is whispering under her breath.

Crowley goes on: 'I hear the cries in your heart, the cries of ordinary people. God hears your cries. God moves within every one of us. God brings us love – love and strength enough that we might rise up in unison and prepare ourselves for a new world, a world in which we might be free of the warmongering of politicians and army men!' His face is as pink as a shaven pig's, eyes popping.

'The world is turning and there will be revolution. The revolution of universal love. That love is with you already. It is in every man, woman and child. It is in every creature. And we must share it! We must spread the message. Each and every one of us has a duty, a calling. He has brought you here today to awaken you!'

There are calls from around the room. Some of the men laugh and swear, others nod solemnly. I squirm on my stool. This is not what is preached in Pendarves's church or Kiffin's meeting room.

'Christ is preparing to walk among us once again. And we must ready our souls! Do you feel His love? His love knows no bounds. It is not to be kept hidden by rich churchmen and given out on a whim. We are not divided from it by altar rails and popish ceremony. His love cannot be contained in a church, so why do we need one? Why should we torture ourselves with questions of sin and righteousness? If His grace is within us, then we are free – free to act according to conscience, knowing that we act before God! Knowing that all comes from God!'

Suddenly Lizzie is on her feet, knocking over her stool. She flings her arms outstretched, like Jesus on the cross, her face tilted to Heaven. The colour has drained from her cheeks and she is pale, grey-green, as if she is under water. She is quivering all over. 'I can see!' she cries. 'I can see!' Tears seep from her eyes. 'He comes to me!'

The room falls silent. Crowley is rapt. There is nothing but her voice, wavering above the crackling of the fire.

'There is light . . . many-coloured light. There is an angel in the light. I see . . . terrible things. I see armies of blood! I see the righteous cut down and raised up again! The dead! The dead are walking. There will be a time of ghosts and a time of miracles. He will walk among us once again! He is coming!'

Her eyes roll back in her head, her body convulses and she falls to the floor, her skirts ballooning around her. I'm by her side in an instant, cradling her head and calling, 'Lizzie! Lizzie!'

'Oh, Lord!' Crowley bellows. 'Thank you for this sign! We see how you work among us and we are humbled!'

Others join him in praise. I fan Lizzie's face with my hand and her eyes flicker behind the lids. Thomasine kneels beside me. 'Is she well?'

'She needs air. Don't crowd her.'

She backs away, shooting me a black look.

Crowley continues his rant. His fiery talk ignites the room. There is cheering. One or two of the drunken men climb onto the table and clank their cups together. I cannot listen to any more of this.

Lizzie opens her eyes.

'Lizzie, are you all right?'

'Oh, Ruth . . .' she breathes. 'It was wonderful . . .'

'You are not well. We must go home.'

'Did you see it? It was so – beautiful!'

'Can you stand, do you think?'

'Stand? Oh, yes.'

She sits up. Immediately Crowley grabs her hand and hauls her to her feet, away from me. 'Praise be!' he says. 'Bless this woman that she may be your vessel!'

People clap and flock to her, touching her shoulders and grasping at her hands. Her eyes are wet and shining. I watch as she makes her way to Thomasine, who enfolds her in her arms and whispers into her ear. There is nothing I can do but watch as Crowley asks question after question. What did you see? What did you hear? How did it feel? Thomasine holds Lizzie's hand and listens to her answers with such pride, as though she herself has been chosen.

At length, Crowley finishes his preaching and praising. He shakes the hands of the townsmen and asks them to spread the word of the miraculous happenings they have witnessed. The drunken men fall to lazing by the fire. The two sisters have long disappeared. I did not notice them slip away. Only Dot remains, seated in the corner, her dark little eyes taking everything in.

Chapter 29

Back at the house, recovered, Lizzie installs herself at the kitchen table with a sheaf of paper and fresh ink. Her quill scratches down the thoughts in her head. Her face is set with concentration and every now and then she stops and closes her eyes, remembering. When she opens them again, they glow with inner light.

I prepare a rich broth for our supper, using the best mutton that money can buy. I scent the pot strongly with rosemary, and add hyssop and camomile – not enough to taste but enough to calm an agitated mind.

I try to draw her out, to bring her back to me. 'What are you writing?'

She does not answer.

'Is it a tract?'

'Ruth, please . . .'

'Supper is ready.'

'I'm busy. You can see that.'

'But you must eat. You need the strength.'

She shakes her head and goes back to her writing. I stir the pot. The flavourful broth steams and my stomach groans, asking for food.

'The butcher said this is his best. And fresh too. Does it not smell good?'

She rolls her eyes and slams the quill on the table, sending spatters of black ink across the wood. 'I do not want it.' Her teeth are clenched, like a child refusing to swallow a cure.

'Come, share a meal with me, and then I'll leave you to work. Everyone must eat.'

'Not I. Not today.'

'But I made it for you.'

'Ruth, you do not understand. What happened today was . . . was everything I have hoped for. It is what I have prayed for, all these years, that God might use me to spread His word. And now that He has chosen me at last, it is my duty to carry His message. I must tell people what I know. It is my chance to make up for the past.'

I frown. 'But you have led a blameless life. You must not heed what others think. You must not take gossip to heart so. If Pastor Kiffin will not relent—'

'I do not care about him.'

'Then what is there to make up for?'

She sighs. 'There are some things I would rather forget, but I cannot, things for which I owe a debt, in the eyes of Heaven. I'm sure you have heard the story of my mother. Charlotte will have made sure of it.'

I nod. 'She did. But surely you do not blame yourself for that.'

She shrugs and I see the pain behind her tight lips. I recognise it as mirroring my own. I think of the nights I have spent cursing myself for my failure to save my own flesh and blood. I sit down next to her and put my hand on hers. 'My love, you are not to blame. I have always known you are a truly good soul, blessed even, but you are not an angel yet, thank God. So, you must eat.'

She pulls her hand away. 'I cannot. I am full. Full of His love.'

She takes up her quill, pulls a fresh sheet of paper towards her and begins again.

I see that I cannot reason with her, so I fetch a bowl for myself and ladle a good helping of broth. As I sit down to eat, a splash of liquor spills from the bowl and slops onto Lizzie's paper. We both stare as the liquid seeps across the page, the wet ink losing form and running into a senseless mess.

'I'm sorry . . .' I reach across and try to blot the words with my apron but I make it worse.

She is still and silent but her eyes slide to mine and they are filled with a look I have never seen from her before. It is contempt, as if I am the Devil himself.

She stands and gathers the papers, all except the spoiled one. Then, without a word or a glance, she takes up a candle and goes into the parlour, closing the door behind her, shutting me out.

I feel like a child, scolded by an elder, as tiny as an ant, crushed under her heel. I am sick with shame. For such a small, silly thing, my feelings are so big.

She does not sup at all that night but stays in the parlour working on her papers until late. The broth turns cold in the pot, the butcher's best mutton stagnant and tough. I scrub the kitchen table, but the mess of black ink has sunk into the grain and left a mark there, like a reminder of my misdeeds.

I go to bed alone. I cannot sleep. The bed feels cold and damp without her to warm it. I lie and stare into the darkness. I know it is wrong, but I am jealous of God.

Chapter 30

The winter months are hard for many. The rain starts in February and does not stop. The roads turn to mud and farmland is lost to the swollen Thames. People talk of more fighting to come. Royalist pamphlets, filtering through from London and Oxford, tell of growing support for the King and turncoats in the Parliament ranks. I cannot believe it will come to this. I cannot believe that people have the stomach for more killing. Besides, now Master Oliver has the army and the ear of Parliament men, I know he will do what he can to prevent it. He is a good man. He will do right by the country, as he has done right by me.

We do not see Master Oliver again, but the money arrives, delivered by a notary in the days after Candlemas. With it comes a letter, sealed with red wax and addressed to me. Lizzie opens it, reads it once and tosses it into the fire.

'Pleasantries,' she says. 'Nothing of consequence.'

I watch the flames take it as though it is a piece of rubbish, or one of the tracts that she has abandoned, wondering what it says, wondering that she can toss away such proof of our good fortune.

Each pamphlet that Lizzie brings home, I scan the frontispiece, looking for a certain printer's mark, waiting for the day I see it there and know that it is Joseph's work. That day does not come. With the passing of time I wonder what has become of him, and what might have happened between us had he not been poisoned by Isaac Tuttle's lies. There is no point in these daydreams, but I cannot help myself. For every choice I have made, a hundred possibilities have closed to me; for every path I follow, other roads are barred; Joseph is just one. There is a sore bitterness in me when I think of him now, and a sad regret that he will never know the truth. His lack of faith in me and his belief in Isaac Tuttle have tainted every good thing that passed between us.

I try to join Lizzie and Thomasine in their work but, truth be told, I do not have the burning passion for preaching and prayer that they share. Now I have coin in my purse and a warm fire at nights, I give as much as I can to their cause, but I'm not one for speechifying in the marketplace or going from tavern to tavern, talking to labourers and soldiers who are more interested in a woman's good looks than her godly words.

Whenever I am with them both, I feel as if they are two parts of a great truth that I do not understand. My letters are well learned, but I do not have Lizzie's fine hand, so cannot act as scribe for her. I am of no use to her. In the evenings when she sits, bathed in candlelight, quietly toiling at her papers, there is a hollowness in my heart. She is here with me and yet I miss her.

As winter turns to spring and the woods creep into life, I spend my time searching the sodden pathways for early herbs and preparing my kitchen for the drying and boiling and distilling that will mark the summer months. I would rather serve God in my own small way, by helping those who need it, the dying and the sick, than by trying to save the souls of those who do not want to be saved.

When May Day comes I am determined to mark it. This year it will not be a day of fear and flight, of happiness shattered, but one of celebration, just like the old days. There may be no drunkenness and no dancing, but there will be Lizzie and me, and good food, and togetherness. It is one year since we left London, one year since that night in the woods when she first held me in her arms, one year since her lips first touched mine. That is something to celebrate.

I spend the day preparing, walking out to fetch the best foodstuffs I can find and collecting flowers to decorate our table, and our bed. I make a pie and spend a whole hour fashioning miniature pastry vines to twine about the crust. I sweep the kitchen and rub the table with beeswax until it shines. Once the pie is baking, I make a thick gravy and spice it with pepper to give it a pleasing heat that makes my nose tingle. I lay out trenchers and knives, cut a chunk of manchet and set the daisies I have picked in a jug of water. I am about to call her from the parlour when she enters, dressed for the street, tying her cap under her chin.

'Are you going out?'

'Yes. Thomasine asked me to attend her this evening, so that we may study together.'

'Again? But I have made supper . . .'

She looks at me blankly. 'You know I'm fasting today.'

'I got beef from the butcher. He saved it for me. I made a pie.'

She sniffs the air. 'That may be, but I'm fasting.'

'It's May Day.'

'Ruth, you must leave these old country ways behind.'

I search her face for some recognition. I find none. 'It is one year since we left London. Almost to the day.'

'Oh.'

'I thought that perhaps we might celebrate.'

'Celebrate? What is there to celebrate in that?'

I have a hard, flat feeling in my chest. She does not understand me. 'Can we not share a meal before you go? You must eat some time.'

'God will sustain me.'

She looks tired and has dark shadows under her eyes. In bed at nights, I notice that she is losing the flesh from her bones and I watch, transfixed, as her ribs move under her skin like ripples on a pond.

'Perhaps just this once?'

'I promised Thomasine,' she says, wrapping her cloak around her shoulders.

'You have been with Thomasine every night this week.'

She puts her hands on her hips. 'Are you trying to tempt me from God's work?'

'I . . . I just want to see you. Perhaps I could come with you?' I make to collect my shawl. 'I can wrap the pie and take it with us. Perhaps a gift to Thomasine—'

'You are not invited.'

I'm used to her tempers, but now she is cold and indifferent. It cuts.

'Besides,' she says, 'we cannot be together all the time.'

'We are not together all the time. I'm here, cooking and cleaning and keeping house for you. You treat me like a servant still!'

Her eyes are icy. 'And what are you, if not indebted to me?'

'I am not your servant now.'

'I took you off the streets when you had nowhere else to go. I fed you and clothed you when you had nothing. I left my home to come here, to this poverty-stricken, pitiful little town, to protect you. And you want me to celebrate that?'

'You said that things are different now. You said that we are equals.' I feel tears springing and I blink them back.

'Things *are* different. You have a home, food on the table, and you are respected here. I have raised you up from nothing. What more do you want from me?'

'I thought . . . I thought you loved me. Till death . . . remember?'

'By God, Ruth, you are like a leech! You will drain me before you are done.'

She turns and swoops down the corridor, her cloak billowing like dark wings. The front door slams. I crumple to my knees and let sobs shake me.

She has snapped at me before – it is her way – but I have never answered back. Now I feel a rage in me. She *had* said those things. She *did* promise a new life and, for a while, we have had it, together. I do not understand what has changed, but I know it is not I.

The more I think about it, the angrier I become. It is true that Lizzie saved me once – I will always be grateful for the charity she showed me then – but it is my own connection to Master Oliver that keeps flesh on our bones now. Have I not proved my devotion again and again? I was ready to face the gallows, choosing to stay by her side when I could have fled for my life. I have sworn on the memory of my mother that I will never abandon her. Even now, when she depends upon me for all her worldly needs, she can still make me feel insignificant, like the supplicant begging endlessly for favour.

I pull myself up off the flags and slam about the kitchen, crashing pots onto shelves and tossing the daisies out into the mire of the back lane. I leave the pie baking in the oven. It will burn and end up in the slop bucket but I no longer have a taste for it. Maybe I will fast too. Maybe I will show her that I am just as strong as she, just as good.

It is all she talks about now, with that light burning in her eyes – being good. Her preaching and her pamphlets, her angels and her visions, they are all she wants, all she cares about – that and Thomasine. It is Thomasine who takes her away from me.

Then a thought comes to me.

Once, it was the most precious thing I owned. Now it belongs to Lizzie. Suddenly I long to smell the leather binding and feel the stiff crinkle of the paper. I want to hold it to my chest as if it were a child's poppet, as if it contained my mother herself. Would it be so very wrong to take the book back? Would it be so wrong to use it?

I creep up the stairs, candle in hand, a thief in my own house. I go to the chest in which Lizzie keeps her things and prise open the lid.

It is full of her clothes, petticoats and grey overdresses mostly, some stitched and mended by my own hand. Underneath is her green brocade, shining like treasure beneath the dull wools and scratchy serge. At the bottom I find a pile of pamphlets and letters and the one piece of jewellery she owns but never wears: a tiny gold cross, threaded on a faded velvet ribbon. Beneath this is the book.

I clutch it to me, snivelling and wiping my tears on my sleeve. I sit on the bed and hold it in my lap, stroking the battered brown cover. I turn to the page I want and find what I'm looking for.

I think of Thomasine and trace diagrams with my fingers, whisper the words under my breath. I make a mental note of the herbs I might need. Then I close my eyes and pray. I pray to the spirit of my poor dead mother. If Annie Flowers can curse her killers from beyond the grave, then surely she will do her worst for her own daughter.

I'm mindful of time passing. I do not expect Lizzie back for hours, but she may repent her harsh words and come home to make her peace. I begin to pack away her things, a little guilty now at my actions. But as I pick up the book once more, a letter falls from between its leaves and lands on the floor. It is dirty with curled edges and smudged with remnants of black sealing wax. I cannot stop myself. I open it and read.

Devonshire Square, May 1647

My dearest Elizabeth,

I do not write to excuse my actions, but to beg that you heed my warning.

Your presence in my congregation has stirred me in ways I never knew before. I have believed our friendship to be a rare gift. But I am married, bound by oath in the sight of Our Lord, to another until death. What we have done, what you ask of me, is sin, and now I am punished for it. My wife lies abed as I write, sick with the loss of another child. She is punished for our sins. I see now that I have been under the influence of a darker force.

I fear for your immortal soul. That is why you must go. For your sake and for my own, that the Devil within us both might be banished and this affliction might be lifted. If you ever loved me, you will go. And if there are other men, I pray you do the same for them.

Beware, my Elizabeth. The eyes of the world are upon you. God is benevolent, but the world does not forgive or forget.

Burn this paper, for it condemns us both.

God have mercy.

William

I read the letter three times and then I weep. I weep for Lizzie and her lies. I weep for Kiffin and his poor tortured wife. But, most of all, I weep for myself.

I am a fool. I have believed her innocence utterly. I have raged on her behalf. I have believed in her purity.

I am deceived.

My mind whirls. I thought I knew her heart. It seems I do not. If she has lied about Kiffin, what else has she lied about?

I wipe my eyes and put the letter back in its hiding place. My hands shake as I fold the clothes carefully so she will not know they have been disturbed. I try to reason with myself. One lie does not mean there have been others. But all I can think of is Thomasine's face. I must know the truth. I must know it at once.

Out in the street the rain comes down hard. Fast-moving clouds blot out the moonlight. I forgo the comfort of a lantern. I do not want to be seen.

As I near the Pendarveses' house I feel dreamlike, as though I am moving without will, a greater force carrying me forward. My stomach is twisted in a great knot of anxiety. I must know the truth, but I fear it too. I am driven on by a certainty that what I find there will bring me pain, but not knowing is even worse.

Visions of Lizzie and Thomasine take away my sense and reason. I see her copper hair tangled with Thomasine's dark locks. I see Thomasine's skin like tallow wax next to her pale, creamy flesh. I imagine fingers meeting, lips touching. What I see in my mind's eye becomes reality and I must see it. I must know for certain that I am betrayed.

I dare not go to the front door and, besides, what is the use in that? If I want to know the truth it must be by other, more secret means. So I sneak from window to window, keeping myself low, hidden by the shadows. There is a light in the kitchen where the hearth smoulders and Dot snoozes on the settle. I see more light from a downstairs casement at the back of the house.

I'm weak with the blood rushing in my limbs. I hold my breath. As I peer over the sill I swear my heart thumps so loudly that they will hear it.

I see Lizzie.

She is sitting on a bench by the fire with a book in her hands and she is watching Thomasine. Thomasine is pacing back and forth, talking and gesticulating wildly. I strain to hear what she says but the noise of the rain covers her words. I see Lizzie speak, although I cannot hear her, and she points at something on the page.

There is no passionate embrace, no naked skin and no ecstatic clinch. The only heat here is in the debate.

Now I am double the fool. Jealousy has turned my mind wild.

At home, I sit and stare into a single candle flame until the wick burns itself out. I think hard. I think back.

I realise she never lied to me about Kiffin. She never denied, absolutely, the rumours that caused him to abandon her. I believed that she *had* denied it because I wanted to believe it. If she did love him, her heart must have broken when he turned from her. Her desire to flee London, to put many mud-soaked miles between them, makes sense now. How she must have suffered, alone and deserted, unable to speak her pain. I know how that feels. I wonder if she loves him still.

And yet she has done what he asked. She has turned away from her sin. And she has come to me for solace. I have picked up the pieces of her broken heart and made them mine. Perhaps there is a kind of comfort in that.

When she comes home, an hour or two later, I take her into my arms and stroke her hair. Her body is hot and feverish, and I'm sure she has rushed home to be with me.

I feel closer to her, now I know her secret, closer than ever, and the warmth between my legs tells me that I want to be closer still. But she sighs and falls asleep with her head on my chest.

I will not mention the letter. It is best to let it stay in the past, along with all the secrets of my own.

Chapter 31

The rain does not stop all summer long. Now the leaves are turned and the crops are failed and there is famine in the west. Even for those with the coin to pay, there is little to be had at market. Many believe God is punishing us for the war, for taking a king off his throne, but not Lizzie. It is the darkness before the dawn, she says. The righteous will be saved. I dare not ask if I am one of them. I fear my sins are too many.

I am eating my supper alone again, watching the day's last light fade. The rain drums against the windowpane.

There is a knock at the street door. It is too late for company. Likely it is one of Lizzie's eager new friends, seeking words of solace from her perfect, godly lips. Well, they will be left wanting. Lizzie is with Thomasine, and they will have none such from me.

The banging comes again, louder this time.

'Open up!'

It is a man.

'Is anyone there?'

'Who is it?' I call.

'Ruth? Is that you?'

'Who's there?'

'Ruth, let me in. I have urgent news.'

I slide back the bolt and open the door. There, red-faced and utterly dishevelled, is Joseph. He is soaked to the skin and struggling to control a sweating horse that stamps and steams beside him. 'Ruth . . .' He tries to doff his hat but succeeds only in knocking it to the ground.

I feel as though I've opened the door to a ghost. My mind is blank with shock but my body gives me away as I stumble over my words. 'What . . . what are you doing here?'

'I've come to find you. I've ridden from London on this damn fool of a horse . . .' The mare nudges his arm. 'I bring bad news.'

'Oh . . . well, come inside. You can tie the horse over there.' I point blindly to a stake where people often tether animals on market day.

He does so and follows me into the house, trailing mud. I lead him into the kitchen and draw him some beer while he catches his breath. My hands are shaking. I try to calm myself. A thousand thoughts run through my mind. What terrible thing has driven him here? What does he want with me? Has he brought Isaac Tuttle with him?

Joseph drinks deeply. He looks tired, older, glowering with the darkness I first saw in him. He can barely meet my eye.

'Is Mistress Poole at home?' he asks.

'No. She'll be back later. Why are you here?'

'The news is for her ears.'

'Tell me.'

He slumps onto the bench by the fire and drains his mug. He rubs his face, streaking the dirt. 'It's Master Poole. He fell sick with a fever not a week since. Three days ago, he died.'

'Oh . . .' I sit on the bench next to him, my legs suddenly too weak to stand.

'Margaret wanted Elizabeth to know. She could not rely upon the post, with the fighting.'

'Margaret sent you?'

'If the mistress does not come home, the house will be sequestered and she and Charlotte will be turned out. So here I am, riding like the Angel of Death.'

'Oh, my Lizzie . . .' I put my head in my hands. I know what is it to be orphaned.

'Will she come home?' Joseph asks.

'Home?'

'Back to London.'

The idea silences me. This is my home now. This house, this kitchen stocked with my own money, good linen on a shared bed and enough cut wood to warm the winter nights ahead. London seems a lifetime away.

'Will *you* come home?' he says.

My mind is racing. 'Why would Margaret ask you?'

'When you didn't come, that night at Broken Wharf, I tried at West St Paul's for news of you. Margaret told me all. She has been good to me since then.'

We are both silent awhile. At the mention of Broken Wharf, my head spins with questions, but it is Joseph who asks first, his voice gruff and cracking.

'Why didn't you come?'

The old bitterness rises within me.

'Isaac!' I spit the name as if it is poison on my tongue. 'Your friend is a liar. Whatever he told you, it will not be the truth.'

Joseph's eyes are stormy. 'He told me enough.'

My heart is pounding.

Joseph puts his mug down on the flags. 'Isaac Tuttle is no friend of mine,' he says fiercely. 'He was a good man once, but this war has made beasts of us all. He told me what he believes, what he did to you and your kin. From that day to this, he is no friend of mine.'

'Then . . . you did not believe him. I thought . . .'

He stands and warms his hands at the fire, his back to me.

'You should have trusted me, Ruth. You should have known me better.' I can tell by the hunch in his shoulders that he cannot trust himself to look at me.

I am wordless for some time, reeling in my confusion. I can hardly believe it. Have I been so mistaken in Joseph all these months? I feel as though the surface of the earth, which I once thought solid, is shifting beneath my feet.

'Where is Isaac now?'

He shrugs. 'That's no business of mine. I've not seen him since that night. Nor do I wish to. It's Mistress Poole I set out to find. That is my business today. And it was not so hard to find her in the end. She is well known in these parts, it seems.' He reaches into his pocket and pulls out a folded, crumpled paper. He flattens it and hands it to me. I need only a glance to know that it is Lizzie's work, one of her printed pamphlets. She will take solace in knowing her words have reached London.

Lizzie. She must know about her father. But this means the end of everything, the end of our life here. I am afraid to think too far ahead.

'I must go to her,' I say. 'Will you come with me that you might tell her yourself?'

He nods.

I throw a shawl around my shoulders and we hurry up St Helen's Street. I rap sharply at the Pendarveses' door and Dot answers.

'I must speak with Mistress Poole,' I say.

Dot's black eyes pop and she shakes her head.

'I have urgent news. This man has come all the way from London.'

I make to enter but Dot blocks my way.

'What is it?'

She makes bleating noises that I cannot understand and flaps her hands.

'I know your mistress asks not to be disturbed when at prayer, but she'll forgive you this once. I promise you'll not get into trouble.' I put my hand on Dot's shoulder to reassure her, and she moves aside reluctantly. She whimpers and I wonder what Thomasine does to put such fear into her.

With Joseph close behind me, I make my way to the parlour, where I know the prayer meetings take place. As I reach the door and lift the latch, I think only of Lizzie and the great sorrow that is to come. I wish I could bear it for her.

The fire is stoked high, sending shadows dancing.

Thomasine sits in a chair before the hearth. Her cap is off and her dark hair spills down her back. Her head is tilted back slightly and her lips are wet and parted. Her stays are unlaced and her shift is pulled open. Her breasts are large and full – wine-coloured tips on white skin. She lolls with one leg over the arm of the chair, her skirts hitched up. One hand is buried deep under her petticoats.

Lizzie stands before her. She is naked.

Her skin glistens with sweat in the heat. She is touching herself, showing herself to Thomasine. Her eyes are glazed with lust. She is Venus made flesh, lit by flames.

There is a moment of silence, so pure that I can almost hear the workings of my mind. One last moment before the walls of my world come tumbling down.

Then Thomasine is screeching, 'Get out! Get out!' and grasping for her clothes. Joseph is stumbling back into the corridor, and Lizzie, frozen still and perfectly beautiful, is locking eyes with me.

It seems that I go outside my body then, as though the pain that pierces me is too great to bear, and I simply drift away, as a great hubbub goes on all around me.

* * *

Later, when Lizzie and Thomasine have made themselves decent and Dot, red-eyed and blubbering, has been sent to fetch spirits, Joseph delivers his news. Now it is Lizzie's turn to hurt.

She turns to me, crying out, 'Oh, Ruth! What am I to do?' and clutches at me like a wild thing with desperate eyes.

My heart is twisted. How I hate her. How I love her.

When, after a time, she has the strength to walk, I take her home, propped up by Joseph and calmed by drink.

I help her upstairs and give her syrup of poppy to help her sleep. Her eyes leak tears, even though she makes no sound. As the dose takes effect, I turn to go but she grabs my arm. 'Forgive me,' she whispers.

I do not answer.

'Please don't leave me. I need you now. I need you . . .'

She looks so feeble, her face pale and drawn against the bolster, her eyes full of despair. She is like a clinging child in her grief. I cannot help the constriction of my heart. I reach out and stroke her hair. 'Sleep now. We will decide what is to be done in the morning.'

'We . . .' she says. 'Yes . . . *we* will decide.'

I make my way downstairs to the kitchen where Joseph is laying new logs on the fire. As I enter he straightens and looks at me.

I do not stop to question. I go to him and let his arms come round me. I lean my head against his chest and weep my heart out for the death of my dreams.

Part Four

London
November 1648

Chapter 32

Master Poole is buried one week later at a small parish church on the edge of the city, one of the few we could find where there is still space in the yard. The black and white morality of Kiffin's congregation and Lizzie's new mysticism are not for him. A plain man in brown cloth says simple words over the grave.

There are few of us in attendance. We are joined at the graveside by two men from the Haberdashers' Guild. They both wear tall hats and good black clothes and nod their condolences to Lizzie.

Charlotte weeps and snuffles into her handkerchief, clinging to Margaret. The older woman, who overcame her terror of the plague to nurse her master in his last days, is stony-faced.

Lizzie clutches my arm with bird-like fingers. She does not cry but closes her eyes and whispers her own private prayers.

I find I cannot hate her for long.

Through the journey from Abingdon and the parting from our life there, she has been meek and placid, seeking my constant approval in small things. She says that God is punishing her for her sins and He has taken her father as a warning. She is determined to do penance for her wrongs and goes days without eating. She says she is sorry. I believe her. I can see her struggle. It is written in the hollows under her eyes and the creases on her brow. In her suffering, she is beautiful, her pale skin almost translucent. In her grief, she is ghostly, ethereal. She needs someone now, to keep her rooted on this earth. She needs me and I cannot abandon her.

Although my heart is broken, and I cannot forgive her, the ties that bind us hold fast. My charms have more power than I knew. Not only have I bound her to me, but I have also bound myself.

As the minister speaks his words, it occurs to me that the man in the plain wooden coffin never knew his daughter. He knew nothing of the passions that rage inside her, the tenderness of which she is capable, the boiling love that spills into her preaching and into our bed. As father and daughter, they had been affectionate but remote. He doted on her, granted her wishes and did his duty. He was a good provider but I doubt he really understood her. I wonder how he felt when she cut herself off from him so completely. Did he feel the blade of Lizzie's selfishness, as I do now? I'm sorry that, in my own selfishness, I did not think of him, left behind in London, brought low by worry and uncertainty, never knowing the fate of his only child. Now Lizzie will never have the chance to know her father better, as I have never known mine. We are both alone in this world.

We leave the gravediggers to finish their work and make our way back through the streets. At Holborn we come across a crowd of people walking east. Children dart, playing games and calling to each other, but the adults are solemn, mirroring our own mood.

'What's happening here?' Margaret asks a ragged woman.

'The procession is passing along Cheapside, so I'm told,' the woman says.

'What procession?'

'The funeral. Thomas Rainsborough. They bury him today at Wapping.'

'Colonel Rainsborough?' Lizzie's face is ashen. 'Colonel

Thomas Rainsborough?'

The woman reads our confusion. 'Yes. Haven't you heard?' She doesn't wait for an answer, but bundles past us into the crowd.

Lizzie turns to me. 'Oh, Ruth, surely it cannot be true?'

I pray God it is not, but already I see the evidence: men among the crowd wearing green patches on their sleeves, matching bands around their hats, women adorned with ribbons in emerald, jade and blue-green – the colours of the Levellers. Some carry sprigs of rosemary for remembrance. Beneath hats and caps, faces are grim, and I know then: these people have lost their greatest hope.

'Come,' Margaret says. 'This is none of our business. We've our own mourning to do today.' She takes Lizzie's arm and tries to lead her away.

Lizzie shakes herself free. 'No, I must see it.'

Cheapside is overflowing with people. The street is bustling with hawkers and taverners selling ale from trestles. Despite the sombreness of the occasion I feel the camaraderie that grows from shared loss. A gathering sups and sings rebel songs around Cheapside Cross, refusing to be tempered by the presence of soldiers, themselves decked out in sea-green sashes, their weapons turned.

As we make our way towards the Cross I recognise faces from the churchyard and the shops around the Pope's Head.

'Ruth!' A woman's voice rings above the throng. 'Ruth!'

It is Sal. She has clambered up onto the Cross, arms waving madly.

I wave back, glad to see her, and pull Lizzie through the crowd towards her. She climbs down to greet me with a hug. 'Well, God be blessed! I didn't know you were back.'

'Not two days since.'

'Joseph found you?'

'Yes. Yes, he did.'

She turns and calls, 'Lads! Lads! Over here!'

Benjamin and Charlie have green ribbons dangling from their hats. They greet me with smiles and pumping handshakes. Benjamin stares at Lizzie and blushes deeply when I introduce them. Despite her pallor and shadowed eyes, she still has the power to capture a man's heart.

'What do you make of all this?' Sal says.

'We've only just heard,' I say. 'What happened? How did Colonel Rainsborough die?'

'That's the question on all of our lips.' Benjamin raises an eyebrow. Seeing our blank looks, he tells us, 'He was murdered, two weeks ago, in Yorkshire.'

'Murdered?' Lizzie gasps.

'By Royalist spies. That's what they would have us think anyway.' Benjamin hands a pamphlet to Lizzie. 'We have different ideas.'

Lizzie studies the paper and I peer at it over her shoulder. The title reads, *The true nature of the murder of Colonel Thomas Rainsborough and other conspiracies done by the Army Grandees.*

'Certain of the army leaders wanted our good colonel out of the way. Certain old enemies that needed him silenced for their own ends.' Benjamin raises his voice and spreads his arms as if to take in the crowds around him. 'But Thomas Rainsborough will not be silenced. Not while there are those who believe in justice and freedom!'

People are watching and listening; there is a smattering of applause.

'Who?' I say, breathless. 'Who would do such a thing?'

'Cromwell, Ireton, among others.' Benjamin looks pleased with himself. 'That pamphlet is my own work, and if you read it you will see for yourself.'

Lizzie, swaying slightly, leans against me to steady herself.

Before I have time to defend Master Oliver, Joseph comes pushing through the crowd.

'The coffin is coming,' he says, and then, seeing me, 'Oh, Ruth . . .'

I glare at him. 'Why did you not tell us?'

'One death in a week is enough,' he says softly, acknowledging Lizzie with a hand to his hat. 'Besides, what is Thomas Rainsborough to you?'

'We knew Colonel Rainsborough,' Lizzie says. Despite her fingers trembling on my arm, she speaks loudly, drawing the ear of those nearby. 'I spoke with him quite intimately and found him to be the very best of men.'

Joseph is stunned. He looks at me. 'Is this true? You knew him?'

'Knew him and loved him, as one of God's true souls loves another,' Lizzie says.

Her voice begins to waver. She gasps for breath, putting her hand to her heart. People around us are staring now. I recognise the signs. I have seen this enough times in Abingdon to know what comes next. I hold her tight, willing her to stay calm. I do not want attention on us today, not so soon, but she pulls away from me and climbs up onto the plinth that holds the old Cross. Her shawl falls to the ground and she flings her arms out wide, face turned to the sky, eyes rolling.

'The Lord comes to me!' she cries. 'He tells me this great man has not died in vain. It is a sign, a sign that His people must rise up. We must prepare ourselves for a new dawn. Do not despair, but fill your hearts with the love that is within you!'

There are jeers from the crowd and one of the men lifts the hem of her skirts and play-acts peering beneath. Benjamin curses and pushes him away. She ignores them both.

'Our God will walk among us once again and there will be a

new age of love and freedom. I am come to tell you the truth –
the truth that Thomas Rainsborough fought for, that we all fight
for. God's truth!'

I see the admiration in Benjamin, as I have seen it so many
times in Abingdon: a boy, captured by her beauty, enthralled by
her words.

Lizzie begins to pale and shake. 'God has blessed me with the
Sight. I tell you now, He has shown me the path we must follow
and it is paved with love! Universal love! There is no sorrow in
this world. There is no sin when all comes from God! Take heart,
my friends, and rejoice in God's love!'

Joseph is by her side to catch her as she faints and falls, to the
mixed sounds of laughter and a few quiet utterings of 'Amen'. All
eyes are upon us. Charlotte stands useless and wide-eyed, her
hands clapped to her cheeks. Margaret wears a look of horror. I
realise that, in one year, Lizzie is much changed. Those who
loved her before barely know her now. They do not know what
she has become.

'She is overwhelmed,' I say, to no one in particular. 'She buried
her father today.'

Joseph lifts Lizzie into his arms. Strands of her hair have come
free from her cap and trail across his shoulder, like threads of
cotton. She looks like a child, cradled against his chest. 'Come,'
he says. 'We'll take her home.'

'I can look after her,' I say. 'You'll miss the coffin.' I indicate
the street, where people have cleared a path for the procession.
The first flanks of soldiers come, dragging their pikes behind
them.

But Joseph just shakes his head and makes for West St Paul's.
I grab Charlotte by the hand and set off after him.

Chapter 33

Later, after all Margaret's questions are answered, and she and Charlotte are gone to their beds, Joseph and I sit before the kitchen hearth. At last the place is silent, save the crackling of the fire.

He crouches before the coals, poker in hand. I'm glad to be alone with him: there is still so much unsaid between us, and many questions I must ask.

'Before you came, Benjamin showed us a pamphlet.'

Joseph snorts. 'His conspiracy?'

'Is it true?'

'What? That Cromwell is the murderer of Rainsborough?' He stokes the fire angrily, then sits back on his haunches, gazing at the blaze. 'I don't know.'

'Well . . . what do you think? The colonel was a hero of yours, was he not?'

'He was, but so was Cromwell at one time. I think there are many wanted Thomas Rainsborough silenced and all the Levellers along with him.'

'But why doubt Cromwell, when he leads the army, and half his men are Levellers?'

He shrugs. 'There are divisions within the New Model. Two camps. Those who still believe in the great dream, and those who don't.'

'But surely this fight has been all about that dream.'

'In the beginning. Now the fight is all but won, and the King is a prisoner. What comes next?'

'The world is turned, just like you wanted.'

'Is it?' He sits next to me on the bench and rubs his forehead with soot-stained hands. 'If the King is tried as a man of blood, and found guilty, who then holds the power?'

'Parliament.'

Joseph shakes his head. 'Those who convict the King will hold the power. And that will be the army grandees – Cromwell, Fairfax, Ireton and the rest of the Army Council. That's where the power lies now. Parliament is nothing but the army's puppet, as it was once the King's.'

I think of the kindness in my old master's eyes when he last bade me farewell in Abingdon. I think of the favour he has shown me, and my mother's fond loyalty to him. I trust he is a good man at heart, and surely even such great power cannot change the heart of him. 'Might that not be a good thing?' I say.

'The Army Council does not believe in the dreams of radicals. They rejected most of the Levellers' proposals and now, with Rainsborough gone, there is no one of stature to fight for us. They would see Parliament made up of propertied men, selected by propertied men. Where is the revolution in that?'

'But England will be a republic. Is that not revolution enough?'

'England will still be led by blue-bloods with wealth and land. Where is the dream that we fought for? Where is the voice of the common man who died on the field?'

I pour more beer for us both. 'And you think they will try the King for treason?' I ask.

'I can see no other end to this. While he lives, he remains a living, breathing symbol of the past. There will always be those who want to return to that. There are those whose money and power depend upon it.'

My blood runs cold. 'You think they will kill him?'

Joseph stops contemplating his cup and looks at me. 'If he is found guilty of treason, they will have no choice. And I cannot see that they would try him unless they were sure of the verdict. There is too much at stake.'

I take a swig of my beer, wishing it were something stronger. 'They will make a martyr of him.'

'Aye. Some say it would be better to let him live, to exile or imprison him. If they kill him, the army grandees themselves become tyrants. That's certainly what the twins think. What they choose to print now runs close to treason. These are dangerous times for those who challenge the power of the army.'

'And what do you think?'

Joseph raises his eyes to mine and I see that they are ringed with shadows. He looks exhausted, hopeless, a man beaten. 'I don't know what to think any more.'

His expression reminds me of the night we sat and talked in the rain, on our way to London. The darkness that dulled his eyes then is present now. I wonder where his fire has gone.

'But this is what you fought for at Naseby,' I say.

'You remember that?'

'Of course.'

A smile plays across his lips.

'This is what your brother died for.'

'And many thousands more.'

'Master Oliver is a good man. I cannot believe he ordered the murder of Colonel Rainsborough and I cannot believe he would kill the King. He has a good heart. He will know what to do.'

'What do you know of Cromwell?'

My eager tongue, loosened by ale, has betrayed me. Now, tired and grieving, I long to share the truth with him.

I take a deep breath. 'General Cromwell was once my master.'

A coal pops and breaks in two, sending sparks flying. 'I grew up in his household in the Fens. My mother and I were servants there.'

'By God . . . you never told me.'

'No.'

'So, when we met in Cambridge, you had come from there?'

'Yes.'

He is stunned. 'Then, you know him well.'

'I know him as a servant knows her master.'

'And you say he is a good man?'

'He was a good master. Firm but fair. Always honest.'

'Good Lord, Ruth, how can you have kept so quiet about this? Does Mistress Poole know?'

'Of course.'

'And who else?'

'No one. Master Poole was an old acquaintance of the general's mother. It was she who sent me here.'

'Margaret and Charlotte?'

'They must not know.'

'Why not? You grew up in the household of one of England's greatest men. You can use this. You could get a better place, you could petition him for help . . .'

'There is no need.'

'But don't you see? With Master Poole gone, there will be lawyers to deal with. You will need money. He could help you . . .' Seeing my flushed cheeks, Joseph stops short. 'He already does . . .'

'You must tell no one of this. It's a secret.'

'I won't tell a living soul, if you'll tell me how it came about.' His eyes are full of wonder. He is looking at me anew and I like it.

'Master Oliver came to us in Abingdon. He said it was his duty to make amends for what happened to my mother, and to me, while I was in his service. He said that the Lord had guided him to find me. He talked of restitution. He offered to support me. I would have tried to refuse but he arranged it with Lizzie. And, in truth, I've been grateful for it. It's not much, just a small income, but enough to keep bread and meat on the table, when it can be got. Lizzie and I will not starve. He is a kind man, with a good heart. I believe that.'

'Do you ever see him? Cromwell, I mean.'

'Only that once, in Abingdon. Never since then.'

'Could you see him again?'

'I don't know. Why?'

He sits forward. 'If you could speak with him, you could petition him on behalf of the people. You could raise our concerns again.'

'I know nothing of politics.'

'But you are close to him. You could go to him on behalf of others. You could persuade him to meet a new delegation. You could help him, warn him, tell him what people are saying.'

'And why would he listen to me?'

'Why does he give you money?'

'What do you mean?'

'I mean, Ruth, that you may have his ear.'

'But I'm nothing to him – an obligation, a duty.'

Joseph gets to his feet and starts pacing. 'Just think, a young woman comes to him, guileless, with truth behind her eyes, a woman he has known all her life, someone he loves. What a difference from jaded men in torn uniforms.'

'He doesn't love me.'

Joseph takes me by the shoulders. 'But he must care.'

'I thought you said that the cause was all but lost.'

'And maybe it is. But maybe you are a new chance. You are a new route to the general.' He is excited by his idea.

'I don't know what I could do, even if I could see him.'

Master Oliver's visit in Abingdon had proved that we have

little to say to one another, and I fear offending him, thereby risking our income. The thought of begging yet more favour troubles me.

'It's worth a try, is it not?' Joseph says.

'I don't know.'

'Will you think about it?'

I shrug assent. He will have to be satisfied with that.

He sits back down on the bench but fidgets, his boot tapping out a rhythm on the floor. 'And now you are back, will you stay in London?'

'I suppose. We have little choice if Lizzie is to keep the house.'

'Well . . . I'm glad of that.'

I think of Lizzie, asleep upstairs. I think of how he carried her here and laid her down, gently stroking hairs away from her face, his fingers brushing her cheek. My heart twists with jealousy. The feeling is familiar now. 'She needs to rest, undisturbed,' I say. 'It will do her good to be at home and away from . . . others.'

'She is much influenced.'

'Yes.'

I feel my cheeks colour. I'm ashamed that Joseph saw what I saw in the Pendarveses' house, that he was there to witness the breaking of my heart.

'She has not been well lately,' I say, swallowing the lump that rises in my throat.

I feel his eyes on me.

'So . . . that is why you stay with her, even now. Even when she betrays you.'

'I don't know what you mean.' As I say the words, tears well in my eyes. I fight them back. I will not let him see my pain again.

His gaze is steady. 'You love her, don't you?'

Suddenly I am angry with him. Of course I love her. I love her more than my life. It is a love that brings me anguish, but I'm fated to endure it. Lizzie and I belong to one another, bound by promises deeper than love – promises made before the souls of the dead, promises made before God. I made a hard bargain with the Fen spirits when I tied my heart to hers, and I must keep my part, for to break it will only bring more suffering. That is why I stay. I have no choice. I'm trapped by my own selfish wishes, destined to be with her until the end.

I want to rage at him, to beat my fists against his chest, to let this staggering hurt out into the open. Instead I sit with my eyes fixed on the stone flags, too afraid to open my mouth.

'So what happened between us – it meant nothing to you?' he says, drawing the words out slowly, as if it pains him.

I had not thought he would ever speak of it, that long-ago, dreamlike day in the meadow, the kiss that held me fast in his arms.

'Things have changed,' I say.

'I have not.' His voice is thick with the feeling behind his words. 'I thought you would come, that night, to Broken Wharf. I was sure of it. When I learned that you'd gone, and without a word, I tried to put you from my mind. I thought I could forget you. But I cannot.'

I have no answer to give him, none that he will want. 'I'm grateful to you,' I say. 'You are a good man. There must be some other girl more fitting . . .'

He shakes his head, turning away from me. 'A good man indeed,' he says, under his breath.

'What? You do not think so?'

'I know it's not so. And I think you know it too. That's why you turn from me. I should have known that you would see through me. I should have known it from the start. You were right to distrust me from the moment we met.'

'What makes you say that?'

He will not meet my eye. 'God has cursed me. I cannot be happy. You know this, I think.'

'Cursed? Why should that be?'

'You are not the only one with a past you'd rather forget.'

'A curse is a serious thing, Joseph, but it can be broken. If you tell me—'

'No. It's done and I must suffer for it.'

His eyes are ink-black. His hand goes to his chest, to the site of his old wound, as if he cannot prevent it. I realise that, whatever his secret, it is become part of him. His passion for the rebel fight is a distraction, his love of the press a whim. His dreams of the New World are his escape. This is the one thing that drives the heart of him, and I am determined to know what it is.

I rise from my seat and make as though I'm collecting more beer from the jug. While my back is turned, I whisper a truth charm. 'Now you know my secrets,' I say, returning to the bench, 'and I trust you with them. If you would share yours . . .'

'I cannot.'

'. . . you will have my confidence. I promise.'

'I have carried this for so long,' he says, as he hesitates. 'If there is anyone who might understand, it would be you . . .'

'I will try.' I give him my warmest smile.

He takes a great gulp of beer. 'Naseby,' he says. 'I am for ever damned by what happened there.'

'The loss of your brother? That was not your fault.'

'No, there is more. I didn't tell you the whole truth.' His forehead is creased in a frown and he rubs it, as if to erase the lines.

I stay silent, giving him the time he needs to find the words.

'They don't tell you,' he says. 'They don't tell you about the madness that happens after blood is let, when men run wild like animals. No one speaks of the depravity a man will sink to, to stay alive.'

He takes another long draw from his mug.

'Jude was already dead when I found him,' he says, voice cracking. 'He'd been hit by a gun. I could barely tell it was him, my own flesh and blood. Something happened to me then. I fought on, filled with rage and vengeance, looking for something to hurt, an enemy to kill. And I found them. I found the women.'

'Women? On the battlefield?'

'Not soldiers, camp followers. Wives and whores. Once we had killed their men, we killed them too. All of them.'

At first I don't understand. 'But surely the women are protected . . .'

'Codes of honour make no difference when the stench of blood turns a man wild. The word went round the field that there were witches among the King's followers, witches using their magic against us. God help me, I went along with the rest. We hunted them down and drove swords through them, like they were nothing more than meat. We were no better than hunting dogs, killing with no mind for aught else.'

My stomach turns. There is a place for death on a battlefield, but this does not sound like the honourable victory that has become almost legend in the hands of the Parliament print men.

Joseph puts his head in his hands and covers his eyes. 'I swear the Devil came into me. If there were witches among them, I don't know, but some were just girls, younger than you. And children. One girl . . . I left her alive but I took my knife to her face. Oh, God . . . I left her bleeding. I left her to die . . .'

Tears wet his cheeks, but I feel no pity. I feel disgust. He has spoken the word I fear so much, a word that holds so much power and spreads such terror. Those women were not witches. They were guilty of no more than their sex. I imagine wives and daughters, following their men to battle, cooking their dinners and mending their clothes, believing themselves safe, protected by the unspoken laws of the battlefield. I imagine them fleeing, stumbling over the bloodied bodies of their husbands and sons, cut down as they run. Even the basest camp whore does not deserve such an end. No one deserves it. I asked to know this, but now I wish I had not – I have meddled too close. I taste bile in my throat.

And still Joseph goes on: 'It was a woman who cut me. This scar was made by a cleaver, meant for the kitchen, not a soldier's sword. There is no honour in my war wounds. I cannot forget what I did in the name of vengeance. I will spend the rest of my life atoning for it.'

'And so you should,' I say coldly. This is not the man I thought I knew. That blackness in his eyes, now I know what it is – there is a devil in him. No friend of mine could commit such an act. If he can do this to a stranger, what might he do to me? He belongs with Isaac Tuttle and his ilk; those twisted men with a taste for blood, learned by battlefield butchery. There is a word for what he is, a forbidden word, marking out the very worst of sinners: murderer. I want him away from me, away from this house.

At last he wipes his eyes and looks at me. 'How is it that even now, even when I know there is no hope for us, you can still draw out my darkest secrets? Perhaps there is something of the spellbinder in you after all.'

My skin crawls. I stand and walk away from him, my back turned. 'And if there was, would you assign me the same fate?'

'Ruth—'

'I want you to leave,' I say, struggling to level my voice.

He says nothing for a moment and then he sighs. 'You see? I'm right. I am not a good man. And now you will never forgive me.'

I will not look at him, or turn to him, or answer him.

'Well, then . . .' he says, standing. 'I'll leave you . . . if you are sure that's what you want?' His voice is as unsteady as my feelings.

I nod.

He gathers his hat and jacket. As he reaches the door, he looks back at me one last time. 'I cannot blame you. How can I expect forgiveness when I cannot forgive myself? But I hoped you might understand. I would forgive you anything . . .' Then he leaves, without bidding me goodnight.

It is only when I creep to Lizzie's room and slip under the coverlet beside her that I let the tears come. She is deep in red-poppy dreams, lips parted, sweet night breath upon my cheek. She does not stir to comfort me. I watch her sleep for a long time, but I cannot join her.

Is there anyone on this earth who is really as they appear to be? I'd thought I knew Lizzie's heart, but she keeps its depths hidden. I'd thought I knew Joseph, but my belief in him has been turned about, and about again, until I no longer know which part of it is true. Lizzie is warm and soft next to me, but I find no consolation in her; I am more alone than ever.

In the morning Lizzie puts on her green brocade and goes out into the street without her cap. At the conduit an old woman spits at her feet and calls her 'holy whore'. Lizzie does not answer. She holds her head high, shakes out her hair and smiles.

She is brazen. She is beautiful. I have never felt more strangely proud of her, or more afraid of what she has become.

Chapter 34

The weeks that follow are bitter. The winter comes on fast and the Thames freezes over by early December. There is no snow, just the ice and biting winds from the north that still the city streets. The conduit is frozen and each morning children make a game of breaking up the water with stones.

After the rally at Colonel Rainsborough's funeral, there is a brief lull, as if people are drawing breath, waiting to see what will happen next. The King is brought home to Windsor, and the newsbooks argue over whether this is a good omen or not.

I consider Joseph's belief that I could have an influence on those great men, in these turbulent times. I hear that Master Oliver is returned to Whitehall and I wonder if he would see me. But what would be the use in that? I have nothing to say on matters of state, so I put the thought aside.

I think of Joseph often, sometimes with disgust, sometimes fear and sometimes guilt. His admission has culled any sentimental feeling I might have harboured, as I realise how close I have come to the Devil once again. Images of the story he told, of those poor innocent women, plague me when I close my eyes at night. But I cannot marry up these pictures with my own memories of the man, and I wonder if I ever truly knew him. People have so many parts that it is impossible to know them all.

Lizzie is consumed by events, visiting the churchyard, even in the cold, eager for the latest news. Her thoughts turn to the

King's fate and she seeks out the Whitehall gossips daily. She tells me that she must know if the King is to be put to trial. I do not understand this obsession, but I have come to see that Thomasine was right about one thing: there is much I do not understand about Lizzie.

Away from Thomasine and her prayer meetings, Lizzie searches for a new way to spread her gospel. She will not countenance a visit to Kiffin to beg a place in his congregation, and I doubt that he would take us in any case. Instead she says God is always at her side, and she needs no church and no minister to find Him.

As in Abingdon, she works hard to find her audience, and she finds it in the taverns and the marketplaces at St Giles and Smithfield. She goes to St Paul's Cross and speaks out amid the vagrants and gossips, drawing crowds of dissidents who are ready to believe her words. And they love her for it, as they must, for her passion matches her beauty, and the people need someone to believe in now.

Lizzie refuses to take up her old trade, and while I spend my days turning away Master Poole's old clients, she works on her writing. I often find her sitting in reverie, or poring over some new tract she is scribbling, ready for Benjamin's press. Her pamphlets find their rightful place in St Paul's Churchyard, amid the penny broadsheets and the countless religious treatises of London's most radical thinkers. It is the only thing that gives her pleasure now so I encourage it, and welcome Benjamin when he comes to collect her work.

Over those weeks, we pick up the threads of our old life but, with Margaret and Charlotte in the house, it is impossible to live as freely as we did in Abingdon. I do not return to my old room in the eaves, with the truckle bed and the straw mattress for which I had once been so grateful. I stay with Lizzie now, curling up next to her once the others are gone to bed and I do not care who knows it. It is nobody's business but our own. And yet there is a distance between us, our love a broken bridge that has not yet mended. The strings that tie our hearts together are frayed. I don't know if time will heal them but I pray it will clear my mind of the torturous imaginings that visit me whenever we are apart.

It is harder to establish my new place in the household. I'm no longer a maid, working alongside Margaret and Charlotte and I see resentment in their eyes whenever I ask a favour of either of them. I cannot slot back into the place I left all that time before. Perhaps it is prideful, but I feel myself elevated. I am no longer the frightened girl I was when I first arrived here. Eighteen months as mistress of my own house, and the knowledge that the food on the table is paid for from my own pocket, makes sure of that.

One afternoon I am in the kitchen, banking up the fire, when Lizzie comes hurtling through the door, calling my name. The urgency in her voice tells me that something is amiss. She unwinds her cloak and abandons it on the floor. She has gone out without a cap again.

'Oh, Ruth, what am I to do?' She falls into my arms and starts to sob.

I hold her for a moment. Tears splash my neck. I guide her to the bench before the hearth.

Gasping for breath through her tears, she tells me the news. The army has seized power in the Commons. Anyone who would treat with the King is gone. It is said that the Army Council is determined to try Charles Stuart for treason. The churchyard is buzzing with the gossip.

So, I think, Joseph is right. They will cut off his head. I soothe Lizzie, stroking her hair. 'But this has nothing to do with us,' I say. 'Why should you care so much?'

'It has everything to do with us. They will kill the King, and when they do, they will kill me too . . .'

'What do you mean?'

She steadies herself a little. 'There is something I have not told you. A secret . . .'

More secrets. I'm sick of them. But I hold her hand, noticing how tiny it feels, and ready myself for bad news.

'I have had dreams,' she says. 'Dreams that are so vivid, so real, I hardly know if I am sleeping or waking. The King comes to me, but he comes as an angel, sent by God from the heavens, shining with a light so bright that I can barely look at him. It is like looking into the sun. He tells me that he and I are one, that I am tied to him and that his fate will be mine. He asks me to help him in the name of God. I have to help him . . .' She presses the heels of her thumbs to her eyes as she tries to stop the flow of weeping.

'He tells me that if he is killed, God will be angry. A great calamity will come and the country will fall into chaos and destruction, the like of which has not been seen since the days of Sodom. And then I wake up and I cannot move. I'm lying on the bed and you are next to me and I cannot reach out to touch you, or call your name. It is as though I am already dead and lying in my grave, and there is nothing but darkness, and I know that what I have seen is a true vision of what is to come . . .'

I do not know what to say. I have grown accustomed to her fits and passions. I have seen the way she performs her visions, paling and trembling like a mystic. But this is different. Her eyes speak not of holy bliss but of earthly terror.

'It's just a dream,' I say.

'No . . . it is much more than that.'

'We all have nightmares—'

'You are not listening. You have not heard me.' She pulls away, insistent. 'This is real, and it comes again and again, night after night. God is speaking to me. The King is speaking to me. You have to believe it.' She twists her dress in her hands, knuckles white as bones. 'You have to help me.'

'You know I will do anything I can.'

She looks hopeful. 'Anything?'

'Yes. I will go to the apothecary tomorrow, and seek out more of the good poppy to help you sleep. Or perhaps the poppy is to blame. Perhaps a little comfrey and camomile will calm you better.'

'I do not need your cures, Ruth. I need your help. I want you to go to Cromwell.'

'Cromwell?' I cannot help but smile. 'Master Oliver is an influential man, but I doubt even he can banish bad dreams.'

'You must listen, Ruth. I must take what I know to the highest authority. Cromwell is the one who can help me now.'

'Lizzie, I don't—'

'Don't you see? The message is meant for him. God has chosen me because of my connection to you. It is *our* duty to take His message to the general. It all makes sense.'

First Joseph, with his politics and persuasion, now Lizzie, both wanting more from me than I'm willing to give.

'Oh, yes, this is a perfect idea,' Lizzie says. She is dry-eyed now, a hint of colour warming her pallor. 'I must present my case to him. He is a godly man, guided in everything. He will surely pay heed, once he knows we are in earnest. You must go to him, Ruth. You must ask him to grant me an audience with the great men of the Army Council.'

'I doubt he will want to see me. After all, there has been no word from him for so long. Perhaps he has forgotten me.'

'Don't be such a fool. He will never forget you. You have his ear, I'm sure of that.'

I cannot imagine myself standing before my old master with such a tale. He has little tolerance for time-wasters. Thinking of it makes me feel like the child I once was, ever wary of the wrath of her betters. 'I'm sorry, I cannot do it.'

Lizzie's nostrils flare. 'But you must. I must be allowed to speak out. God has given me this great task. I cannot fail him.'

'I cannot go to Master Oliver with stories of dreams and imaginings.'

She gives a cry of exasperation. She stands and paces the room. There is a wild, distracted look in her eye. 'Why do you not believe me? Do you not trust in God?'

'Of course I do.'

'Then why hesitate?'

I ask myself the question. For a long time I believed blindly in Lizzie. I placed her higher upon this earth than any other. But now I see a desperate intensity in her that I do not recognise – something behind her eyes, as though somebody or something else resides there. She is taken over with such fire, set alight by God. Where once that fire was all for me, all for our bed, now it is all for Him. The fierceness of her conviction frightens me; I do not trust it.

But she is insistent. 'General Cromwell is my best hope. You must go to him. He will listen to you.'

'I doubt he will see me. I will not know what to say.'

'I will tell you. You will carry God's message. You will be my angel, just like I've always said. You will be my saviour once again, my darling.'

She comes to me and puts her hand on my chest. I feel the familiar lurch of my heart. But it is a broken heart now, and the sensation brings pain.

'No. I won't do it.'

She freezes for a moment and the wildness in her eyes sparks with anger. Then she lets out a great wail. 'So you condemn me to my fate! I cannot live with this pressing down upon me, knowing I could have done something to stop it. Knowing that you would not help me!'

She stumbles to the table, where Margaret has left out her

kitchen knives for sharpening. She picks up the largest. 'You said you loved me. You promised you would do anything for me. How can you turn from me now, when I need you more than ever? After everything we have been to one another. Do you not care for me at all? I cannot go on if you have abandoned me.' She pushes up the sleeve of her dress and holds out her wrist. The blade glints as she puts it to her flesh.

'Lizzie, no!' I shout, but I'm too late.

Blood wells over the silver blade and streaks down her arm to puddle in her palm. I'm with her in an instant, grabbing her hand and forcing the blade away from her skin. For a moment her grasp is strong and we grapple, neither willing to give way, but then, as her blood begins to drip, she lets the knife clatter to the flags.

I press my free hand over her wound. The cut is not very deep but she has opened a vein and I must stop the bleeding. She slumps to the floor, her face draining.

I crouch and gather my own skirts, pressing the fabric to her wrist. 'By Christ, what are you thinking?'

'If you will not help me, then I cannot live. My fate is tied to that of the King, and they will kill him. You know there is no other end to this trial. But the army men are wrong. Your Master Oliver is mistaken. This is not God's will. I know it.' She looks at me with such pleading. Her skin has taken on a sickly grey sheen and her hair plasters to her damp forehead, like riverweed. 'I know that I am a sinner,' she says. 'I know that I have done you wrong. God has given me this one chance of redemption, this one task to make amends. If I cannot complete it then I do not *deserve* to live.'

I look deep into her eyes, and I see that she believes, absolutely, what she says. Something has happened to her; something beyond my understanding. I feel as though I have been struck a blow to the chest. Whatever this terrible thing is that she has seen, and

wherever it comes from, it is no fantasy. I cannot ignore it. If I
have doubted her before, I do not now.

'Who else will help me?' she whispers. 'You are so much better
than I. You are my only hope . . . my good angel . . .'

'I will help you,' I say. 'Of course I will help you.'

Chapter 35

The next morning I set out early, leaving Lizzie in bed. She is weak and frail and refuses to eat, saying she must remain pure to receive God's message. Nothing I say or do will tempt her. I tend her poor cut wrist, using a little salve to help the healing, and wrapping it with linen so the wound will not open again. I leave her with a chaste kiss on the forehead and a promise that I will do what I can to help her.

Outside the air is chill and the sharpness of the wind on the Thames takes my breath. At Blackfriars Steps I take a wherry upstream. So early in the day it is empty and the boatman whistles an old tune from the days of Queen Bess. It is one I know well: it takes me back to Ely, and the song of the men bringing in the sedge harvest, drifting across the flatlands. My memories carry me out onto the water, back to the Cromwell house, back to Master Oliver.

As we make our way, I watch the river waking up. People board the ferries that cross from bank to bank, patterning the waters in their wake. Barges sail alongside, making the most of the winter winds, taking goods from the docks in the east to the merchants and towns inland, to Abingdon and Oxford.

Here and there, on the north bank, smartly decked boats with liveried boatmen wait to take rich owners from their riverside homes. Behind me, the bridge looms in the mist. Charlotte, ever the lover of macabre gossip, has told me stories of boatmen killed in the currents as they try to shoot the tide between the great stone pillars. It looks ghostly enough now, wrapped in morning mist, like a winding sheet. I'm glad I do not need to travel that way.

The banks are silted, sludgy, like week-old pottage. The sky is flat and grey and the water is full of dead things. Bloated rats and carcasses of mangy dogs bob past, and I pray I will see nothing worse. The river might be the city's lifeblood, but it can also be its graveyard.

Soon we come to a gathering of buildings on the north bank, topped by a hundred red-brick chimneys belching smoke into the clouds. I have arrived at Whitehall.

I have always imagined this palace of kings to be the most splendid of all, but it is almost as ramshackle as the Minories. As I make my way through a maze of alleyways, the place seems a chaos of buildings much like anywhere else in London. The people here go about their business with intent. I pass kitchen-boys, ostlers, gardeners and countless soldiers, but no one stops or questions me. I have to ask for Master Oliver's quarters several times before I find a boy willing to show me the way for a few pennies.

The boy takes me away from the riverbank and we walk through dark-shadowed lanes and along cold stone corridors until I begin to think he is taking me out of the palace altogether, as some sort of trick. But then he shows me into a small room where a clerk broods behind a great wooden desk.

Black-clad men sit lined up on a bench, like crows on the branch of a tree, eyeing me as I approach and ask to see General Cromwell. I'm told to state my name and my business and the clerk makes much work of writing down my answers. He cannot say whether the general will see me and I must wait my turn with the rest.

I perch at the end of the bench. The men stare; one makes sucking noises and blows me foul kisses. But my wait is not a long one and they all gape when my name is called before theirs. A soldier takes me through more doors and corridors and into a large, plush room with high windows. He tells me to sit before the fire.

I have never been in so grand a room before. The ceiling is the height of three men, with swirling plasterwork painted in red and gold. The walls are panelled in richly carved oak. Tapestries of glittering yarn hold images of long-forgotten kings and queens. I long to run my fingers over the shimmering threads. Nothing so fine ever passed through Master Poole's front parlour.

The fireplace is the largest I have ever seen. The mantel is covered with carvings of roses and vines. I notice a witch's mark, scratched into the blackened wood near the floor, a talisman from the old days. There is a good blaze and I choose a chair, then sit and rub my hands together to banish the chill. The horsehair cushion creaks and rustles as I move. I cannot get comfortable. I do not belong in such a place. But there is no time to dwell on this. A door opens at the far end of the room and there is Master Oliver. He comes towards me, smiling, and enfolds my cold hands in his.

'Ruth, it is good to see you again,' he says.

I'm pleased to see that he wears the plain buff coat common among the army men and looks just as he did in Abingdon. There is no change in his bearing, no gold upon his jacket or jewels upon his fingers. His face, always craggy, is perhaps more deeply lined and his nose is reddened, as though it has been bitten by a Fenland gale, or warmed by too much wine, but I'm satisfied that he is not changed in essentials.

I drop into a deep curtsy. 'Sir, thank you for seeing me.'

'Please, sit. Will you breakfast with me?' He beckons a boy and orders bread and cheese.

As we wait, I sit down again on the chair and he stands, rocking on his heels and warming himself before the flames. 'What do you think of the place?' he asks. 'Quite splendid, is it not?'

'Yes, sir.'

'Quite unlike what we are used to.'

'Yes.'

'Do you ever think of our time in Ely? Of the old house and the times we had before all of this?'

'Of course.'

'There were some good times, long ago. Perhaps you were too young to remember.'

The boy enters with a tray of food. He places it on a small table at the fireside.

'I prefer to eat by the hearth,' Master Oliver says. 'Somehow I cannot seem to get warm in this place. The wind whistles in the chimneys so.'

He dismisses the boy and cuts chunks of bread and cheese, filling one pewter plate and passing it to me before filling his own. I have not yet eaten but my stomach is clenched with nerves and the food sits untouched on my lap.

'Are you well?' he asks, taking the seat opposite mine.

'Well enough.'

'Good. And Mistress Poole?'

'She is . . . she is recently bereaved. Her father . . .'

'I'm sorry to hear that. I will pray for him. Is that what brings you back to London?'

'Yes.'

'And your house in Abingdon?'

'Abingdon is finished for us.'

'I see. Is that why you have come?'

I take a deep breath. 'Sir, you have been very kind to me in the past.'

He flaps his hand as though dismissing the idea.

'And you said to Mistress Poole that if we ever needed help we were to come to you.'

'Indeed.'

'I come to you now, sir, to ask for that help. For you were always a kind master to me and I believe you are a good and godly man.'

He puts his plate aside. 'What kind of trouble are you in?'

'None, sir. I come to petition you, as your humble servant, on behalf of Mistress Poole. She has received messages from God. I'm come to you in her stead, to beg that you listen to them.' I'm trembling as I speak.

'Calm yourself,' he says. 'Take a drink. No one will harm you here.'

He studies me as I take a sip from my mug.

'Mistress Poole believes that she is chosen, sir. It is her purpose to speak out. If you listen to her messages, then she may be able to help you, in matters relating to the King.'

'I see. And what form do these messages take?'

'She has visions and dreams of what is to come.'

'I will not lie to you, Ruth. I have heard her name mentioned in certain circles. My good friend and ally General Ireton collects her pamphlets, I believe. He takes a keen interest in such things, keeps a watchful eye on our radical friends. She claims to be a prophet, does she not? She draws attention to herself, I think.'

'She has been blessed with this gift for some time. You will find none other so earnest.'

'Tell me, what is the content of these visions?'

I bow my head, recalling the words now learned by rote. 'God has warned her that the fate of the country is tied to the fate of the King. He has asked her to speak out.'

'In support of the King?'

'To ask for his life, sir. And to warn you of what evil will come to pass if that life is taken. She is to warn you of a terrible fate if God is so displeased, for no good can come of it.'

He stands and moves closer to the fire, hands behind his back. 'I'm going to ask you a question, and be careful what you say, for you know I will not suffer pretenders. Is she truthful?'

The image of Lizzie, naked before the Pendarveses' hearth, eyes glazed with lust, flickers in my mind. I swallow the lump that rises in my throat. 'In this matter, I believe she is.'

He gazes into the flames. 'They say such things in the streets, you know. The agitators still press their arguments. But all must submit to the God-given power of the army. God has brought us here.' He turns to me. 'Tell me, why should I listen to yet another prophet of doom, when I could pick from a hundred more out there on the streets? Why should I question my actions when I am convinced of Divine Providence?'

'Because, sir, you are a man, like any other. And, in the matter of the King, you must have your doubts, just like the rest of us.'

He seems shocked at my boldness. Then he sits, wringing his hands. I notice that his fingers are gnarled and scarred with old wounds.

'You have known me a long time,' he says. 'You knew me when I was but a simple farmer and you have seen me raised, by God's grace, to this seat of power in which I now find myself. I never asked for aught of this. You know that, don't you?'

'Sir, I know you only as a servant knows her master.'

'And yet you see into the very heart of me. You are right that I doubt. These last months I have spent many a night on my knees, praying that God grant me the wisdom and strength to do what must be done. I fear for the future, Ruth. I fear what must be done to secure peace in this country, what must be done in the name of God. All I can ask now is that He grants me the courage to see this thing through to the end. I am His servant, nothing more.'

He is silent then. After a few long minutes, he sits back and takes a swig from his cup. 'I will see your friend,' he says. 'I will send for her when the time is right and we will see what is to be done.'

'Oh, thank you, sir. Thank you.'

He puts up a hand to silence me. 'Do not thank me. I take my guidance from God in this, as in everything.'

'You will find us at Mistress Poole's house at West St Paul's,' I say. 'If you send word, we will be honoured to come whenever suits.'

He nods. 'Indeed, but now you must go. There is much to be done.'

'Of course.' I stand and wrap my cloak around me. 'Sir, I am grateful—'

'There is no need for that between old friends.' Again he takes my hands in his and holds me still for a second. I see sadness in his eyes and I know he is thinking of my mother. 'I am pleased to see you so grown-up,' he says.

My heart warms. It comforts me to know that Master Oliver, a man with such a great burden to bear, still has a care for me. Perhaps there is one person I can rely on after all.

A boy is waiting outside to take me back down the winding corridors and stinking passageways of the palace to the river steps. This time I'm glad to board a boat and set out on the gliding grey waters of the Thames, for it will take me east, home to Lizzie, with good news at last.

Chapter 36

My joy is presumptuous. We hear nothing from Master Oliver for weeks. Christmas comes and goes and January begins in the same way as December ends – with bated breath, the whole world waiting to learn the fate of the King. The trial is set, the commissioners who will sit in judgment are gathered, and the King is brought to Westminster. I begin to think that my visit to Whitehall was in vain.

But a letter comes at last, delivered by hand, stamped with Master Oliver's seal. Lizzie, flushed with excitement, reads it aloud to me.

My dear Madam,

Would you be so good as to attend upon myself and my fellow Commissioners, tomorrow at Westminster Hall. This summons is issued in the understanding that you have received providential visions in matters relating to the trial of Charles Stuart. You have some support among the members of the Army Council, and we would hear what guidance you have for us in this most serious of undertakings.

Oliver Cromwell

Lizzie has what she wants. She will take part in the trial of the King. She hugs me. 'They believe me, Ruth, they believe me!'

'Master Oliver is a good and true man. I knew he would help us.'

'Oh, Ruth, I am to be Parliament's prophet. The whole world will see. Can there be better vindication than this? Just think, if I can help prevent such an awful fate, the whole country will be indebted to me. This cannot fail.'

'If it is God's will . . .'

'Oh, Ruth! It is to you that I owe this. After everything, you have stood by me. You truly are my blessing, my own angel.'

Joseph was right. It seems I do have the ear of the most powerful man in the country. I am pleased by this, and glad that Lizzie has what she wants, but somehow I cannot share in her celebration. The anxiety that makes my stomach churn and my heart beat that little bit faster stays with me all that day and into the next.

And so it is as God's messenger that Lizzie attends Westminster the next day. Of course, I go with her. We will never be parted. And, indeed, she squeezes my hand as if she will never let go.

Westminster is the centre of the world now and it seems that half the world is here. The public galleries in the Great Hall are full to bursting with people hoping for a glimpse of the King. They will be disappointed, for today's court is a private one, held in the Painted Chamber and the King will not attend. Lizzie is not to have the audience she longs for.

After a long wait, we are shown into a grand room with a high, carved ceiling and whitewashed walls, hung with tapestries. At one end of the room, a great flock of judges makes up the Commission, every head crowned with a tall black hat. Word is that it has taken bribery and threats to persuade these men to sit in judgment upon their king. I am not surprised – I would not wish such responsibility on the worst of them. I find Master Oliver's face among them and try to catch his eye. I wish I could thank him for keeping his word to me, but he is deep in conversation with the man next to him. I draw courage from the fact that he is here, and try to still my nerves.

In front of the Commission, two men sit behind a desk. One wears a thick red robe and leather hat with a band of iron. This must be Bradshaw, president of the High Court, whose name is on the lips of every gossipmonger in the town. The other, then, is Cooke, the solicitor, who is already made famous in the public galleries for his addresses to the King these last two days.

'Mistress Poole, please step forward.' Cooke sweeps his hand in a half-bow.

As Lizzie obeys she lets go of my hand and I have to stop myself bleating and reaching out to her, like a frightened child. She stands before the table. She looks so pale, with round spots of high colour where the blush rises. The thick layers of clothing that I have insisted upon have gone some way to padding out her thin body, but nothing can disguise the spindly bones of her hands or the slice of her cheekbones where once her face was plump. Standing opposite Bradshaw, who is seated like a lord on a red velvet chair, she looks as if she is the one on trial.

In that moment I care nothing for our quarrels; the pain she has caused me falls away. I feel nothing but love for her. My own cheeks burn and my skin prickles with nerves. I look to Master Oliver for reassurance, but he is staring intently at Lizzie.

Cooke addresses the room. 'This woman claims to be the recipient of diverse visions and messages regarding the outcome of this trial. She wishes to recount these visions before the Commission as the Word of God, which is within her.'

I notice several of the judges frown. Bradshaw shows no reaction but inclines his head in assent.

Cooke turns to Lizzie. 'Mistress Poole, you may begin.'

Lizzie lifts her head. I can see the blood coursing in the vein at her neck, and I know that her heart is pounding along with my own, but when she speaks, her voice does not betray it.

'Good sirs, I am here to deliver a message from God Almighty,' she says. 'I am a humble woman, weak in body and in mind. But it is that very weakness that keeps me near to Him. I do not come to tell you what is right or wrong, for nothing can determine that save your own consciences, but ask only that you listen to His humble servant, that I might be a vessel for His Word. Sirs, although you may find Charles Stuart guilty of tyranny and treason against his people, you must let him live.'

I'm impressed by the strength and surety in her voice.

'God would have me warn you that the death of the King would bring a great downfall for those who would wield the power in this country. A time of great suffering and retribution will follow, a time of boundless sin and devilry, unlike any we have seen before.'

A man in the stalls behind me mutters, 'Superstition and nonsense. What has this to do with the law?'

'I put it to you,' Lizzie goes on, 'that the King has care of his people, as a husband has care of his wife. We have bowed down to him and trusted him as our lord and protector, as a wife will obey her husband. It is true that Charles Stuart has broken these bonds of duty, and has betrayed his people, who entrusted him with their safekeeping. Indeed, any man might betray his wife in sin. But I never did hear that a wife might rise up against a betraying husband and cut off his head.'

A ripple of amusement runs through the men on the bench. There is spluttering and sniggering in the stalls behind me.

'A godly wife would do best to pray that her husband may see the error in his ways and forsake his sin. In that same way, I say that we subjects have no right to break away from our half of the contract, and take this betrayer's life, any more than a wife has that right over her betraying husband. We must rely on

God and pray that He will deliver us safely and without more bloodshed.'

She pauses, swaying gently. I pray she will withstand, for if she faints now, it will be the end of her chance to be heard.

'Mistress Poole,' Cooke says. 'You spoke of a vision of what will happen, should the King be put to death for his crimes.'

'Yes.'

'Pray tell us about that.'

'The message I bring is this. The King is treasonous in his actions against his subjects, but that does not give you the right to take his life and set another in his place. You make yourselves the same as him by such an act. You will replace one kind of tyrant with another. And then there will be nothing but discontent and suffering among the people.'

The great black body of the Commission stirs as the men turn to one another, shifting in their seats. Someone cries out, 'This is nothing more than sedition!' He is hushed by those around him.

'Mistress Poole,' Bradshaw says. 'We do not meet here to listen to rantings of a radical bent, but to determine the matter in hand, your communion with Our Lord. I ask that you leave your political leanings outside this room, and if you have nothing more to say, kindly leave us, that we may move on.'

'I am His humble servant,' Lizzie says, raising her voice, 'and I come to you as only that, and nothing more. I speak for no one but God. I implore you to look deep into your hearts and know the truth. If you kill the King, you will be nothing more than traitors yourselves. And all traitors will meet the same fate in the end. All traitors will have a place in Hell . . .' Her voice wavers. I will her to hold back her tears. These men will not suffer a weeping woman.

'Mistress Poole,' Bradshaw fails to hide the irritation in his voice, 'it seems your message is founded in nothing more than the malicious accusations to be heard on every street corner from here to Smithfield. This court does not have the liberty to indulge false prophets. Are your words truly the result of a divine intervention or are these opinions merely your own?'

Lizzie does not hesitate. 'Both, sir. They are both!'

The commissioners erupt into a sea of catcalls and eye-rolling. But Bradshaw looks grim. He shakes his head. 'Take her away,' he says. 'I will hear no more of this.'

Two guards step forward and take Lizzie by each arm, as though she is a prisoner. She shrugs them off. Still she is defiant. 'You will suffer for this, sirs! You will all burn for this!'

As I follow Lizzie to the door, I look for Master Oliver. Surely he will defend us now. But I cannot find his face among those on the bench.

Chapter 37

Benjamin brings us the news two days later. Charles Stuart, the man who was our king, is named a traitor. He is to have a traitor's death. They will cut off his head.

Lizzie, who has neither eaten nor slept since her shaming in the Painted Chamber, blanches as he tells us. Her legs give out and she drops to the floor, like a puppet with severed strings. The papers she has been working on fan around her on the floorboards. Benjamin gathers them up while I cradle her and call for Charlotte's help.

Charlotte and I struggle to help her to her bed.

'Mistress Poole,' Benjamin calls, as we take her from the room, 'are these ready for the press?'

For an instant Lizzie seems to wake from her trance and fixes him with a look of intent. 'Yes, Benjamin. You know what to do.'

The crowd is massed at Whitehall, every man, woman and child waiting to witness the death of their king. The press of bodies cannot warm the January chill and breath steams and curls above people's heads like smoke, as if they have fire burning in their bellies.

Sal and I press onward, weaving our way between merchants, servants, apprentices and the filthy poor. It seems that the whole of London is here; rank and file do not matter today. The fine clothes of the wealthy rub up against the stench of beggars' rags.

Apprentices stand shoulder to shoulder with their masters. Hucksters ply their wares from stalls set up outside the alehouses to well-dressed ladies.

Today the natural order of things is turned upside down. It has taken the death of a king to do it.

I have seen my share of public executions: condemned men hanged in the market square at Ely, processions of the damned making their way along Cheapside from Newgate to Tyburn. And I was witness to another, more lawless death, only too close at hand. In all those cases, the crowd was ugly, chisel-faced and flint-eyed, baying for blood. But there is none of that here. Even those who want the King dead, even those who despise him as the cause of so much bloodshed and suffering, even they dare not raise their voices now.

There are groups of men deep in discussion, some in prayer. Here and there a lay preacher speaks words of hope to a makeshift flock. There is no jesting or jostling, no banter and no laughter. People do not even complain when Sal pushes our way to a spot near the Banqueting House, where a scaffold has been put up overnight.

The wooden structure is draped in black cloth and protected by a wall of grim-faced soldiers. Behind it, with high glazed windows and white columns, the Banqueting House sits proud and splendid, like a palace from a fable, amid the tumbledown squalor of Whitehall. It is like a great block of ice, the glass in the casements reflecting back a pale winter sun. Today makes a mockery of the power and wealth of the kings who built it. Behind the windows, I can make out row upon row of snowy lace collars and tall black hats. These are the men who hold that power now.

Already the pamphleteers are at work. Sal refuses them again and again. She catches me looking at her in puzzlement.

'Not yet,' she says, keeping her voice low so only I can hear.

'Today is the end of the old world,' I say. 'I thought you and the twins looked forward to the new.'

She shrugs. 'A king dies today. No matter how many people tell me it is necessary, no matter what has happened in the past, it's just that in here . . .' she puts her hand to her heart '. . . I cannot make it right.'

I know what she means. It is for the same reason that Lizzie cannot rise from her bed these past three days, the same reason that she bade me come here and see the thing with my own eyes, and carry the details of it back to her. Even now it is hard to imagine that the years of the old order can ever be undone, that England really can be made new. Even after all the fighting and all the death, there is still doubt. I must see this thing done in order to believe it.

I think of Master Oliver and his admission to me in that fine room at Whitehall Palace. He believes that God has brought us here, but even he has doubts, even the very man whom people say is responsible. I wonder if he is sure of his actions now. I will not believe it is all due to him. The man I know is not a cold-hearted killer.

We wait for some time and rumour of a reprieve starts to circulate. Some say that Parliament is meeting to overturn the verdict. The crowd shuffle and sway, losing patience, limbs aching from standing so long, and I have to cling to Sal's arm to keep from losing her in the crush.

But then there is a commotion inside the Banqueting Hall. People turn and crane their necks. Two men step out onto the platform, dressed entirely in black, hooded, faces hidden. One carries a long sword that glints as though it has been polished, as though it has never seen blood before. Following them come two soldiers and the King's chaplain. The crowd falls silent, all faces upturned. After a moment's pause, Charles Stuart steps out onto the scaffold, blinking against the afternoon light.

He looks nothing more than a frail old man, with a thin grey face. Can this be the great tyrant? Can this be the man of blood who cares only for his own power and greed and wealth? For a moment I think I must be mistaken and that the terrifying figure of the King is yet to come, but people about me are bowing their heads and he is coming forward to address the crowds.

I strain to hear his words, but the breeze buffets them away.

The black drapes hide the block, but I watch as the King removes his cloak and hat and insignia and hands them to his chaplain. He is given a small cap and puts it on, tucking his hair inside as though he wishes to save it from the sword. Then he turns and addresses the executioner.

I feel as though I'm watching a stage play, as though the scene before me cannot possibly be real. I glance about me to catch the laughter in people's faces, to understand the joke, but there is none. I cannot believe that this man has held the fate of the country in his hands, that this man has set brother against brother and brought us to the very edge of Hell, that this man is anything more than just that. He may be proud, he may be flawed, but he is still just a man, with a life that can be taken by the fall of a sword. He is not so different from Master Oliver.

The King speaks and the crowd waits silently, his words snatched away by the wind. I notice a tiny glimmer beside his cheek. A small pearl earring hangs there, gleaming in the light, a fragment of glamour remaining.

Then he puts his hands together in prayer and lowers himself to the block and out of view.

The hooded man steps forward. Seconds run by and I hold my breath. The executioner raises his sword and brings it down in one hard, sharp swipe. Then he stoops and lifts up the head of the dead man. He holds it at arm's length and shows it to the crowd.

'Behold the head of a traitor!' he cries.

There are no cheers, no celebrations, bells do not ring out. Instead, the sound that comes from the crowd is deep and resounding, a primal moan of despair. It is a sound I know well. It is the sound that Esther Tuttle made when she birthed her cursed offspring. It is the sound that welled up inside me as I watched my mother's body turn and twist beneath the branches of the willow tree. It is the sound that Lizzie made when she learned of her father's death. It is horror. It is grief. That is what I hear now, as the black-hooded man holds up the head of Charles Stuart and lets the blood drip upon the scaffold.

Moments later the crowd begins to shift and swell. Those at the front rush the soldiers, desperate to be closer to the platform, holding out rags to catch any royal blood that might spill between the planks. There are sudden cries from all quarters, 'God save the King!' and, in answer, 'Let the tyrant be damned!' Scuffles break out nearby and soldiers draw their swords.

I am mesmerised, head spinning.

'Come!' Sal pulls at my arm. 'We've seen enough blood for one day.'

We try to push through the crowd, away from the scaffold, but the press of people is too dense. The silent spell is broken: people shout and shove.

Next to us a man yells, 'The tyrant is dead!'

His companion tugs at his sleeve. 'And, look, here comes another . . .'

I turn to where he points, back towards the Hall, and see a small group of army men upon the scaffold. Among them I think I glimpse the crumpled face of my old master.

'A tyrant and a traitor!' Sal says. She pulls a sheaf of pamphlets from her satchel and presses one into the hand of the man. 'Oliver Cromwell is the true traitor!' she cries. 'A traitor to God! A traitor to us all!' She hands out the papers to those around her.

I catch her arm. 'Sal, what are you doing?'

'What I must,' she says. She clambers onto a nearby barrel to raise herself above the heads of the crowd. 'Listen! Listen all of you! Oliver Cromwell has killed a king so he can put himself on the throne in his place. He uses the word of God to fool us all. He says this is God's work, but it is the work of plotters and schemers who want power and riches for themselves. He promised us a new England. Where is that promise now? Is this what we fought for? Is this what our loved ones died for? For Oliver Cromwell to betray us all? Read the truth – read it here!' She hands out pamphlets to eager hands in the crowd.

I snatch one from her. I need hardly read the words to prove what I already know in my heart. These words are not Sal's. They are not even the twins'.

There it is, as bold as anything: her name upon the page.

Oh, Lizzie. What have you done?

I leave Sal ranting her accusations at Master Oliver and the Army Council, doling out Lizzie's pamphlet to anyone with a mind to read. I push my way through the crowd, jabbed and jostled, the world a blur of elbows and fists. The air is thick with fury, as if the stinking coal smoke is poisoned with it. I cover my face with my shawl and take shallow breaths; I have enough anger brewing in me already.

Yet again, I'm astonished, and hurt, by Lizzie's duplicity. How dare she speak out against Master Oliver when he has been so good to us? He has singled her out, giving her the chance to be heard, when so many voices like hers are ignored or ridiculed. He could not have foreseen the shameful outcome. He could not have known that those men would not listen. He gave her what she asked for and now she sullies his generosity with slander. I know her well enough to understand that this is her means of revenge. I must get away from here. I must see how to limit the damage she has done.

I'm deep in my own thoughts, trying to make my way through the rabble, when someone grabs at my arm. Thinking it a beggar or a cutpurse, I pull away, but strong fingers dig deeper and then I hear my name. I falter as I recognise his voice. My heart tilts. I know it's him before I turn. I know it because I have been dreading this meeting for weeks.

Since the day Joseph told me his awful secret, I have imagined this moment. I have run it through in my mind over and over, planning to spurn him, this man who is dead to me. I would not give him so much as a word or a nod. I would turn my back and walk away, and he would never know how it pained me to do so. But here, in this place, with the world gone half mad about me, I have no such composure. The corruption that poisons the air fills every part of me, simmering under my skin, until I don't know whether to rage or to cry.

I spin to face him, Lizzie's pamphlet aloft. 'Did you know about this?'

Joseph takes the crumpled paper from me. 'Not until today.'

He glances behind him. I follow his gaze and see the twins, Benjamin and Charlie, a few steps away. Just like Sal they have packs strapped across their chests, and are handing out pamphlets to the crowd. Like Sal, they are fired up with sedition, eyes wild, cheeks flushed.

'I think they're making a mistake,' Joseph says. 'It's not a good time to make enemies.' He looks back over the crowd, towards the scaffold.

'Can you not stop them?' I say.

'It's not my place. They are their own men.'

I snatch the pamphlet back from him and turn on my heel.

I fight my way up Whitehall, away from the Banqueting House.

'Ruth, wait!'

I am pulsing with fury, fighting back tears. I don't want to speak to him, or even look at him, but he keeps pace by my side.

'I know you don't want to see me, but I am glad to see you,' he says. 'I must speak with you, alone.'

'Leave me be.'

'There is something I must show you . . . something you will want to see.'

'I have seen enough today.'

'Please, Ruth, you must trust me.'

At this I want to spit at his feet, right there in the street, like some godless wilding.

'I promise you will want to see this,' he says, catching at my sleeve.

I slow, curiosity piqued despite myself, but still I refuse to meet his eye. 'What is it?'

'Come away from here,' he says, tugging my arm and leading me into a side-street, until we find a place where the crowd has thinned. He stops before a tavern. The door is closed and barred, a lone man sitting on the sill, quietly weeping. Close by, three whispering women huddle, subdued children about their feet. Two lads hurtle past, armed with fire-stokers, boots splashing in the wet street drain. The air rings with the shouts of the Whitehall crowd, the tolling of a single church bell.

Joseph fishes inside his jacket and brings out another pamphlet. He hands it to me. 'I found this a few days ago. I knew if I came to West St Paul's you would not see me, but I think you are meant to have it.'

It is an account of the trial and hanging of one Michael Mitchell, who met his end at Tyburn not a month since. On the frontispiece, under the lettering of the title, a crude black figure dangles from the gallows, tongue lolling. Such stories make common fodder for the presses, feeding the clamour in St Paul's Churchyard for scandal and horror. I have seen dozens of the like in Lizzie's hands.

'What do I want with this?' I say.

'Read it . . . here.' He points. 'The second page.'

Although I'm desperate to be away from him, I glance at the type: . . . *Mitchell, a man of such evil wrongdoings, having led a life of sin and devilry, brought to justice at last by the grace of Our Lord* . . .

'This has nothing to do with me,' I say. 'I don't know this man.'

I hold out the paper for him to take it. He does not, so I let it fall into the dirt. I curse myself for allowing him to persuade me here.

Immediately he rescues the paper from the mud. 'For God's sake, Ruth, just read it.'

I hesitate, wanting to walk away, afraid of what might happen if I stay, but my feet will not do as I bid them. I take the paper and read.

At an inn on the Portsmouth Road in the month of September, the villain did engage in acts of violence against one Isaac Tuttle, a vagabond known thereabouts for his drinking and lewdness, and did use a blade against that same man Isaac Tuttle, inflicting grievous wounds until his victim fell to the floor with bleeding and was taken from this earth.

All my reason is taken away. My legs give out beneath me and I sink to the ground, gaping like a lunatic. My stays feel unbearably tight and I cannot breathe. At the same time I feel the world shrink about me. I am back there again, on the banks of the Ouse, watching a body swing beneath the boughs of a willow tree. But this time it is not my mother whose limbs are cut and bleeding, it is not my mother whose face is twisted in a death mask. It is Isaac Tuttle.

Joseph's arm comes round my shoulders, supporting me, stopping me sinking further into the shit and piss of the street drain.

'Can it be true? Is it him?'

'I believe so.'

I grasp at Joseph's jacket, pulling him close. 'I must know for certain.'

'I went to the courthouse and found out the lawyer who took the case against this man, Mitchell. He could not tell me much, but he did know that Mitchell's victim, this Isaac Tuttle, was indeed a Fenlander.' He nods. 'I think it must be him.'

Suddenly I cannot control my breathing. It comes in great shuddering, spluttering gasps, as though I'm drowning in the air. Strange strangled cries erupt from my throat. I paw at Joseph's chest, like an animal. He wraps his arms around me and rocks me back and forth as my body is racked with sobs.

This is not weeping for sorrow, for how can I mourn that man? Nor is it weeping for joy, for there is no gladness in my heart. It is as though I am taken over with all the ills and horrors of the world. Perhaps I should be grateful to have the vengeance that I have so longed for, but now, on this day, I feel as though God has abandoned us all. Death himself broods over London like a storm cloud, and he will not let me be.

When my tears have lessened, Joseph puts his hand on mine. 'Come, you cannot sit here in this muck.'

My mind reels and I doubt I have the strength to stand. My limbs feel numb and I shiver as the cold takes its grip. But with Joseph's arms about me, I struggle to my feet.

'I thought you should know,' he says. I have dropped the pamphlet and he bends down to retrieve it from the mud. He holds it out to me.

I shake my head. I want never to see Isaac Tuttle's name again. 'No. The knowing is enough.'

Joseph nods, as though he understands. He puts the paper into his pocket and stares at me. His eyes are black; black with sorrow, black with guilt. But I have no patience with his turmoil when I am consumed by my own. I am shaking, the chill eating into my bones.

'I . . . I must go . . .'

'Let me take you somewhere safe,' he says.

'No – I must go to Lizzie . . . and do not follow me. I'm grateful for this knowledge, but it changes nothing. Please, do not speak to me again.'

'You need to be with someone who can help you. *She* cannot help you.'

'I don't need your help.'

'Ruth, please. You've suffered a great shock today.'

'So has all of London.'

I walk away, leaving him standing there alone, palms outstretched like those of a stone statue.

Chapter 38

By the time I reach West St Paul's I have recovered myself. My eyes are red and sore with crying, and I have a sense of the unreal, as though I see the world in reflection, but my anger with Lizzie still burns, driving me on. I find her in bed, wrapped up in blankets and talking quietly with Margaret. In my fury I am unable to check myself. I rush in and throw her pamphlet upon the bed. 'How could you do this?'

Margaret is shocked. 'Ruth?'

'It's all right, Margaret.' Lizzie is calm, measured. 'Leave us awhile, would you? Ask Charlotte to fetch us a posset. I've a hankering for one.'

Margaret looks pleased. This is the first thing Lizzie has asked for in days.

'I'll fetch it myself. That girl is nowhere to be found today.'

She leaves us, throwing me a warning glance over her shoulder. But I don't care. She understands nothing. She knows nothing.

'How could you do this?' I ask again. 'When he has been so good to us?'

'So good indeed . . .'

'Do you know that Sal is out there this very moment, spreading these lies to anyone who will listen? And Benjamin and Charlie are doing the same. This is nothing more than dangerous deceit. You will bring trouble down upon all our heads.'

'Calm yourself. What does it matter? People are already saying such things. The printers' boys will be hawking a hundred of the same by morning.'

'It has your name on it, Lizzie – your name! What do you think will happen when he sees it?'

She picks up the pamphlet and flattens it. 'You think this is lies?' she says, her eyes hard.

'You accuse Master Oliver of treachery. You say he is a traitor to God, to the people. How can you say such a thing of the man who keeps you housed and fed? Or have you forgotten that we live by his charity now?'

'Listen to yourself. You are living in a falsehood, Ruth, living in a memory. You do not understand the man he really is.'

'I know him better than you. I have known him all my life.'

'And do you like what he has done to me?'

'What do you mean?'

'You think he really wanted me at the trial? You think he really meant to listen to what I had to say?'

'Of course. That is why I went to him. Why else would he ask you there?'

'To discredit my cause. To shame me and cast me out, so that everyone will think me a fool, a charlatan, a holy whore. As I stood in that court, it all came clear to me. He knew those men would give no credence to a woman, and he wanted me silenced, along with any other who would speak out for the life of the King.'

'That is nonsense. I won't believe it.'

'I'm just one of the voices he seeks to suppress. There will be more. You'll see. This is not over. Today he silenced a king. Well, this is just the beginning.'

I shake my head. 'You are wrong. He wants peace, just like the rest of us. He told me so.'

'But at what cost?'

'We depend upon him, Lizzie – this house, our food, wages

for Margaret and Charlotte. Everything comes from my pocket now, and that money comes from him. You have jeopardised everything!'

'What care I for that? I would rather starve on the street than take money from a traitor.'

'It may come to that. Would you take us all down with you?' I feel tears welling. 'I cannot go back to that life. I cannot.'

'Calm yourself, my love. It is done and I cannot take it back.' She smiles and smoothes the coverlet next to her. 'Come here.'

I sit upon the edge of the bed. 'Why? Even if you think these things, why must you do this? Why make yourself his enemy?'

'I have no choice. It is God's will.'

'That is exactly what Master Oliver said.'

'And only one of us can be right, I suppose,' she says. 'Which one of us will you choose?'

Margaret returns with a posset and a dish of curd-cakes. She puts them down next to the bed.

'Ruth, a word, if you will,' she says.

I follow her to the threshold.

'She's weak,' she says. 'There is something in her now that reminds me of her mother during her times of great sickness. I've seen well enough what she did to herself . . .' Margaret's hand wanders to her own wrist, as though she is imagining what might have been, what might still be. I have never seen her look so worried. 'There's no one can cheer her, except you. I will see to it that you are left alone. Please . . . she needs your kindness now.'

I go back to Lizzie, and Margaret closes the door, shutting out the world. I light the candle in silence.

'Let us not fight,' Lizzie says. 'Not tonight.' She takes my hand and squeezes it. 'We must hold fast to each other now, no matter what.'

I sigh and nod. I am angry with her, but she is right. In a world of uncertainty, we must cleave to what we know. Besides, I made a promise to stay by her side, and I still mean to keep it.

'Tell me, did the King make a good death?'

'Yes.'

'Was it clean and quick?'

'Yes.'

'Did the people mourn?'

'Some.'

'Then I can only pray that my end will match it.'

'Lizzie, you cannot really believe that the King's death has any bearing on your own. There is no reason for it.'

'But I know it is so.'

'How?'

She shrugs. 'Let us not talk of it. Just be with me. I don't want to be alone tonight. I want things to be as they once were, in Abingdon.'

How I long for that too. I wish with all my heart that we could be back there now, collecting posies in the woods, laughing in the sunshine, wrapped up in nothing but each other, safe and content in a world of our own making. How simple things were before others ruined it. I want to cast out all thoughts of the day and lose myself in our shared memories. I'm suddenly exhausted. I do not want to think of the dead King, or Thomasine, or Joseph, or even Isaac Tuttle. I want to escape back to that blessed time, when all I needed to make me happy was Lizzie's hand in mine.

Lizzie reaches out and gently strokes my head. 'Take off your cap and comb out your hair.'

She has not looked at me so for months. I feel the familiar quickening dawn in me, like the traces of a dream. I do as she says. Then I unfasten my stays. As I undress, I feel her eyes on me and the warm, flooding river inside me begins to ebb and flow.

We lie face to face. Her fingers creep to my lips. By the light of the single candle, her eyes glitter, reflecting the flame. Her cheeks are flushed. Her lips part and she slicks them with the tip of her tongue. 'Will you kiss me?' she whispers.

I answer by leaning in close and touching my mouth to hers. Despite my betrayed heart, she still holds such power over me that my body wakes in an instant. I kiss her face, her eyelids and her neck. I bury my face in her hair, breathing in the smell of her. Her arms come round me and she pulls me so close I can barely breathe. I am so glad to hold her again that tears threaten. She kisses them away and whispers, 'I know . . . I know . . .'

The pleasure we take in one another that night is unlike any time before. It is forgiveness for all our sins and faults and arguments. I put all guilt and resentment from my mind and feel only the sweet sense of belonging that I have always craved and striven to find with her. It is like coming home.

Lizzie has a sadness about her that makes her tender and slow, her fingers gentle on my body and her eyes holding mine. Even in her starved and weakened state, she is beautiful to me – she will never be otherwise – but her body is changed. Her ribs jut and her skin feels papery thin. Her breasts, never large, are half full, nipples drooping like pale berries. Where there was once smooth flesh, there are dips and hollows. I untie the linen bandage at her wrist and kiss the wound there, as though my lips can kiss away all trace of past hurts.

As we lie together, I know that the bond between us is still strong, and that our love cannot be destroyed by anyone but God. It is not the same love as before: it is no longer simple or untainted. Now, as she loves me, I yearn for the innocence that is for ever lost. But there is still pleasure, there is still such tenderness, and Lizzie's eyes say the things that her lips cannot.

★ ★ ★

We are woken before dawn by noises in the street. There is a loud rapping at the front door and a gruff voice calls, 'Open up! Open up!'

It is dark in the bedroom, the candle long since sputtered out, and I sit bolt upright, eyes straining in the gloom.

'What is it?'

Lizzie is awake.

'Someone at the door.'

The knocking sounds again.

'Open up, or we shall enter by force!'

As I struggle into my shift, I hear the roll of Margaret's step on the stairs. I hear the bolts slide back, then muffled conversation.

Lizzie clutches at the bedclothes to cover herself. I grab her chemise, from where I tossed it to the floor, and throw it to her. 'Get dressed.'

But there is no time: heavy footfalls thunder upon the stairs.

The door of the bedroom flies open. I am momentarily blinded by the glow of a lantern and the shine of a sharp sword. Four men, dressed in the colours of the local Watch, come into the room, sniffing the air like dogs. The one with the lantern is the captain. He thrusts the light into the hands of one of his men and comes towards me, touching the point of his sword to my belly.

'Are you Elizabeth Poole?'

I shake my head.

'Ruth Flowers?'

I choke on my answer.

'Are they the ones?' He turns to address a figure in the doorway. In the cast of the lantern, I see that Charlotte has returned. She nods meekly.

He turns his sword back to me, catching my shift and tearing it at the shoulder. He looks from me to Lizzie, who cowers on the bed.

'As if we need more proof than this,' he says. 'Take them both.'

His men move across the room and suddenly my arms are twisted behind my back, a pistol pointing at my face.

'What is this?' I say, gathering my senses. 'What right have you to come here? This is our house.'

Lizzie cries out as she is dragged from the bed and hurled to the floor. The men are rough with her and she crumples at my feet, a sprawling tangle of skinny limbs and fiery hair. She looks at the captain, anger blazing. 'With what charges are you come here? Who sends you? Tell us or leave this house now.' She struggles to her feet and stands tall next to me. The men, hesitant to touch her nakedness, keep their hands off her. I see her skin pucker into goose bumps. 'We have friends,' she says, 'and when they hear of this, you will fear for your life.'

The captain turns his blade on her, setting it to her neck. Slowly, he moves it downwards, the tip pressing the skin between her breasts and the hollow of her belly until it rests on her navel. It leaves a white trail where it scratches that quickly turns red.

'Your friends will not be able to help where you are going . . . witch.' He lands a hawk of spittle at her feet. 'You and your whore.'

He makes for the door. 'Cover them, bind them, and bring them down.' He points to one of the men. 'You, search the house. Bring anything that might be proof.'

The men throw clothes towards us and we pull our dresses on, with pistols at our backs. I hear Margaret shrieking downstairs as she argues with the captain. By the time we are bundled to the door, shoeless, our mouths stopped with hard leather bits, she is on her knees in the street, wailing and pleading, 'Do not take her, sir! Please, do not take her!'

We are put into a closed cart that waits outside. Lizzie and I both strain to reach the tiny barred window, just in time to see Margaret collapse in the dirt as we are taken away.

Charlotte, it seems, has disappeared into the night.

Part Five

London
February 1649

Chapter 39

Newgate Prison lies only a short distance from West St Paul's, but I have never felt so far from home. It is an unholy place, plagued by damp, chill winds that come off the river. In the cells, ancient stone walls drip with centuries of moss and mould. When it rains, the floor floods with drain waste and rats search for dry islands among the sewage. The air is foetid. Death is carried on the draught. Gaol fever takes lives every day.

The inmates are debtors mostly, and dissidents – forgotten remnants of the war, left here to rot. Among the women there are prostitutes and beggars, murderesses and cutpurses. There are those who have broken the new laws on maypoles and merry-making, or are shut away for cursing or licentiousness. There are those poor wretches who have cut the throats of their own babes to keep them from the pain of hunger, turning over their care to God. There are false prophets and radical preachers who speak out against the new rule. And then there are those who put fear into even the basest criminal: those covenanted with the Devil, no longer quite human but half-women, capable of anything. I speak of the witches, of which I am one. Or so I stand accused.

For two weeks I have been shut up here, counting the days by the thin light that filters down from the one small window, set deep in the thick walls. There is no glass or covering at the bars and at night the wind howls like a crying child.

I am barefoot and filthy, the very picture of what they would make me. I have no shawl or cloak, nothing but the dress in which I arrived. At night, we must all press together for heat. I must make new friends among the whores and thieves for, alone in this place, I will die. Not three nights since, a woman sat alone, afraid of contagion, and when we awoke she was stiff, blue and beyond our help.

I am given food once a day. A mean portion of bread is all that reaches me from whatever Margaret leaves at the gatehouse, after the gaoler has had his pickings. The flesh is already falling from my bones and I cannot bear to think how Lizzie does in this place. I have not been allowed to see or speak to her since we were brought in.

When I arrived, I shouted and screamed for her, but the keeper put the bit on me and threatened me with beatings. I spent three days unable to eat or sleep with the foul leather thing strapped into my mouth and my hands tied so hard they turned numb and blue. I have been still and silent since.

In the third week the keeper comes to me. He ties my hands with rough rope, gags me with a blackened rag and leads me from the dungeon room, along corridors and up winding staircases until we reach an upper floor. Here are the cells and apartments where the wealthier inmates live – men who can pay their way into the gaoler's favour. The air is cleaner and, although it is still icy, no fire lit in the whole place, I gulp deep breaths, clearing the stench of decay from my nostrils.

He takes me to a large cell, with high, barred windows, where two women and a gentleman wait.

'Here she is, Master Ponder.' The keeper addresses the man, holding out his palm.

The man covers it with coin, then waves him away.

By my reckoning, Mason Ponder is about thirty years old, but he has the stature of an old man. He leans heavily on a cane. He limps and holds himself stiffly, as if his twisted body gives him pain. He has flinty eyes and a bitter turn to his mouth that lends his face a sour look beyond his years.

The keeper unties my hands and takes the gag from around my neck.

'If she be any trouble, sir, send for me. There's a boy outside the door to keep the lock for you.' He leaves the room and I hear the key turn.

I look from Ponder to the women. Both avoid my stare. They seem the godly sort, perhaps mother and daughter, dressed primly with their caps tied tight under their chins.

'Do you know why you are here?' Ponder asks, his voice high and wheedling.

I shake my head.

'Do you know of what you are accused?'

I do not answer. After three weeks of starvation and sleeplessness, I do not trust my wits.

'You are brought here to undergo examination. These good women will search you and then you will be watched. Do you understand?'

I have heard stories of women such as these, paid by the witchfinders to seek out the marks of the Devil on women's bodies. Paid by the hour to watch them, allowing them neither food nor sleep, until the Devil's imps come to suckle. The printers' stalls are always full of pamphlets, telling how witches are found out this way.

'But I'm not guilty . . .'

Ponder snorts. 'Then you can have no objection to an examination.'

'Please, sir, it is not needed . . .'

'I shall be the judge of that.'

He moves to the door and raps upon it with his cane.

'Mistress Wheeler, please begin your work. I shall wait outside.'

Once he is gone, the two women look to one another.

The older woman, whom Ponder addressed as Mistress Wheeler, sneers at me, her nose wrinkling. 'Undress,' she orders.

I peel off the clothes that have not left my back in three weeks. Already the damp has eaten into them, turning them to rags. But even this spare covering is better than nothing. The freezing February air bites at me as if it would snap my bones. I shiver and spasm, teeth chattering.

Mistress Wheeler indicates a table that stands to one side of the room. 'Lie down.'

I do as she says, lying naked on the wood. I try to cover myself with my hands but they have me move this way and that as they inspect all parts of me. They bid me spread my legs and pull myself open for them. They hold a candle up close that they might see into my very insides.

I feel like a slab of meat, put out for display in a butcher's shop.

Mostly they are silent, giving little away, nodding and grunting as if they have some secret way of speaking together.

Finally, when they have shamed me enough, they tell me to dress. Back in my rags, I wait for Ponder.

He enters, followed by a fidgety younger man – a clerk, judging by the paper and quill he carries. Ponder raises an eyebrow to the women.

'There is nothing, sir,' Mistress Wheeler says. 'No marks or teats.'

Ponder frowns. 'Are you sure?'

'Yes, sir, as sure as I can be.'

'Then we shall begin the watching at once.'

He bids me stand in the middle of the room, while the women take up their stations on stools by the door. The clerk sits at the table upon which I have just lain, and fusses over his paper and ink.

Ponder paces in a slow circle around me, his stick tapping on the flags, his piercing gaze taking in my body as though he is judging a sow at market.

'You are Ruth Flowers, are you not?'

'I am.'

'And you live with one Elizabeth Poole?'

'I do.'

'This you freely admit?'

'Yes.'

'How did you come to meet Elizabeth Poole?'

'She was my mistress. I was her maidservant.'

'Are you her servant still?'

'No. I have independent means. Master Cromwell—'

'So what are you to one another?'

'We are friends.'

He stops his pacing and studies my face. 'I think you are more than that,' he says.

'What do you mean?'

'Do not play games with me, Ruth. I know what you are.'

His tone makes the hairs bristle on the back of my neck.

'We have evidence against you. We have witnesses. It is well known that you are guilty of grievous sin. Will you not confess it, seek redemption and forgiveness? We know about Elizabeth Poole. We know what she has done. And we know that you are her partner in this despicable, filthy, devilish magic.'

'Magic?'

'Confess it, Ruth. Confess and you may yet find mercy. You were led astray, perhaps. Does she control you with her spells? If you tell us what you know, the Lord may smile on you yet.'

'I know nothing of any spells.'

'Come now, the jury will surely understand how a sweet innocent like yourself could be bewitched by one so plainly evil. You are in thrall to this witch, Elizabeth Poole, are you not?'

'She is not a witch, sir.'

'Then you deny it? You deny that you are a member of her coven? You will protect this – this adulteress, this murderess?'

'Murderess?'

'Do you deny it?' He bangs his fist down hard on the table, making the women jump.

I meet his eye. 'I deny it.'

He begins his pacing again.

'You are proud, I see,' he says. 'But pride will not save you.' He takes off his hat and places it upon the table. 'We searched the house at West St Paul's, and found several items that would indicate your guilt. Among these was a book, a compendium of pagan charms and spells. Among these spells are detailed rituals and instructions that claim to sustain or take away life. Do you not consider that ungodly? Do you not consider that magic?'

'No, sir. They are remedies only.'

'Ah! So you know the book. It was penned by one Annie Flowers. I must assume, by the name, that she is a relation of yours.'

'She was my mother.'

Ponder smiles, his lips peeling back over his teeth in a gargoyle grimace. 'Now we have some truth! And where is your mother?'

'She is dead.'

'How did she die?'

At this I remain mute, despite his probing and prodding. I will give him no help. I will not bring the past into the present. I will guard the story of Annie Flowers for as long as I can: I know it will only condemn me. Eventually he gives up and changes tack.

'Also in your possession was a quantity of coin. Tell me, how does a poor servant such as yourself come by such wealth?'

'I have a benefactor, as I have told you. General Cromwell.'

Ponder laughs. 'Do you hear this, Harding?' he says to the clerk. 'Be sure to note it down. She has the protection of the general himself!'

Harding smirks and scribbles obediently.

'It's true. I grew up in his service and he gave me the money. If you speak with him, he will tell you so.'

'How dare you?' Ponder roars, turning on me. 'How dare you blacken the general's name with such claims? Impudent, sluttish wench!'

'If you will speak with him – please . . .' My strength gives out and my knees buckle beneath me.

'Stand up, girl!' Ponder swipes at me with his stick.

I struggle to stand, but my feet are so numb from the cold that they will not hold me. I begin to sob with frustration, thin, stringy mucus dripping from my nose.

The younger of the two watcher-women, who has not spoken a single word till now, drags a stool to the centre of the room. 'She does not have the strength to stand, sir,' she says softly. 'Let her rest and she will more likely have the wherewithal to call her imps to her when the time comes.'

'Thank you, Grace,' Ponder says, and raps the seat with his cane. 'Sit.'

I pull myself onto the stool and look over to the young woman to thank her. Her eyes are fixed on the floor. She is expressionless, her hands neatly folded, chewing her lip.

Ponder takes up his hat and beckons to Harding. 'Very well. Let the watching begin.' He jabs me in the ribs with his cane and hisses, 'I will find you out . . . Devil's child.'

He leaves me imprisoned with the watcher-women.

For the rest of that day, and the whole of the next, I am kept in the cell, without bread or even a drop of water. The two women, Grace and Mistress Wheeler, keep watch over me day and night, taking turns to sleep upon a lousy straw mattress. They have rest and regular meals while I have neither.

At first I'm glad to be away from the stinking dungeon, but

without the warmth of other bodies, and my meagre serving of bread, I soon long to be back there.

My mouth is dry and my tongue feels large and rough. My lips crack and begin to bleed. My stomach gnaws with a pain so great that every inch of my body aches with it. But the worst thing is the wakefulness. Whenever my head hangs low upon my chest and my eyelids slide shut, one of the women shakes me, or forces me to walk about the room with her, so that it is impossible to rest.

Ponder visits several times, sitting and rapping his cane against the flags in a rhythm that drives me wild with agitation.

By sunset on the second day, things start to change: the gnawing in my stomach disappears and instead I feel nothingness there, as though the middle part of me does not exist. I am hollow, empty.

I begin to have waking dreams. I see an army of rats scurry across the floor where there are none. I see the beer that the watchers sup glitter and sparkle like cupfuls of jewels. I see a great black cloud, buzzing with flies, sitting above Ponder's head and following him about the room. And once, just once, I see a golden light, hovering high in a corner. I am convinced that this light has sense and reason. Goodness pulses from it. I believe it is the spirit of my mother, who has come to give me strength.

I say nothing of these things. I say nothing at all. I don't know what is expected of me so I cannot give it. Fear keeps me sane, dragging me back again and again to wakefulness and clarity whenever my mind begins to slip. But some time near dawn on the third morning, my body will take no more and I fall, like a helpless babe, from the stool onto the floor.

Grace is awake and watching and is by my side in an instant. She fixes her arms under mine and hauls me up until I'm sitting with my useless legs tangled beneath me. I think she will make me stand and walk with her, but instead she fetches her cup of ale and holds it to my lips. She darts quick looks at Mistress Wheeler, who lies snoring upon the mattress.

I drink as much as I can, panting and snorting in my desperate greed.

'Can you eat?' Grace says.

I nod. She goes to her own plate and brings back a hunk of bread. It is dry and turning stale but I don't care. My tongue is so swollen that I can hardly get it down, so I nibble at it, taking gulps of beer, until it is all gone.

Grace watches me with her brow creased. As she takes the cup from me, my fingers brush hers. She does not snatch them away.

'Thank you,' I whisper.

She shakes her head. 'You are not a witch, I think.' From the corner of her eye she watches the sleeping figure of Mistress Wheeler.

'Lizzie?'

'Your friend? She is watched also.'

'She lives?'

'Yes.'

I feel my heart take a great leap and I swoon. Grace's arms come round me again, catching me.

'Come, we must get you back on the stool.'

'Wait, please, tell me how she does.'

'I have not seen her. But I know that you are both in a great deal of trouble.'

'But what is the charge? Please, no one will tell me.'

'Your friend is accused of using witchcraft to seduce men and to commit a murder.'

My head spins. 'But . . . that is not true . . .'

She hushes me. 'That is not for me to say.'

'And me?'

'They say you are a witch also, and that you are seduced by

her. They say you are unnatural with her and that you aid her in her magic. You will be tried for a witch.'

I always feared it would come to this. It seems, no matter how hard I try, I cannot escape this fate. Even in death Isaac Tuttle has won. But my mind is as hazy as a Fenland fog. If Joseph is right, and Isaac is gone, then who sent the Watch to West St Paul's? It makes no sense. I am so tired, I cannot think.

'Please,' Grace begs, as Mistress Wheeler stirs, 'if you are watched three days and nights and the Devil does not come to you, they will have little proof. You may be spared the rope . . .'

But, despite her coaxing, I cannot find the strength to stand. I feel nothing but an overwhelming desire to lie down upon the freezing flags and let my bones turn to ice.

I am not the Devil's plaything, of that I am sure, but some of the things Grace said are true: I have loved Lizzie; I have been bewitched by her. I have lived with her and shared her bed, thinking it to be the finest, most beautiful thing. And, for a time, it was. Even though those days are past, lost along with my trust in her, it seems I must pay a price for them.

Perhaps there is a kind of balance in this world: for every good thing I have, I must give up something else. For every joy, there must be pain. For the simple, uncomplicated love of my mother, I must suffer the grief of her end. For the fleeting moments of affinity I have felt with Joseph, I must bear the disappointment of his failings. For the rapture of my passion for Lizzie, I must suffer a broken heart. Nothing comes free, not even love.

My shrivelled stomach reacts violently to the food and I retch onto the floor until bloody green stuff comes out. The noise wakes Mistress Wheeler and the last thing I remember is the sound of her scolding, and the blur of faces in the glow of candle flame, before I close my eyes and let blackness take me.

Chapter 40

I am feverish for some time. I do not know how long. I lose count of the days.

I am put back in the dungeon and am glad of the company and warmth of others. One girl brings me my bread each day, saving it from eager hands, and helps me to eat. I do not ask her name, or why she is here, but I'm grateful there is some kindness to be found in such a place.

I begin to think I may die here. My mind is so frenzied I am ready to lie down one last time, but thoughts of Lizzie stop me. Since Grace told me that she lives, and although the keeper will not answer my questions, I will not give up while there is still that hope. When, at last, the fever breaks and my head clears, I think that perhaps God has plans for me yet. When Master Oliver hears of this, surely he will help me. He will tell them the truth, and they will not dare to go against him. The truth is what matters now. The truth will save us both.

The assizes are held in the first week of March, when I have been here a month.

The keeper gives no warning, but when the court bailiff comes to fetch me, the other women shout and rattle their chains. In my time here I have seen others go to meet their fate before the magistrate. None has come back. I am dragged from the room, bound at the wrists and shackled with a heavy iron collar. These things are to keep me from bolting, as if I have the strength for that. As I pass her, the girl who nursed me through my illness gives me a sad smile.

The Newgate courthouse is full to bursting. In the public gallery the gossips are gathered, chattering as if they have come to see a play. With the theatres closed so long, London finds entertainment where it can. I dare not look among them for a friendly face, for fear I will find none. So I keep my eyes to the floor until I am led into a gated box and forced to sit and wait my turn before the court.

The jurymen are lined up on benches, the magistrate on a raised platform before them. He is a big man, ruddy-faced and fat, his skin bearing the old marks of the pox. He confers with Mason Ponder, his bulk a stark contrast to the lawyer's wizened frame.

Next to me is another woman, a ragged specimen with dirty fair hair that might once have been golden, hanging in matted clumps. Her eyes are wild and she gives me a sneer of a smile.

At last, Lizzie is brought up. I barely recognise her, she is so wasted and stooped. Her dress, dirty and torn, hangs from her bones. Her face is smeared with the filth of her cell and her beautiful hair is tangled and faded, all the fire gone from it. She looks like a beggar. I would have passed her by in the street.

I struggle to stand as she enters the box, but the bailiff pushes me down and threatens me with a cudgel. She sits, just a few feet away and looks at me. Although her eyes are dull, she gives me a small, secret smile and it is enough to make my heart sing. I'm surprised by a tear leaking down my cheek. I'd thought I had none left.

They put Lizzie up first and make her stand on a small raised step before the jurymen.

'Swear her in,' the magistrate says.

Ponder brings the book to Lizzie. She puts her hand upon it

and recites her pledge before God. There is much muttering and whispering among the crowd and the magistrate orders silence before he begins.

'Are you Elizabeth Poole?' he asks.

'I am.'

'Elizabeth Poole, you are accused of witchcraft. You are accused of entering a covenant with the Devil and using the powers granted you to seduce men and commit adulterous acts. You are accused of using the powers granted you to commit a murder. You are presented before this jury as a witch, an adulterer and a murderess. Do you understand?'

Lizzie nods.

'You must speak, madam.'

'I understand.'

'And what is your plea?'

'I am not a witch.'

The crowd stirs.

'Are you guilty or no? You must plead.'

'I am not a witch,' Lizzie repeats.

'Very well. The prisoner pleads not guilty.' The magistrate waits for the clerk to scratch this into his ledger. 'Mistress Poole, we have witnesses who will testify to your guilt. Before we bring them up, do you have anything further to say for yourself?'

Somehow Lizzie manages to stand tall. Only I, who know her so well, would detect the waver in her voice.

'Who gives you the right to judge me?' she says. 'Who gives these men the right to judge me? I answer to God alone. He will judge me. He alone knows the truth in my heart. I will answer to none other.'

'A pretty speech, madam, but a sentiment that holds no sway in a court of law, as we have all learned of late.'

He turns to Ponder. 'You may begin, sir.'

Ponder calls for his first witness. A young woman enters. She is short and fleshy with the dour, sensible garb of a servant. She holds her head high and simpers, as though she knows all eyes are on her and is ready for it. It takes me a moment to realise it is Charlotte.

I should not be surprised. I knew she had played her part in this from the moment the captain of the Watch asked her to name us as she stood mute and mouse-like in the doorway of our chamber. She has never forgiven Lizzie for giving me the place by her side that she believed rightfully hers. She has never forgiven me for taking it. These things are no secret. She speaks them every day in her petulant looks and spiteful words. But I had thought her loyal, if not to me then to Lizzie.

Ponder gives the room no time to settle. 'What is your name and occupation?'

'My name is Charlotte Stoker. I am maid at the house of Mistress Poole at West St Paul's.'

'And how long have you lived there?'

'Eight years, since I was twelve.'

'Mistress Stoker, I would like you to tell the jury what you have told me, regarding your mistress.'

'Which part, sir?' Charlotte whispers, causing snorts and laughter in the gallery. She is as demure and lovely as a girl on her first maying. My fingers curl in anger as I wait for the lies.

'Tell us about your mistress's relationship with a certain gentleman.'

'Oh, yes, of course.' She clears her throat. 'Mistress Poole has a taste for certain company. More than is seemly.'

'Which person in particular?'

'Some time ago she did meet with Pastor Kiffin, in secret. She was very intimate with him.'

'Did you ever see them together?'

'Yes, I saw them.'

'Where did you see them?'

'I saw them several times in our front parlour and once when I was down by the river. I saw them go into an inn and take a room there.'

'And what exactly did you see?'

Charlotte flushes. 'I saw them in sin.'

'Did you see them performing adulterous acts? It is important that you are clear and specific.'

'I did, sir. I saw them together, kissing and touching.'

Lizzie is staring vacantly at the floor.

'And when did you see these things?'

'It was about two years ago.'

'And did you report this to your master at the time?'

'No, sir.'

'Why not?'

Charlotte shifts from foot to foot. 'I don't know. I did tell some others, at the church.'

'Is this the only time you have seen your mistress engaged in such sinful behaviour?'

'No, sir.'

'You must tell us what you know, every part of it. Do you understand?'

'Yes, sir.'

I hold my breath. I know what is coming.

'I know she has committed shameful and licentious acts with one other.'

'And who is that person?'

'It is Ruth Flowers, who is sitting there.' Charlotte points at me.

I feel a hundred eyes turn on me. Like Lizzie, I stare at the floor.

Charlotte's words come tumbling out. She has prepared her act well.

'I have seen them many times, kissing and holding hands like sweethearts. Ruth was nothing but a kitchen girl when she first come, but the mistress made her maidservant and ran off with her to set up house like husband and wife, leaving us poor servants to look after the master in his last days.'

'Living like husband and wife, you say?'

'Yes, sir. They share a bed, even now in London, and are most licentious together. It is no secret. They do not try to hide it.'

'And have you seen them committing these lewd acts?'

'I have heard them and spied them naked together. The Watch found them just so on the night they were arrested. You can ask the captain. I know what it is they do. Everyone knows.'

A man in the crowd makes a bawdy comment and there is laughter, the crowd rippling.

'Thank you, Mistress Stoker. But now we come to a more serious accusation. Murder. Please tell the jury what you told me of your suspicions.'

Charlotte squirms. 'But you said I wouldn't have to—'

'It is important and you are sworn to tell the truth.'

Charlotte glances at Lizzie, her mouth hanging open as though she cannot find the words. Then she looks to the crowd. I follow her gaze and find Margaret there, seated at the front against the barriers. She looks stricken, eyes wide with panic. She clutches at a soiled rag. She is crying.

Ponder softens his voice. 'God knows you are doing the right thing and He will bless you for it.'

'It is a rumour, sir,' Charlotte says, 'but many people say that Elizabeth Poole killed her own mother.'

So, this is the murder charge I have been so afraid of. I am relieved it is nothing worse. Charlotte told me the story of Lizzie's mother and how she disappeared. No one knows if she lives or dies. I have heard it from Lizzie's own lips. Lizzie may blame herself, but I know it was not her fault. The woman was sick in body and mind. Only God knows her fate. There is no truth in the charge.

'And where did you hear this rumour?' Ponder asks.

'It is common among the servants hereabouts. And once I heard Margaret say it, when she was weeping and in her cups.'

Margaret freezes, holding the rag halfway up to her eyes.

'And who is Margaret?'

'Our cook, sir. She sits yonder.' Charlotte points.

'And have you ever heard your mistress speak of it?'

Charlotte glances sideways at Lizzie, who sits silent and unmoved.

'Once, when I first came to the house, I overheard Margaret and her whispering. They spoke of someone who had died, of a body. I'm not certain who it was they spoke of, but I believe it was Mistress Poole.'

'So you believe the rumour is true?'

'I – I don't know.'

Ponder pauses, letting the crowd whisper and gossip.

'There is one more thing I must ask you,' Ponder says. 'Your mistress has been found to have the marks of the Devil upon her body. Have you ever seen her receiving strange company, imps or dark creatures or such?'

'No, sir, but if I did, I would cast them out.'

'Tell me,' again Ponder wheedles, 'do you believe that your mistress is a witch?'

'I believe she has the power to bewitch people, sir.'

'Thank you, Charlotte. That will do.'

Charlotte is taken from the room. As she passes, she slips me a sly look. She has the better of me and she knows it. I want to spit at her, to set about her with my teeth and nails, like a wild cat. Behind all her play-acting coyness, she knows exactly what she is about. I wonder who has paid her off, what riches she is promised, to betray her mistress in such a way. For her greed and her petty jealousies, she will see us both hanged.

Chapter 41

William Kiffin enters the courtroom with his wife upon his arm, the picture of respectability. It is the first I have seen of him since the day he abandoned Lizzie all those months before, but he has changed little in that time. He is as handsome as ever. It must pain Lizzie to see him, when she is so reduced. But she does not look at him and sits with her head bowed, her lips offering up silent prayers, as though he is not there.

Ponder has Kiffin swear by the book that he claims to live by, and wastes no time in pleasantries.

'Pastor Kiffin, this jury has heard an account of your sinful and unsavoury relations with Elizabeth Poole. You are a religious man, are you not, with a congregation of men, women and children who look to you for moral and spiritual guidance? Pray tell us what you have to say of these accusations.'

Kiffin puffs out his chest, as if he is about to preach. 'I believe it is Elizabeth Poole who is on trial, not I.'

Ponder smirks. 'Indeed, sir, but we must have the truth of it from your own lips. What was your friendship with Elizabeth Poole?'

'Elizabeth was a special case in my flock. I believed that she needed more guidance than most. She came to me first to ask for supplementary ministry. I believed she was devout and seeking a spiritual life.'

'So you became her pastor?'

'For a time.'

'Where did you meet?'

'At Devonshire Square, along with many others.'

'Did you ever visit her at her home in West St Paul's?'

'I visited on several occasions and met her father and other members of the household. The servants worshipped with us too. That is no secret.'

'Did you ever meet Elizabeth Poole alone?'

'Yes.'

'Did you ever meet Elizabeth Poole at an inn by the Thames and take a room with her?'

'Yes. For the purpose of spiritual discussion in privacy only.'

There are snorts and catcalls from the crowd.

'Did you ever engage in adulterous acts with Elizabeth Poole?'

'The Lord knows my heart in this matter, sir, and he knows that I am devoted to my wife.'

'Why then, Pastor Kiffin, did you expel Mistress Poole from your congregation in May 1647 and soon afterwards write to her, expressing tender and intimate feelings?'

Ponder pulls a single sheet of paper from his pocket and brandishes it like a flag.

I know only too well what is in that letter. It splintered my own heart not so long ago. I remember tucking it safely back between the leaves of my mother's book – the book that is now in the possession of Mason Ponder.

Ponder begins to read: '"My dearest Elizabeth, I do not write to excuse my actions, but to beg that you heed my warning . . ."'

I have to listen to every last word of it, as if it were not already branded into my heart. But what pains me more is knowing that as this piece of paper condemns Kiffin it condemns Lizzie too. I had my chance to destroy it. I wish I had taken it.

When Ponder is finished, he slams down the letter before Kiffin. 'Tell me, Pastor Kiffin, this is your hand, is it not?'

Kiffin darts a look at Lizzie. His face turns red. He looks to his wife, who has covered her mouth with her hands. 'It is.'

'The Watch found this letter among Elizabeth Poole's belongings. Tell me how such a missive came to be there.'

Kiffin gathers himself. 'Early in that year I began to hear rumours about Elizabeth. People were saying that she was sinful and licentious. They accused her of fornicating with strange men. Members of my church came to me and asked that I eject her from the congregation. I did as I was asked.'

'Did you attempt to ascertain the truth of these rumours?'

'I did. I spoke with Elizabeth myself and, although she denied it, I felt that she was not truthful.'

'Come, come, sir. From this letter it seems to me that you knew the rumours were true. You knew because you were one of the men. Is that not so, Pastor Kiffin?'

'The letter – the letter was meant as an explanation—'

'Is that not so?' Ponder thunders.

Kiffin falls silent. The crowd falls silent. Lizzie shuts her eyes.

'I was one of the men.'

A great gasp goes up from the gallery.

'Wait,' Kiffin says. 'I must explain myself.'

'Please do so.'

Kiffin turns to the jurymen. 'The Lord knows, my flock knows, my wife knows that I am a godly man and a truthful one. I have proved my honesty here today.' He uses his sermonising voice. 'The Lord compels me to speak now, not to clear my name or save my reputation, but so that the truth may be known to all. The truth is that I am a man, plain and simple, and I am powerless against the forces of evil that plague this land. The truth is that this woman,' he points to Lizzie, 'is a whore of the Devil. I saw the Devil in her when she first came to me, and had to try to help her. The Lord brought her to me that I might save her. That is why I paid special attention to her, why I gave her ministry whenever she required it. But the Devil's manipulation was too strong and, God forgive me, I fell. I fell from His grace and was seduced. She is not natural. She has ways and means to tempt a man and drive him half out of his wits. The Lord knows my intentions were good. He knows I am not to blame for the evil magic she worked upon me. That is why I expelled her. I could not have such evil among the good people of my congregation. I had to send her away so she no longer had hold over me or any under my protection. God forgive me my sins. She is a succubus, a harridan. She is a witch!'

When he stops, he quivers with emotion, just as he does in Sunday worship. Such is his passion, his eloquence, that the crowd is in awe.

But I am not. I know him for the fraud he is. I can take no more. Before I know it, I find my own voice. 'You are a liar! You are a liar and a coward!'

Then the bailiffs are upon me, dragging my chains until I have no choice but to sit. I weep in my anger. I weep with frustration, letting the rage out of my heart. Why doesn't Lizzie stand up and scream with me? Why does she sit so still and accepting?

I shout at Kiffin over and over until the magistrate orders me gagged. As the bailiff ties the bit into my mouth, Lizzie looks to me at last. Her eyes are deep pools of sorrow and love, but her face is calm, almost serene. She reminds me of the ancient paintings of the Virgin Mother I used to see in the cathedral in Ely when I was a child. She looks like a martyr. She looks like a saint.

As Kiffin is dismissed, the gallery erupts with chatter. There are calls of 'Hang the witch!' and 'Send her back to Hell!' The magistrate is forced to call order to the room. He consults Ponder, then asks Margaret Small to take the stand.

Margaret looks around the room like a startled animal, eyes darting between Lizzie and me, as if we can do something to help her. At least she is not part of Charlotte's plot. I can tell by her shock that she has not been coached for this by Ponder or anyone else. She loves Lizzie as if she were her own child. She will not betray us.

A bailiff brings Margaret up before the magistrate and Ponder swears her in. She is unsteady on her feet and a stool is brought for her.

Ponder circles, his stick tapping the floorboards. 'Mistress Small,' he says, 'how long have you known Elizabeth Poole?'

'Since she was born.'

'And what is your relationship to her?'

'I have been cook, and kitchen maid before that, at Master Poole's house since he was wed.'

'And what is your opinion of Elizabeth Poole's character?'

'She has always been a good mistress, sir. Even when she was a child she was kind and good and always quick to make up after an argument.'

'And were there many arguments in the household?'

'Oh, no. Mistress Lizzie has a quick temper but she's always quick to make amends, if ever harsh words are said.'

'And what say you to the charge of witchcraft?'

'I say that is not possible.'

'But we have found the Devil's marks upon her.'

'I have known her since she was a babe, sir, and there are no such marks upon her.'

'Are you saying that I am a liar?'

'Oh, no – no, of course not, but I never saw such marks.'

'And when was the last time you saw Elizabeth Poole unclothed?'

'Not for a good many years, I'd say.'

'Not for many years,' Ponder repeats, and pauses, allowing his insinuation to settle. 'Did you ever see her acting strangely, performing rituals or receiving strange visitors?'

'Never. She has always been a singular sort of girl, but nothing ungodly.'

'Singular? How so?'

'Set apart, on account of her quick moods, I would say, sir. She was always a difficult child, but very dear to me.'

'Please go on, Mistress Small.'

Margaret is flustered. Her eyes flick to Lizzie. 'She was an excitable girl and changeable, more so after . . .'

'After what?'

'After the loss of her mother. But any girl losing their mother so young would be so.'

'She is unsteady? Wilful?'

'I just meant that she is . . . she is . . .'

'She is unstable in her mind. This is a woman who has a weakness in her. A weakness professed in her own words, spoken aloud before a court of law at the trial of Charles Stuart. Put down in print. It is this weakness that allowed the Devil to take her. Is that not so, Mistress Small?'

'I – I—'

'I turn to the testimony of William Kiffin. We have heard from that godly gentleman the tale of how he tried to save her from this fate. He is your pastor, is he not?'

'He was for a time, sir.'

'And do you believe he is a good man?'

'I did, until he turned Mistress Lizzie out and abandoned us all.'

'And what do you think of him now? Do you believe him?'

'No. My Lizzie is no witch.'

'But we have had a confession from the man himself. See how he sits before us now, a good man, eager to undergo scrutiny and speculation so that the truth might be heard and justice done. Why do you not believe him?'

'I think he is false.'

'Can you prove it?'

'No, sir.'

'You call him a liar without proof. That is a serious accusation.'

Margaret's face is blotchy and swollen. Her eyes swim with tears. 'I only know what I know, and I know nothing of any witchcraft.'

'Mistress Small, you are a godly woman, are you not?'

'Of course.'

'Do you believe, as the scriptures tell us, that we will answer for our sins on the Day of Judgment?'

'Of course.'

'And do you know that it is a sin to lie before God?'

'Yes, sir.'

'Very well. We have already heard from Charlotte Stoker the rumour surrounding your previous mistress's disappearance. What do you know of this rumour?'

'It's just a rumour, and Charlotte Stoker is an ungrateful girl. Mistress Lizzie has been nothing but kind and charitable to her all these years.'

'Your loyalty is admirable, but you have been known to speak of this rumour yourself. Do you believe it to be true?'

'No, sir.'

'Then why would you say such a thing? Remember, God is listening, Margaret.'

'I . . . I don't remember.'

'Do you remember the night of Mistress Poole's disappearance?'

'Yes.'

'Can you tell the jury what happened?'

'I don't know. Nobody knows. It was a normal night, the mistress was unwell, and we had all gone to bed. When we awoke, she was gone. She could not be found. We never saw her again. It was a long time ago, and my memory is not good.'

'And so the story goes . . . I want the truth, Margaret . . . the truth.'

Margaret shivers under Ponder's gaze.

'Remember, the Lord is watching you now. This may be the most important moment of your life. This is your chance to prove yourself a true Christian, a true servant. We must have the truth, and if you lie, you will be damned for all eternity.'

Margaret starts to blub. Through her tears, she chokes the words, 'But she is my Lizzie . . . my Lizzie . . . I raised her like my own . . .'

Ponder pounces. 'And where was her mother?'

'Her mother was a weak and useless thing, always sick, no strength for such a lively child. She was no good . . . no good at all. But Lizzie never meant it. It was an accident . . .' Her shoulders shake as she covers her face with the rag.

Thin shreds of foreboding twine down my spine and sit twisted in my stomach.

'What was an accident? You must tell us, Margaret. Remember, the Lord is all-seeing . . . He already knows.'

'Lizzie thought she was helping . . .'

Ponder puts his hand upon Margaret's head, like a priest of the old faith. 'Margaret, all will be well if you tell the truth.'

Margaret raises her eyes and looks longingly across the room to Lizzie. Lizzie meets her gaze. Very slowly, she gives Margaret a single nod. That one small action speaks louder than any words. In it there is permission, and truth, and forgiveness. Margaret calms herself, breath slowing, as if comforted. Then Lizzie looks away.

'Mistress Poole was abed all that day,' Margaret says. 'The physician had been in and given her henbane to help her, but it didn't work and she moaned all night long. Lizzie couldn't sleep and went in to her mother to give her a dose. She didn't know that henbane is a dangerous herb. It can kill as well as cure. Lizzie bade her drink too much, and the poor woman died in the night. It was not murder . . . It was a mistake, sir, such as anyone might make.'

'A mistake – or a calculated act to rid herself of a burdensome mother?'

'She was barely more than a child. She didn't know what she was doing.'

Ponder's cheeks twitch. 'Go on,' he says.

'Lizzie came to me. I didn't know what to do. The poor child was so distraught, saying she would hang for it. But I had an idea to rid us of the body. We hid her in a barrow and took her all the way to the river. We tied her down with stones . . . I never told a soul until now . . .' Margaret doubles over on the stool. She rocks back and forth, back and forth, whispering, 'God forgive me . . . God forgive me . . .'

After this it takes Ponder only moments to seal Lizzie's fate. I am dimly aware as he turns testimony into truth with his slippery tongue. He talks of the Devil's work, speaks of heresy and witchcraft, says she is an unholy and unnatural thing. He talks of enchantments and poisons, as he poisons the room with his words.

With the bit still tied tight, straps chafing my cheeks, I cannot make a sound. But there is still the tiniest flutter of hope in me. I have a protector. When it is my turn on the stand I will scream his name and they will have to listen. I will Lizzie to think of him. I will her to do the same. Then we will see who are the liars and the cheats. Then Ponder, Kiffin and the rest will be dead men.

The jurymen return their inevitable verdict. Lizzie is guilty.

'Elizabeth Poole. Stand up.' The magistrate is sober.

Lizzie stands. Her eyes are unfocused and she sways.

'You have been found guilty of those crimes of which you stand accused. Before I sentence, will you plead?'

Say his name, I think. Say his name and they dare not harm you.

But she does not.

She closes her eyes and shakes her head.

The magistrate pulls a black felt cap from his robes and covers his head.

Chapter 42

I am taken back to the cells and left in a small chamber, alone, bound and gagged. A man is put outside the door to guard me through the night. My fate is to be decided on the morrow and the hangings are set for the day after that. I do not need to stand before a jury to know that I will join Lizzie at Tyburn Tree, unless I can find a way to Master Oliver.

I think of Lizzie's last pamphlet, and wonder how far her accusations have spread. Even if they have reached Master Oliver, surely he will forgive her transgressions if I explain how she is afflicted. Her words against him are not the Devil's work, but a distraction of the mind, brought on by disappointment and grief. He will understand that. And they are only words, after all. How much harm can words do in the end? She deserves his pity, his Christian charity. I need a chance to speak with him. Then, surely, he will not abandon us.

I have no money to bribe the gaoler, so I must give up the one thing I have left to sell.

With the foul leather bit in my mouth I have no words, so I bang on the door with my shackles over and over until the guard knocks back and yells for quiet. But I do not stop. I keep on and on until at last he slides back the bolt, comes into the room and threatens me with curses and harsh words.

I size him up in seconds. I have seen others like him over these last weeks: mean-spirited men handed power beyond their station, selfish men of low morals with no compassion for those in their care. He has an ugly, unshaven face. The Newgate stench comes off him as though it seeps from his skin.

He finds me on my knees. I clasp my hands together and beg.

'Stop your racket,' he says, 'or I'll shut you up myself.'

He knocks me backwards, but I scrabble after him and clutch at his breeches. At first he tries to shake me off, but I reach my hand up between his legs and gently hold it there. He hesitates. Again I beg, showing the chains that bind my wrists. I nudge up against him until my face is level with his navel. I touch him, looking up with pleading eyes, as if I am some practised whore, at work in a Southwark bawdy house. I feel him shift and harden beneath my fingers.

I wait until he moans with pleasure and then I lie back on the cold floor and lift my skirts. I show him my bound hands one last time, to make sure he understands me, and keep my knees together until he nods and says, 'Yes . . . Yes.'

He is rough and quick. He reeks of liquor and unwashed clothes. He calls me slut and filthy bitch, pushing hard into me, bruising my thighs. He is large and it hurts, high up inside, as though he will split me in two. Tears spring to my eyes. When the pain forces a groan from my throat, he takes pleasure in it. He puts a hand over my face so he cannot see my eyes.

When he is done, he stands and wipes himself. Shaking, I hold out my hands for him to unlock the chains.

'Stupid wench,' he says, and laughs. 'I have no key.'

He leaves and slams the door.

They call me a whore, but they have made me into something worse. I have sold myself for nothing.

I pull my skirts down to cover my legs and curl myself into a ball. Deep in my gut, I ache with a pain keener than that of my monthly courses. My body shudders uncontrollably, but it is not because of the cold. I think he has made me bleed, but it is just the hot wetness of him, seeping between my thighs.

I am too exhausted to feel disgust, or shame, or any of the things that a prison preacher would tell me I should feel. I do not pray. I do not even cry. Instead, there is just despair – empty, black and endless.

So, this is how it feels to look death in the eye. This is how it feels to be abandoned by God. This is how it feels, when all hope is lost.

In the bleak hours that follow I wish for the end. I am hollowed out, numb and weak. I cannot face the long hours of night, let alone the dawn and the fate that the rising sun will bring. Perhaps they will let me die next to Lizzie. Perhaps we will end together after all. When I made my bargain with the Fen spirits I did not know that I would pay such a heavy price. In binding my heart to Lizzie's, I have given away my life. The spirits answered me then, but where are they now? Not here, in this dank, foetid cell, in this city that God has forgot.

As I lie there, Joseph's last words to me echo and taunt: 'Let me take you somewhere safe. You need to be with someone who can help you. *She* cannot help you.'

I should have listened to him. But where is Joseph now, when I need him most? Sudden longing drives needles deep into my chest.

Pictures crowd my mind, images of that long-ago day in the meadow, how the May sun haloed us both, a smile lighting Joseph's face as he spoke of the future with hope. I recall how he held me fast, that night by the fire in Abingdon, while my heart cracked into pieces. I remember his arms tight about me, on the day of the King's execution, when he brought me the news of Isaac's death, protecting me when I could not protect myself. I imagine his eyes, clouded with sadness and regret, on the night he admitted the truth about Naseby, the night I sent him away. All these memories make up the past but none of it seems to matter any more. I will never see him again, and that pain cuts sharper than any other.

My mother was right: I should not have meddled with the hearts of others, especially when I did not even know my own.

It is the early hours when I hear the sound of leather boots on stone and the scrape of rust against rust as the bolts are drawn back. I am stiff with cold and sore between my legs. I have no fight left. I do not struggle as powerful arms drag me upwards. They can take me anywhere they want. What does it matter now?

Outside the cell another man is silhouetted in the dim glow of a lantern. He wears a dagger at the hip, glinting like a looking glass.

'Take that thing off her,' he says, and the gaoler unties the bit.

Freed, my jaw aches and my tongue is raw. I swallow gulps of air and cough up the foul stuff from my throat. Before I can right my senses, dark sackcloth comes down over my head, blinding me.

'Please . . .' My swollen tongue is unwieldy in my mouth and my voice does not sound like my own. 'Please . . . No . . .'

'Quiet yourself, Ruth,' the man says. 'You will not be harmed.'

With my hands still tied, and my legs trembling so much they can barely carry me, I am led away from that stinking cell.

Newgate is quieter at this hour, prisoners sleeping or wiling away the hours in whispered conversation or silent terror. The sound of our passing wakes a few and there are calls and hisses from the men's cells.

I feel the cold bite of outside air as I'm led through a door, then lifted into a carriage and placed on a wooden seat. I hear the stamping of a horse and the jangle of its harness. The carriage lilts as someone else climbs in and closes the door. I cower in the corner.

'Don't be afraid. You are safe now.' It is the same man. I feel a thin thread of recognition. There is something in his voice that I know but cannot place, like trying to remember a dream, or the answer to a riddle that keeps slipping away. But his words do little to soothe me. Bound and robbed of my senses, I am his prisoner.

The man taps on the roof and we move off.

The night-time streets are frozen. I shiver as I am jolted about, the horse skittering on the ice. It is some time before dawn and the city sleeps. I hear no sounds that I recognise or can use to right myself. I think we have not crossed the river but fear that we are headed there, or some other place where they might easily be rid of me.

When the carriage finally draws up, the man takes my arm and guides me down the steps, through a doorway and along stone-flagged floors that freeze my bare feet. His touch is gentle but he does not say a word.

We reach a place with a wooden floor and, through my blindfold, I see patches of candlelight at intervals along the walls. Soon we turn off this gallery into a room. It is brightly lit and the warmth of a good fire hits me, the first such I have felt in weeks. There is rich carpet underfoot.

The man orders his companions to wait outside, and I hear the clatter of the latch as he closes the door. Then, the creak of his boots as he guides me to the fireside. I feel the full heat of the flames and see the glow of the hearth at my side. Despite the warmth, I am trembling.

'Be still, Ruth,' he says. Then, with a deft swipe of a blade, he cuts away the rope at my wrists, and slowly lifts the sacking from my head.

I know him. His name is Henry Ireton. He is an army man who often visited the Cromwell house in Ely, and was betrothed to one of the older daughters. He looks more fretful now, and bears the scars of battle upon his neck, but it is surely he.

'Do you know me, Ruth?' He smiles, and it seems the kindest, sweetest gesture in the world.

'Oh, sir . . .'

He puts his hand on my filthy shoulder. 'Sit and be still. All will be well.'

I do as he says, looking about me and realising that I am in the same grand room at Whitehall where I had visited my old master to beg for help, not so long before.

A door opens at the far end of the room and Master Oliver enters. With him is Old Bess, dressed all in black with her creased, round face, just as I remember her. I could faint with relief.

'Thank you, Henry,' Master Oliver says. 'You have done me a great service and I will not forget it. You may leave us now.'

Ireton makes a curt little bow and steps outside the room, closing the door quietly.

For a few moments, the three of us remain still and silent, while the clock on the mantel clicks and whirs and the wind moans in the chimney.

'Oh, Ruth, my poor girl, you are frozen to the bone . . .' Old Bess pours something hot and steaming into a mug and places it on a low table next to me. 'Here, a drink will take off the chill.'

She bends and takes my hands in hers, one at a time, turning them about, stroking them where the ropes have cut into my flesh. She tuts and shoots a dark look at her son. Then she rubs my shoulders to warm me, as if I am a child.

Master Oliver perches on the chair opposite. Although the night is cold, he takes a red kerchief from his pocket and wipes beads of sweat from his brow. He tucks it away but at once fetches it out again to wipe his nose and dab his forehead. 'You are safe here for now,' he says, his eyes fixed on my trembling fingers.

I believe him, just as I have always believed him. 'Thank you, sir. I knew you would help us . . .' Suddenly, and without warning, my body is shaken with sobs that double me over. Old Bess tries to soothe me, stroking my back and my matted hair and making cooing noises as if she is tending a babe.

'I am truly sorry for what you have suffered,' Master Oliver says. 'I did not know of your plight until today. There have been so many pressing matters . . . You owe a great debt of gratitude, I think.'

'Yes, thank you, sir . . .'

'No, not to me, child. To your friend, the one who came here and would not leave until he had seen me. The stewards could not turn him out these three weeks. And thank God for it. You have a good friend in him, I think.'

'Who?'

'His name was Oakes.'

I can hardly believe it. Would Joseph the deserter dare to stand before his general? Would he risk so much for me?

'Joseph?'

'That was his name. Indeed, we are both in his debt. Without him, you would be facing a stiff sentence today.'

Despite all my blindness, all my cruelty and judgement, can it be that Joseph has not given up on me? Even now he still fights, not for God and glory, not for liberty and justice, but for my life. Perhaps there is hope yet. Perhaps our story is not done.

Master Oliver stands, paces to the fireside and leans on the mantel. 'Why did you not send word to me yourself? Why did you not tell them?'

'I tried, but no one would believe me. They bridled me and mocked me and would not believe I had your protection. When I called out your name, they laughed at me.'

He snorts and shakes his head. 'Well, you are safe for tonight at least.'

'What about Lizzie?'

'Lizzie? Elizabeth Poole?'

'Have you sent for her too? They will hang her if you do not stop it.'

He stares into the fire. 'I cannot do that. I have some powers, but I am not above the law. Elizabeth Poole has been tried and sentenced by the court.'

'You could pardon her.'

'I am not the King, Ruth.'

'But she will die!' My breath comes too fast just thinking of it. 'She may have done wrong but she does not deserve this. She is not well. She needs your mercy. Surely a lesser sentence—'

'Listen to me, Ruth. I have risked much to bring you here.' Master Oliver's eyes are stormy. 'There are many who would see me fall now. Half the country, which once cried for the blood of Charles Stuart, the traitor, now calls me by the same name. I am watched closely. Do you understand? I risk all to save you. No one must know of it. No one. Do you understand?'

He is my last hope. 'But you must save her . . . you must.'

'Elizabeth Poole is a witch!' he bellows, and immediately I am that young child back in Ely, fearful of her master's unpredictable wrath. 'She is a dangerous influence on you,' he says. 'She speaks seditious and traitorous lies. She has set herself up for her fate.'

'The pamphlet,' I say, a curling dread clenching my stomach. 'I know she has spoken out against you but she is not in her rightful mind. She means you no harm. If you give her a chance you will see—'

'She has had her chance! She uses the word of God to speak against us, against me. She twists the words of the Bible and flaunts her Devilish opinions in public. She is a rebel and a false prophet. It cannot be borne. Once I saw what she was, I had no choice.'

Suddenly I realise who has brought these charges to our door. I feared that Lizzie's dangerous words would bring us trouble, I knew she had gone too far, but I had never dreamed it would come to this. With horror, I understand that Lizzie may not have been right about everything, but she was right about the man who stands before me now.

The knowledge knocks the wind from me, like a punch in the stomach.

'You . . .'

'If there had been any other way then, believe me, I would have taken it. You were never meant to be part of it, and I was assured you would be safe. Mason Ponder took his brief too far. For that I am sorry.'

The heat from the fire is suddenly stifling and I struggle for air. My body trembles, but anger gives me new strength. 'You are not sorry. If you were truly sorry you would stop it now. You would not do this.'

'I must.'

'Then she will hang and her blood will be on your hands.'

'It is cruel necessity.'

'Then it's true what they say. By this action you make it true. The King, Lizzie – who will be next? How many more lives will be lost before your path is clear? You will lock up your enemies, you will crush them with your army. You will not listen to the people as you promised. All you care about is money and property and power!' I fall to my knees before him.

'Ruth, you must desist. I had hoped you would see the sense in it. I see you have been greatly influenced.'

'No! I have my own mind!'

Old Bess kneels beside me and tries to put her arm around my shoulders. I do not want to be touched and I shrug her off.

'If I am beyond all hope, why not give me up to the hangman too?'

Old Bess stops trying to comfort me and stands, giving her son a look of displeasure. She walks to a cabinet at the side of the room and, from it, draws out a bundle. She brings it to me where I sit on the floor. Even before I unwrap the linen, I know what it is. I recognise the size and weight of it. I know the smell of the battered old leather and the feel of the crisp, frayed edges of the paper. It is my mother's book.

'How did you get this?'

'I had it brought from the court,' Master Oliver says. 'It seems even Mason Ponder can be persuaded to part with valuable evidence, once it has served its purpose.'

As I turn the book in my hands, it falls open at a page that is marked with two lengths of faded red ribbon. I hold up the ribbon to see it shine in the firelight. It is curled and spotted in places with dark stains.

A chill runs through me, my skin puckers to goosebumps. The last time I saw these ribbons they were tied into the hair of my mother's bloody corpse.

'Go to her, Oliver,' I hear Bess say. Her voice sounds like an echo.

But he does not move. He stares at me until I feel he can see inside me and read my thoughts. Then he speaks and I understand.

'There was a time, before you were born, when I was a different man from the one you know now. I was young, I was impetuous, and I was stupid. I was the very chief of sinners, made up of base wants and lusts. My soul was plunged into darkness for punishment of the things I did then. But that time did pass, and I found the light of God's elect in me. I do not apologise for what I did then, or for what I do now, for God leads me in my path and knows better than I what is right.'

He bends down and puts his hand upon my shoulder. As he

touches me I feel the essence of him running all through my body. 'I cannot acknowledge you, Ruth, but I have done what I can for you. God knows I will always regret what has happened to you and your mother.' A shadow passes across his face. 'You are very like her.'

And then his hand leaves my shoulder and I am alone again.

The room is suddenly very still and very quiet. No one speaks. I hear the blood rushing in my ears and the whisper of my own breath.

I feel as though I am standing on the edge of a great, dark void, into which I might fall, down and down into turmoil and madness.

But then I think of my mother. I think of her dancing with Master Oliver, eyes shining, crimson ribbons gleaming in her hair; of her unquestioning loyalty and trust; of the love pledge, the very promise I made to Lizzie, lettered upon the pages of the book I now hold in my lap; of the binding charm my mother forbade, for fear of what payment the Fen spirits might demand. She knew too well the terrible debt that must be levelled. I think of all the things that, as a child, I did not understand, the questions I dared not ask, answers she did not offer. She did not need to tell me the truth because it was plain for me to see. Only I did not see it.

'We buried her. We made sure she had a proper burial,' Old Bess says, as if she can follow my thoughts.

'Why did you send me away?' My voice is small, the rage gone out of it.

'I had to, Ruth. You were in great danger,' she says.

'As you are in danger now.' Master Oliver strides across the room and draws out a leather bag from the cabinet. From the chinking sound it makes, I guess it holds coin, and plenty of it. He brings it to me and holds it out. 'There is a ship leaving Southampton in eight days' time. The *Seaflower*. It sails for

Virginia. You will be on it. You will take this money. Half of it will pay for your passage and the captain's silence. I have sent word to him and he expects you. He is an old friend and can be trusted. Use the rest to feed and clothe yourself as you see fit. If you are frugal, there is enough to keep you for some time.'

My anger has died. I am empty. Spent. I cannot feel anything any more. For the first time I look him in the eye as an equal. 'So, now you want me gone.'

'Ruth,' Old Bess says, 'Oliver has done what he can, but you will never be safe here. You are known. They will find you and, when they do, they will hang you, just like your friend. Just like your mother. We cannot protect you for ever. If you go, you have a chance at life. Please . . . take it.'

She takes the moneybag from Master Oliver and places it in my hands. 'Please, Ruth, your mother would want you to live. As does your father.'

I do not want to take their charity. It seems I have depended upon the Cromwell family all my life. I could walk from this room and disappear for ever. I could hide, like a child running from punishment, knowing all the time that punishment will eventually come. But penniless, with bare feet and dressed in rags, I will not get far.

As Whitehall Palace begins to stir, I slip from a side door, silent and unnoticed, just as I had arrived. I carry nothing with me but an old book, two scraps of stained crimson ribbon and a leather purse, hidden in my skirts.

Chapter 43

I make my way to the riverside and take a boat to Southwark. During all my months in London I have visited the south bank of the Thames only once, with Lizzie by my side, brave and unflinching on one of her expeditions among the illegal printing presses and booksellers that ply their disreputable trade to the sailors and merchants come into the docks. Then I was frightened of cutpurses and charlatans but now I am every bit as ragged and despicable as they are. They will take me for a whore or a beggar. No one would imagine the riches hidden in my petticoats.

I find an inn on a back-street, away from the bustle of the wharf, where the floor is spread with clean rushes and the landlord's daughter smiles at me with pity. The taverner does not trust me. He demands payment before he will accept my business and I enjoy the surprise in his eyes as I show him a shiny new crown and ask for a good room with a fire and no questions asked. He is willing to strike the deal.

Southwark is a good place for pawnshops and moneylenders and, out once more on the streets, I soon find what I'm looking for. The shopkeeper, seeing my Newgate rags, tries to shoo me away, but I silence him with the sight of a few coins and he takes me to a trunk of musty clothes at the back of the shop.

There is fine stuff here, made by talented seamstresses: ladies' dresses in brocade and lace, petticoats of delicate yarn and a gentleman's coat with brass buttons. There are moth holes and a few threads dangling, but these things will serve until I can buy better. I pick out a good serge dress, the deep purple of a bruise, with a bodice cut lower than anything I have dared wear before. I try not to think too much on the owner of the dress and why she had to sell it.

Then, beneath the faded breeches and threadbare cloaks, I spy the gleam of emerald satin. There are a few tears in the skirt, that I won't have time to mend, and Lizzie is so tall that the hem might not reach the floor, but the dress was once fine enough to match her beauty. It is almost perfect. I will take it.

I find all I need and, back at the inn, eat my first proper meal in weeks. I ask the girl for a tub and hot water to be brought up, and a looking glass, if such a thing can be found. She sends up a clean copper tub and pails of steaming water, fresh from the kitchen fire. The tinder is lit in my room and she brings her mother's hand glass and places it lovingly on the bed.

Alone at last, I throw my rags into a pile in the corner of the room – I will have them burned – and step into the tub. The dirt comes off in flakes and I scrub until my flesh turns pale pink once more. I rub hard between my thighs until I am sure that the crusted dirt of the Newgate gaoler is gone from me. I take a fresh pail of water and pour it over my hair, teasing out the knots with rosemary soap. Only when the water is cold and floating with scum do I step out and stand before the fire, savouring the heat of the flames as they dry my body.

I dress in the purple serge. It is a good fit, as though it were made for me. I comb out my hair and leave it loose to dry. I study my reflection. There is something different about my face. My cheeks have hollowed in these last weeks, and are flushed in the firelight. My lips are red where they have cracked and bled, as if they are rouged. But there is something more than that. I stare at myself in the glass until I know what it is.

The fear has left my eyes.

I am no longer the frightened little girl from the Fens. I am a runaway. I am a felon. I am a whore. I am my mother's daughter, with nothing to lose but a bag full of gold from a father who has broken my heart.

I am Cromwell's witch.

I expect to feel hatred for the man who has made me what I am. But my heart is more complicated than that. I cannot put a name to what I feel.

A long-ago memory comes back to me, like a half-remembered dream. I am six years old, playing in the yard, grubbing in the dirt with the chickens, too young yet for any real work. I sense eyes on my back. He is there, leaning against the doorframe. He watches me, frowning, as though he is trying to find the answer to a puzzle. Then he calls my name and beckons.

I run to him and dip into the awkward little curtsy I have learned from his daughters. It makes him smile. He crouches, so that his face is level with mine, and puts his hand upon my shoulder. 'Are you happy here, little one?' he asks.

I nod slowly, unsure of what is required.

'Then you will always have a place in my house. I will always look after you. Will you promise to remember this?'

I look at the pouch of coin that sits upon the table. I do not recognise the man in my memory. I feel no love, respect or gratitude, such as I always imagined a girl must feel for her father. I blame him for too much. I blame him for my mother's half-lived life. I blame him for Lizzie's brutal fate. I blame him for the aching disappointment that crawls under my skin like a curse. But, despite all this, I find I cannot despise him.

He will have his wish at least. I will take his money and he will not see me again. He has paid out his promise to me in gold. But I still have my own promise to keep, and I cannot rest until it is settled.

* * *

I wait until night falls and the city streets are peopled only by those brave or careless enough to defy the curfew. The men in the taproom are too drunk to notice as I slip from the inn, and the drabs are too busy to care. They take me for one of their own and are glad for less competition.

I take a boat to Blackfriars Steps and from there I make my way on foot. As I near the gates my heart starts to pound. It is less than a day since I was saved from this place, and now I choose to go back.

The doorkeeper is easy. A quick smile and a wink persuades him that I'm here on business. I slip him a few coins and press a finger to my lips, as if I have done this a hundred times before. He lets me inside.

Through the door, the stench is like a bad memory, making my stomach turn and my head spin. A woman's screams echo from the dungeon below. I want to turn and run, my nerve failing, but I must go on. I will never forgive myself if I do not try.

I tell the gaoler the old lie – that I'm Lizzie's cousin, come to say my final goodbyes – and slide a good stack of coin across the table. I keep my hood pulled down low and my face in shadow, but it is clear he has no idea who I am. I must be changed indeed.

He turns the key in the door to Lizzie's cell. 'Go on,' he grunts.

There is no window to let in the moonlight and I am made blind by the blackness.

'A candle, sir,' I say, and the man hands me his lantern.

'Make it quick,' he says, glancing over his shoulder. He shuts the door and slides the bolts back into place. I am trapped.

'Ruth?'

Her voice is cracked, a whisper. She is curled up in the corner, like a pile of mouldering rags. In the lantern's dim glow, her eyes shine white against her filthy skin.

I gather her in my arms.

She cries and murmurs, 'My angel . . . my angel . . .'

I wonder that she still has tears left to shed. Since I left Master Oliver, mine have dried.

'Am I dreaming?' she says.

'No, I'm come to take you away.'

'But how?'

Quickly, I tell her about my meeting with the Cromwells and the truths I have learned. As I reveal the story of my beginnings, she nods and smiles to herself.

'You are not surprised,' I say.

'I could think of no other reason for his interest in us – in you. It is plain he cares nothing for me. I am nothing to him. Worse than nothing.'

'Why did you never speak of it?'

'It was your innocence I liked.' She looks sad as she remembers.

'That is lost now.'

She takes my face in her hands. 'But you are more beautiful than ever.' Gently, she puts her lips to mine.

I feel my heart splinter, shattered by the loss of her, but there is no time left for such talk. 'I have money and clothes for you. If we are quick we can leave now. The gaoler, he—'

She puts her hand up to my mouth to stop my words. She shakes her head.

'I will speak with him,' I say. 'I will offer him everything I have, if that is what it takes. It is a lot, he will not refuse.'

'No, Ruth,' she whispers.

'But in the morning . . .'

'I know. Take your money and fly away with it. I will not be the reason for your end.'

'Come, dress quickly.' From the bundle I pull out the green satin. 'See? It may not fit but it will do for now.'

'And if you give your money away, what then? You cannot sail to the New World without coin. A life of poverty, a life on the run, is not what you want, not what you deserve. Nor I.' She raises an eyebrow in the way I used to find so enticing. Now it frustrates me.

'I will find a way,' I say. 'I will not stand by and see you hang. I will not let that happen to you . . .'

She catches my hands. 'Oh, my angel, it is meant to be this way. Did I not tell you that my fate would follow that of the King?'

'There is no sense in that. It doesn't have to.'

'Oh, but it does. Don't you see? They have made a martyr of the King. It will be the same with me. The truth will come out and my death will not be in vain. I die for every man, woman and child who has suffered in this hateful war. I sacrifice myself for those who are yet to suffer under the yoke of England's new chains. There are many who will speak out now against those conspirators and traitors who would keep us shackled in fear, your friends among them. I am their new cause, their new hope. I was made for this. It will be a glorious death, Ruth. Just wait and see . . .'

I recognise the otherworldly shine in her eyes. She looks beyond me, through me, and sees nothing but her God. I see she is determined to go to Him.

'It is what I want,' she says.

'You don't know what you are saying. You've been here too long. They have driven you half mad. You will see differently once you are away from here, once you are recovered.'

I stand and try to pull her up. Although she is nothing but bones, she is a dead weight. I hear movement in the corridor outside the cell. Someone is coming.

'You must come now, Lizzie . . . please!'

Still, she does not move.

'Until death, remember? You promised me.'

'Death is already here,' she whispers.

I let go of her hands. 'If you ever loved me, you will come with me.'

She gazes at me, her eyes swimming with tears like fat pearls. 'I do love you . . .'

I know it then, as I have known it all along. I have known it and buried the knowing deep inside, because I could not bear the truth.

'Yes, you love me, but not enough . . . not enough.'

There are voices outside the door. The bolts are drawn back. The spell is broken. The thread is snapped. My time is up.

'Madam,' the gaoler hisses. 'Say your goodbyes.'

I leave the green satin and a handful of coin on the floor next to her. I hold her tight and breathe in the smell of her one last time. I tangle my fingers in her filthy hair and feel her bones press against my body. I press my lips to hers and taste salt and blood.

And then I turn, scoop up the lantern and walk away. I do not look back and I do not stop until I have crossed the river and am safe again, inside my room at the inn.

Chapter 44

Towards dawn I pull myself up from the bed. A thin light filters through the panes and I can hear the sounds of people stirring below.

I open the casement and breathe deep of the cold air, clean and still, not yet polluted by the smoke and stench of the day. A dank, marshy smell rolls in off the river and for a moment I shut my eyes and think of home. I will never see those flat, flooded lands again. I will never catch the salted scent of the sea on the autumn breeze, never lie on my back and gaze at summer skies of purest blue, watching swallows dart, never climb those worn stone steps to the top of the cathedral and stretch my hands up to the never-ending heavens. I have made up my mind. Later, I will leave London for ever and travel south, to the coast.

I watch the glow of first light rise over the rooftops and think of what I am leaving behind. Then I go in search of the innkeeper's daughter.

I find her in the kitchens, sweating over the bellows and setting a cauldron of water on the fire to boil. I ask for paper and ink and she nods, wiping her forehead with the back of her hand. She runs to find her father.

Soon after, she comes to my room, carrying the writing things I need and a plate of oatcakes.

'Your pardon, mistress,' she says, dipping into an awkward curtsy, 'but you look awful pale. Are you sickening?'

I shake my head.

'Shall I light the fire?' She glances at the open window as though she longs to shut out the cold air.

'No. No fire today. Please tell your father I'll be leaving this morning.'

'Please, eat something.' She pushes the plate towards me. 'They are yesterday's but they're still good.'

'Thank you. Now, please, if you will leave me . . .'

I sit down to write.

I have never been one for fancy words and, until now, have saved my romantic notions for Lizzie. A simple question will have to be enough.

I seal the letter with wax from my candle and write Joseph's name on the front. I know where to find him. There is only one place he will be this morning and it is the same as half of London, the same as me. Today is a hanging day, and I am going to Tyburn Tree.

Despite the bitter winter morning, the crowds along Tyburn Road are merry. I keep the hood of my cloak down low and wear a veil. I carry a small bundle containing my mother's book and one warm blanket, bought from the inn. With my money stowed in my skirts and my letter to Joseph tucked into my stays, I travel light.

As I check my reflection in the hand glass before leaving, I barely recognise myself. Still, if I want to live the life I have been granted, it will pay to be wary and I keep my eyes to the ground as I head west through the gatehouse. If I am caught, I have no plan, no means of escape a second time. But I cannot help myself. I must see Lizzie. I must see, with my own eyes, how it ends.

Will London never tire of blood? Even after these years of chaos and death, hanging days are still a holiday. Men, women and children revel in the prospect of a day out. Groups of young apprentices sup ale outside the taverns. There is already a crowd gathered when I reach the crossroads and see the gallows, marked out against the sky.

Tyburn is a mean sort of place, with tumbledown houses built next to the road and wooden scaffolds put up all around for the crowds. People hand over pennies to buy a seat, hoping for a better view. Hawkers and street merchants sell beer and bread. People spill from the nearest inn.

I'm put in mind of the King's execution, just a month before. But today is quite different. Then the mob was quiet, deferent, hardly believing their eyes. Today there is no King upon the block to deserve their prayers. The unthinkable has been done and these people have witnessed it. Now London cannot be shocked.

I find myself a place in the crowd where I can see the gallows. People jostle for space and, more than once, I nearly lose my footing. I search for Joseph's dark curls but find none like him. I watch pamphleteers handing out their wares to an eager public, hoping he is among them, but I cannot see him. Instead, there is another I recognise.

She is brightly dressed in her favourite red and green, fair curls bubbling over her shoulders. She hands out pamphlets to any who will take them and asks for no coin in return. I push through the crowd towards her. At first she doesn't know me. She presses a pamphlet into my hand and says, 'Read this, madam, and see that justice is undone today.'

'Sal . . .'

She falters, peering through my veil. 'Ruth?'

I shoot a look over her shoulder at the soldiers stationed before the gallows and put a finger to my lips.

She grabs my arm. 'Oh, my Lord! My good Lord! We thought you were surely dead!'

I pull her close to me and together we move away from the crush.

'How are you come here?' she asks.

'Joseph . . .'

'He said he could save you. That boy knows more than—'

'Where is he? Is he here?'

'He's looking for you. Gone to Whitehall as soon as we found out you had clean disappeared from Newgate. He seems to think the general had something to do with it.'

'I thought he would be here.'

Sal shrugs. 'This is the last place we thought you'd be. Lord, it's good to see you safe. Let me fetch the boys. They are somewhere hereabouts.'

'No.' I pull her back. 'Sal, I have to leave. Today. I'm not coming back. The less you all know the better. I just had to see . . .'

'I know. I'm so sorry, Ruth. We all are.' She puts her hand on my shoulder, and it is as if, by this show of kindness, she breaks a barrier in me and my pain comes flooding out. I collapse into her arms and let her hold me. She strokes my back.

A few people around us jeer, and a woman says I should not be taking up the space if I cannot stomach the spectacle, but Sal soon silences them with her wicked tongue.

'Are you sure you want to stay?' she whispers.

I unhook my veil and wipe my eyes. 'I must.'

'Then I'm not leaving your side.'

'Please, don't put yourself in danger.'

She gives me a withering look. 'And what do you think I'm doing with these?'

She passes me a pamphlet from the bundle she carries. It is Lizzie's work, the very words that Master Oliver could not swallow, the words that convicted her, the words that will kill her.

It is what Lizzie wants.

Sal grins. 'You should be proud.'

'Can I keep it?'

'Keep as many as you like,' she says, and hands out more to eager hands around us.

I slip the pamphlet inside my mother's book. It is a tiny, precious piece of Lizzie.

Then I remember my own heartfelt scribblings.

'Sal, will you do something for me, something important?'

'Of course.'

I take out the letter. 'Will you make sure Joseph gets this, today if you can?'

She hesitates. 'He's suffered enough heartbreak. If you're leaving, perhaps best let it be. I can tell him you're safe.'

'Please, you do not need to protect him from me. I've done all the hurt I can do already. I think he will want to read this. Please do this one last thing for me.'

She takes the letter and nods. 'I'll find him.' She puts her arm around my waist and holds me close.

Just then I hear noise coming from Tyburn Road: the cheers and catcalls of the mob as the convicts are brought to the gallows. Straining to see over the heads of the crowd, I can make out the cart and the figures inside, tethered together like cattle. At first I cannot see Lizzie and I think that perhaps Master Oliver has reconsidered, but then I catch a glimpse of green satin, shining bright in the sun.

She is like a jewel. She has washed and her skin is pale again, stripped of Newgate grime. Her hair gleams with the lustre of burnished copper. I thank God she is still sensible enough to have used the money I left to buy a few last comforts. As they draw near I see her face. Her eyes are large and glittery and, to my surprise, the corners of her mouth are upturned, not quite a smile, but an expression of defiance. Even though her hands are tied, she holds up her head and tosses her hair. She looks for all the world as if she has come to watch the day's justice, not be a part of it. I marvel at her. She has more strength than I knew.

My own heart feels as though it is being pushed up into my throat and I can hardly breathe. I pant and quiver, like a frightened dog.

The crowd heckle and spit at the cart.

Soldiers on horseback clear a path to the gallows and the cart draws up beneath. The hangman wastes no time. Ropes are made ready and the prisoners are lined up without a moment's reprieve.

I cannot feel my body. I am numb. Sal keeps her arm tight around me and I am glad of it.

The people nearest the cart are shouting and arguing, some of them waving Lizzie's pamphlets in the air. A woman falls to her knees, crying out, 'She is innocent! She is innocent!' But those around her laugh, and someone pushes her onto all fours in the dirt.

An officer reads out the charges. When it is Lizzie's turn a man behind me yells, 'Witch! Traitorous whore!' He takes the pamphlet Sal gave him not moments before and tears it into pieces. Then he throws it into the air and points a finger at Lizzie. 'See the witch!' he cries. 'See how she does not repent! She is the Devil's plaything!'

'Pay no heed,' Sal whispers to me.

But the call is catching.

'Witch!'

'Devil!'

'Holy whore!'

As more people join in, they take Lizzie's words and tear them into little pieces until the air is filled with floating print. Sal looks as though she does not know whether to run or to fight. 'Where are the boys?' she mutters.

But the mocking crowd cannot halt what is happening, and nothing can tear my eyes from Lizzie's face.

She stands, glazed and detached, watching the crowd before her. I see her shiver, betraying a little of her doubt. In that moment, I would gladly give my life for hers. I long to call out that it is me they want, that I am the witch, I am the whore, and I will take her place, if they will only let her go. The thought grips me and I free myself from Sal's grasp and stumble towards the gallows.

But then Lizzie's eyes, scanning the crowd, find mine. I am transfixed. Her mouth opens slightly and a small crease appears between her brows. I swear she mouths my name. She smiles, sweetly, joyfully, and I see her lips move, forming the words 'Thank you'.

Whether she thanks me or she thanks her God I will never know, but as the hangman puts the noose around her neck, she keeps her eyes on mine.

A preacher reads from the Bible, his voice drowned by the roar of the crowd. More and more people rip up the pamphlets and throw the pieces to catch the wind until the air flutters with them, like black and white butterflies.

I remember my promise: 'Where you go, I will go; where you lodge, I will lodge; your people shall be my people, and your God my God. Where you die, I will die – there will I be buried. May the Lord do so to me, and more as well, if even death parts me from you.'

It is a promise I will not keep after all.

Lizzie tips her face towards the sky, towards her God. And then the hangman whips the horse, the cart is pulled from beneath her feet, and it is done.

Chapter 45

My story started with a hanging and so it ends with one.

In the moments after Lizzie's death I am robbed of my reason. I am faintly aware of the crush of bodies and feel as though I will suffocate in the rage and violence of the mob. I see Lizzie's lifeless body, cut down by the hangman, her head lolling like that of a rag doll, her beautiful neck raw and bloody. I see hands grabbing for the fine green satin and her copper spun hair as she is carried away to a sinner's grave. I see Sal's lips moving, but I cannot hear what she says.

And then, before I know it, I am away from Tyburn and sitting on a grassy bank by the roadside, while Sal fans my face. 'There, you've some colour now,' she says. 'Drink this.'

She hands me a flask of liquor.

I thank her and she shrugs. 'It's nothing. Best get this veil on before we go back to the city.' She reaches up and clips the black gauze into place.

'I'm glad you were here with me,' I say.

She still has a few copies of Lizzie's pamphlet. She picks them up now, folds them and puts them inside her satchel. 'We'll print more, you know. We'll keep going. They haven't silenced her, not while I'm still here.'

'Thank you, Sal. She could not ask for more. But, please, be careful. I fear for you, and the others. There are still hard times ahead.'

Sal sighs. 'Perhaps you are right,' she says. 'But we are used to such times, and what would life be without a cause to fight for?'

She takes my hand and squeezes it.

'Have you seen Margaret?' I ask. 'And Charlotte? Do you know what's become of them?'

'Mistress Small is taken ill, I'm told. Brought low by the shock of it all.'

'Is it bad?'

'I don't know. The Cutlers have taken her in.'

'She is a good woman. She never meant for aught of this. I'm sorry for her.'

'Indeed, but with such care she has as good a chance as any. And there is no one left now to bring charges against her.'

'If you ever see her again, will you tell her . . . I'm sorry?'

Sal nods. 'But no one has seen Charlotte.'

We sit in silence for a few moments.

'What will you do now?' Sal asks.

'I make for the coast today.'

'So soon?'

'The sooner the better.'

'Where will you go?'

It will be better for her if she does not know.

'Abroad.'

She raises her eyebrows. 'So far away.'

'It has to be.'

'I see. So, you'll leave us all behind to carry on the fight. What about Joseph? What's in this letter of yours?'

'Give him the letter, Sal, and then it is up to him.'

She smiles. 'I understand.'

She reaches down to a patch of small green shoots that nose their way through the earth. She picks one and gives it to me. I stare at the tiny white flower, so delicate, so pure and yet so hardy among the last frosts of winter. It is the first snowdrop I have seen this year. Sal does not need to say a word.

We part at the river. Sal leaves me to make her way to Whitehall, while I take a wherry to London Bridge where I will meet the carrier to Southampton.

I hug Sal tight and she kisses me hard on both cheeks. Then she watches me go, standing on the riverbank with her hand held to her heart, where she has tucked my letter to Joseph beneath her stays.

Chapter 46

Southampton
March 1649

I stand at the prow of the ship, watching the sun play upon the waves as they lap against the dockside. It is a cold morning and I am wrapped in a woollen blanket that scratches my face. The air smells of brine and space and the promise of new beginnings.

We sail on the noontide. The crew has been at work since dawn, loading the hold with crates and bundles that we will take to Virginia. The dock rings with the calls of men. Rigging plays a beat upon the mast and sails slap. Gulls circle overhead, their mournful cries echoing the unceasing ache in my heart.

The captain has been good to me. He has asked no questions. I have a hammock and a place to keep my things below deck. That is all I need.

I am one of many passengers, starve-eyed labourers and young families seeking a new and better life. There is a buzz of excitement among them as we settle into the place that will be our home for these coming weeks.

I have been in Southampton for three days and in that time I have barely eaten or slept for fear of discovery. Threads pull me back to London, back to Ely, back to a life that no longer exists. I long for the impossible. I suppose, in time, this will pass, as all things must.

This morning, as I climb aboard the ship, greet my fellow travellers and wander the decks, impatient for the off, I feel a new sensation – the smallest bud of hope growing inside. I think of Sal, and the snowdrop, and the letter I gave her. I run the words over and over in my mind.

> *Joseph, I owe you my life and I will never forget it. I am leaving England on the Seaflower out of Southampton, Tuesday next. I go to your New World. I was wrong to send you away. I forgive you. Can you forgive me? Ruth.*

Sometimes love comes like an arrow, sudden and swift, an unforeseen shot from an unheeded bow. Sometimes love comes slowly, like the first small sparks of a green-wood fire, smoking and smouldering for the longest time before the kindling flares and the heart of the blaze glows with fierce, consuming heat.

I loved Elizabeth Poole. I loved her as a friend, as a sister, as a sweetheart. She was all these things to me and more. She saved me when my first and only love was lost. The passion I felt in return gave me courage and meaning, mending the tears in my tattered heart. I will hold this love inside and I will take it with me. It is part of me now, something I will carry until the end of my days. I have not wasted my love, for love given freely is never wasted, but she could never love me in return. She simply could not do it. I see now that there was something broken in her. She was not strong enough to give herself to me completely so she gave herself to God. And it seems I am a jealous lover. I would never have been happy, always being second best. But I am grateful for one last gift; by choosing her own sad fate, she has set me free.

I look out to sea and take in the wide expanse of water. I notice a gull riding the wind, the same wind that will take me to the New World. I watch as a fat man in an embroidered coat and periwig directs the crew. He is a merchant by the look of him. They are winching up crates and hauling them over to the ship for stowing. Ropes creak and the men shout instructions to one another. The fat man is red-faced and fretting as each crate is lifted.

A rope snaps and a crate hangs in mid-air. Children, come to watch from the dockside, clap and cheer as it swings. The fat man is beside himself, shouting at the sailors as they lower it. New ropes are attached and they begin again.

As I watch this, I see him. His head is bare and his dark curls shine in the sun. He has a knapsack slung over one shoulder and wears a smart coat and new boots. He comes along the dockside, skirting the merchant and his crates, looking up at the ship. He shields his eyes against the light.

He sees me. His eyes meet mine. He smiles.

I know then that I have a friend, a true friend, who never lied to me, who was never false or selfish, who has saved me from the world and from myself.

He will come with me from this old life into the next.

He will give himself to me, body and soul.

All I have to do is ask.

Acknowledgements

This book is a work of fiction, grounded in historical research. I owe a great debt of gratitude to those historians who inspired and informed my work. Any bibliography is too long and varied to reproduce here but for those interested in further reading about the period and some of the themes explored in this book, the works of Christopher Hill, Diane Purkiss, Blair Worden and Malcolm Gaskill will prove fruitful. I must give due credit to Antonia Fraser's masterful biography of Oliver Cromwell, which influenced my initial impressions of that controversial figure, and where I first encountered Elizabeth Poole. Articles by Manfred Brod and Marcus Nevitt were especiallly helpful in putting together the details of Elizabeth's life. Particular thanks are due to Mark Stoyle whose work on the Naseby massacre helped determine Joseph's story. Any mistakes or alterations are entirely my own.

Huge thanks must go my editor Claire Baldwin, to the whole team at Headline and to my agent Annette Green. Without these people Ruth, Lizzie and Joseph would have remained forever my imaginary friends.

I am indebted to Lorna Fergusson and Clare Smith for giving advice and feedback on early drafts and to Suzannah Dunn for generously sharing her experience and wisdom. Heartfelt thanks go out to all the friends and family who have supported and encouraged me while this book was born. You know who you are. Particular thanks to John Clements, Caroline Clements, Jeremy Prosser, Claire Holloway, Ian Madej, Maxyne Ryan and Mark Rose. And lastly, special thanks must go to my mother, Janet Clements, to whom this book is dedicated, for her red pen and her unfaltering belief that Ruth's story is one worth telling.

Author's Note

The Crimson Ribbon is set during one of the most turbulent times in England's history, in a century that saw great change. The mid-seventeenth century witnessed the awful horrors of civil war, the persecution of witches, an era of uncensored journalism and the emergence of new, radical religious sects and revolutionary political thinking, all of which played a part in the creation of this novel.

We don't know much about the real Elizabeth Poole, who she was or why she was given a voice during one of history's most controversial prosecutions. Pamphleteers of the day suggested that she was a fake, perhaps stage-managed by Cromwell and Ireton, but this is probably Royalist propaganda. This novel is my attempt to answer these questions, using a mixture of research, conjecture and imagination; but it is a work of fiction and story must be paramount. To that end, I have invented certain things and altered others.

Several other characters are based on real people: members of the Cromwell family, William Kiffin, Thomasine Pendarves and Thomas Rainsborough among them. But my imagined versions of these people are exactly that.

Joseph Oakes is of my own making, but represents the experience of many men who fought against, or for the King (and due to the changing fortunes and allegiances of their leaders, sometimes both). The brutal slaughter and mutilation of female camp followers fleeing the Battle of Naseby was, perhaps, the worst atrocity committed by Parliamentary forces during the early years of the New Model Army – a blood-soaked stain on the famous victory that was to effectively determine the outcome of the English Civil War.

The 1640s also saw the infamous witch hunts led by self-styled 'Witchfinder General', Matthew Hopkins. His means of discovering witches, experienced by Ruth, were used to identify and prosecute hundreds of men and women, in an unprecedented climate of suspicion and recrimination. Many lost their lives. Belief in, and fear of witchcraft was a very real concern for ordinary people, who occasionally took the law into their own hands.

Ruth Flowers is my own creation. There is nothing in the historical record to suggest that Oliver Cromwell ever had an illegitimate child, other than, by his own admission, allusions to the 'sinful' behaviour of his youth. But then again, I like to think that there is no way to confirm that he did not.

The Crimson Ribbon

Bonus Material

Cromwell and His Monstrous Witch: The Real Elizabeth Poole

You justly blame the King for betraying his trust, and the Parliament for betraying theirs: This is the great thing I have to say to you, Betray not you your trust . . . Stretch not forth the hand against him: For know this, the Conquest was not without divine displeasure, whereby Kings came to reigne, though through lust they tyranized: which God excuseth not, but judgeth; and his judgements are fallen heavy, as you see, upon *Charles* your Lord.

Elizabeth Poole, 'A Vision', 1648

The real Elizabeth Poole is a shadowy figure; like many women of the early modern era, the details of her life must be pieced together using fragments in the historical record. While much of what we know about her is uncertain, her published writing, coupled with convincing circumstantial evidence, is enough to create a sense of who she was.

Elizabeth Poole was probably born in London and baptized at St Gregory by St Paul in the autumn of 1622. Her father, Robert Poole, is recorded as a householder at the West End of St Paul's in the late 1630s, so it's likely that Elizabeth grew up in the midst of the printing, pamphleteering and bookselling trade in St Paul's Churchyard.

As a young woman Elizabeth came under the influence of Particular Baptist leader William Kiffin. A controversial, charismatic figure, Kiffin was accused by Robert Poole of 'seducing' Elizabeth, and others of the Poole household, away from Robert's orthodox religion. A pamphlet, penned by Kiffin in his own defense in 1645, proves that the relationship between the two men was troubled. But this was only the beginning of the scandal. By 1648, Elizabeth had been accused of heresy and licentiousness and expelled from Kiffin's congregation. Details of the allegations are hazy.

Relocating to Abingdon, Elizabeth fell in with Thomasine Pendarves. Thomasine and her husband John, vicar of St Mary's, were in contact with William Kiffin around this time, but the reasons for Elizabeth's move and whether she and Thomasine had any prior acquaintance is unknown.

Thomasine is an interesting character. Actively involved in radical religious networks, she caused John some embarrassment due to her links with prominent Ranters (a libertarian group, frequently accused of sexual immorality, drunkenness and blasphemy). Elizabeth's friendship with Thomasine is likely to have affected the ideology of both women. Whatever the case, Elizabeth seems to have become assured of her own spiritual vocation by this time.

But it was not until the winter of 1648-49 that Elizabeth attempted to influence events on a larger scale. What is certain is that she appeared twice before the General Council of the Army – that close circle of military leaders who were to determine the fate of King and Country – in the month leading up to Charles I's execution.

During her first visit, on 29th December, Elizabeth described a providential vision wherein the Army, appearing in the shape of a healthy man, cured the State, personified as a sickly woman. The officers agreed that this auspicious revelation had indeed come from God and Elizabeth was thanked for her contribution.

Elizabeth's second appearance was quite different. On 5th January she returned to present a paper directly opposing the execution of the King. Using a metaphor that would have been familiar to her audience – of the King as 'husband' to his subjects – she argued that the Army should 'Bring him to his triall, that he may be convicted in his conscience, but touch not his person'.

The message was clearly political. Elizabeth was closely and repeatedly questioned about the origins of her directive; whether it had come from God or from herself (the answer was: from God). When she failed to address more complex enquiries about the legality of the King's trial, admitting that 'I understand it not', she was dismissed.

Contemporary writers and historians have argued over why and how Elizabeth gained access to such an influential group of men at this crucial time. Some claim that the role of prophetess was enough to invoke the god-fearing reverence with which she was first received, while others assume that she must have had an influential patron and have put forward various names, including members of the Army Council, as candidates.

Later pro-royalist factions accused Cromwell and Ireton of stage-managing the whole affair. A pamphlet of 1660 describes Elizabeth as 'a Monstrous Witch full of all deceitful craft' who 'had her Lesson taught her before by *Cromwel* and *Ireton*'.

There is evidence of one further possible meeting with Ireton, and perhaps some truth that both men were still doubtful about the King's fate at this point. But it does seem unlikely that Elizabeth was positioned by either to sway the more determined proponents *away* from execution, especially given her hasty dismissal, the outcome of the Council's deliberations, and Cromwell's eventual determination to follow such 'cruel necessity'. If either Cromwell or Ireton coached Elizabeth, it seems she didn't stick to the script.

A more convincing theory is that Elizabeth was working closely with the Levellers. Her first appearance before the Council was followed immediately by the presentation of a petition by the Leveller leader, John Lilburne. At least one contemporary describes Elizabeth as 'one of Lilburne's doxies'. Elizabeth herself referred to the Leveller document 'The Agreement of the People' hinting that she was at least sensible of current debates. Perhaps Elizabeth's vision, flattering the Army as the saviour of the country, was meant to smooth the way for Lilburne's audience and the ongoing negotiations that had recently broken down between the Levellers and the Army. But this doesn't account for her subsequent visit or the message she then delivered.

It seems unlikely that Elizabeth would have gained access without some sort of patronage, but the contrast between the two appearances, and the dramatically different reception, is striking. It's not unreasonable to say that in the patriarchal society of early modern England, divine prophecy was one way for women's voices to be heard and heeded, and prophetesses had meddled in politics before.

Not to be cowed, Elizabeth quickly published a written account of her 'Vision', soon followed by 'An Alarum', in which she set out her version of both visits to the Council. There are four surviving publications to her name, but all are editions of the same, with various supplements and amendments. One 1649 copy is printed to emphasise her name on the frontispiece, perhaps suggesting some level of notoriety.

A VISION:

Wherein is manifested the disease and cure

OF THE

KINGDOME.

BEING

The summe of what was delivered to the
Generall Councel of the Army, *Decemb.* 29. 1648.

TOGETHER

With a true Copie of what was delivered
in writing (the fifth of this present *January*) to the
said Generall Councel, of Divine pleasure concerning the KING in reference to his being
brought to Triall, what they are there-
in to do, and what not, both concerning his Office and Person.

By *E. Pool* herein a servant to the most
High GOD.

Jan: 9th LONDON,
Printed in the Year, 1648.

Most striking is the inclusion of a lengthy polemic by Thomasine Pendarves, supporting Elizabeth's claim to be the genuine article, and defending her against those old accusations by Kiffin's congregation of 'scandalous evils'. A further section written by an anonymous contributor (with some similarity to Elizabeth's own style and sentiments) does not deny Elizabeth's follies, 'committed many years ago and long since repented of'.

One version includes a section by Elizabeth herself, directly addressing her accusers, wherein she references the charge of 'seducing' and defiantly vindicates her actions. It was fairly common for allegations of sexual promiscuity, licentiousness and heresy to be leveled at women acting outside social norms, but it's clear Elizabeth believed it was for God, not her fellow men, to judge, and she had God on her side.

We hear nothing more of Elizabeth until 1653, when a 'Mistress Poole' preached from the pulpit of Somerset House in defense of John Lilburne, then on trial for his life. If prior claims that Elizabeth was a Leveller sympathiser are true, the conclusion that this is our Elizabeth is a tempting one, but contemporary sources are conflicting.

In 1668 she was living at the Mint in Southwark when she was arrested for housing an unlicensed printing press and imprisoned at the Gatehouse. This is the final trace of her; there is no known record of her death or burial.

Historians have argued over Elizabeth Poole's significance, most disregarding her as the agent of one or other political faction or specific male figure. While it's true that ultimately she had little affect on the thinking of the Army Council in those critical winter days of 1648–49, her treatment does cast some light on the political position of ordinary women and the limits of their influence.

Through her own writing we catch a glimpse of a strong

character: passionate, defiant, and fighting for justice. Her political savvy might be questionable but no one can argue that she didn't try to have her say at a time when governmental decision-making was the domain of men.

Elizabeth was not the only prophetess to attempt to influence events. In fact, the years of civil war and Interregnum saw a marked increase in the number of women claiming prophetic visions concerning the state of the nation. That this coincided with revolutionary and social upheaval and an explosion in uncensored print media is no coincidence. But ultimately, any real influence was finite and dependent upon the advocacy of men. Where such women might sometimes be regarded with respect and reverence, they might just as easily be shamed, stigmatised and silenced. By attempting to have her say, Elizabeth, and others like her, put themselves in a precarious position.

In her writing Elizabeth uses the patriarchal view of the differences between men and women to strengthen her own arguments: if women are unstable, emotional beings, incapable of rational, intelligent judgment, weak in mind and body, then surely they are more susceptible to the influence of some greater power; that such power might be for good or for evil meant that prophecy and witchcraft were equally possible consequences.

KAREN MAITLAND

The Vanishing Witch

The reign of Richard II is troubled, the poor are about to become poorer still and landowners are lining their pockets. It's a case of every man for himself, whatever his status or wealth. But in a world where nothing can be taken at face value, who can you trust?

The dour wool merchant?
His impulsive son?
The stepdaughter with the hypnotic eyes?
Or the raven-haired widow clutching her necklace of bloodstones?

And when people start dying unnatural deaths and the peasants decide it's time to fight back, it's all too easy to spy witchcraft at every turn.

Praise for Karen Maitland:

'A ripping tale . . . full of colour and detail' *Daily Telegraph* on *The Gallows Curse*

'A richly evocative page-turner which brings to life a lost and terrible period of British history, with a disturbing final twist worthy of a master of the spine-tingler such as Henry James' *Daily Express* on *Company of Liars*

'Scarily good. Imagine *The Wicker Man* crossed with *The Birds*' *Marie Claire* on *The Owl Killers*

978 1 4722 1501 7

headline
review

LYNDSAY FAYE

Seven For A Secret

1846: KIDNAP, MURDER, LOVE AND BETRAYAL
ON THE LAWLESS STREETS OF NEW YORK.

Timothy Wilde, copper star in the newly formed NYPD, thinks himself hardened to the darker practices of the city he's grown up in. That is, until he encounters the 'blackbirders', slave-catchers with a right to seize runaways from the Southern states.

When a woman reports her family has been stolen, Timothy and his wayward brother Valentine find themselves plunged into an underworld of violence and deceit, where police are complicit and politics savage. If he's to protect all those he cares about, Timothy must unravel the corruption at the heart of the authority he was hired to defend . . .

Praise for Lyndsay Faye:

'Reanimates a menacing 19th-century New York' *The Sunday Times*

'Vibrant' *New York Times*

'Lyndsay Faye's command of historical detail is remarkable and her knowledge of human character even more so. I bought into this world and never once had the desire to leave' Michael Connelly

978 0 7553 8680 2

headline
review

Now you can buy any of these other
fiction titles from your bookshop or
direct from the publisher.

FREE P&P AND UK DELIVERY
(Overseas and Ireland £3.50 per book)

The Yonahlossee Riding Camp for Girls	Anton DiSclafani	£7.99
A Discovery of Witches	Deborah Harkness	£8.99
Shadow of Night	Deborah Harkness	£8.99
The Gods of Gotham	Lyndsay Faye	£6.99
Seven for a Secret	Lyndsay Faye	£7.99
The Paris Winter	Imogen Robertson	£6.99

TO ORDER SIMPLY CALL THIS NUMBER

01235 400 414

or visit our website: www.headline.co.uk

Prices and availability subject to change without notice